Rise of the Antichrist

PENTIAN

Grant Leishman

Rise of the Antichrist

Rise of the Antichrist

Edited by: Pentian

info@pentian.com
www.pentian.com

Printed in Spain
ISBN: 9781635030389

Dedication

This book is for the three lovely, young ladies of my life—my daughters: Angeline, Charmaine and Amelia-Rose

Jan 23, 2017
Dear Dette & Thomas
Enjoy [illegible]!!!
[illegible] Grant

Acknowledgment: This novel would not have been possible without the constant input of character ideas, character arcs and plot twists by Chris Leishman. I thank you for your ideas and advice Chris — many of which have found their way into this book.

Disclaimer

This book is a total work of fiction. Any similarities to real events and / or real people, is purely coincidental, except where indicated below:

Although the towns, cities, and institutions named in this novel are real, they are only included to provide realism and nothing about them or their activities should be construed from this work of fiction.

Any mistakes, factual or otherwise, are totally of my own making and I take full responsibility for them all.

Grant Leishman: Author-July 2015.

Índice

Chapter 1

Neither Samantha nor Damien knew they were different; "special" somehow — that revelation would come to them much later in life. For now they were happy and content to grow and develop in the caring, warm, comforting environment that was their mother's womb.

Damien, the more active of the twins, lifted his almost fully developed eyebrow at his sister, as if to say; "how's it going Sis."

Her lips morphed into a smile as she replied; "I'm cool Bro. Any idea how much longer we gotta stay in here?"

He responded the way he always did to her impatience. "Hey Sis, what you want to leave for? We got everything we could ever want in this place. I don't wanna find out what's waiting for us out there, anyway."

Samantha kicked away and floated around, so she was not looking directly at him anymore. "Well, I'm just bored! I want to find out what's in store for us."

He reached out one of his perfectly formed, little, arms; placing it gently around his sister's waist, being extra careful not to bump the cord that provided her with all the nutrients she needed.

"I'm just happy here with you Sis. I love you!"

She felt the comfort of her brother's body gently lapping against her back, and relaxed; as they both fell into a deep, restful sleep.

. . .

Maria Manyanan-Castillo rolled over on the bed. Damn those kids are getting restless, she thought.

Her husband, JC, lay beside her, on his back, gently snoring; his lips softly fluttering with each intake of breath. Her heart swelled with wonder and with love that she and JC were finally together forever and inside of her was, rapidly growing, the fruits of their love. They'd been shocked initially to discover they were expecting twins — but the shock lasted all of two seconds before the excitement kicked in. The last scan had confirmed what they'd hoped for all along — a perfect set; one boy and one girl.

Ma chuckled as she remembered her reaction to the news. She'd screamed and jumped up on JC, grasping him around the neck, wrapping her legs around his waist, and kissing him passionately; without any thoughts of what other people might think. From the very first moment, she had loved JC passionately, and now they were married; she didn't care who she showed it to.

The Doctor had stood there and watched it all, smiling. This was one of the best parts of her job, imparting the good news to the prospective parents. Dr Annabelle Silorio, a highly respected Manila obstetrician, had seen most things in her thirty odd years of practice, but she felt there was something a little odd about this pregnancy; something she'd never seen before. Pushing her glasses back up her nose, brushing a stray, prematurely greying hair back into its rightful place, she gestured for JC and Maria to take a seat. Maria noticed the slight furrow on the Doctor's brow.

"Doctora," she began; "what's wrong? Is there something wrong with the babies? Did you see something in the scan? Please tell us. What's the matter?"

The doctor leant forward so she was close to them, and smiled reassuringly. "No... no... no, please don't get worried — both babies look absolutely perfect in the scan; too perfect actually."

JC placed his arm on the Doctor's white lab coat; "too perfect? How on earth can two babies be too perfect?"

The Doctor laughed; "perhaps that's not the right word. Here's the thing though. According to everything you told me Maria, you should be six months pregnant now... right?"

Ma looked up at the ceiling and mentally counted the months since she and JC had made love that first time, when they had returned to Davao, from Pangutaran Island. "Absolutely, it was almost exactly six months ago. I'm absolutely sure I know the date I conceived;" she added,

"Well... both of your babies are already full-term. They're completely developed; everything is already there and fully functional. If I didn't know you and I looked at your scan, I would say you were just about to deliver."

She paused and looked hard at Maria; "In fact Maria, I would say you're at least two weeks overdue."

Maria jumped from her chair and shouted; "If you're suggesting what I think you're suggesting Doctor, then you're totally wrong. There's been nobody since I met JC — he's my everything!" She buried her face in her hands and sat again; "No... no... no... you're totally wrong," she cried.

JC reached over and placed an arm around her shoulder whilst the Doctor raised her hand to try and placate Maria.

"No Maria! You misunderstand me. We both know who JC really is. Goodness me — for the past year, everyone in the world has known exactly *who* JC really is. No... all I'm thinking is that although he's given up his immortality and become wholly human, perhaps his genes are still those of an immortal. Perhaps your children will be special in some way."

Looking at them opposite her; worried and confused, she spread her arms and opened her hands wide. "Look guys! I just don't know — maybe you'll give birth tomorrow Maria, or maybe you'll go the full nine months; it's just a total mystery to me."

She got out of her chair and squatted down in front of them, placing one hand on JC's knee and one hand on Maria's knee. "Just don't worry please... okay? The babies are perfect — trust me".

They stood up, their smiles almost complete, but doubts still nagging in the corners of their minds. After hugging Dr Silorio and thanking her for her help, they left the surgery and headed to the nearest coffee shop for a much needed boost of sugary donuts and coffee.

. . .

JC looked across the coffee-shop table and took both Maria's hands in his. "Honey, neither of us gave much thought to any ramifications that might follow my decision to return to earth and become fully human. We assumed that fully human would mean just that — but the Doctor's right. I am still Jesus Christ; the Son of God, and who knows what that might mean in the future, for our children... but hey, you heard Annabelle... right? She said the twins looked perfect."

Maria grinned and grasped his hands; "yeah, she did, didn't she. JC... we're going to be parents very soon — damn that's scary!"

He laughed; "Well hon, for now we better head back to Mindoro and our hideaway, until the time comes."

Maria looked concerned; "Do you think I'll do the full nine months JC? You heard what she said — but I don't feel like I'm ready to give birth yet, I think it will be full-term."

He nodded and smiled reassuringly at her, before they left to head back to their little hut in the hills of Northern Occidental Mindoro. They had been living amongst the native Mangyan people; engaged in bringing basic education and health care services to the tribe.

. . .

Maria pulled herself wearily out of the bed. She'd slept well, but she *was* indeed a full nine months pregnant now and the strain of carrying these twins to full term was starting to wear heavily on her.

She grinned as she recalled the doctor worrying she would not make the nine months. It was now nine months and two weeks!

"Time you little ones put in an appearance;" she muttered, patting her stomach lovingly, as she trod wearily to the outside tap and their washing area — little more than a drum filled with rainwater.

. . .

Samantha tapped her brother on the shoulder; "you awake kiddo?" she thought directly into her brother's mind.

Damien giggled to himself and pretended to still be asleep, until she kicked him hard on his left buttock.

"Owww!" he protested angrily; "that hurt, you bully."

Samantha just ignored his complaint and continued. "I think it's time we got out of here Bro! What do you say we give it a go, eh? I reckon if we start heading downward we can squeeze through that tiny, little, gap down there."

Damien twisted his head to look and his thoughts carried his incredulity to Samantha; "through there? Damn girl! You gotta be kidding — we can't fit through there."

Her reply was to just kick with her feet and start trying to force the opening apart with her hands. "Just watch me — I'm going! Are you coming with me?"

. . .

Maria was bending over, scooping water on her face when she felt the sharp pangs of the twins moving again; "awful early for you two to be awake," she chuckled down at her stomach, continuing to wash her face.

She gasped, as a pain like a knife cutting through her pelvis, lanced at her. Sinking to her knees she managed a strangled scream for help. The call brought a bleary-eyed JC, who tore through the door; still pulling his pants on.

"Hon, what's wrong? Is it the babies?"

Maria looked up and grimaced. Through clenched teeth she muttered; "It's time JC! Oh... Oh... Oh... God! It's definitely time! These two are on their way out."

JC, like millions of men before him, panicked. He ran around barking instructions to nobody in particular, turning this way and that, as if seeking some sort of divine inspiration.

Maria grabbed hold of his leg and shouted at him; "JC, we haven't got time to get to Manila ha — just get me to the Mamburao District Hospital. They have good doctors there. Come on, pull yourself together man!"

Her sharp tongue snapped him to attention. "Right, right, okay — we can do this! Now... can you stand honey? I'll get some of the boys to get you onto the back of the truck and then we'll go."

The trip down the mountainside was like a never-ending nightmare for Maria.

JC sat beside her on the bed of the flat-deck, holding her hand and whispering encouragement in her ear. As the truck jolted and swayed its way down the narrow, dirt road from the Mangyan village to the main road, Maria clutched, desperately, to his hand.

Every few minutes she would be seized by another contraction and would dig her fingers mercilessly into JC's vulnerable flesh. He may well have been the son of God, but at this moment he was like every other man in this situation — completely helpless and totally terrified.

Fortunately, as the truck skidded to a halt beside the emergency entrance of the hospital, Maria was still holding on. She assured JC after her last contraction that she could feel the baby's head coming out. A quick check confirmed what she'd said and he was mightily relieved to hand control over to an efficient group of hospital personnel. They quickly bundled Maria onto a gurney and headed for the maternity suite.

At 8.45am on June 22nd 2015; Samantha Manyanan Castillo entered the world; to be followed five minutes later by Damien Manyanan Castillo.

Samantha, swaddled in a blanket, and already on her mother's breast, when her brother joined her on the other breast; looked warily around the delivery suite before declaring to Damien; "So this is what the world looks like Bro — Damn! It 'aint half bright is it?—"

. . .

Chapter 2

<u>Seven Years Later:</u>

It was early evening, high atop the mountains in the Mangyan Village that Maria and JC had called home for the past seven years. They sat on an old, wooden bench he'd fashioned out of a fallen tree; arms around each other's shoulders, staring at the delightful vista that opened up in front of them. They adored ending their working day here together; soaking up the atmosphere and the peace of village life.

A gentle, cooling, breeze wafted up the valley from the West Philippine Sea; keeping the heat to a bearable level — the air, fragrant, with the sweet smell of the many fruit trees that encircled the village. Maria had often thought, at this time, it was the most beautiful place in the world.

She looked sideways at her husband; his eyes were half-closed and he appeared to be dozing, but Maria knew he was doing what he always did at this time of the evening; communicating with his Father.

She leaned in and rested her head on his shoulder, as she watched the sun begin its slow dip beneath the horizon. She had seen it many times, but it never failed to excite her and capture her imagination. She gasped in wonder, as the sky exploded in a glittering array of oranges, yellows, fiery reds and deep violets, near the edges of the sea; as the sun made one last dip into the wispy clouds hanging low on the water's surface.

"This truly is paradise;" she muttered to herself.

In the gathering gloom she looked at the shadowy profile of her beloved JC and knew it was because of him that she had this endless well of happiness inside of her.

"It's all your doing my love!"

He smiled, and opened his eyes, to look down into his wife's adoring face. Leaning over slightly, he kissed her; forcing her lips apart with his insistent tongue.

"It's dark!" he exclaimed; when they finally came up for air. "Where are the kids? They should be back by now."

She smacked his arm. "Why do you worry so much honey? They have an army of friends who would never let anything happen to them..."

His query was answered; by the trilling sounds of laughter they both recognised as belonging to Samantha. She was shouting something at her brother. As usual, she appeared to be teasing her "younger" brother.

"Come on slowpoke, is that the fastest you can run?"

They grinned at each other as Samantha appeared from the trees, running full tilt into her Daddy's waiting arms. Damien, not far behind, came puffing up to fall, exhausted, into his Mama's embrace.

"Righto you two; time to get dinner sorted. Sam, you get the fire boosted, and Damien, you go and help your Mother with the *kanin* (rice). I'm going to sit here for a bit more in peace and quiet." JC announced.

An insistent wail sliced the air and JC laughed;

"So much for that plan, what I'm *actually* going to do is; see to Angeline and Angelo." Pushing himself upright he went into the house to check on the couple's third set of twins; born eighteen months ago.

Following on from Samantha and Damien, three years ago had come; Shannen and Sean. All three sets were fully developed within the first six months of conception, but all went the full nine month's gestation period.

Once everyone was fed, happy, and contented in their beds, Maria and JC went for their evening stroll through the village. They were able to leave the children in the care of their "adopted" Mangyan daughter Marielle; a fourteen year old orphan who absolutely adored the children and loved her new life as their caregiver.

They ended their walk atop the cliff that marked the village's boundary. There they sat, like young lovers, and talked about the past, their plans for the future, and their hopes for their children.

The moon shone brightly as JC gently helped Maria to sit down on the cliff edge; with their legs dangling off into space. Looking at his wife's face, illuminated in the pale light of the moon, his heart soared; the same way it had all those years ago when he first saw her in Tito Awe's Bar. Their journey had begun that day.

"I love you Ma, I have from the very beginning."

She turned to him and kissed him briefly on the cheek; "I did too honey. When I saw you there standing, so tall and determined, calling for people to volunteer for a mission to save the world; it really wouldn't have mattered what you wanted us for — I would have followed you anywhere."

They sat in silence, before JC finally broke the spell. "The others will be here next week honey. I'm really looking forward to seeing them all and finding out what the year has brought them. So much has happened in the past seven years — and yet sadly so much still remains the same."

Maria nodded; "I know what you mean hon; you came to change the world, and although we made an impact; sometimes I think nothing has really changed at all. All we can do is to do our best babes — and that's what we're doing. You have to remember, you're just a normal man now; not the Son of God anymore. You gave *that* up for me."

The stark reminder of what he had given up to marry her and become the father of their children brought a tear to her eye, which she brushed away impatiently.

"Honey, we're truly happy here; raising our family, and helping these wonderful, warm, people finally embrace the twenty-first century. Isn't that enough for us?"

Looking down at her, he nodded; "yes babes, this is more than enough."

The conversation had reignited thoughts of their "mission" together. JC knew the world was no longer under threat of destruction by a vengeful and angry God. His decision to relinquish his immortality and return to earth had seen to that, but he still felt a deep need to make a difference; as a man. To leave this planet a better place than when he arrived.

Oh yeah... they'd been such an idealistic band of *"disciples"* when they'd first marched out from Manila, to change the world. They had gone out fearlessly to Davao City to unmask and dethrone a usurper to the title; "The Son of God".

JC chuckled softly to himself as he recalled how the imposter Adonis Quanico, had become one of JC's greatest followers and "disciples" and was even the pastor that had married him and Maria. They'd built a beautiful, wonderful, caring, and loving

Church and community in Davao, on the ruins of Adonis' false Church. They'd then moved on to Manila where JC had declared to the world, on television, that he indeed was the true Son of God and unless the people changed their evil ways quickly, God was going to destroy earth and everybody in it — declaring humanity to have been a failed experiment.

He grinned. All hell had broken out after that announcement and the hardy band of "disciples" had had to get out of "Dodge" in one big hurry. They'd chosen to go to beautiful Pangutaran Island in the South Sulu Sea; where they had restored a delightful, but broken and decrepit, old chapel.

He reached across and embraced Maria. Of course Pangutaran was where he and Maria had been married; so it held wonderful memories for him. Cradling his wife's head in his arms, he leaned over to kiss her passionately. As she pivoted to return the embrace, they both remembered just where it was they were precariously perched; on the edge of a three hundred and fifty foot drop. JC slid back rapidly pulling Maria with him until they were safe from any danger. Laughing aloud at the close call, they rolled on the ground as their passion began to rise.

JC broke the embrace, as he sat up and giggled at Maria;

"Hey babes, it just won't do for the village nurse and teacher to be caught 'in-flagrante' with the pastor, now would it?"

She chuckled back at him. "Well, big boy, it seems like you're ready, so we better get ourselves back to the privacy of our hut then." Standing up and brushing the dust off their clothing, they skipped back to the village, swinging their held hands, like teenagers on their first date. That's what their life still seemed to them — one long, exciting, first date.

. . .

Both their dreams were filled that night with thoughts of the reunion with their closest friends; the ones they had been through hell with. After it was all over, Angelo and Gabriel had stayed behind on Pangutaran to help with the school, the medical centre and to keep the refurbished Church alive and vibrant.

For all of them Pangutaran was something special. It was where they had all become a true band of brothers; where they had faced their worst fears, and survived. Ronnie also had stayed on the island, but for a totally different reason to Ange and Gabs. He'd also gotten married that same day as Ma and JC. He'd married a local girl; Delia, and he had helped turn their struggling, little, farm into a thriving agricultural enterprise. He, Delia and Delia's *Lola* (Grandmother) were doing exceptionally well. JC and Ma were thrilled to see how happy and contented their friend was, with his new life.

Even in the sweetest of dreams, there lurks an element of evil and that was represented by Dan-dan and Chog; their two friends from Batanes, in the far north of the country. It had been a bitter blow to JC when they'd realised that their two "brothers" had broken the trust they'd placed in them and absconded with over a hundred million dollars of the funds that belonged to Adonis' previous Church. It had been their betrayal that had prompted JC to return to heaven and await his Father's decision on Earth's fate.

He'd been devastated and but for the love and support of Ma, and the others, it was likely he would have just given up and allowed his Father to destroy the world. Love, though, is a powerful emotion. Their love was strong enough for him to make the ultimate decision — to abandon his life in Heaven; to abandon his immortality; and to return to earth and live the simple life they now lived.

A smile crossed the sleeping JC's lips and his arm unconsciously tightened around the waist of his beloved Ma as the vista of his friends' faces faded from his dream world and was replaced by the image of his best friend; The Archangel Michael. Michael had been the most distraught at JC's decision to return to earth permanently. It was Michael that JC missed the most; especially in the early years back on earth. Michael had always been JC's "guardian" angel.

They'd been inseparable in Heaven and JC found, to his utter surprise, that he truly missed Michael's arrogance, rudeness and bossiness. He chuckled in his sleep as he recalled Michael's total unwillingness to accord JC the respect JC always felt he deserved; as the Son of God.

Michael would slap him around his shoulders and say; "Sonny boy — respect is earned, not born. When you deserve my respect then damnit, you shall have it!" He'd always laughed aloud and grabbed JC in a bear hug; just so JC knew what his true feelings were.

Despite it being forbidden for Michael to cross between the two worlds; he still did it on occasions, not out of any sense of defiance; more a sense of need. He genuinely needed to keep the bond with JC alive and thriving.

On those wonderful occasions when Michael was able to visit, usually once or twice a year, everything else was put aside for them to be able to spend as much time together as they could. Ma, JC, and Michael would spend hours just sitting around reminiscing. For Ma, it was especially interesting, as although JC had tried to explain Heaven to her, she'd never really understood what it meant. By sitting in with the two boys and just listening, she began to at least get some inkling—.

. . .

Chapter 3

The telepathy that Damien and Samantha shared wasn't something Damien thought about until he was around four years old. Samantha had always been there, in his head. He never wondered how she was able to do this, or how he was also able to invade her space as well; it just was.

It was true, there were times he didn't appreciate his sister's ability to invade his mind. A number of times, when he had been annoyed with his sister, she had thumped him on the arm. The reason was obvious! She knew he was angry because she was inside his head. It was a great skill to have when they were playing games; like hide-and-go-seek, or jungle tag. Knowing where each other was gave them an advantage over the other children. He loved his sister, but as time went on he became resentful at her unceasing presence.

Damien and Samantha were almost carbon copies of their parents, except in reverse. Damien looked like his Mother; while Samantha looked like her Father.

Damien was deep olive in complexion. He had the shiny, jet black hair of a native Filipino and yet it sat on top of his head in a glorious mass of curly locks. He had the large, inquisitive, almost doe-like, hazel-brown eyes of Maria, and his skin was as smooth as the proverbial "baby's bottom".

A nurse at the hospital had once remarked when Maria had been feeding him, that if there had been a model for Batoni's painting of the "Virgin Nursing the Child"; the pair would have fit the bill perfectly. As Damien grew older, his beauty flourished. Retaining his curly mop of dark hair, his cheeks were infused with dimples that creased whenever he laughed.

He was a fun-loving, active, toddler who revelled in playing games with the other village children. He was always to be found around the communal well, sitting in the dust, with the other boys, playing *Bahay-Kubo* (a hand-clapping game) or *Buwan-Buwan* (a tag game).

He had his serious side though, and he would often disappear for hours at a time. When one of his parents realised he was missing and they went in search of him they would often find him sitting on the edge of a cliff, staring out at the sea — off in the distance; a far-away look in his eyes. When queried as to why he was there, he would just smile that enigmatic smile of his; dimples creasing, and reply;

"Just thinking Mama" or "Just admiring the beauty of the world Papa."

His parents would smile and placing an arm around him, would lead him back home.

During one of these trips into the forest Damien began to become annoyed with his sister's presence in his mind. "How can I be alone to think about things?" he had shouted at Samantha in his mind; "Leave me alone!"

Sam's response had been to laugh and shout back equally as loud; "You can't be alone Damien, you're stuck with me — we're one person, not two."

Damien had furiously screamed back at her; "*NO!* I am my own person and I will prove it to you one day! I am *ME*!"

As they started to grow both children had been slow to pick up the attributes of vocal speech — they didn't need it to communicate with each other. It had come as quite a shock to the pair when they realised, that in fact, they were unique in this skill. They'd just assumed everyone else was able to communicate this way. They could invade anyone's mind at will; so why wasn't the reverse true? It was this cognizance that convinced them they had better start using their mouths to talk; if they wanted to communicate with their parents or anyone else in the village.

By the time they had reached five years old and were attending the village school, run by their mother, Damien had reached the point where he was trying to block Sam from his mind. It had always seemed that it wasn't a case of Sam entering his mind; more, her always "just being there". He didn't understand the thought processes involved, but he knew that he couldn't continue to worry about his sister intruding on his thoughts. There had to be a way to stop her.

He tried a number of techniques; ranging from placing a mental brick wall around his brain, to trying to separate his thoughts into different compartments and then locking them, but nothing worked. Samantha was always there. It became obvious to her what he was doing and she became quite derisive of his efforts; laughing at him when he would try some new technique to shut her out.

Sitting on a tree stump one morning contemplating techniques to shut out his sister, he was feeling frustrated at his inability to beat her at this. He stomped in annoyance; "Grrrr;" he mumbled to himself; "there has to be a way to keep her out of my head!"

The idea, when it came to him, was so obvious he thumped his hand on the tree trunk. He remembered when he was listening to music on the radio in the hut and his mother had been calling him to help her with the fire; he'd been oblivious to her calls. He'd been swaying and rocking to the music, so wrapped up in it, that he didn't even hear his mother's voice.

He knew his mind was an amazing thing and he could do almost anything with it... so! "What if I set up a continuous loop of loud music playing in my mind — maybe... then, Samantha won't be able to hear my thoughts?"

It seemed like the perfect solution, so he ran back to their hut to turn on the radio and record some music into his mind. He chose a rock station because he figured the louder and trashier he could make it, the better. Once he heard the right song to fit the bill, he mentally switched on the recorder in his brain and soaked it up. Replaying it and turning up the volume, he looked for indications that Samantha might not be able to tune into his thoughts anymore. Concentrating, he said to himself; "Samantha *I HATE YOU*! You are an *EVIL* little girl." He waited for the expected response, but none came. It worked! He grinned in triumph.

There was one problem with his plan. With the music blaring in his head, he found it difficult to think coherently. The thrash metal song that he had chosen was vibrating his brain so intensely that after a few minutes his head began to hurt. Okay, he thought, so I can't use it too often, or for too long, but when I need it — I can shut Sam out of my mind; at least for a while.

He lay back on his bed and savoured his minor success; swinging his legs to the rhythm of the song. "Ha, ha, ha... I got you this time — I win;" he chanted to himself, in time with the music.

. . .

Samantha was physically very different from her twin. She had taken on her father's attributes; down to the sandy-brown hair and the blue eyes. To look at Damien and Samantha, you would never have picked them as brother and sister, let alone twins — but twins they were. Sam had long, flowing sandy-brown hair that cascaded down her back. By the time she was four, it was down to her waist. Her skin was much lighter than her brother's and although tanned by the tropical sun, it still had that underlying, pale, almost translucent, sheen to it that made her look sickly. It was her face that really caught the attention though.

She had a high brow, with an aquiline nose; not at all Filipino — her lips were ruby red and looked like they were permanently made up; but most startling of all was her sparkling, deep blue eyes. Her eyes had a way of just drawing you in — almost trance-like. They were so bright, so blue, that you felt it impossible to resist anything she said to you.

When she smiled, her perfect white teeth, framed by those shiny ruby lips and her twinkling eyes gave her a beauty that was reminiscent of Western standards of beauty and far removed from anything Asian, at all. Amongst her peers in the village she stood out as being "different" far more than her brother. Whereas her brother was fun-loving and thoughtful, Samantha could best be described as cheeky and mischievous.

Her way of fitting into the group was to be the practical joker. From an early age she was constantly getting into trouble with her parents, her brother and the elders of the village.

From the moment Samantha was able to crawl, she was independent — scared of nothing and willing to try anything. At age four she had wandered off from the family hut one Sunday morning; when everyone else was occupied with other things. She had gotten it into her head that she wanted to play a trick on the local villagers as they headed down the short track to the

Village Chapel, which sat on an outcrop of rock, overlooking the main Occidental Mindoro highway; far down in the valley below.

With absolutely no concern for her own safety she began to shimmy her way up a small coconut tree that overhung the path. Its crown was fifteen to twenty feet above the ground; but it represented no challenge to the fearless, determined little madam. Even when her foot slipped and she grabbed the tree to stop herself falling to her death, it didn't faze her. She took a deep breath and continued upward. Stopping every so often to gather her strength, she reached the top and cosseted herself amongst the leaves that emerged from the central crown.

Looking around at the magnificent view that was afforded her from her lofty vantage point, she began to shake; not from any fear over the height she was above the forest floor, but from excitement at her planned trick. She giggled, as she heard the first of the villagers heading to church that morning. "Hehehe... they're in for a big shock today."

As the first family of five people passed under her tree, Sam began to wiggle her first coconut free, with her fingers. It fell, silently to the track below, landing with a resounding thwack before bouncing harmlessly away into the undergrowth. It had missed the group by mere inches and they had all dived for cover when it hit the ground beside them.

The father was the first to lift his head and scan the tree from where the coconut had fallen. Sam was invisible from the ground. Shaking his head at the closeness of the call, the father pulled his family to their feet and pushed them rapidly in the direction of the Chapel.

"We'd better get going, before another one falls;" he urged them.

To emphasise the point, Sam nudged another one free from its grip and it crashed to the ground a metre behind the party. Without looking back they high-tailed it off down the track. To Sam, they looked hilarious, as they sprinted, dressed in their Sunday finery. She waited till they were out of sight before roaring with laughter.

She sensed Damien in her head. They were looking for her. Well of course they were; she thought. Daddy's the preacher after all — there's no Sunday Service without him there. She sensed and heard Damien;

"Sam, you naughty girl — I know what you're up to. You'd better get yourself back here quick smart before Daddy gets angry. We're all ready to go."

She sighed heavily; so much for my fun, she thought. Reluctantly she wormed herself over to the tree trunk, and grasping it firmly between her legs she slid effortlessly and smoothly to the ground. Patting her Sunday-best frock down, as best she could, she turned sadly toward home and trotted back down the track.

Still... that was so hilarious, she giggled, as she ran.

That little escapade was one of many she would indulge in over the next year or so. Much of her time, it seemed, was taken up with planning ways to annoy Damien and his friends. She resented the fact that the boys wouldn't let her play with them. She didn't want to play with the other girls, as she had explained to her brother one day;

"They're all such boring creatures;" she complained. "All they want to do is sit and play with their stupid dollies. It's just not fun. I want to play with you guys."

She'd been hurt by his response. She felt Damien's reply even before he articulated it. "You're a girl Sam — act like one.

No! Us boys have important things to do and girls are neither required nor necessary."

From that point she made a decision to be a constant thorn in her brother's side. She vowed she would never stop annoying him, constantly cutting into his thoughts and badgering him; but more importantly she would plot ways to sabotage their games and adventures. The best thing about being telepathically connected to Damien was she always knew where he was and what he was doing.

Her sense of "mischief" caused much pain and hardship for Damien and his "gang" of boys. The boys decided they would make a trolley to ride down the twisting track. They'd found some old pram wheels that had been discarded, so they set to building a base, on which to set their wheels.

The project took on a community feel when some of the parents offered their skills to help them build something, "extra special". Over the course of a week they sawed, hammered and bolted together a machine that would have made the engineers at *MIT* (Mapua Institute of Technology) proud.

The result was a vehicle that had room for a driver, two passengers and a brake-man. In shape it resembled a Winter Olympic bobsleigh despite none of the children even knowing what snow was, let alone how bobsleighs looked and worked. The trolley was christened, by each of them painting their own special design. When the masterpiece was completed it was displayed to the village with pride and anticipation of its maiden "voyage".

They drew lots to decide what to name their trolley. The winner, Tobias; chose the name *"Bagyo"* (Typhoon). After painstakingly painting their new name on the trolley; they argued who would be the first team to take it for a spin.

Again it was decided by ballot. Damien would be driving; the two passengers would be Ken and Coey, with Agustin in the rear to man the brakes. There was great excitement in the village, at the first run of the boys' wonderful creation. Everyone who had helped, in the construction, wanted to see how they handled their trolley on the perilous descent down the mountain track. Nobody appeared overly concerned about the risks and dangers the boys were taking.

Samantha was furious at the fuss being made over their stupid trolley. She'd decided they *weren't* going to have a successful run with their new invention. The previous evening she'd snuck out and loosened, almost to the point of being undone, several of the nuts that held the steering wheel and column to the front axle.

"Let's see how well they can steer this hunk of junk when their steering wheel falls off in their hands;" she'd giggled to herself.

People were lined up and down the track waiting to cheer on the first band of intrepid riders. Samantha had grabbed herself a prime position, halfway up a Mango tree, just beside the first real bend on the track. If anything was going to happen, she reasoned, it would be here. She made sure she had a perfect view of the coming carnage and settled in her perch to wait.

At the top of the track the boys positioned themselves carefully and gently, into their respective seats on the trolley. They all took a deep breath as Damien announced; "right... we're off!"

With a gentle push from one of the spectators the trolley began its stately descent down the track. Erring on the side of caution, the brakeman was leaning heavily on the lever that controlled the brake pads. Frustrated at their speed Damien flicked his head around; "Agustin, ease up — give us some speed ha!" With that, the speed increased rapidly and the four boys were whooping and hollering as they rocked their way down the rutted cart track.

With the first corner coming up fast; Agustin lent heavily on the brake lever to slow their barrelling descent down the hill. As the trolley slowed to a manageable speed, Damien, his lips drawn in a grimace that reflected the exhilaration and joy of the ride, lent slightly right and turned the steering wheel to the right — but nothing happened. The trolley continued to head for the apex of the corner. In desperation, he twisted his hands hard on the steering wheel, but it just spun freely.

With screams of horror they careered off the track, clipped the Mango tree where Samantha was perched, before flipping and barrel rolling twenty metres down through the undergrowth, slamming to a stop against the trunk of a tree. Bodies were flung from the trolley, as soon as it began to roll. There were four crumpled forms lying on the forest floor — some softly moaning, but one in particular, ominously still and silent.

Samantha watched, horrified, as her brother and his friends were flung from the cart-wheeling trolley. She couldn't believe the carnage and devastation she'd been responsible for. She hadn't thought it would be anything like this — she just thought they would have a little crash and they'd all be embarrassed. By this stage people were crowding around all four of the broken bodies, trying to assist them and help them to their feet. They all seemed conscious, but at least two had broken arms and it looked like Agustin had broken his ankle. His foot was at a right angle to the rest of his leg, and Sam knew that wasn't right.

Damien was lying further down the hill, near the wrecked trolley and he still wasn't moving. The rescuers had reached him and were crouched beside his prone body. She scrambled down the tree and ran headlong toward her brother.

"Damien!" she screamed, "Damien... please be alright!"

That was the point Samantha discovered another special bond she and Damien had. Damien stirred on the ground and groaned in pain. To Samantha it was like being struck by a hammer — she felt Damien's agony, to the very depth of her being. She sank to the ground clutching her head and moaning incoherently. The pain lanced through her — her head felt like it would explode and she rolled on the ground mewling softly.

That day she discovered whatever physical pain Damien felt — she felt too. The reverse was true also, as Damien would discover for himself when Samantha had to be rushed to Manila for an emergency appendectomy, several months later.

Damien was at least alive. She hung onto that thought as she experienced the intense pain of Damien's gaping head wound.

"I promise never to do anything like this ever again," she swore as she lay there; "just as long as Damien's okay."

The voice that answered her was her brother's; sarcastic and cutting. "Thanks big sis. Don't for a second think I'm gonna forget what you did today. You will pay — trust me!"

Samantha smiled; "well... at least if you're angry, I guess you're going to be alright."

The four "wounded soldiers" all required medical treatment beyond that which Maria was able to provide in their rudimentary village health-centre. It was onto the back of a pickup for the four, and a bumping, painful journey to the Occidental Mindoro District Hospital in Mamburao. At Damien's insistence, Samantha accompanied them to the hospital.

"I don't know if this shared pain thing works at a distance Sis and I want you to feel everything I feel on this long trip," he had whispered to her as they loaded him onto the flat bed of the truck. She'd smiled wanly at him and climbed in beside him obediently. Everyone assumed it was a case of "inseparable twins"; but Damien and Samantha knew better.

. . .

Growing up in a hill-top Mangyan village, far from the maddening rush and crowds of Manila, or even San Jose, was an idyllic lifestyle for the children. It had been when they first attended the school run by their Mother that they realised another of their special talents. It became apparent that they didn't actually need to be attending school. Everything their Mother was teaching — it seemed they already knew. When the class was learning the alphabet, numbers, reading, writing; everything, Samantha and Damien, already inherently knew how to do it. There was nothing they didn't instinctively know, or understand.

Damien raised the issue over dinner one night;

"Papa, there's something weird happening. You know when Mama's teaching us... well... we sort of already know it even before she tells us. What's that all about Daddy?"

Maria and JC exchanged furtive glances. They'd known there would be things that were different with the children, but they'd not known what. This was their first discovery.

"What exactly do you mean Damien?" JC asked his son.

Samantha cut in; "Like... when Mama was teaching us about the world today; you know continents, countries, capitals, all that sort of thing — well... I already knew it all. I know all the countries of the world, I know all their capitals. It's nothing new to me."

JC pursed his lips before speaking. He looked at Maria, but she just shrugged her shoulders and said; "Well... maybe it's time we told them the 'facts of life' honey — though just not really the normal 'facts of life'."

He was worried about the impact it might have on the kids, but that evening he related the story how he was actually Jesus Christ, the Son of God and how he had surrendered that to become a man and to marry their Mother. He told the children the story of the "disciples" and their mission on earth. He finished by saying;

"You know guys, when you two were created, I was still Jesus Christ, so it was always possible that something special might be passed on to you — and that sure does seem the case. It looks like you've inherited my collective knowledge of everything that's ever happened. I've witnessed the full gamut of history first-hand kids. There's nothing that's ever happened on this planet that's escaped my notice. I know it all... and... it seems... so too do you."

He smiled reassuringly at his two precious children; "and that's a good thing guys — don't ever think it's not. You're infused with the knowledge and the wisdom of the entire history of this planet. That makes you uniquely positioned to carry on the work of your Mama and I when... ahhhm....well... when we get too old to do it anymore."

They'd listened attentively to the whole story and not interrupted once. When their father had finished and sat back waiting expectantly for their response, they sat there silent and mute; but communicating furiously with each other within their minds.

Eventually it was Samantha who spoke up. Looking at her mother and then her father, she said softly and quietly; "yes, we always knew we were different — special somehow; so it's a real relief to finally know why. Do you know there's one other thing we can do that nobody else can do?"

JC and Maria sat up attentively; "What's your other special ability Sammy?" Maria pressed.

Samantha grinned at her; "well... Damien and I can communicate without talking — through our minds. We're telepathic;" she added.

Maria looked at JC excitedly. "Wow, that's awesome honey;" she offered, "but can you read my mind?"

Samantha was about to answer when she felt Damien's insistent "*NO!*" screaming in her head. She could, "sort of", read other people's minds but clearly Damien didn't want her to say that.

She shot back a thought message; "why? What's wrong with telling them?" Damien's response was to interject in the conversation.

"No Mama, we can't, it's just between the two of us".

Maria nodded and looked to JC, as the twins Angelo and Angeline began to cry from the other room.

He laughed at Maria; "Well honey, I can *never* read your mind, but I think I know exactly what you're thinking now — do Shannen & Sean and Angelo & Angeline have the same abilities ha?"

When Maria nodded, he continued. "Well, I guess we'll just have to wait and see on that one, but for now I suspect at least two of them need their nappies changed".

He pulled himself to his feet and wandered across to the source of the crying.

When Samantha urged her brother to explain why they hadn't told everything about their telepathy, Damien whispered to her; "we need to keep some things private Sis, just between you and me, right?"

Samantha screwed up her face in doubt, but eventually nodded her agreement.

It was agreed the children would continue to attend school — to do otherwise would have drawn extra attention to them, especially as their Mother was the school-mistress. Instead of studying what the other students were studying, Maria agreed they could do whatever took their minds that day.

"You've absolute freedom to be as creative and innovative as you want," she had told them. She was terribly excited about what they might achieve and what a difference, her two genius children, could make in this world.

That night as she and JC lay softly talking in bed, she pulled him tight to her and whispered; "Ohhhh... JC we are truly blessed... I know our kids will change the world.—"

. . .

Chapter 4

They arrived at the village in two separate groups. First, was Adonis and Jonny, who had flown into Manila from New York, where they had been supervising the establishment of a massive, new, Church in the centre of Manhattan.

After the initial group had split up, Jonny had made the decision to remain in Davao with Adonis and help to build up the wonderful community they had established out of the ruins of the false Church.

The Davao Church and community was now known worldwide and millions of visitors toured the property every year; marvelling at the wonder and grandeur of the Crystal Cathedral. It was more than the gloriousness of the buildings that attracted people to the Church in Davao — it was the community. In the seven years since the Church was rebuilt, they had worked tirelessly to create a safe, caring environment where anyone, from anywhere, was welcome to come and settle down, to live out their future; worshipping God and enriching each other's lives.

JC shied away from the word "commune" because of the connotations it had inherited over time, but boiled down to its simplest terms; that is exactly what the Church had become — a commune. A community of like-minded people dedicated to the glory of God and the advancement of their fellow human beings.

JC was extremely proud of the work his friends had done over the past seven years and he and Maria made it a point to visit the community in Davao at least twice a year. At last count there were fifty thousand souls living, working and caring for each other in the Davao community. The most amazing thing, especially to outsiders, was the total lack of any trouble, greed, envy, or avarice among the community members. There was no security on the premises — just a group of leaders headed initially by Adonis and Jonny, who oversaw the day to day operations of the massive organisation. Adonis especially was very proud of the fact that in seven years not one person had ever been asked to leave.

Such utopia could not go unnoticed by the rest of the world and there was a constant stream of media visiting the compound, talking to the people, and querying the leaders on how they had achieved such a perfect, balanced, community. This free advertising ensured a regular supply of visitors and also new members. Many tourists would arrive, and just never leave. It was that type of place — once you went there, it got under your skin. You wanted to stay, because it offered the closest thing anyone had ever seen to "paradise on earth".

Four years ago, Jonny, who controlled the finances for the massive community, bailed JC up during one of their reunion meetings on Pangutaran Island. "JC;" he'd begun. "We love all the new members that are joining, but we're going to have a problem, sooner rather than later. We're simply running out of room."

JC considered the option of buying more land in Davao, although nothing was available in the area immediately surrounding the existing compound. Perhaps they could open a new compound further out of the city — buy some farmland and develop it, he suggested to Jonny.

Jonny chewed his lip thoughtfully; "Well, it's certainly an option JC, but let me talk you through my thinking — and see how it strikes you."

For just over an hour Jonny laid out the most ambitious building plan ever undertaken on the planet. There was no doubt he had a vision — a vision that would see the Kingdom of God Church spread its tentacles to every corner of the world. His main qualm with expanding in Davao was that it would split the community into two separate factions.

"I don't think that's the best way to go. No! What I envisage, is the creation of a great and marvellous, missionary Church, spreading the word of peace and love to the rest of the world."

It was impossible for JC not to get caught up in Jonny's enthusiasm and excitement for the new idea. It was clear Jonny had thought this through and had spent many hours preparing plans, budgets, feasibility studies and a timeline for expansion that covered the next thirty years.

"JC!" Jonny implored him; "What we've created in Davao is amazing. We've shown the rest of the world, that given the right environment, the right people, and most importantly the right motivation; human beings can live in peace, happiness and joy. Surely we owe it to everyone to share this recipe with them?"

JC shook his head in amazement and suggested that they show the others, Jonny's plans, over dinner that evening.

"What does Adonis think of the idea Jonny?" JC enquired, as he busily wrapped up the plans he had drawn up.

Jonny looked up and grinned; "Oh, he's more excited than me. You know, he's become one of the greatest leaders I've ever met. It's almost impossible to believe now that he's the same man that pretended to be 'The Son of God' and fleeced his people, just a few years ago. He's a changed man JC."

JC chuckled; "yeah, a near death experience can do that to a man!"

Jonny's plans had been enthusiastically received by the others that evening. They involved the systematic development of communities similar to Davao, all over the world. They would start in Europe; building communities in England, France, Germany, Poland, The Ukraine and Russia; before turning their attention across the Atlantic to build new communities in every State of the United States. After that it was to be Africa, South America and the Pacific that would benefit from the largesse of the Kingdom of God Church.

The community that Adonis and Jonny had been setting up in New York was the sixth community in the US; with Churches already opened in Washington, D.C; Los Angeles, California; Chicago, Illinois; Las Vegas, Nevada; and Charlotte, North Carolina. The undertaking was massive, the cost phenomenal and the workload for Adonis and Jonny crippling, yet each community was being established, opened, and run, with no significant problems.

It was like the work was preordained and blessed. Both Jonny and Adonis thrived in the opportunity this presented. Everywhere a community had been set up people had flocked to it and joined en masse. Jonny remarked that many of the members were former tourists to Davao.

"They came to Davao; they saw what we had and they knew it was special — but for a variety of reasons they felt they couldn't join. You know; family, jobs, commitments etc. So... when we gave them the chance to join a similar community in their own area; Wow! They just jumped at it. It's incredible!"

. . .

When Adonis and Jonny jumped from the SUV that transported them up the mountain, there was a tearful reunion. For JC and Adonis the reunion was poignant, as it always was, when the two met. When JC had saved Adonis' life all those years ago, an unbreakable bond had been forged between the two men.

After they'd hugged it out, JC pulled back and with both hands on Adonis' shoulder looked hard into his friend's eyes. "My friend, you look incredible — despite the massive workload and stress you've been under. I can see it in your eyes; you're excited, vibrant and full of joy."

"Adonis, you look younger than you did when I first met you. Hell man, you just got off a twenty-hour flight from the other side of the world and yet you look as fresh as a daisy."

Adonis laughed, in that deep baritone of his; "What can I say JC? When you're doing something you absolutely love and it's such a great thing — well... you just feel awesome all of the time."

JC put his arm around both of them and led them toward the hut. "Come and have some food; Maria and the kids are dying to see you again. Gosh, it's gonna be great to have us all together again... Ohhhh! And I have something special for us tomorrow night; something *very* special."

Jonny looked at him questioningly; "Spill boss, what's up?"

JC chuckled; "Nope, this one stays under wraps until everyone's here."

. . .

The next morning; Angelo, Gabriel, Ronnie and Ronnie's wife Delia arrived at the village; after their long and exhausting, trip from Pangutaran Island.

"Finally the gang's all here again;" JC exclaimed happily.

Angelo smiled a little wistfully and added; "Well, not quite all JC — what about Dan-dan and Chog?"

At the mention of the two friends who'd betrayed the group, a look of disappointment flashed across JC's face.

He forced a small laugh; "Ah well, wherever they are, I hope they're happy. You know, I may never get over their betrayal, but I still love them both and I still want the best for them. Maybe they're satisfied now. I hope so anyway."

He looked around his band of "disciples", with intense pride.

As she always seemed to be; Delia was pregnant again — about six or seven months by the look of it. He clapped Ronnie on the back; "Sheesh man, haven't you figured out what causes that yet? What number's this one going to be?"

Ronnie grinned sheepishly. "What can I say JC, she's a vixen, that woman. She just won't leave me alone. Ahhhh... this will be number six I guess... hehehe."

They wandered inside, out of the heat, and sat around the kitchen table reminiscing for the rest of the day.

Angelo was excited to meet his namesakes; JC and Maria's third set of twins, Angelo and Angeline. He rushed into their bedroom to gaze down at the little ones who were sleeping soundly.

"Ohhhh... JC," he whispered; "they're so beautiful... and to think you named them both after me. I'm so humbled."

JC wrapped his arms around his old friend and hugged him tight. "Ange, you were always the one that kept our spirits up — you never let us down. It's me that's honoured to be able to name them after you."

Angelo dragged a hanky from his pocket to dry his eyes and to blow his nose.

Samantha and Damien were excited to see all their *Tito's* (Uncles) and *Tita* (Aunt) after such a long time. They were constantly running in and out of the room, seeking attention and approval from all the visitors.

Everyone indulged them. Adonis, in particular, exciting the children with his *pasalubong* (gifts) all the way from New York — real M&M's; not the fake ones you could buy in Manila, but real M&M's. They were delighted and rushed out of the house to find their own private places where they wouldn't have to share their precious bounty with anyone. Both the twins managed to eat their entire giant-sized packets in one sitting.

As the evening drew in on the mountain top, JC suggested they repair to the rock overlooking the West Philippine Sea; so they could all enjoy the gorgeous sunset, as the sun would sink beneath the horizon in its usual fiery display. It was a laughing, jovial group that walked down the track to the couple's "special place".

Samantha and Damien skipped alongside them, both grumbling about their "upset tummies", but neither willing to forego any time with their beloved *Tito's* and *Tita*. Damien was grasping firmly onto Delia's hand, helping her negotiate the winding and rocky track whilst Samantha was content to skip along between Adonis and Gabriel, holding each of their hands. Jonny tapped JC on the shoulder before saying;

"Hey mate! What about that big surprise you were promising me yesterday ha? So... where is it?"

JC grinned at him; "Aha... have patience my friend — all will be revealed in the fullness of time. Now come on, the sooner we get there, the sooner I can unveil it."

He began to jog down the path, prompting Maria to shout; "Hoy, boss man, wait up for me ha!"

By the time everyone had gathered around the rock, the sunset was reaching its peak. The sky exploded in a riot of colour so vivid, that all of them were compelled to just utter the word; "Ahhhh!" They sat in a circle, holding hands; nobody saying a word, as they marvelled at the incredible wonder that was God's creation. The glistening sea, far off in the distance was changing colour also; reflecting the kaleidoscope in the skies. It was a magnificent display of nature's beauty and everyone felt blessed to have been privy to it.

As suddenly as it had begun, it was over, and darkness settled quickly on the group. JC had come prepared, and until the moon would rise, bright and soft, in about an hour's time; he lit the three hurricane lamps he had brought with him. They sat, in contemplative silence, enjoying each other's companionship. No amount of time apart could dim the friendship and love of this group — they were committed to each other for life.

Jonny, the impatient one, broke the spell of silence; "Okay, enough already JC — what's the big surprise? Come on; give man!"

JC stood to his feet, feigning a weariness and resignation that he did not feel.

He wanted this to be dramatic; partly because he had a flair for the theatrical, but partly because it really *was* dramatic. He was about to reveal to his friends one of the true secrets of heaven. Lifting his head to the dark skies, already twinkling with a billion stars, he raised his arms above his head; imploring the dark vault of the heavens.

Maria looked up at him in wonder and awe. She had no idea what he was going to do tonight; but she had long ago ceased to be surprised by his magnificence and just the sheer loftiness of his actions. What does he have in mind tonight? She bit her lip to stop herself from trembling.

Framed in the starlight, with a hurricane lamp in one hand, reaching for the heavens she could only think of one person that he reminded her of — he looked like pictures she had seen of Moses standing on the mountain prior to receiving the "Ten Commandments" on the tablet of stone. This man; this Demi-God, was her beloved JC, her darling husband. She was consumed with overwhelming emotions of love and adoration. Hugging herself with both arms she waited to see what this big surprise could possibly be.

JC dropped his arms to his side and bowed his head — waiting... just waiting.

Suddenly, in a burst of light, the sky erupted in flames as the heavens opened and regally, majestically, a figure began to descend toward the group. They stared upward, mouths open, as the figure began to take shape. It was a man; no doubt about that; but oh... what a man! From the flowing, golden, locks that cascaded around his head; to the tips of his winged sandals, he was the summation of everything any of them had ever considered an Angel should be.

Gently, without a sound, he settled down in the middle of the circle of awestruck people. Throwing back his head he let out an ear-splitting laugh;

"JC... you young puppy; you always did have a penchant for the theatrical."

He walked across to him and lifting him effortlessly in an enormous bear-hug he swung him around unceremoniously before depositing him back on terra-firma. Grabbing Maria he lifted her to her feet and kissed her; "and my sweet, sweet Maria, what did that reprobate ever do to win your fair heart? He doesn't deserve you, you know."

Maria giggled in his embrace and slapped him playfully on his shoulder. "Put me down, you naughty, naughty man... I'm a married woman you know."

JC went over, and placing an arm around his shoulder, turned to the others; "Guys, I'd like you to meet my best friend — outside of earth; The Archangel Michael; or as I prefer to call him; Mickey."

After introductions, Michael took a seat between Delia and Maria.

JC turned to Jonny; "Big enough surprise for you mate?" Jonny's jaw was still somewhere down around his ankles and it was all he could do to stutter an answer;

"Ttthat's Mmmichael? A... a... a... real Angel?"

JC giggled and nodded. "Actually, I asked Michael to come tonight because I want to ask him how our work is being viewed up there. I need to pick his brain, so we know we're on the right track. It's getting a bit chilly though, so time we went back to the house and talked tactics and plans eh?"

As they wended their way back through the village; Maria was worried. She'd seen JC like this before. Oh sure, he loved his work here among the Mangyan's, but every so often, she knew he got annoyed he wasn't able to get out and do more.

"Surely everyone will have forgotten who I am," he would frequently exclaim. "I feel jealous of Adonis and Jonny. They're making a real difference and I can't do anything but stay here, in anonymity."

As they walked, she clutched onto her husband's arm and whispered to him; "Mmmm... so what are you up to ha? What's with Michael's visit? Darling... you know I love you so much... but... I think you're hiding something from me."

He bent down and kissed the top of her head. "Hush now my love; all will be revealed shortly."

She knew that was all she would get out of him for now, so she just tightened her grip on his arm and leant against him until they reached the house.

JC stretched out the suspense by insisting that they all eat dinner before discussions. Marielle had cooked them a massive pot of steamed, fresh, *lapu-lapu* fish caught that very day, *gulay* (vegetables) and *kanin* (rice), while they had been at the rock, watching the sunset. They suddenly realised just how hungry they all were and there was little time for chat, as their mouths were too busy demolishing the feast placed in front of them. When dinner was complete and the dishes all cleared away, everyone looked expectantly at JC to begin.

He cleared his throat; "Mmmm... One of the reasons I asked Michael to come here tonight, apart from meeting you all, was to pick his brains. I want to know how things are going in Heaven and I really want to know what my Father thinks about what we're doing here on Earth."

Turning to the Archangel he grinned; "So Mickey... the floor's all yours."

Michael brushed his long blond hair out of his eyes before taking a big draft of the cool water Marielle had spread around the table for everyone.

"Well... what can I tell you about what is happening in Heaven? Ummm..."

He looked directly at JC. "First of all... let me just say this JC; your Father was pretty damn impressed with that speech you gave him the day you left."

JC appeared about to interrupt, but Michael just held his hand up imperiously; "You'll get your chance young fella, I thought you told me I had the floor. Right... now... I think it's fair to say he wasn't too happy when you suggested that life on earth was better than life in heaven — more real, more exciting, more spontaneous were the words I think you used. Well... he sure didn't like that — *but,* I'll tell you what JC, he sure did respect you for having the courage to say it. He's mellowed a fair bit and he seems to accept now that you've chosen to live here, with Maria and your growing brood."

"Well that's cert..." JC began to say, but again Michael waved his hand airily;

"Man... You haven't changed much have you — still got far too much to say for yourself. Didn't I just tell you to shut up for a bit and let me finish? You'll get your chance soon enough. Now where was I?"

JC hung his head in shame, but a wry grin creased his lips as he mumbled; "yeah... and you haven't changed much either — still the big, bully-boy."

Everyone around the table, except Maria, tittered at this exchange. They'd never seen anyone prepared to speak to JC like that, or to take him to task. Maria had seen it all before from Michael, and she wasn't averse to giving JC an earful herself (in private of course) when she felt he deserved it.

"As I was saying;" Michael continued on, "before I was *rudely* interrupted. The Father *has* mellowed a fair bit, but he did complain the other day that he felt you, JC, just weren't doing enough to justify returning to earth to continue the work you'd begun."

JC looked up angrily; "Not enough!" he shouted.

Michael giggled, but didn't bother to wave JC to silence again, as he was now just sitting there glaring.

"Yeah... JC... Not enough! He's super impressed by the work of Adonis and Jonny. He said the communities they're creating show that man really does have a chance to live and work in peace and harmony. He has high hopes that all of humanity will one day live in loving, caring communities like those."

Jonny and Adonis both looked at each other and then high-fived. Johnny spoke for both of them when he said;

"Michael, if only you knew how much those words meant to us. God is pleased! Wow! What more could we ask for?"

Michael grinned; "the rest of the team; Gabriel, Angelo and Ronnie all made personal decisions to stay on Pangutaran and do what they could there. The Father understands that, and accepts that they have all made a wonderful difference in that community."

He looked at JC, who was resting his head in his hands, looking downcast; "and don't look so forlorn JC — he said you and Maria had done a wonderful job with the Mangyan people; that you'd brought them into the twenty-first century with dignity and pride. He's happy with you!"

"*But...* he thinks it time you moved on; moved out of your comfort zone and spread the message further and wider. After all JC, the other guys are doing great, but at the end of the day it's *you* who's 'The Son of God', it's *you* who's 'Jesus Christ'...So... he just feels you should be doing more. "

Michael picked up his glass and drunk deeply before spreading his arms wide; "Okay, big boy... it's your turn to speak now — let's hear it!"

JC looked up at his old friend before replying. "I agree! It frustrates the hell out of me that I can't do more, but you know what happens if I leave here — people recognise me and it becomes so difficult to deal with. I wish I knew what to do."

Michael stood up and walked around the table until he was standing directly behind JC, placing one hand on each shoulder. "It's simple my friend — just do it! If people recognise you, then deal with it. You don't have to go to the big places anyway, to spread the word. The sort of work you are doing here's wonderful, but you could do it in so many other places as well."

He walked slowly around the table, taking his seat again; "anyway, that's for you and Maria to discuss. I can't force you to do anything JC, but you have such power, such magnetism and so much to share with the world, it just seems a bit of a shame to spend it all here — worthy as that may be. On that note, I think we should all take our leave and you guys get some sleep — I rather suspect our friends JC and Maria have some talking to do."

Michael stood up and without another word just slowly ascended toward the ceiling. With a quick wave of his hand, he was gone; out of sight. Nobody moved for an eternity, until Angelo broke the silence.

He slapped Gabriel on the back. "Come on you, time we were in bed. I'm tired."

They all slowly got to their feet and wandered into the bedroom at the back of the hut; each of them wrapped up in their own thoughts on the wonders they had witnessed that evening. Finally there was just JC and Maria sitting there.

Maria looked at her husband and smiled; "Well honey, he's right about one thing — we do have a lot to talk about."

Their discussions lasted into the early hours of the morning, before they both dragged their weary bodies to the bedroom also — being extra careful not to stand on the prone, sleeping, forms of their friends, on the floor—.

. . .

Chapter 5

When they all stumbled out to the breakfast area for their reviving cups of coffee the next morning, there was a palpable air of expectation. Things were about to change in their organisation, they had no doubt about that. They knew JC intimately and they knew he wasn't going to take, the even veiled, criticism from his father, lightly. Each of them had experienced JC's true personality over the years — they all knew he was a man of action and that as happy a picture he always painted of their life in the Mindoran hills, they knew, deep down, that he really wanted to be out there with the rest of them.

There was a happy, breathless, bubble of conversation from around the table as they awaited JC and Maria to emerge, and put them out of their misery. When a smiling and sheepish JC finally entered the room, with Maria by his side, all faces turned to the couple expectantly.

JC placed him arm around his wife's shoulder and drawing her close to him he whispered; "look at that honey... everyone's waiting to hear what the plan is. We're so blessed to have such true and loyal friends, who have stuck by us through thick and thin".

Maria's answer was to kiss her husband softly on the cheek, and push him toward the waiting pack.

Sitting down, he spread his hands on the table, as if in supplication. "Good morning my brothers," he began.

Infuriatingly, for everyone who was hanging on his every word, he poured himself a large mug of coffee, from the well-used and slightly battered coffee urn. Breathing on his drink to cool it slightly, he took a large sip; exhaled, with deep satisfaction, and glanced at the faces surrounding him at the table.

He chuckled at the look of impatience on Jonny's face, the look of slight annoyance on Ronnie's, but also at the look of bemusement and slight humour on Angelo's. Aha, JC thought, Angelo at least understands the theatricality of the moment.

His reverie was broken when Maria slapped him, unnecessarily hard on the back of his head, before taking a seat beside him.

"Come on, you big lummox, don't keep everyone in suspense... just tell them what our plans are. There's no need for the amateur dramatics — you just love it don't ya?"

He grinned and rubbed the back of his head in mock pain. Holding his hands up to quell the rising revolt he announced; "my Father's right!"

He smiled. "It is time for Maria and I;" looking around he spotted Damien and Samantha peeking between chairs; "and the children," he added; "to get more involved with the ministry."

After a long pause, as chairs began to shuffle, and mutterings were heard, JC continued on. "As Jonny and Adonis well know, our Davao community is chocka. We couldn't squeeze another soul in there if we tried. Now both of them are fully committed to building new communities all over the world."

He looked at the pair, seated at the head of the table and gave them both a soft nod and a smile. "It's not only my Father who's pleased with them, it's me also. I think these two have done more to change the world in the last seven years, than all of us put together and for that I give them all my thanks, all my admiration and all my undying love."

Jonny and Adonis stood as one and walked round the table to hug both Maria and JC. With tears already flowing down his cheeks, Adonis managed to squeeze out; "you gave me a new life JC, I will happily spend the rest of it in yours and God's service. Thank you so much."

JC squeezed his arm and turned to Jonny, who just shrugged his shoulders in that self-deprecating way of his. "JC... this is my dream! Not only do I get to organise and run some of the biggest projects in the history of the planet, I'm doing God's work. What could be more fulfilling than that? I thank you too, for the trust and faith you've put in us."

After they'd returned to their seats JC continued on; "Maria and I have talked about this and here's what we plan to do..."

JC explained they would purchase a number of large buses and fit them out as accommodation units. They would pack up the children and tour around Asia holding, what he referred to as, "Revival Meetings". He smiled widely at everyone;

"You remember the meetings that were held in baseball stadiums all over America, back when I put my golden cross in the sky? Well..that's the sort of thing I want to recreate."

He took a long sip of his coffee before continuing. "What we have in mind is to tour all over Asia for the foreseeable future and to stay in each city for one month, holding meetings every evening for the locals to attend. When we leave a city we want to have in place a group of townspeople committed to, and ready to establish new communities like Davao, in their own cities. Obviously we'll fund it all, but the money's not the issue. What we want to create is the same loving, caring, environment we have in all our other communities."

He sat back and looked at them. "So guys — opinions, ideas, criticisms? Let's hear them."

They sat and pondered the proposal for several minutes, before Angelo spoke up.

"But what about the children's education JC? It will be pretty hard to teach them anything on the move."

Maria interjected; "Ahhhh... now that's certainly not a problem for Sam and Damien; they already know everything there is to know in this world — something they inherited from their Dad."

Casting a glance at the room where the other children were sleeping, she continued. "It's too early to know about the other two sets of twins, but if they're the same — then great; but if not — then I'll teach them myself. No problems!"

They answered other questions about timing and about itineraries before everyone finally agreed that it was an exciting and feasible proposal.

Angelo and Gabriel appeared to be locked into non-verbal discussion with each other at the end of the table. There was nothing said, but lots of shrugs, raised eyebrows and the occasional shaking of the head. JC noted with a smile, that those two were as good as married — they could communicate their feelings without words now.

Finally it was Gabriel who spoke up. "JC... Ange and I want to come with you... if you'll have us. We love what we do on Pangutaran, but sometimes we feel we should be doing more, also."

He chewed his lip a while before continuing. "The only problem is we can't just leave the people and the Church there — they need us."

Delia spoke up; "Ronnie and I are more than happy to take over what you guys do there. Our business interests are not important and besides we have good managers. We'll move to the Church and help with the medical centre and the school, if that will allow you and Ange to follow JC."

She looked at her husband Ronnie and noticed a tear squeezing from the corner of his right eye. "I know Ronnie would like to come with you also; he won't admit it... but he does miss the lifestyle you all had back then."

Ronnie leant over and hugged Delia, shaking his head. "No," he said, "not yet... when the kids are old enough, we will *ALL* join you guys." He looked quickly at JC; "that's assuming you want us ha!"

JC was weeping unashamedly. He buried his face in Maria's blouse and sobbed, as she gently stroked his hair. Looking up and smiling she said; "I think we can take JC's response as a *yes*. We want you all to come with us — as many as can do at this time, anyway."

JC looked up and wordlessly went around the table pulling each of his friends to their feet and hugging them tightly, before moving on to the next. When he reached Adonis and Jonny they stood and faced him.

Adonis, in his booming, deep voice announced; "Wish we could go too JC, but we know what we're doing is the right thing. We'd still rather be with you guys though."

JC nodded and placing an arm around each of their shoulders drew them both to him and hugged them for several minutes.

Once everyone had settled back to the table; he announced; "time to start planning guys. There's a lot to do if we're going to be ready to hit the road on the first of next month."

The realisation of the tight schedule sobered everyone instantly and they began to put together concrete plans for purchasing and outfitting their new mobile homes.

. . .

Damien and Samantha had been listening to the conversation and now the adults were busy with their preparations, Damien looked at Sam and arched his eyebrows. "So... it looks like we're about to start a big, new adventure ha! Excited?"

The thought response from Samantha was not what he was expecting. "Excited? No... more... enthralled. This is our big opportunity Damien — we can be part of this. We can participate in the rallies with Mum and Dad. We can speak to thousands of people. It's more than exciting, it's stupendous!"

Damien hadn't considered that possibility, but the more he thought about it, the more he realised he and Sam were probably the most qualified people to do that. After all... didn't they already know everything there was to know? Didn't they have all of the wisdom and knowledge of their father?

"You're right Sam, it's an amazing opportunity — all we have to do is convince Mama and Papa of that... hehehe! Anyway, we'd better go and tell our friends we'll be leaving."

At that thought, Samantha's face fell; "yes... I hadn't thought of that; that's so sad."

With the adults deep in conversation, nobody noticed the youngsters' departure outside.

. . .

Damien headed to his private hiding place to do some thinking. This turn of events had taken him by surprise; more so, Sam's reaction. Could they really be expected to participate in the rallies? The more he thought about it, the more he grew as excited about the possibilities, as Sam clearly was. He smiled to himself; yes, this could be wonderful — no more boring school, no more pretending to learn what I already know. He felt Sam's subtle presence inside his head and waited for her interjection.

"So... Damien, finally you see the light ha! Well, forget about it — I'll be greater than you! I'll be more important than you! I'm the true heir to Dad's legacy; just you wait and see."

Damien shook his head sadly; "Samantha... game on girl! See you on the road."

He tuned into his own personal stereo to block her from his mind, for a while. He needed time to think — time to develop some plans for the future. He sure as hell wasn't going to let his annoying "big" sister get the better of him this time.

Samantha was already putting her half-designed plans into play. Re-entering the house, she made a bee-line for her father's chair. Pulling herself up on his lap she stared at the multitude of documents and drawings spread across the dining room table. Her father indulgently rubbed her hair and gently caressed her shoulders, as she squirmed closer, into the comforting crook of his arm. In a brief pause in proceedings, she judged her time to perfection. Looking up into her father's kindly face she wheedled in her best "little girl" voice;

"Daddy... I've been thinking."

Absently, JC leant down and placed his hand under her chin. He lifted it until they were looking eye to eye. JC marvelled at what a beautiful, young girl he and Maria had conspired to create. As he looked deep into her crystal, blue, eyes his heart surged with the intense love only a father can know for a daughter.

"And... Just what is it you've been thinking... my little pumpkin?"

Intrigued by the interplay between father and daughter, the adults sat back in their chairs and waited for Samantha to enlighten him, and them.

Maria chuckled softly to herself. She knew that look of Sam's exceptionally well. Although it never worked on her, she was well aware JC just couldn't say no to her when she put on this act. She giggled — she can wrap that grown man around her little finger like he's her puppy dog. She, though, was also fascinated to know what cunning plan her daughter had hatched this time.

Sensing the moment perfectly, Samantha leaned back and gave her father a look that was always guaranteed to melt his heart. She favoured everyone seated at the table with their own personal look, and winning smile. When she came to her mother she couldn't help but notice the sly grin on her mother's face. Hmmm... she thought... Mama knows me too well... hehehe.

Allowing the anticipation to rise even further she paused before speaking; "well Daddy... if we're to be off on a tour around Asia, it's going to be very hard for Damien and I to do any schoolwork." She shook her long locks playfully; "and besides Daddy, you know we already know everything there is to know anyway. So..."

JC chuckled softly; even he was aware now that he was being played.

"So..." he urged her on.

"Well... What I was thinking was... Damien and I could be part of the revival meetings. We could speak and help people find the right way. I know we can do it Daddy... and just remember what you said two thousand years ago...'out of the mouths of babes' ha? So... what do you think?"

Maria laughed aloud at her daughter catching her father with his own words, albeit those spoken a very long time ago.

JC though, was moved by Samantha's sincerity, and kissed her softly on the head, before looking to his wife for confirmation.

Maria held up her hands in mock surrender. "What can I say? The child has a good point. There's nothing more for them to learn and they could be incredibly inspirational speakers, as we tour Asia. It's an unqualified yes from me."

Sam just grinned at her mother and jumping off her father's lap she ran to her and threw her arms around her waist. "Thank you Mama, I know we won't let you down."

Maria shook her head softly. "It's not just up to me Sam... Everyone has to agree, right JC?"

JC tried hard to look serious. "Yes, of course. We're a team here, so any big changes need to be approved by us all."

He looked around the table at the rest of the friends. "Does anyone want to give their opinion on Sam's idea?"

Nobody spoke, but each one of them was smiling and nodding their heads in approval. Finally, Gabriel spoke up.

"JC... you have two of the most gifted children in the Universe in Sam and Damien. I think I speak for everyone when I say allowing them to participate in the rallies would be awesome. The power of beautiful, eloquent, and truly sincere children will melt even the hardest of hearts. I think..." he looked around and spread his arms wide. "*We* think it's the best idea we've ever heard. Wow! This is going to be some tour."

Samantha made a point of going round each of them and hugging and kissing them, whispering her thanks. She turned finally to her father and burbled excitedly; "Ohhhh....I'd better go and find Damien and tell him what we'll be doing for the next few years. I know he'll be as excited as me."

They smiled indulgently as Samantha turned and ran outside, without a backward glance.

She focused her mind to find her twin. Initially she had no success and her brow wrinkled in annoyance. Hmmm... Why I can't focus in on him? She sat down on an old tree stump and put her head in her hands — focusing all her energy and thought on Damien Castillo. After much concentration and with sweat dripping from her forehead; she began to feel herself creeping back inside of his mind.

"Hey you!" she shouted in his head. "What you think you're doing ha? You trying to block me out now are you?"

All she got in return was a muted giggle. Hmmm... she thought... this boy needs teaching a lesson — but that will have to wait.

"Damien," she purred; "Guess what? We're going to be part of the revival tour. We're going to be speaking at meetings and making altar calls. How about that ha? Everyone at the meeting thought it was a wonderful idea. I'm so looking forward to it — to doing something really meaningful."

She waited for Damien to respond but there was an eerie silence inside of his head. She couldn't even seem to zero in on what he was thinking. Was she losing her power, or was Damien blocking her still?

"WHAT!"

The response from her brother was so loud, so violent and so unexpected that she jerked upright and fell off the side of the old tree stump. Laying in the dirt, blinking to clear her head she noticed Damien looming above her, looking down at her. The shout had come from his lips, not from his mind, as he had crept up behind her.

Grinning just a little ruefully he offered his hand to help her to her feet. Brushing it aside angrily she pushed herself up and grabbed him by the shoulders. "Why the hell'd you do that for Damien? I almost wet myself."

Damien laughed; "well... why did you volunteer me for something without talking to me about it first. I don't think I can speak in front of a big crowd Sam. I'm not sure I have the confidence to do it. Ohhhh... Sam; why didn't you tell me you were going to do this?"

Noticing the tears in the corners of his eyes, she was immediately overcome with contrition. She moved her hands from his shoulders to around his waist and hugged him tightly. "Damien, don't worry — we'll do it together. We'll be amazing — the twin preachers. Please don't be angry with me. I just wanted us to do something special; together. This will be wonderful, trust me; I'll be by your side always. We're a team ha! Inseparable!"

She felt Damien relax and relent.

"Well... if you're sure I can do it Sammy, then yeah, I guess it's a lot better than pretending to go to school and learn things we already know." He pulled back and looked his sister directly in the eyes. "You promise me we'll always be together — come on... promise me."

Samantha grinned. "Oh Damien, we're one person in two bodies, we've always known that. Of course we'll be together forever."

That settled; the pair headed off for some fun with their friends before they were due to leave the village — possibly forever. They wanted their last few weeks there to be memorable. They skipped away, hand in hand to seek out their friends—.

. . .

Chapter 6

Las Vegas, Nevada USA:

It was a tad ironic that the newest, most glorious construction site in Las Vegas over the past few years had not been a glittering edifice to man's greed and debauchery; but rather a magnificent crystal temple, and a village, dedicated to the Kingdom of God Church. Just a few miles away from the bright, neon lights of the Las Vegas strip, with its ostentatious and gaudy hotels and casinos, aimed at fleecing the unfortunate, who sought the dream of instant wealth; was raised a completely different monument. On the outskirts of the dusty city; rose a testament to something better in man's psyche — The Kingdom of God Church and the village of Ezraville.

Pastor Jhoemar Nolasco was intensely proud and protective of the sanctuary they had created, in the midst of this city dedicated to hedonism. He saw his role partly to guide people who were down on their luck — who had lost everything at the Casinos' relentless tables and machines, to a place where they could recover and regain their sanity without any pressure on them.

The Las Vegas, Ezraville community had become almost a transient camp, where people would come and recover, before heading back to their families and the realities of life. It never ceased to amaze him however how many of these transients would return, months later — family in tow, declaring they wanted to permanently join the Church community. He saw his mission to love and nurture everyone who came to the community. Whether or not they later returned was between them and God, but so, so many of them did.

Joe Nolasco was one of the original members of the Davao Church and had at one time been a close confidant and friend of the Reverend Adonis Quanico. Having witnessed the miracle of Davao, Joe, like his mentor, had committed his life to serving the true Church. When he was offered the role of Pastor to the Las Vegas community it had been the pinnacle of his life. He expected he would never leave this wonderful place that he was now privileged to serve. Helping humanity in a wonderfully, beautiful setting had made him a truly contented man.

That Sunday morning he was standing on the balcony of his cottage, sipping his coffee, looking across the vast expanse of the community's building and grounds; thanking God, and the Reverend Quanico, for such a wonderful opportunity. His gratefulness regime was interrupted by the insistent chirping of a cell-phone. A quick glance assured him it was the front gate calling.

He grinned to himself — new arrivals no doubt. Joe had made it a rule that he would always be the first to welcome new members to the community. At times it seemed an onerous responsibility, having to drop whatever he was doing to head for the main gate and greet the newcomers. For him though, there was nothing more important and more lasting than the first impression a potential member of his flock had, of the Kingdom of God Church. It was a responsibility he took very seriously.

A quick chat to the person at the front gate assured him that, yes, there were new arrivals that sunny morning. Donning his wide-brimmed panama hat, to protect himself from the harsh desert sunlight, he sauntered happily down the main road toward the front gate. Entering the air-conditioned office he smiled at the two gentlemen seated at desk.

"Welcome, welcome, welcome... my friends... to the Kingdom of God Church. I'm the Reverend Joe Nolasco — I'm in charge here. Now, how can we help you today?"

Taking a seat beside them he began to study them. They seemed somehow familiar. There was something in the slant of their heads, or perhaps the eyes, that banged away at Joe's memory cells. Do I know these two men, he wondered? Thoughts of recognition were quickly swept away as he examined the two "strangers" more closely. His heart went out to them — they'd obviously been through some tough times.

Both of them looked like "down on their luck" drifters, with their torn, dusty clothes and their wide-eyed appearance. They both seemed relatively young men, perhaps in their mid-thirties, but it was clear to Joe that their lives had been far from easy. Their hair was long and greasy, with the shorter of the two having made some concession to attempting to tie it back in a ponytail. They both sported long straggly beards and moustaches that hid half their face from view.

As he surveyed them, the taller of the two removed his crushed, wide brimmed Stetson and wiped his grimy, sweaty forehead with an even grimier cloth he'd pulled from his pants pocket.

When the man spoke, Joe jerked up and looked him in the eyes. The man had a Filipino accent; he was sure of it. *"Ikaw ay Pinoy"* (You are Pinoy) he ventured.

The man appeared to give a slight flash of understanding before shaking his head and replying; "Nah Reverend, we're

Mexican, from Guadalajara. We've been working on the farms up and down the south for the last three years, until about a month ago, when my friend Chito and I decided to try our luck in Las Vegas."

He looked down at his clothes and shook his head sadly. "As you can see Rev. our luck wasn't with us this time." Suddenly, as if remembering his manners the man jumped to his feet.

"I'm sorry Reverend, how rude of me. Let me introduce ourselves. I'm Jesus Magtana and this here is my friend, Chito Guerrero."

He thrust out his hand for Joe to shake. "We sure would appreciate some help to get back on our feet Reverend. Someone at the casino suggested we might try here. Is that true?"

Joe quickly became business-like with the pair. "Absolutely right! You guys are welcome to stay here for as long as you need and if, after a while, you decide you want to stay permanently, by all means. But... if you want to move on, we'll understand."

The look of relief on Jesus and Chito's faces was reward enough for Reverend Joe. Putting his arm around Jesus' shoulder he began to lead the pair toward the door to the compound.

"Right, first things first — let's get you boys cleaned up and fed and then we'll sit down and discuss what we can do to help you." Sniffing the air slightly, he added; "now come along; showers first I think."

Jesus and Chito exchanged an unseen knowing nod and conspiratorial smile as they allowed Reverend Joe to lead them into the compound.

. . .

Several Weeks Earlier: Mexicali (Baja California)-Mexico:

As seedy bars go, this particular one was no worse than the hundreds the pair had frequented over the past couple of years. Located in the seediest part of the seediest border town in Mexico, it was nothing more really than a tin shed; with a patched, corrugated iron roof that kept out the worst of the rains, on the odd occasion that it did actually rain. The walls were covered with fifty year old posters proclaiming the glory days of Mexican football and although the single window gave some pretence of letting in light, it probably had not been cleaned, in the same amount of time.

It was dim and it was dingy; but that was the way the serious drinkers that frequented this establishment preferred it. Anonymous people, in an anonymous world; wrapped up in their own problems with just one desire in life — to get hopelessly drunk and forget, if only for a day, their miserable, pathetic lives.

Down one side of the small shed was a rough, wooden counter behind which leaned a sweating, grossly overweight, barkeeper who would regularly mop his forehead with the same cloth that he would assiduously polish the cracked and chipped glasses, from which the drinkers downed their shots of rot-gut, home produced, and vile, whisky.

In one corner of the room a faded beauty from the past; her wrinkles clearly giving away her advanced years, sat at a piano softly singing an old Mexican folk song — out of tune, and with her rough, gravelly voice grating over each word. That morning there were three tables of serious drinkers in the ten table establishment. Each group was separated from each the other by as far as was humanly possible in the tiny bar. They each had their own secret, *important,* discussions happening that they didn't want to share with anyone else.

Occasionally a raised voice would break the low mumble that emanated from each table. A glass would be slammed down on the rough-hewn timber tables and chairs would scrape, as combatants prepared to defend themselves, their honour, or the validity of their argument. Most of these contretemps would invariably end without punches being thrown, knives being drawn, guns being wielded, and blood being spilt on the bar's sawdust floors. Most arguments would end with the protagonists hugging it out and laughing, before signalling to the bartender for a refill.

Once in a while though, real violence, would erupt and the bartender would haul himself upright to his full, imposing six feet six inches and waddle his over twenty stone toward the miscreants; ready to bash some heads. Pablo was known to deal quickly and none too pleasantly with patrons who insisted on taking their arguments to the next level. Usually the mere sight of this giant man lumbering toward them, with violent intent written all over his face, was enough to calm even the most argumentative of would-be, drunken brawlers.

At one table, nearest the door they sat; leaning back on their fragile plastic chairs, feet on the table, sipping their cold Corona's. With no ventilation in the bar, and with the sun beating down mercilessly on the old tin roof, the heat was almost unbearable. Both men were sweating profusely and one took off his battered Stetson to wipe his forehead with the grubby handkerchief he'd wrapped around his neck. Draining the last of the precious, cold liquid he signalled the bartender for a refill.

Reaching under the counter he handed two more ice-cold Coronas to a little Mexican girl of no more than eight years of age.

She ran to the table and placed the beers in front of each man. Smiling at her, the man reached into his shirt pocket to produce a small coin for her efforts. She giggled and tucked the coin into her skirt pocket before skipping back to her sanctuary behind the bar.

One of the men looked up from his bottle, which he'd already half-drained in just one swallow, and smiled ironically at his companion. "How the fooking hell did we end up like this Danny boy?"

His friend grinned back at him; "Well Chog, it seems to me maybe this is that thing called karma ha! Maybe we're just getting out just desserts."

Chog laughed so loud that even the other patrons ignored their own sorrows long enough to lift their heads and glare across the room at the pair. He took another swig from his bottle before replying; "Well mate... you might be right. I know they say karma's a 'bitch', but I reckon we did this to ourselves alright."

Nodding sagely, Dan-dan continued to sip on his beer.

Chog cast his mind back to that fateful day in Zamboanga City when he and Dan had made the decision to betray their friends and go on the run, with over $100M of the Church's funds. It had seemed so easy back then and even so right. He remembered when Dan had first raised the idea with him.

He and Danny had been friends forever; since they were boys growing up on the isolated island of Batanes in the South China Sea. All their lives they had been inseparable and when Dan suggested they should help themselves to the funds and make a new life somewhere else, Chog not only agreed with his friend, he'd quickly rationalised exactly why they were justified in doing so.

That was all ancient history now though and it hadn't taken too long for them both to regret what they'd done — but... you can never turn back the hands of time and you have to live by your decisions.

It was ironic that they'd spent the first few years of their escapade looking over their shoulders, wondering when someone from the Church or from law enforcement would tap them, and take them into custody. They'd no idea that JC and the rest of them had actually forgiven them and had no intention of chasing after them. As far as they'd been concerned, they were wanted criminals and they behaved exactly like that.

They sought out the remotest, most unlikely place for anyone to look for them. For the first four years they'd used their immense wealth to purchase a lifestyle for themselves on a Pacific Island wonderland. They had purchased Katafanga Island; a small, partially developed private island in the Fiji group of Islands. The island already had everything they needed for their South Pacific fantasy.

They'd hired a full complement of workers, from the mainland, to live there and cater for their every whim. This included any number of pretty, young Fijian girls who would act as "hostesses" to the wealthy eccentrics (which was how the locals viewed them). Living in paradise worked well for them for about four years, but then both began to feel the meaninglessness and boring routine of island life. Even in the midst of absolute luxury, both began to crave more excitement and action.

Chog wasn't sure if it was his or Dan's idea to sell the island and go sailing, but one day, while they were relaxing on sun loungers by the pool, sipping their cold vermouths, it was agreed. They would buy a large cruising yacht and spend time travelling the world and experiencing everything it had to offer.

Chog had read extensively as a child and had always been fascinated with the lifestyle of the Caribbean; "I reckon we should head for Jamaica first mon and try out their Rastafarian ways — what do you say Dan? Let's blow this place and hit the world running."

The decision made, it was only a few short months later that they travelled to New Caledonia, to pick up their newly refurbished 62-footer touring yacht. The former "Mistress Mary" was quickly renamed by Dan-dan, tongue firmly placed in his cheek, as; "Gift of God".

Coming from an island background both of them were well indoctrinated in the art of sailing from a very early age, yet neither had ever seen a yacht of this size, beauty or splendour before and they were captivated by it. Her spacious teak joinery interior gave an aura of warmth, comfort and unabashed luxury. Fitted out with all the latest technology and electronic gizmos, Chog was confident they could handle it themselves, but Dan-dan was adamant they should hire a local skipper.

"Hey mate," he'd insisted; "do we really want to be bothered with all the actual work of sailing. I thought the idea was to have fun." Allowing the idea to sink into Chog's head, he added after a short while; "besides, we're going to be way too busy entertaining the lady friend guests we pick up along the way, to be worried about mundane shit like sailing — right?"

Unable to disagree with him, they'd hired a grizzled, old retired sea captain by the name of Francois Duaphane, they'd met in one of the many bars that littered the Noumean waterfront. He'd assured them he had years of experience in ocean-going yachts... and... that was good enough for the boys, especially in their current state of inebriation. After agreeing a salary package they headed back to where the yacht was moored, to prepare for their first epic voyage; across the Pacific, north first to the Hawaiian Islands, where they planned to rest and recreate for a month or two; before continuing on to somewhere in Central America — they 'd decide on the way.

After that it was just a quick side trip through the Panama Canal and into the Caribbean. It seemed so simple when you looked at it on a map. Just across the limitless sea and then hug the coast. What could be so hard about that, the boys thought? After a week of stocking up on supplies, purchasing all the necessary charts and refilling the yacht's substantial wet-bar, the brave trio were ready for the off.

Once sober, Francois had proved to be an efficient and effective organiser. He was adept at harnessing the locals to load up supplies, freeing up the boys to just relax on their sun loungers on the deck of the yacht, watching the hive of activity around them and sipping on their cold beers.

When all was ready "Gift of God" sped out of Noumea harbour, under her own engine power, before hoisting sails and setting sight for the islands of Hawaii.

On their final day before departure Chog and Dan-dan had again done the rounds of the local waterfront bars of Noumea, but this time they were looking for some suitable feminine "company" for their long sojourn across the ocean.

As luck would have it they struck up a conversation with two twin sisters; Natalie and Angeletta. Twenty-two years old, incredibly beautiful and nubile, these island princesses said they were sick and tired of their boring lives with no real future beyond marriage. They had long dreamed of escaping one day to America. With the promise of a "free" ride to Hawaii, both jumped at the chance and rushed home to pack a few things before joining them back on the dock.

For the first leg of their journey the infamous Pacific Ocean and its weather lived up to its name. Hot, balmy day followed hot, balmy day as the days drifted into weeks and the weeks into months. The wind proved weak, but reliable, and "Gift of God" sailed unerringly through the endless expanse of ocean, heading for its ultimate goal.

The two girls proved their worth in many ways. They were wonderful eye-candy, as well as warm, willing and comfortable bodies to wrap around at night; but they were much more. They willingly helped with all the chores and did more than their fair share of the scrubbing and cleaning necessary to keep an ocean yacht in tip-top shape on a long sea voyage.

As they neared the coast of Hawaii, Chog and Dan-dan ruefully realised their little companions would soon be departing them. When Chog asked Angeletta how they planned to get around US Customs officers, she just laughed in her high-pitched tinkle.

"Oh you needn't worry about Nat and me. We'll just dive into the sea when we're near one of the islands and swim to shore." She favoured Chog with a cunning look; "you know Choggy... we have ways of getting what we want. Don't worry about us, we'll be fine and thanks for bringing us — it's been fun." With a toss of her long black hair she rushed off to find Natalie and organise their gear for the departure and swim to the mainland.

The two girls jumped into the sea just off the island of Kaho'olawa. With a quick wave to the watching trio, they struck out for the distant shoreline. Having spent all their lives in and around the sea, Angeletta had explained that she and Natalie could swim for hours, so they really didn't need to worry about them. Nevertheless, "Gift of God" stayed in place until they could see the small figures emerge from the surf, onto the beach. Chog turned to Dan-dan and he could see conflicting emotions in his eyes.

"Yeah; me too bud — I'm going to miss them as well."

He clapped Dan-dan on the shoulders.

"No time for misery my friend — we have more adventures and more girls to meet in Honolulu ha, so let's get there—."

. . .

Chapter 7

After Chog and Dan-dan had spent a week of drunken debauchery ashore, in Honolulu; Francois had "Gift of God" fully provisioned and ready for the final push to Puntarenas in Cost Rica. They would land there before heading through the Panama Canal and into the glorious Caribbean.

Chog and Danny were a sorry sight as they struggled up the gangplank, just twenty minutes prior to their planned departure time. Both looked like they'd been through the wringer of the washing machine — their clothes dirty and sweat-stained, their faces haggard from hours of no sleep; both sporting four day old fuzz on their chins. They swayed from side to side as they hauled themselves up the gangway.

"Casssssssshhhhhht us off my good man;" Dan-dan waved at Francois, watching the pair from the bridge, with a look of wry amusement on his face.

"Coshhhhta Rica — here we come."

Danny fell flat on his face on the deck and lay there flapping helplessly, like some giant marlin hauled up from the depths of the ocean. Laughing uproariously at his friend's predicament, Chog tripped over Danny's flopping frame and fell right on top of him, where they both lay, writhing away, each unable to stand.

Francois, walking down from the bridge, chortling away to himself; none too gently nudged the pair with his boot before heading to the bow to release the lines. By the time "Gift of God" was pointed toward the harbour entrance and steaming gently toward the open sea; Chog at least had managed to haul himself to his feet, fall down the stairs to the main salon and thence to his bunk, where he collapsed; still fully clothed, to sleep the sleep of the dead for the next sixteen hours.

Dan-dan wasn't going anywhere — he remained on the open deck, curled up in the foetal position for the next six hours, before the chill of the evening sobered him enough to pull himself to his feet and make his way to his cabin where he also collapsed on the bed, for the interim.

Francois noted with a sad shake of his head that there'd be no feminine company for them on this leg of the voyage. Although he wasn't able to participate in the sexual gymnastics he knew was taking place in the bedrooms; he enjoyed the pleasant sight of often topless young ladies accompanying them across the ocean.

"Ah well," he muttered to himself; "those lads were probably too pissed to even attract any self-respecting girl to come with them". He tittered quietly to himself.

When Chog finally emerged from the cabin some sixteen hours later "Gift of God" was well out of sight of land and wallowing in suspiciously deep troughs in the middle of the Pacific Ocean. Leaning over the balustrade he dry-retched over the side of the yacht, before wiping his mouth and turning to Francois, who had come down to check on his condition.

"What's with this sea Fran? God, I feel so sick!"

Francois looked at the southern horizon and scratched his chin thoughtfully. "Well my laddie, if the forecast's to be believed, we have a Category Four Pacific hurricane barrelling toward us."

That sobered Chog instantly and he jerked upright. "Shit Fran! Shouldn't we maybe head back to Honolulu and ride it out there?"

Francois laughed long and loud. "How long do you think you've been asleep young man? Nah! We're a hell of a long way from Honolulu now. Our best bet is to head north and try and outrun it." He looked at the southern horizon again and pursed his lips.

Joining him at the rail, Chog also looked south. What greeted him was a sight that all sailors know and fear. The sky was gun-metal grey and he could see an almost impenetrable wall of falling water rapidly bearing down on them. "Can we beat it Fran? It looks bloody scary."

Francois looked silently at the oncoming hurricane wall and clicked his false teeth loudly. "Nah boy... I don't think we can outrun it, but if we're lucky we can avoid the absolute worst of it and outflank it. Still... whatever we do... it's going to be a rough next thirty hours or so, so if I was you I'd scurry back to that safe, warm bed you just emerged from and hunker down for a couple of days."

Chog took a last, worried, glance at the fast approaching storm and with a tight grin to Francois, nodded his head and headed back down the stairs to the relative safety of his cabin.

With Chog and Dan-dan hiding in their cabins and unwilling — unable to help in any way, it was left to Francois to stay on duty on the bridge for the next three days straight — but, he relished it. He'd spent a lifetime battling typhoons in the Western Pacific, on one vessel or another, and this approaching Hurricane (Ethel) was no different. Standing at the wheel, lashed to a stanchion, so the constant battering of the waves and spray wouldn't sweep him overboard; Francois grinned at the approaching Hurricane. He knew by now "Gift of God" was a wonderfully built vessel and he backed himself, and his new baby, to make it through the storm intact.

He was thoroughly enjoying the opportunity to pit his skills and his fine vessel against the fury of nature's damndest. It was a battle that was playing out all across that part of the ocean — skippers proving their worth against everything the violent weather could throw at them. Pointing almost due north, Francois knew the Hurricane would likely bear more westerly than nor' westerly, so he fancied his chances of sliding around the northern fringes of the storm, unscathed. It was a long three days, but excitement and adrenaline kept him alert and on point.

On only one occasion did he consider the weather may have gotten the better of him and the yacht — well, at least momentarily, anyway. Seemingly out of nowhere, in what had been a predictable if mountainous series of waves and troughs, "Gift of God" was hit full abeam by an, out of sequence, out of tempo, "rogue wave". When it struck, the yacht heeled over at an almost impossible angle, dipping its masts deep below the sea's surface.

Clinging desperately to the wheel Francois shouted "Sacre Bleu!" and prepared for the final moment when the boat completely turned turtle. This was not some poorly built, native vessel though and its natural buoyancy and automatic tendency to try and right itself took over. Slowly, inexorably, it began the roll back to an upright stance; water pouring from the decks as the yacht almost seemed to shake itself dry, like a dog emerging from a bath.

Gulping his first breath of fresh air since the wave had struck; Francois gave up a quick prayer to his God and surveyed the damage all around him. The main mast was snapped in two about a quarter of the way up. Everything stored in and around the deck was simply gone; swept into the churning waters of the Pacific Ocean. The two life-rafts, stored on either side of the bridge had been ripped from their protective cages and tossed away like mere confetti. Most of the forward rails had also just disappeared, as had all the radio antennas and the satellite dish on the roof of the bridge. It looked like the entire boat had received a swabbing from some giant Ogre, who had just casually brushed everything into the sea.

Water had poured down into the main cabin and Chog and Dan-dan emerged through the swing doors, battling to open them in the howling gale. The sheer terror the two men felt was clearly evident in their wild-eyed looks. They scanned the boat, before grabbing hold of a nearby ladder step, as the yacht reached the crest of another giant wave, before hurtling down the other side at breakneck speed.

"Wwwwhat the ffffuck just happened, Francois?"

Chog was the first to recover his wits, although his voice was shaking and his teeth were chattering in sheer fear. Francois looked down at the pair and grinned.

"Ahhhh, t'weren't nothing this little beauty couldn't cope with — although... we did cop a fair bit of a thumping and we'll need to get to shore as quickly as possible and get repaired."

Chog and Dan-dan stood there shaking their head in amazement as they gazed at the broken mast and the absolutely spotless deck.

"I've plotted a course for Manzanillo in Mexico. We can organise repairs to the boat there;" Francois continued.

Dan-dan shook his head several times and rubbed his jaw. "Have we got enough fuel to get there Fran — we sure as hell can't sail, can we?"

He grinned at the pair; "Don't worry — while you two were busy getting shit-faced in Honolulu, I made sure we were fully resupplied. Yeah... we'll get there no problem." His attention was drawn back to the wheel as another giant wave swept under them and lifted them high in the air, depositing them unceremoniously in the next trough.

"Now... I suggest you two just go back to your cabins and wait out the storm. When it blows out, we'll all have a shit-load of cleaning to do, so you'd better grab what rest you can now. You're no bloody use to me out here and knowing you two, you'll end up getting swept overboard, and then where the hell would I be? I wouldn't get paid, would I?"

Dan-dan grinned embarrassingly and then placed a hand on Chog's shoulder, gently steering him toward the swing doors to the cabin. "He's right my friend, we're bugger all use here — let's get some sleep."

As a new wave deposited them deep inside another trough; Chog lost his footing and bounced down the few steps to the main saloon, on his arse. Sitting in two feet of water he looked up at his mate and started laughing maniacally.

"Yeah... you're right... best we go to bed and ride this one out ha!"

The next day dawned calm and beautiful; the seas still very lumpy, but the worst was over. Francois was beyond exhaustion. He stood, like a statue, holding the wheel with a deathlike grip keeping the little yacht pointing directly away from the following swells. He knew it would only get better from then on and soon he could entrust the wheel to either of the two guys, but until that time he wasn't leaving his post. It was his job to make sure they all made it safely to Manzanillo and by God; he was going to do his job.

When Dan-dan and Chog saw fit to make an appearance, the seas were dropping. The sun and the soft breeze ensured that very quickly life would return to normal aboard "Gift of God". Chog and Danny quickly set about clearing up the mess down in the main saloon and cabins and before too long Chog came up to offer his assistance to steer for a while.

Francois had trouble releasing the wheel from his vice-like grip, but once he managed to pry his fingers loose, one by one, he gratefully handed control over to Chog. He wearily trudged toward the warmth, safety and sanctuary of his cabin, where he would sleep for the next fifteen hours — the sleep of the grateful sailor who has once again defied the worst that his beloved sea could throw at him. "Gift of God" motored on relentlessly, the engine never missing a beat, toward the port of Manzanillo and the much needed repairs.

With all their radio and satellite equipment swept away in the storm the three of them had no way of knowing that Hurricane Ethel had cut a broad swath across the eastern Pacific. It sent six ships and yachts to an early watery grave, before slamming into Hawaii and causing massive loss and devastation, especially on the Eastern side of the Big Island. "Gift of God" had done extremely well to survive Ethel; the first of the season's Pacific Hurricanes.

As they limped into the Mexican port of Manzanillo they all offered up prayers of thanks for their safe arrival — ironically for Chog and Dan-dan, but nevertheless there was great relief and satisfaction on setting their feet on solid earth again.

As Dan and Chog made their first tentative steps onto Mexican soil they realised Francois had made an excellent choice in heading for Manzanillo. The city of over 100,000 people was a bustling port City whose entire focus appeared to be centred around the sea and industries related to it. They would have no problem finding a suitable establishment to repair their beautiful yacht for the trip through the Panama Canal to the Caribbean.

Despite the trials and tribulations they had not been put off the idea of cruising through the Caribbean islands. "Hey mate... it's just a short distance between islands over there — we won't get caught out in the open again like we did this time." Chog had reminded Dan.

Nodding his agreement Dan-dan winked at his friend before adding; "Well let's leave all that to Francois shall we? I fancy some cold tequila and some hot Mexican poontang. There must be some waterfront dives around here. Let's party my friend and celebrate our survival."

Caught up by Danny's enthusiasm, Chog clapped him on the shoulder and pushed him toward the first seedy establishment he saw, as they exited the wharf area.

Starting at the first seaman's dive, the pair embarked on a drunken orgy that would last three days and span numerous bars, brothels and hotel rooms, until eventually they found themselves waking up together in a grimy, cockroach-infested, hotel room on the edge of town. Wiping his eyes and attempting to stand Chog quickly fell back onto the bed, as a team of little men inside his head rapidly beat their hammers against his brain.

"Oh my God," he murmured; "that was some blow-out."

Ascertaining that he and Danny were alone in the room he shook his friend's shoulder. "Hey! Wake up you drunken prick. I want to know what the fuck we've been up to."

The response was just a grunt as Dan-dan rolled to the other side of the bed.

Gingerly, Chog tried to stand again, this time using the bed as added support. The black, lacy panties and bra hanging unceremoniously from the bedpost assured him that they had not been naked alone, in the room, all night. They must have picked up some lady or ladies somewhere along the way. He shook his head to try and dredge up some memories of the previous few days and instantly wished he hadn't as the pain shot through his skull like an electric discharge.

"Owwww! Shit! That's some bloody hangover I've got."

He had a vague recollection of a tall, black-haired, woman whose arm he had been holding the previous evening. Try as he might though he couldn't conjure up any images of what had taken place. The only clear mental picture that came to him was of the woman's eyes — they were deep brown pools, of mystery and intrigue. He smiled wryly to himself; I do remember she was gorgeous.

Walking across the room to the washbasin he turned the tap to splash some water on his bristly, grimy, face to try and bring some semblance of normality to his mind. There was an enormous gush of air from the tap, before a thin, brown trickle emerged briefly, followed by another massive blast of air — and then nothing.

"Damn!" he cursed. He wandered over to his still sleeping mate and showing zero concern for his friend's rest, or his comfort, he proceeded to pull the filthy, off-white sheets from the bed, depositing Dan-dan on the floor; with a loud crash, that reverberated off the cheap, plywood walls.

Danny sat up and screwed his face up in anger.

"Wwwhat tthe ffffuck are you doing? His face turned bright red, with fury, at his friend's cavalier treatment.

Chog tried to laugh, but it came out more as a wheeze, quickly followed by a loud, hacking cough. Running to the sink he managed to dry-retch up what little was left in his stomach.

Weakly, he turned back to Dan-dan, who was still looking furious.

"Settle down buddy;" Chog whispered softly.

"Where the hell are we? What happened last night? Shit... I feel like the last thing I really remember was walking down the gangplank — everything else is just a blur."

Dan-dan pulled himself to his feet, brushing off the dust he'd accumulated from the floor — "So... you don't remember anything ha? You don't remember the lovely Conchita Morales? Wow that was some woman." He wandered to the end of the bed and picking up her flimsy panties he chuckled; "Looks like Chita left something behind when she left this morning... hehehe".

Chog swallowed heavily to keep down the bile that threatened to return yet again. "Hmmm... well... I do sort of remember a woman — just her eyes really, they were so deep."

Dan-dan grinned and stared into space wistfully. "Yeah! Yeah! She did have nice eyes for sure, but she had many other nice things as well... hehehe." Realising he still had her panties in his hand, he put them down gently on the bed and looked directly into Chog's eyes. "You do remember the poker game though, right?"

Chog looked blankly at him; "poker game — what effing poker game?"

Danny sat down on the edge of the bed and sadly shook his head.

"Ohhhh, now let me think — just the poker game you lost our fucking boat on! You stupid, useless, twat!"

Chog's expression went through a variety of phases; from shock, to horror and finally to disbelief. "You're having me on right? You're messing with me head?"

Dan-dan looked at his stricken friend. "Oh Choggy boy, I wish I was... but no... last night, you bet our beautiful boat on a nine high straight — a nine high straight for Christ's sake, what were you thinking? You goddamn idiot!"

The reality of the situation finally broke through to Chog and he did have a flashback of sitting in a smoky room, surrounded by grinning Mexicans looking like characters out of some B-Grade western; dealing cards.

"I bet the boat?" he almost begged Danny to contradict him.

Nodding his head slowly Dan-dan smiled; "Ah well... don't let it get to you — they probably cheated us anyway. So... you lost the boat, we've still got shitloads of money. We'll just find something else to do. No problem my friend — and anyway, it was great fun."

Relieved his friend was taking it all so well Chog was still mentally beating himself up. How could he have gotten so incredibly drunk and stupid as to bet their boat on a poker hand? But Danny, bless his soul, was taking it in his stride. "So, what are we going to do now Danny boy? Where will we go?"

Dan-dan got up from the bed and walked to his friend. Placing his arm around Chog's shoulder he led him toward the bed and pushed him down on it. "Well Choggy;" he began; "I've been thinking and I reckon I have a new career path all mapped out for us."

Dan-dan explained, while Chog had been playing, he'd been chatting to the Mexicans around the table. "Everyone says if you want to make some real money here there's really only one way."

Chog looked at him expectantly and waved him to continue. "Drugs is where it's at here in Mexico, Chog. Juan told me, if you have money for the initial purchase, you can make a fortune smuggling drugs across to America and the beauty of it is; you don't take any of the risk. You buy the drugs, deliver them to a courier and then get paid for them. It's that bloody simple Choggy! Juan said we can double or even triple our money in just weeks. So, what do you think? Time for us to become big-time drug lords? So Chog... ha? ha? ha?"

Chog sat there for a while, letting the idea ruminate in his still aching brain. He wasn't in any condition to think clearly, but he'd always trusted Dan, so if Dan thought it was a good idea — well... then it simply must be. He smiled painfully at Danny and nodded his head. "Okay my friend — let's become Mexican drug lords for a while."

They high-fived before Chog turned to Dan-dan and said; "but first, can we please get some greasy food inside me to try and settle this stomach? I feel like I did during that bloody, big, storm."

Dan-dan laughed his agreement and they walked to the hotel room door with their arms around each other's shoulders.

After a breakfast of three greasy tortillas Chog was feeling, if not renewed at least a member of the human race again. As they returned to the port area they noticed a short, fat, Mexican man standing at the gangplank of their yacht, arguing with Francois. "That's the guy you lost the boat to;" Dan-dan quickly explained. "We better get over there and sort it out."

After quick introductions and an explanation to Francois, they all boarded and adjourned to the main saloon. Breaking out a bottle of tequila, Chog toasted the boat's new owner and added; "Right! We'll get our stuff and head off — she's all yours Miguel. Enjoy her!"

Miguel had a grin, underneath his gaucho moustache, as wide as the Rio Grande. "Thank you Senor Chog — I surely will"

Taking Francois aside, Chog gave him full payment for the year's contract and said ruefully; "sorry it all had to end so quickly, but that's life, especially when you get shit-faced drunk and gamble away your boat... hahaha! Are you sure you'll be alright?"

Francois laughed along with him. "Ahhhh, don't you be worrying about old Francois now. I'll find a berth back to New Caledonia and with this money I won't have to work again for a while. I'll miss you two though. You take care; ok?"

Chog nodded and wiped his eye to hide his emotion. He'd miss the old-fart, too; and the boat... but... that's history now, he thought. Time to get organised for our new career and he headed to his cabin to pack his meagre personal belongings.

They headed north to the border town of Mexicali where their ready access to large quantities of cash enabled them to easily buy into, and infiltrate, the local drug-smuggling trade. It was an easy life. They rented a luxury apartment and all they ever had to do was buy the drugs, pass them on to the designated courier and then wait for the payment — it couldn't be simpler and the returns were staggering. From an initial outlay of just US$1M, they had quickly, in just six months, parlayed their "working capital"; to an amazing US$20M.

"It's money for jam my friend....couldn't be easier!" Dan-dan murmured to Chog one afternoon, laying on sun-loungers on the balcony of their luxurious apartment. They sipped long, tall, cold, margaritas and fondled the breasts of two compliant, young ladies. Chog leant over to place his lips around the dark, full breast of his current, sleeping partner — Maria? Or was it Marietta? He could never quite remember.

He felt, rather than heard, the bullet that whistled past his right ear and slammed into the middle of Marietta's forehead.

Falling limp in his arms, an expression of shock in her still wide-open, eyes, she flopped forward onto Chog's lap, pulling him down slightly with her. It was that movement that saved him from the second bullet which slammed into the window just above his head. Chog and Dan-dan rolled to the floor and looked at each other in abject terror.

"Who the hell's shooting at us?" Chog screamed way too loudly, as he gently pushed Marietta's lifeless body onto the balcony deck.

Without waiting for an answer he crawled toward the sliding doors to the apartment's interior, motioning for Dan-dan and his girlfriend to follow him. Once they reached the sanctuary of the kitchen, where there were no visible windows, they rose to their feet. Dan-dan was visibly shaking and his girlfriend was crying and screaming Marietta's name. Dan-dan slapped her hard. "Shut up Rosalita; Marietta's dead — nothing we can do about her now. We need to get the fuck out of here though."

Chog and Dan-dan were brown enough to pass for Mexicans, but their arrival in Mexicali had been well noted by some of the big drug lords of the city. As far as they were concerned, these two; were flashy, rich interlopers who dared to try and horn in on their long-established and hard-won franchises. They were having none of it and plans were quickly hatched to dispatch the two "foreigners" to the graves, rightfully waiting for them. The only surprise being it had taken six months for them to strike, but struck they had and Dan-dan and Chog were rapidly running out of manoeuvring room.

Instructing Rosalita to wait in the apartment for a few hours and then head home, the pair threw what belongings and money they could into a couple of backpacks and headed down the back, service stairs of the apartment complex. Emerging through the rear door of the building they spotted two henchmen watching intently. Spurning that exit, they returned inside the building and headed for the basement car-park where their brand new, BMW M4 was stored. Chog jumped into the driver's seat and turning to his friend said; "This could get a bit hair-raising, so hang on tight and keep your head down. I'll see if I can get us out of here."

They hit the exit of the car-park at 60 miles an hour and swung hard left in a squeal of tyres and smoke. They were definitely being shot at — they could hear the pings, as each bullet slammed into the side of their BMW. Chog wasn't stopping for anything though and floored the super-fast car, quickly outdistancing the shooters. He kept on driving at hair-raising speed through the bustling streets of Mexicali until he was absolutely sure they didn't have anyone following them. He rounded a corner, near the outskirts of town, slammed on the brakes and they slid to a halt in the dusty, street.

The area they were in was unfamiliar to either of them, but there wasn't time to worry about that. It was just another depressingly rundown part of a largely depressingly run down town. Abandoning the car, they noticed the many bullet holes in the sides of it — bullets that must have come perilously close to either one of them. Chog crossed himself in relief, before they headed down the street to a seedy, neighbourhood bar. Slowly they regained their equilibrium over several large, ice-cold Corona's.

Once the adrenaline of the shooting and the escape had worn off both men began to sag a little in their chairs. Chog asked the inevitable question; "so what do we do now?"

Dan-dan removed his hat once more and wiped his sweaty brow again. "Well, one thing's for sure my friend — those bastards want us dead and the only way we're gonna get away is to get out of Mexico and head for the U.S."

Chog nodded, "I think you're spot on there buddy, but we'll need to get new identities and all that sort of shit... and where will we go in the U.S? It's a bloody big place?"

For the first time since their escape Dan-dan's face split into one of his trademark grins and he giggled. "Well Choggy... I've been thinking about that. You know what? I think it's time we rejoined our brothers and sisters in the Kingdom of God Church."

Chog's feet slipped from the table as he sat bolt upright. "What the..."

Dan-dan held up his hand. "Now, just hear me out ha! I read there's a new settlement in Las Vegas. If we go there... with new identities... nobody will recognise us from Adam. I mean none of the 'originals' are likely to be there anyway. Just think Choggy... all those rich people, giving it all up to the Church. We could have a lot of fun."

Chog scratched his bristly chin for a few seconds and then tuning on, his eyes illuminated and the possibilities began to dawn on him also. "Hmmmm... sounds like a plan Danny... it definitely sounds like a plan. I like it!"

A few well placed dollar bills to Pablo the bartender soon elicited a name and address of the best document forger in all of Mexicali. Once they'd organised their new passports; Chog and Dan-dan were dead and buried, to be resurrected as Chito Guerrero and Jesus Magtano. As a final touch they agreed it would be a good idea to have some minor plastic surgery done to alter their appearances even more.

Like forgers, Mexicali was awash with discredited and failed surgeons whose practices these days revolved around altering people's appearance just enough to fool the casual observer, or the latest facial recognition software.

For a small fee, Jose, the man who prepared their perfect passports for them was able to introduce them to a doctor who all agreed was the very best. The reason for his being struck off the medical register had less to do with his incompetence and much more to do with his sexual proclivities — especially with anaesthetised patients. After their face-altering surgery and a two-week recovery period in Dr Martinez's convalescent home, they were ready to undertake the long, arduous trip to Las Vegas.

Unwilling to risk exposure they'd decided to play the part of down-and-outs to the hilt, travelling rough and hitching rides to the U.S. border, before crossing on foot like so many other Mexican workers did every single day. So, it was that Chito Guerrero and Jesus Magtano headed north, for their date with U.S. immigration and their reunification with the Kingdom of God Church.

"What goes around... comes around;" Chog muttered as they slung their backpacks over their shoulders and headed out of Mexicali —.

. . .

Chapter 8

Shanghai, China: 7 Years Later:

Samantha stood on the podium; arms raised high in the air, head thrown back, as she shouted to the heavens — her trim sixteen year-old frame silhouetted by the setting sun. Her yellow dress; a shimmering, diaphanous material, seemed to sparkle and shine with an eerie, golden, glow. The hundred thousand odd people crammed into the football stadium to see her, were as one, swaying and chanting along with her as she offered her supplications and prayers to the Almighty.

Since the very first time she had climbed on a stage, the audience was quickly one with her. Even at seven she had had the uncanny ability to mesmerise and transfix the crowds. When the altar call came, as it would eventually, almost every single person in that stadium would come forward. Such was the power of Samantha Castillo — she played an audience like she was conducting a symphony orchestra.

Lowering her arms she revelled in the absolute power flowing through her. This was her calling, this was her gift and she couldn't be happier; her face glowed with excitement. Behind her and off to one side was her twin brother Damien; a scowl etched on his face. Unlike Samantha, Damien took no pleasure, or excitement, from these rallies. He didn't feel or understand the sheer thrill and exultation that Sam got from the event.

Oh... he played his part and went through the motions, but inside he always felt dead; not really part of the proceedings. Occasionally, when Samantha was in full stride, he would enter her head to try and gain, by osmosis, some of the euphoria she was feeling during her performance. There always seemed to be a wall inside her mind that he couldn't quite penetrate when she was on stage. His inability to experience the joy and emotion she experienced added to his sense of frustration and annoyance.

Standing in the stage wings, the rest of the team watched Samantha's performance with mixed feelings. JC and Maria were justifiably proud of what she had achieved over the past seven years on tour. Within one year all of them had been able to step back from direct preaching and allow Samantha and Damien to take over the rallies.

They were now the children's support crew, and it would be them that would swing into action; counselling, guiding and instructing when the thousands of people poured to the front of the stadium, after the altar call. JC was thrilled with the way Sam and Damien had grown and matured over the years. He watched them, that evening, his face beaming with pride and split by an enormous grin. Turning to Maria and kissing her softly on the cheek he whispered in her ear. "Those are our children; of whom we are so pleased."

Maria grinned and nodded, although she had conflicting emotions about her children's participation in the rallies.

Leaning across to JC she whispered back to him; "It worries me a little though honey; they're both missing out on a normal adolescence — a normal childhood. What about their first crushes, their first loves and all those things that normal adolescents go through. They're missing out on it all; aren't they?"

Her words struck at JC's aura of peace and tranquillity. Turning away from the performance he looked his wife directly in the eyes.

"Ohhhh... sweetheart....you know, I hadn't really thought about that to be honest. I guess because they have so many special abilities, I just assumed they were not like other kids; but yeah, maybe you're right. We need to talk to them ha? Find out how they really feel."

Maria smiled — mission accomplished. "Yes babes, we'll talk to them."

Beside Maria and JC stood the inseparable pairing of Angelo and Gabriel; who rather than watching Samantha, were scanning the crowd for possible signs of trouble. They needn't have bothered — there wasn't a man, woman or child whose eyes were not transfixed on the tiny, wraith like figure on stage, who captivated them.

Angelo smiled to himself. In the early days, when the preaching had been done by JC and Maria, with the children mere props to the two adults, there had been the odd crowd problem. The tour had taken them through some pretty hostile regions over the years and their message often challenged centuries of religious, spiritual, and occasionally state indoctrination. Groups of protestors had been sent to their rallies to cause trouble and create havoc.

Back then, running the security detail had been a fulltime job. They hired locally and trained the men and women on crowd control. Fortunately the worst they'd encountered was some raucous chanting and fist-waving from these groups and they'd been able to handle them with ease. Once young Damien and Samantha had taken over the testimony and preaching the problems had just disappeared.

They were so capable of controlling a mass crowd, the whole issue of security became almost moot. Angelo giggled to himself and turned to his buddy Gabriel.

"Those two have done us out of a job, my friend."

Gabriel grinned back at him and reached down to ruffle the hair on the top of his head. "Yeah Ange, you're not wrong there. Still, it means we can enjoy the rally more and there's always plenty for us to do after the altar call."

They jerked back to attention as they realised the finale was about to happen.

This was always something spectacular to see and although they had witnessed it a thousand times before, it never ceased to excite, amaze and stupefy them. This was Damien's big moment and Angelo and Gabriel focused on the tall, dark-haired, boy moving to centre-stage.

For Damien, this was the part of the programme he despised the most. It had been Samantha's idea to do it, right from the start, but in Damien's mind it was like he was being asked to perform like a circus seal, or something — to do special tricks that would amaze and create a deep sense of wonder and reverence throughout the stadium. Yes, they were special — he knew that. Yes, they did have special abilities and powers that nobody else had — he knew that; and yes, their little show did indeed put the final exclamation point on their performance, but somehow he found it all just a little bit tacky and theatrical.

A hush fell over the audience as Samantha dropped her hands to her sides and bowed her head. That was Damien's cue. He walked toward his sister, his arms held out wide. As he drew alongside of her she lifted her head and smiled warmly at him.

Curtly nodding at her, they reached their arms toward each other. As their fingertips touched there was a visible, blue, surge of electricity between them that shimmered and danced, like an aura, in the now partially darkened stadium. As the sun dipped beneath the horizon the stage was thrown into complete darkness. A single spotlight shot out to illuminate the young pair.

Their fingertips still just barely touching Damien and Samantha began to slowly, almost imperceptibly, rise from the body of the stage. There was a collective gasp from the audience as they slowly ascended toward the heavens. When they'd reached the full height of the stadium roof, they began an almost regal glide around the full circle of the enormous football stadium. This was Damien's star performance though and it was he that began to speak. From one so young, his booming, deep baritone, voice was a shock.

"My brothers and sisters of Shanghai;" he intoned; "the time has come for you all to make a decision; on yours, your family's, your city's and indeed your country's future direction."

They had now completed a full circle of the football stadium and effortlessly glided to the centre of the large bowl, where they turned until they were back to back. Spreading their arms wide, the now twin spotlights illuminating and sparkling off their clothes, Damien continued to speak.

"You have all heard tonight of the glory of God and the great opportunities that the Kingdom of God community can offer you, to live fulfilling, exciting and worship-filled lives. We will build such a community here, in your beautiful city of Shanghai..."

"Tonight you need to decide if you will commit to rejecting your stressful, hate-filled, angry, world and embrace the peace, the tranquillity and the love of our community."

He paused and waited until he could feel the building anticipation of the crowd. A groundswell of murmuring rose, as neighbours began to discuss what they would do. As the hub-bub of noise reached a crescendo; Damien, picking his moment to perfection; boomed:

"WE WILL BUILD IT — WILL YOU COME!"

The response was instantaneous and massive. An enormous chorus of ***"YES!"*** came billowing up to the two teenagers, still floating, basking in the spotlight. Samantha turned and floated around to face her brother.

"Awesome bro," she whispered to him; "just awesome."

With a wry grin, Damien nodded his head.

Grabbing his hand, Samantha slowly glided them back to the stage where they were immediately greeted with hugs and love from their parents. Damien noticed a tear building in the corner of one of his father's eyes, as he hugged his son.

"That was the most inspirational one ever Damien, you were just amazing — your sister too ha!"

Damien shrugged self-deprecatingly and mumbled; "Thanks Dad".

The rush was on for the front of the stage and it was time for the well-oiled management team to swing into action. This was the hardest part and would take the longest, but was also, from the leaders' point of view, the most satisfying. They'd been refining the technique for seven years now and had it down to a fine art.

Every person that came to the altar call would be spoken to, given plenty of written material (in their own language) and encouraged to return, over the next week, to discuss the planned community and their possible place in it. Every leader was trained to look for potential future community leaders among the recruits. It was a tried and true process that had worked exceptionally well for them over the past years.

In seven years the travelling revival show had toured all over Asia; from Uzbekistan, to Siberia; from North Korea to Indonesia; and all the places in between. Spending a month in each venue they'd established no less than eighty, self-supporting communities, under the banner of the Kingdom of God Church — all of them formatted along the same lines as the still, very successful, home Church in Davao.

Initially they'd met some severe opposition from local governments and provincial governments on their tour, especially when they visited communist or dictatorial regimes. The group's message of love, tolerance and community did not always go down well with some of the region's more entrenched and self-serving politicians.

Some of the early rallies had been beset by protests and in one particular rally in Georgia's capital. Tbilisi, the entire company had been briefly arrested and held on suspicion of espionage. Always though, they managed to talk their way out of trouble — JC had become very adept at discovering what it was the regime required of them to allow them to stay. Samantha and Damien were instrumental in manoeuvring the group out of tricky situations.

Without revealing they actually had the ability to enter people's minds; they were frequently able to guide their father to the right response or course of action to defuse a situation. The children were seen as being exceptionally perceptive and able to pick up small nuances that the others missed; without anyone actually discovering the truth of the matter. Samantha was forever telling Damien not to reveal this ability to their parents.

"It is our special secret brother — something nobody but us knows about and we should keep it that way." Damien agreed with his sister's demands.

The smooth running machine that was the Kingdom of God's leadership team completed dealing with the last of the crowd that had come forward, at around midnight. They would all meet together at the end of the evening's work, just to give their own thanks and praise to God. Despite the hectic nature of the work they were doing, everyone was energised and excited. It didn't matter how many times they did this, it still filled them with awe and wonder and by the time they were ready to come together at the end of an evening, there was always an electric atmosphere.

The initial team that started out from Manila seven years ago had been only twenty people, and that included the drivers and roustabouts. They'd recruited locally, in each town they visited and now the leadership group numbered several hundred. Fortunately, they'd found people who were great administrators and able to keep everyone organised, fed, and happy. It was an awesome team, with an average age of just twenty-five.

JC, Maria, Angelo, Gabriel, Ronnie and Delia felt like the old grandparents among this teeming group of young, excited and enthusiastic people. When everyone had found a seat, JC and Maria walked out to greet and congratulate them on their wonderful effort in Shanghai.

JC spoke to the team: "We probably had the best response from a crowd we've ever had tonight; and that's absolutely awesome. I suspect there was maybe a ninety percent answer to the altar call."

He paused briefly to place his arm around his wife's shoulders. "Maria and I are so proud of how you all performed this evening. Despite the incredible numbers, you all handled them like professionals and we know well from past experience that around sixty percent who come forward end up joining and becoming part of the new community."

He allowed the numbers to sink in before continuing. "That means, we can expect something like fifty thousand people to start the community here in Shanghai — and guys — that's mind-boggling. Congratulations! I think you all deserve an enormous round of applause and to pat yourselves on the back for a job well done."

JC and Maria led the rapturous clapping and spontaneous hugging that ensued.

They stood centre stage surveying *"their"* family, and their hearts were filled with joy and love for these wonderful people spreading peace and happiness throughout the world. Eventually JC held up his hands to quiet them. When all was silent and everyone's eyes were focused on him he spoke; "I'm not actually finished tonight though. My beautiful wife Maria has one announcement that we want to make."

Everyone craned forward to hear what Maria had to say, and in the ensuing silence, instead what they heard, was Angelo's overly loud whisper to Gabriel;

"Wow! You don't think she's pregnant *again,* do you?"

Maria threw her head back and laughed loudly. Turning to him she uttered; "no Ange, that's not the announcement — yet!"

That drew another round of laughter from the crew. Smiling, Maria stepped forward to the edge of the stage, where she sat with her legs dangling over the side, just a few feet above her adoring audience.

"No guys... I'm not pregnant, but what JC says is right. We should be immensely proud of what we've achieved here tonight and over the past seven years. The Kingdom of God Church now has..." she paused slightly to allow the excitement to build; "at last count, over one billion members... Yes! You heard me right one billion! We have established over one thousand self-sufficient communities in no less than one hundred and seven countries, all around the globe."

There was a collective gasp, as they allowed the enormity of the numbers to sink in.

Maria continued; "we are the largest, most professional, organised movement in the world and the incredible thing is; everyone living in our communities is able to live a life of purpose, peace and prosperity; free from the evils of poverty, greed and fear."

She took a deep breath before launching into the climax. Standing from her position at the edge of the stage, she walked back to her husband. Putting her arm around his waist, she carried on.

"What we have done is exactly what JC's father asked us to do — *WE HAVE CHANGED THE WORLD; FOR THE BETTER!"* It was just too much for everyone to contain themselves and excited cheering, backslapping and hollering broke out.

Maria waited for them to settle down before raising her hands for complete silence again. "Yes... we have changed the world for the better *BUT...*"

Turning to JC she kissed him on his cheek. "*BUT...* it's time for a rest. We're going to call a halt to our tour, after we finish here in Shanghai, and take a year's break. I know we all love what we do, but despite the power that infuses us in doing God's work, we're all just human and we need to step away for a while and recharge."

A stunned silence greeted her words. Slowly, a groundswell of conversation and shouted questions began to rise from the group. Maria smiled and held up her hands again, for silence.

"I know this has come as a shock, but I want you all to think of it in this way. You're all well-trained, young people, with so much to offer. It's time for you all to return to your homes for a while and share your learned wisdom with your families, your friends and your communities. If... at the end of the year, you wish to return and continue with us, of course, you'll be welcomed back."

She paused and went around the assembled group proffering them each a personal smile.

"But, what I actually suspect is that what you've all learnt with us will become the basis for your future leadership roles in your own communities. You guys and girls are the backbone of this Church and you will take our dreams into the future after this old man and I are long gone to meet his father. We couldn't be any prouder of you than we are right now. We love each and every one of you. Thank you for everything... and we'll see you all again... somewhere. I'm sure of that."

Maria, the tears flowing freely down her cheeks now, turned and grabbed a hold of her husband burying her face in his chest. This was a real turning point in their ministry and everybody knew it.

Nobody would be able to sleep much that night and later, when they were gathered together around the table; Maria, turned to the children and asked; "so you lot, how do you feel about having a holiday ha? Excited?"

Nine year old Angeline clapped her hands together and shouted with glee; "Mama... this will be our first real holiday — wow! What are we going to do?"

JC reached over and ruffled her long, lustrous black hair; "ahhhh... Angie honey... we have some ideas we want to run past you all, but first, I want to know what Damien and Samantha think. After all, they're the ones most affected by the change."

He looked across at his two teenage children who both sat there with totally different expressions on their faces.

Damien was looking thoughtful, but had a hint of a smile playing across his lips. There was no mistaking Samantha's mood, however. She was chewing her bottom lip and her eyes were darting from her mother to her father; blazing with a barely contained fury.

Damien grinned; "Hmmm... well Dad... it's a bit of a shock, but yeah, I think..."

"*THINK* Damien... when was the last time you ever thought ha!" Samantha interrupted her brother angrily, unable to contain her whirling emotions any longer.

They all looked at Samantha, who appeared to be on the verge of exploding. Her normally serene face had reddened considerably and was screwed up as she tried to contain her emotions.

"Mama!" She shouted. "How could you do this to me? This is my life — I live for these performances. How could you take it away from me; just like that — without even a word? I'm not a damn kid anymore Mama; why?"

She looked at her father, and tried desperately to recreate the "little-girl lost" look from her childhood, but failed miserably — she was too far gone down the road of anger; "and Papa, how could you let this happen. This is your mission too. I thought we were a team... how could you allow *her* to wreck our dreams. Ohhhh... none of you understand do you? All you care about is yourselves."

She banged her fist on the table and fled from the room, the tears coursing down her cheeks.

Maria rose to follow, but JC gently placed his arm on her wrist. "Let her be honey, she just needs time to think... she is right in a way though. We probably should have talked to her and Damien about it first; it is sort of their show now."

Maria nodded sadly and turned to the other children. "So... are we ready for a holiday?" They all nodded gleefully, quickly forgetting their sister's outburst.

"So... what are we going to do Mama?" Shannen asked.

Maria and JC explained that first they would head back to their Mangyan Village, for a couple of weeks, to catch up with everyone. Then, they'd have a quick trip to Pangutaran Island, where it all started, for some quiet time together before the fun adventure.

"After that... we'll head to the US and tour around the many communities that *Tito's* Jonny and Adonis have set up there;" Maria finished.

At the mention of America, Angelo leapt from his chair and began jumping up and down in front of his father.

"Can we go to Disneyland pleeeease? I've always wanted to see Disneyland... can we, can we, can we ha... please, please, please."

JC laughed and picked up his youngest son placing him on his lap. "Sure Champ, I'm pretty sure we can find some time for Disneyland along the way."

Damien sat silently while the family discussed the planned vacation. He was furiously communicating with Samantha, but she blocked his entry to her mind.

"Go away Damien; I don't want to talk right now."

Damien could hear and feel the pain she was experiencing. It wasn't physical, but still he resonated with every wracking sob that he felt coming from her body. Standing up he looked at his mother;

"Ma... Sam needs me. I'll go to her; okay?"

She knew if anyone could talk Sam around, it would be Damien. She smiled softly at her son; "Yes honey, I think that's a good idea. If she'll listen to anyone, it'll be you."

. . .

As he entered her sleeping quarters he noticed Samantha curled up on the corner of the bed. Her slim frame was shivering with emotion and every so often she let out a mournful sob and her head would bob up and down. He sat beside her and gently placed an arm around her shaking shoulders.

"Sis...;" he began, but Samantha pushed his arm away and sat up; naked anger evident in her face.

"I thought I told you... I don't want to talk to you."

He reached up and lovingly flicked a stray lock of her long hair, which had fallen across her eyes, back into place. "You need to talk to someone Sis and that someone's always been me. Why is this so hard? I mean, it's only a year and then we'll be back on tour doing it again, just like before."

She shook her head angrily; "You don't get it Damien... this thing we do, it fills me with power. It's the only thing that makes me feel alive. How can I go a whole year without it? This is *OUR* show, don't you get it? We can't just walk away."

He looked at his sister with new eyes. She was not the loving, carefree, fun girl he had always been so close to — this Samantha was something new; a power-hungry, self-centred and unreasonable version of his lovely twin sister. He grabbed a hold of her shoulders and looked her directly in the eyes; communicating this time, not with words but with thoughts.

"Samantha, we're still young — we have all our lives to do this work. You need to compromise and let go of all this for a year. You can have your power trip back in just a short while." He seemed to be getting through to her. He noticed her eyes visibly softening, although still moist with tears.

She gave him a rueful grin and nodded; "yeah I know — we're still kids, we have to do what Mama and Papa say — for now."

Damien visibly relaxed and hugged his sister. It was what she said next that chilled his blood and would come back to haunt them over the next few years. "I'll tell you what though — I won't forget they betrayed me. One day Damien, I *will* get my way; just you wait and see."

Damien's mind struggled with the possibilities that simple statement might have hidden within it—.

. . .

Chapter 9

<u>Las Vegas; Nevada:</u>

Jesus and Chito sat on the balcony of their duplex in Ezraville, Las Vegas. This community had been named after a prophet or leader from the old testament of the Bible, as they all were. Neither Jesus or Chito had any idea who this Ezra dude had been, but they did know the last seven years in Ezraville had been the most satisfying and productive years of their lives. They sat, sipping their daily quota of ice-cold cans of Budweiser, watching the bright, orange ball that was the desert sun, dip beneath the horizon. Both of them felt the calm and peace of living in a community of like-minded people, working together for a common cause.

Chito dropped his legs from the table, where he'd been resting them and regarded his long-time friend and companion, with a quizzical stare. "You're very quiet tonight Danny boy; just what's going through that evil, little mind of yours?"

Jesus chortled; "ahhhh... you know me too well my friend... and how many times do I have to remind you to let our old names go. I'm Jesus, you're Chito and that's an end to it."

Chito waved his arms at their surroundings; "and who the hell's going to hear us here ha... *Dan-dan*?"

Giving up Jesus just grinned; "well, just remember where you are when you use them, that's all I'm saying."

He laughed; "sure my friend, so what nasty plan do you have cooking up in that brain of yours?"

The past seven years had been kind and productive for the boys. Initially they'd worked on the large cattle ranch that the community had established, but before long the lure of the bright lights of Vegas began their relentless pull on them. Community members worked either within the community or found work in Las Vegas and returned each evening — the choice was theirs.

They'd both found gainful employment, working as security personnel, in one of the many casinos that lined the main strip. The job gave them access to their three favourite pastimes; gambling, drinking and womanising — the three things they were unable to do in the community.

Working in a casino meant they had to be a little bit discreet about their "outside work" activities; but luckily, not far from the gaudy, neon-lit, tourist trap that was the Vegas strip, lay the seedy underbelly of the relentless city that never slept. Chito and Jesus were drawn to the dark, dank, backstreet dives, like flies are drawn to carrion. For seven years they had happily lived out their double-lives.

The respectable, security personnel from the Christian Village of Ezraville co-existed happily with the two thugs; quick with their fists when they felt cheated in a game of chance, always on the lookout for some lonely woman who needed their special charms to cheer her up and make her feel special.

Back at the village they had quickly become fixtures and pillars of the community, dutifully attending all the regular Church services and soon becoming lay preachers in their own right. They were well-known for organising events for the community; their regular picnic barbecues being a big stand-out favourite of many and they were always doing small things to help out their neighbours and friends.

At Ezraville, the names Chito and Jesus were synonymous with everything the community stood for; love, peace, brotherhood and community spirit. After they had been living there for five years the idea of standing for the Community Board had snuck up on them. One or two of their neighbours and friends had suggested they would be perfect to take their turn on the Community's governing board. They'd discussed it at length, over several evenings and numerous beers, before coming to the conclusion that this would be a perfect opportunity to put their cunning and quick wits to their own advantage.

The community was run very much like any normal city. Apart from the Community's leader, Pastor Nolasco, who was effectively leader for life, a council of elders were elected by the community's residents on a tri-annual basis. They operated in a similar way to any local council or authority, organising the necessary functions that a community of that size required.

By dint of their experience as security personnel, both Chito and Jesus were prime candidates to stand for the role of the Community's Chief of Police. It was an honorary title really, as they had no authority or standing outside of the community, but within the community, they were the accepted face of the law.

Chito decided he would stand for the position, with Jesus standing for the very important role of Financial Controller or Treasurer. Serving on the community's governing council had always been seen as a duty and an honour. There was no recompense and serving was seen, as exactly that — serving their fellow brothers and sisters. Members of the Council were elected to three year terms, but could not re-stand for election at the end of the term. After their three years the entire Council was re-elected. This gave as many people as possible the opportunity of serving their community.

When Chito put his name forward for election there was little doubt that anyone would bother to stand against him. He was well known and liked throughout the community and besides there really was no crime in Ezraville anyway, so it was just a figurehead role that nobody was particularly interested in. Chito seemed to be the perfect candidate and was elected unopposed.

It wasn't quite so easy for Jesus to secure the role of Treasurer though. Like all the Kingdom of God Communities, Ezraville was literally awash with money. When people joined the community they were provided with essentially, free accommodation and necessities for life, and they actually had very little use for money. What money they earned working outside was often donated, in full, to the Church. Similarly, it was not uncommon for new arrivals to donate all of their worldly savings to the Church.

None of this was required or expected, but it was just the type of environment that encouraged members to donate everything they had, to better their community. The role of looking after these funds, investing them and ensuring they were well preserved fell to the Treasurer, making it an extremely important, powerful and responsible position.

Chito and Jesus had big plans to utilize their positions on the community's board to feather their own nests, and to rebuild the nest-egg they'd essentially lost prior to their arrival. Like most they both donated much of their outside income to the Church, but as Chito remarked on more than one occasion; "it's just a loan

Jesus and when you get elected, I expect a *very* significant return from that loan... hehehe."

Jesus had laughed and added; "Don't worry my friend, I'm going to ensure we get what's due to us — you can be sure of that."

Jesus was up against three other potential candidates for the role of Treasurer and despite Chito and he doing their best to subtly discredit the other three, with rumours and downright lies about the other candidates' credentials for the role, and even suggesting deep, dark, secrets lurking in their past, Jesus ended up the second highest polling candidate for the role. The job went to an ex-banker from Los Angeles.

As they sat on their balcony drowning their sorrows, Jesus bemoaned his performance in the election.

"How did I not win Chito? I thought we did everything to discredit that squirmy, little, wanker. God knows, I even planted a rumour he'd orchestrated a robbery of his own branch a few years ago and had allowed his family to be kidnapped and threatened, just to make it more realistic. I thought that would have done it."

Chito scratched his still long and straggly beard and smiled. "Ah well... that's just the capriciousness of the people Danny boy. Never mind, you can stand next time and you're bound to win. After all you're incredibly popular and you only lost this time by a few votes. We can bide our time my friend. You win next time and then we'll start rebuilding our capital."

Jesus rubbed his forehead; "yeah, I can see that Chog, but the reality is you won't be Chief of Police next time, so you won't be able to run interference for me. It's gonna be harder without you helping me... isn't it?"

He nodded sagely; "you have a point my friend... but what can we do about it?"

Jesus laughed; "I wondered how long it would take for you to ask me that. I've been thinking about it actually. There is one thing we could do Chog — we could just kill the fucker!"

Chito sat upright in his chair; "wooooah down there... slow down mate; I mean killing someone in this community — that's a big call. Are we sure we want to do that?"

Jesus waved his hands airily; "shit, why not — we've killed people before haven't we, and they'll have no choice but to elect me Treasurer, if he disappears, right?"

Chito thought about it for a while before looking at his partner, with an evil grin on his face. "So, you've thought about it — do you have a plan?"

The decision made they quickly put Jesus' plan into play, to rid themselves of the pesky, little, banker once and for all.

. . .

Michael Watman had been with the Ezraville Community for ten years, having moved there with his family, after attending a huge rally, led by Adonis Quanico, at the Los Angeles Coliseum. He was so moved by the simplicity of the message of love and peace that Adonis preached that evening, he'd sought him out personally immediately after the show.

Michael had slowly become disillusioned about chasing the "American Dream". He was a very successful bank manager, earmarked for rapid promotion by the powers that be within the bank, but deep down he felt a void and hollowness in his life — that something was missing. That evening Adonis had provided the missing piece and he was ready to jump into the fray and reclaim the life he felt he, his wife and their three children deserved.

He'd not been able to ascertain just what it was that had been missing from his life, until that moment, when he had sat mesmerised listening to the message of peace, dedication to God, and brotherly love that Adonis had brought, just especially for him.

Adonis explained they were going to establish a community there in Los Angeles and Michael was more than welcome to be one of the founding members. After Michael explained that he couldn't wait for that, and wanted to move him and his family to an existing community, Adonis pointed him in the direction of Ezraville. He was so excited that he had finally found his way in the world he jumped at the opportunity. It was only a mere month after the rally in Los Angeles that Michael, his wife Susan and their three children; Beth. Tiffany and James arrived at the gates of Ezraville; ready to begin their new lives.

Michael and his family had never looked back. They loved their new life in the community and quickly fitted into the neighbourhood they'd moved into. Once the children graduated from College they all, individually, chose to stay within the community and work day-jobs at various establishments around Las Vegas. For Michael, the move to the country had been incredibly liberating. There was no way in the world he was ever going back to a nine-to-five, stress-filled, job behind a desk. He happily took one of the lower-level jobs on the farm and flourished in the freedom and purpose it gave him.

He was responsible for cleaning the milk cows' teats before milking, rubbing them down afterwards and then cleaning the mess they invariably left in the milking shed. It was hard and dirty work but he quickly fell in love with the simple routine and the tiring physical labour. He grew to love the relationships he developed with the individual cows and when one of them finally grew too old for milking he felt the loss personally; like an old friend had passed away. For the first time in many years Michael felt truly alive and part of something important. In time he progressed to actually milking the cows himself; a task he adored.

Susan also decided not to return to work when they arrived and she relished the opportunity to become part of a loving community of women who were dedicated to making life at the village fun and rewarding. Their club, that they jokingly called "God's Angels" met every Thursday afternoon and planned events like dances and parties to keep the residents' amused.

The group of women were close, fast, friends and when they weren't having one of their "official" meetings they would invariably be found at one or other's houses. Once in a while they would take themselves off to town for a day's pampering at a local spa, and dinner at one of the top restaurants in Las Vegas.

As a couple their relationship had deepened and strengthened since the move. They were living a simpler life now and that suited them just fine.

Initially, when Michael had been approached about running for community treasurer, he had been reluctant. It was his neighbour and friend Ephraim Williston who had first suggested it. "We need experienced people like you in charge Michael. With your background, you're the perfect person to look after the community's resources."

Michael protested vociferously that it was that sort of thing that he had left behind in order to join the community. "I'm not sure I want to go back to the stress of that Ephraim;" he'd explained one Sunday morning over coffee.

Ephraim had pushed and pushed, insisting that it wasn't an onerous task — "maybe only half the week needs to be spent on the finances and the other half you can spend with your beloved cows."

The clincher came when Ephraim had reminded him how much the community had given to them. "We have a duty to give something back Mike — and anyway my friend, it's only for three years; that's just a speck of time in the cosmos."

Michael laughed at his friend's analogy and nodded his head. "You're right Eph, I owe this community so much — it saved my life and my marriage. Alright, I'll do it."

That evening the Watman family had invited their closest neighbours around for a "celebration" barbecue, in honour of Michael's successful election. It had been a fun affair with children running around the yard and splashing in the Watman's small back-yard pool. Michael had been truly humbled by the support he had received from all his friends. As they sat around munching hotdogs and congratulating each other on the success, Michael rose slowly to his feet; tapping his glass to garner everyone's attention.

"Friends;" he began, "thank you all for coming here this evening to share this special day with us. Susan and I have been greatly buoyed by all the positive support we've received from you all. I'm not sure if I'm the right person for the job, but I tell you what — I will do my very best to make you all proud. Thank you again."

His face red with embarrassment and from the sultry evening Michael sat down, looking a trifle lost. His speech had been a fitting way to end the night and as his friends came round to embrace Susan and him and to assure him they were certain he would do a fantastic job — the yard slowly began to empty.

Once they were alone he turned to Susan and embraced her. "You go off to bed honey, I'll join you shortly. I just want to sit out here in the starlight and think for a bit." He turned and looked at his loving wife. "Ohhhh... Susan, things will change a little from now on; but two things will never change — how glad I am we came here and how much I love you."

She clung to her husband with fervour; before kissing him softly on the cheek and whispering; "see you soon honey, I have a surprise for you when you come to bed... hehehe."

Michael grinned and added; "just keep it wrapped till I get there eh," before patting her bum and sending her back into the house.

As he sat down on the swing chair, on their deck, he smiled softly to himself. Yep... things couldn't be better — my life really is perfect. He closed his eyes and drank in the warm, soft, Nevadan air. "Ahhhh... what a perfect end to a perfect day;" he whispered to nobody.

When the cold metal end of a gun barrel was shoved hard into the back of his neck his reverie was brought up short. Jerking upright he tried to turn, to relieve the pressure of the barrel pushing into his neck. A meaty hand grasped his skull and turned him back to the front.

"Now don't be getting any stupid ideas about being some sort of hero Mikey boy. Me and my partner; we're just hankering for a slice of your lovely daughter Tiffany, not to mention that little cougar of a wife you got there. Do what you're told or Tiffany and Susan will find out what a real man is like... capiche?"

Michael stiffened with anger. He recognised the voice delivering the veiled threats. It was that Mexican dude, Chito

Guerrero, the guy who had just been elected Chief of Police. "Chito," he began; "what the fu..."

He didn't get any further as Chito smashed the barrel of the pistol into his temple, causing him to slump forward in the swing and roll off the front, smashing his head on the ground in the process.

Chito turned to Jesus standing behind him. "The little shit recognised my voice. Damn!"

Jesus gave a brief chuckle. "So the fuck what Chito... we're gonna kill him anyway — whose he gonna tell?"

Realising the stupidity of his worry Chito laughed softly as well. "Okay, so let's get the prick out of here and into the boot of the car."

They headed out the village gates and set their course dead north to the forbidding lands of the Nevadan desert. Leaving the main highway they drove for ten kilometres to a desolate, rock strewn, valley where they'd already prepared a suitable grave for Michael Watman.

As they strained to get his lifeless body from the trunk of Chito's car, Michael gave a soft moan and a whimper. His eyes flashed open on Jesus, the pistol pointing straight between his eyes. The horror at what was now clearly inevitable, quickly gave way to a questioning resignation. He looked at Jesus and implored him; "Why? Why my friend — what did I do to you?"

Jesus giggled; "Nothing Michael... nothing — let's just say the devil made me do it eh". He shot Michael Watman three times through the forehead.

. . .

Michael Watman's disappearance was a real test for the community's resilience and faith. Nothing like this had ever happened in Ezraville. People demanded answers from their new Chief of Police; Chito Guerrero, and because it was a major crime, local officers from Vegas were also called into investigate. Months of fruitless inquiries yielded nothing — Michael Watman, it appeared, had simply disappeared. There was rumour and speculation (much of it surreptitiously started by Chito) that he'd been involved in some shady dealings, or that there was some sort of extra-marital affair going on.

Over time, the rumours began to have an effect and even the local Las Vegas police consigned the case to the unsolved basket. Nobody would ever know for sure just what had happened to him. His wife and children eventually decided to leave the community; disillusioned with the lack of success of the investigation. The Michael they knew would never just up and leave. They were certain something horrible and foul had happened to him, but what, they would never know.

As expected, Jesus, as the second-highest polling candidate, was duly appointed to the role of Ezraville Treasurer for the next three years. He quickly set about looking for flaws and opportunities he and Chito could exploit in order to "get their share". In the end it was ridiculously easy to rig the system to ensure that they scooped the cream off every financial transaction the community entered into.

It was simple but effective — and the reason it was effective was because there were no checks and balances to ensure faithful and true accounting. There were no audits. Like everything else in the community, it was based on the concept of total trust; something Jesus was quick to exploit. Their simple scheme was to take the top ten percent off any financial transaction. When money came into Ezraville they'd deposit ninety percent into the community's bank account and ten percent into their own. When money was paid out, they'd pay the full account to the supplier and then add ten percent, which they would pay to themselves.

In any commercial establishment such a simple and obvious ploy would be quickly picked up, in the normal course of business, but in Ezraville nobody believed that any of the community members would ever do something so underhand and shady.

They knew it was only a short-term scam and they'd have to leave the community at the end of their terms, but even then they had a plan. They figured if they stood for each other's positions at the next election, they maybe could get another three years of free money. As it was, their little scheme was netting them a considerable windfall every week and both were confident that, if need be, when their three years was up they would have more than enough funds to go anywhere their little heart's desired.

Jesus had just parked his ever expanding arse on one of Chito's leather chairs in the community police headquarters. He sat down with an audible sigh. Every day Jesus would visit Chito's office when he'd had enough of the world of high finance for one day. They'd share a coffee and a chat about the day, before heading for the bright lights of Las Vegas and their customary drunken debauchery.

"Sheesh," Jesus began, wiping his forehead; "been a busy day! I'm certainly looking forward to a night on the town and a hot woman to bed. What I really..."

Chito, held up his hand to silence his friend. He was reading an email on his computer screen. "Oh shit," he exclaimed; "we got problems!"

Jesus jerked upright in the chair. "What's up bud? What's happening?"

Chito looked up from his monitor and regarded his friend with a worried expression. "Ohhhh... nothing much mate... just the big cheese himself is coming here next month. Shit, what are we gonna to do? JC, Maria and their kids are planning to visit us as part of a year-long sabbatical. Bloody hell! We need to leave town, my friend."

Jesus smiled; "really Chog? You think we need to leave, do you? Take a look at yourself in the mirror my friend. Do you *really* think they'll recognise us... God, it's been seventeen years. We've had facial surgery, we have beards, we're a lot older and... some of us are a lot fatter... hehehe. I think we'll be fine."

Chito looked unconvinced and sat scratching the bristly, razor cut, hair on his head. "You might be right Danny boy, but can we risk it?"

Jesus laughed; "risk it — hell, we can not only risk it, who knows it might even offer us up some new opportunities. We 'aint going nowhere bud — besides, I want to see how the years have treated our old friends. Nope... we'll be here to greet them. You worry too much Chog. Now let's go and get us some pussy and some booze, maybe not in that order though."

Jesus stood up and headed for the door. Chito shut down his computer and quickly followed. The next few months would be a real test, was all he was thinking, as he rushed to catch up with his comrade—.

. . .

Chapter 10

Damien lay on his bed, unable to sleep. He'd been thrilled when his Mama had announced the year's break from the tour. He really wanted to spend some time just being a normal teenager and unlike Samantha he wasn't missing the hype and excitement at all. The first few weeks of their break had been marvellous.

They had returned to the tiny Mangyan village in the Mindoran hills for the first time in seven years and Damien felt he had returned home. His friends had grown, just like he had, but it was like the clock had been turned back and they were still young kids having fun and getting into mischief. It had been there that he had truly begun to think about his future and whether he really wanted to be part of this "travelling circus" that his parents had created. While Samantha was moping around, with a long face, and feeling depressed about everything, Damien was enjoying life without the pressures of having to perform each evening.

He lay, tossing and turning, trying to figure out what direction his life should take and how his parents would react if he even suggested he wanted a life of his own, outside of the Church. He noticed a bright, pulsating light outside his window, where none had been before. He looked quickly across at his other siblings — they were all sound asleep. Noiselessly he crept off his bed and padded toward the dining room and then outside.

The light was becoming brighter now and he smiled as he realised just what it was. It had been some time since Archangel Michael had visited the family. Even after all the times he'd watched Michael put in an appearance, the sight of the warrior descending from heaven, in a ball of light and glory, never ceased to amaze and enthral him. He watched spellbound as Michael gently drifted down to stand in front of him.

"Michael;" Damien exclaimed, "it's so awesome to see you again; I'll go and wake Mama and Papa and let them know you're here."

Michael smiled broadly at him and placed one hand on each of his shoulders. "No Damien, it's you I've come to see, not your old reprobate of a father or indeed your gorgeous mother... it's you I want this time."

Damien grinned back a confused smile; "Me Michael? Why on earth would you want to see me for?"

He turned Damien toward the dark, forbidding forest and began pushing him gently down the village track. "Let's go to our favourite place my friend and we'll have a little talk shall we?"

He was powerless to resist and they walked silently toward the rock where he loved to sit, and think, and dream of what might be... that is if he didn't have this curse of being the grandson of God upon him... if he was just a normal teenage boy!

Reaching the clearing, they sat on the rock and Michael took Damien's two hands between his large, meaty fists. "We need to talk young man" Michael began. "I've been watching you these past few years and I realise you're not happy doing what you're doing."

Damien began to answer, but Michael just held his hand up, commanding silence; "just like your old man ha! Always got to have a say. Well, just like I tell him; shut up and let me finish, then you can talk, okay?"

He nodded his acquiescence and Michael continued. "Now, I think what your Mama and Papa have done in calling a halt to the tour is a good thing. You and Samantha need some time out... time to be just kids again, and enjoy life."

"That's exactly..." Damien began, but Michael held his hand up, with a scowl on his face.

"Sheesh Damien, what did I just say?" Damien hung his head in shame and Michael roared with laughter..."like I said, just like your Papa. Now, where was I? Ahhhh... that's right. I don't think you quite understand what your future holds. Let me be crystal clear about this my little friend. *You* are the son of Jesus Christ. *You* are the one who will carry on your father's legacy when he's gone. JC's human now and one day he *will* grow old and he *will* eventually die. You're his successor and heir. Yes, you need to take some time off, but don't ever for a second think you can walk away from the life you were born into. This is your destiny Damien — you really have no choice. Do you understand?"

Damien looked up into his mentor's face and Michael could see there were tears in his eyes. Softly, almost so softly that Michael had to crane forward to hear it, Damien choked out a whisper; "bbbut Michael, it's just not me. I just want to be normal." He swallowed deeply and drew on the depths of courage deep within himself. "Besides which, Samantha's older than me, even if it is by only a few minutes and... most important of all Michael, she absolutely loves this life. She lives and breathes for the rallies, for the adulation, for the conversions. She wants this so much more than I do."

He paused, as the tears overflowed his eyes and rolled down his cheeks. "Let her be the standard bearer Michael... please. I'm happy to be in the background, but please don't put all this on me." He broke down into deep sobbing, putting his head in his hands.

Michael sat there impassively and silently, letting the young man get all the pain and frustration out of his system. Finally Damien looked up into Michael's eyes and begged with such emotion and fear, that even Michael was moved. "Please Michael; please... I don't want this burden."

Michael stood and lifted Damien up to him, enfolding his massive arms around the shaking teenager; "Oh Damien," he whispered, "if only there was a way I could take this poisoned chalice away from you, I surely would." He patted Damien's head softly and then lifted his face, so their eyes were just mere inches from each other. "Sadly, Damien, you're the only one that can do this. Samantha's not suitable, and that's all there is to it."

Damien shook his head; "but Sam loves it Michael — it's like she was born to be a preacher. Why shouldn't it be her... why, why, why?"

Michael's face drooped as he looked at his protégé. "Why Damien? I've been watching these past few years and the problem is; with Samantha, it's all about Samantha. She's not interested in gaining souls for the glorification of the Father; all she wants, is to gain souls for the glorification of Samantha."

He looked at Michael with a flash of understanding. The same thought had crossed his mind on a number of occasions. When they were performing on stage, Samantha seemed to go into a trance-like state and he'd often wondered if she was really calling people to God, or calling them to follow her. "Hmmm; I guess I know where you're coming from Michael... I've sort of seen that myself."

Michael swallowed before continuing; "it's more than that Damien, I truly believe Samantha's fatally flawed — certainly for any role as a Messiah. There's something evil lurking in that young woman; something I can't quite put my finger on." He leaned in close and whispered; "quite frankly Damien... sometimes she scares me."

They sat on the rock in a companionable silence for several minutes, both contemplating the import and gravity of what they'd just discussed. Finally Damien turned toward Michael and hesitatingly queried; "yyyou don't want me to spy on Samantha do you?"

Michael placed an arm around his shoulders before replying; "No Damien, I don't want you to spy on her, but I do want you to accept the role I've given you here tonight. I don't want you shrinking into the background anymore. You have to be more active, more forthright and more up front."

He grinned at Damien; "just take more of an equal share of the show, with Samantha; it doesn't need to be so dramatic. You get me?"

Damien nodded; "I *will* keep a closer eye on her though, than I did before."

Michael stood up abruptly to signal the discussion was over. "Right, my boy, you get yourself back to bed and get some sleep. Make the most of this next year of freedom because when you come back you need to dedicate your life to continuing this work." He laughed softly; "oh yeah, and find yourself a pretty girl as well. You'll need someone to share the burden with. It's time you discovered the joys of girls Damien."

Damien turned bright red; if the truth be known he'd been thinking something sort of similar himself this past year. It was part of the reason he'd wanted out of the movement; so he could meet someone special and fall in love, just like any normal human being. But then... he wasn't just any normal human being was he? He was the son of Jesus Christ. Michael's green light to pursue a relationship was the final thing Damien needed to bring him around. He punched Michael lightly on his arm and laughed back; "you betya Mike — I'm going to!"

Michael's face turned serious again. He spread his arms wide to encompass the moonlit landscape and the stars that twinkled in the soft, warm atmosphere of the Mindoran highlands. "You guys have made an enormous difference to humanity — you must never forget that. There are those of us in Heaven who firmly believe, that within your lifetime, you will reach the halfway point — the tipping point if you like. When that happens Damien, this world will never be the same again. This planet will again rightfully be God's treasure, joy and pride. I want to see that day and so does your Mother and Father, Damien. So... make it so!"

With that he gave a quick wave and began his slow, graceful ascent back into the dark void of the heavens. His words had filled Damien with hope and given him a renewed sense of purpose plus a burning desire to make Michael proud of him. He continued to stare at the beauty of the night sky long after Michael had disappeared from sight.

Eventually he sat down on *his* rock and reflected on just what had taken place that evening. He was filled with wonder and awe at what the future held for him and the others. He was ready, willing, and able, to answer Michael's call."

"ARSEHOLE!"

The totally unexpected curse thrust itself unbidden into Damien's mind.

"You bastard! What were you doing meeting Michael without me eh? What have you two been cooking up between you?"

Despite the fact Samantha was half a mile away and couldn't see him, Damien still held up his hands to try and ward off the vehemence of her attack.

"Sammy;" he replied as soothingly as he could muster. "Don't get your panties all twisted up. Michael just wanted to have a chat with me... talk about the upcoming year off and what we're going to do."

"I don't believe you," the reply came back, but the anger was slightly dissipated this time; "what were you two *really* talking about?"

Damien thought quickly about how much or little he should say to his sister. They'd always been so close he hated the thought of having part of his mind compartmentalised from her. Yet that was the only way he could hide the true nature of their discussions.

"Actually sis... if you really want to know, Michael wanted to tell me it was time for me to find someone — a possible future partner. We were talking about *girls* actually."

He felt, rather than heard, the snort of disgust from Samantha. "Ha... you want girls do you? You want to lose your virginity too I suppose. Oh well... if that's what you stupid boys think is important then who am I to stand in your way?"

Damien relaxed a little — he seemed to have convinced her — this time.

"Anyway, you'd better get back here in case anyone else wakes up."

Damien began to pick his way back down the path to the hut. "Yeah... yeah, I'm on my way, okay?"

When he re-entered the bedroom he found Samantha propped up on one elbow, wide awake and regarding him quizzically.

"Girls ha;" she asked. "Well, I guess even someone as *pangit* (ugly) as you might find someone to love him — if you look hard enough. Maybe it's just as well we're going to America next month; I hear tell the girls there just love brown-skinned, doe-eyed, little boys. Perhaps you'll find your *soul-mate* there... hehehe."

Damien wandered over and cuffed her around the side of the head. "Just coz you're slightly older than me doesn't mean I can't beat you up when I want. Just mind your manners little girl."

Samantha laughed; "yeah, yeah Damien... you and whose army?"

They settled back down to sleep, for what was left of the night. Damien immediately fell into a deep, sleep in which he dreamt of the great crusades yet to come and the part he would play in making this world acceptable to God again. He pictured little Damien called before the Almighty himself to receive the plaudits of God and the hosts of Angels. As he slept a broad smile crept across his face and stayed there until daybreak.

. . .

Samantha's mind was whirling with the possibilities of what might really have taken place between Michael and Damien. Ever since her mother had announced the year-long sabbatical she had been quietly seething inside. How dare they do this to me? Do they not understand how important *my* work is? Do they not understand just how much power I have in my little finger? I can change the world... but now they won't let me. They want to have a holiday — for God's sake! Shaking her head, she realised sleep was not going to come again that night.

Following her brother's example she rose and padded softly outside where she stood looking at the vast expanse of the night sky, marvelling at the myriad of twinkling lights that glittered in the soft moonlight. Hugging herself tightly she exclaimed softly; "Damn it! This is *my* world now, this is *my* birthright. Why are they taking it away from me?" Despite the darkness she sought solace in *her* favourite place — high in the coconut tree where she'd playfully thrown coconuts at the villagers going to Chapel, all those years ago.

Once she'd scampered up the tree and settled comfortably in the crown, she gazed upward at the stars and allowed her sense of the injustice of it all to overwhelm her. She closed her eyes tight and squeezed until the tears began to flow.

"It's just so unfair" she whimpered softly.

"Don't cry, my little cousin." The voice from nowhere was such a shock she almost fell from her precarious perch. Her eyes flew open to look for the source of the words.

Sitting, cross-legged, seemingly on absolutely nothing, just hovering slightly above the leaves was what she could only describe as a "very ordinary looking old man". He looked to be around sixty years old, had grey, balding hair and was wearing a scowl on his face that furrowed his brow into numerous worry lines.

"Wwwhhhooo the fffuck are you?" she managed to stutter out.

The visitor's scowl relaxed ever so slightly as a half-smile almost managed to make an appearance on his lips.

"Who am I Samantha? Why... I'm your cousin... your best friend... and the man who will save you from your idiot family."

She pushed herself upright so she was in a sitting position and able to look this stranger directly in the eyes. Drawing on her courage and her ever present anger she snapped at him;

"So, I repeat my question — just who the fuck are you?"

This time the visitor actually smiled. "Well... I've been called many things in my time Samantha; the Prince of Darkness, the Evil One, Satan, the Devil, the Father of Lies, the Great Deceiver, Beelzebub, and a whole host of others — but my friends, and I do so hope you'll be one of those, just call me Bubba."

He sat back and waited for Samantha's reaction.

"The Devil ha! Well... Papa certainly warned us about you. He said you were a pure-evil Angel who had been banished from Heaven for plotting to overthrow the Father."

This time the stranger laughed out loud. "Hmmm, yes... well... JC would say that. The truth is little lady, I'm your close cousin and I'm also your biggest ally. You see... your father's right about one thing I *was* exiled from Heaven, but not for the reasons he suggests."

Samantha was fascinated by this time and waved Bubba to continue.

"You see... I was in the same position you find yourself in now. I was popular — I had many followers and frankly the others were jealous of me; just like they're all jealous of you — so... they found a way to get rid of me."

Bubba waited, for the words to sink into Samantha's consciousness, before continuing; "What do you think Michael and Damien were discussing tonight Samantha?"

She looked up shocked that he was so well informed.

"Hmmmm... girls apparently."

Bubba threw back his head and roared with laughter that shook the surrounding trees. "Girls you say? Nope... it wasn't girls — and anyway, I'm not sure girls are actually Damien's thing. What they were really discussing was life after the holiday. Michael wants Damien to lead the crusade — he wants Damien to be the inheritor of your father's legacy. He wants to push you into the background; in fact, he really wants you out of the picture altogether. When the holiday's over Sam, Damien's going to be running the show around here; mark my words."

Samantha was in total shock. "No!...No!...No!" she spluttered. "You've got it all wrong. You have to have. I'm the oldest; I'm the one who actually wants to do it. Why would they want to push me out?"

She slammed her fist down so hard, one of the coconuts fell, spiralling down to the ground, crashing and bouncing off into the forest. "Damn it Bubba! I'm the star of the show — without me... it's crap!"

Bubba reached out and patted Samantha on her shoulder. "You don't need to tell me Sam, I agree... *but* the fact is the others are jealous of your charisma, your power and the attention you get. They want the glory for themselves."

She sat in stony silence for a few minutes and when she looked up at Bubba again there were tears in her eyes. "Bubba, what can I do?" I don't want to be pushed out — this is my destiny. When I'm preaching, I'm so filled with power — I just love it. It's... it's... like a drug; it feels wonderful."

He reached down and lifted her effortlessly into his arms, cradling her gently. Kissing her softly on her lips he murmured to her; "there is a path Sam, there is a path."

She looked up into his eyes imploring him; "tell it to me Bubba, show me what I must do." He silenced her by kissing her again, this time with passion.

She felt herself responding. She wrapped her arms around his neck and kissed him deeply, forcing her tongue between his lips. When he broke the contact she frantically sought to re-establish it, but he just put his fingers against her lips.

"Hush now child, there is a path... and we will walk it together, but for now we need to be patient. I'll tell you the same thing Michael told Damien; go and enjoy your year-long vacation. Opportunities will arise — trust me, and we will see each other again soon, I promise you that."

Samantha nodded her head gently and started to speak; "but Bubb..."

He silenced her again with a finger to her lips. "Time will come Samantha — time will come. For now, all you need to worry about is that you have pledged yourself to me and the time will come when that pledge will be consummated. Just trust me."

She was overcome with a deep feeling of love and warmth for this strange, old man. She just nodded meekly. He set her down gently again on the crown of the tree and smiled down at her. "Now go, get home and get some sleep. I will visit you often and we will plan our revenge on them... yes?"

She smiled winningly at him. "Oh yes Bubba, oh yes, I want that so bad." He leant down and kissed her again, this time chastely on the cheek; "Goodbye for now my precious, little, cousin."

Almost as if he was teasing her he brushed the back of his hand against her nubile breasts and flicked her erect nipple with his finger..."time will come Samantha," he repeated — and then he was gone... just disappeared.

She sat there stunned at what had happened. She was aroused, excited, and just a little bit scared. What have I agreed to? Then the memory of Bubba's lips on hers and his finger caressing her breast won through and she shivered in anticipation.

After she had regained her composure she shimmied down the tree and headed back to the hut, where she lay down and was instantly asleep. Her dreams were filled with images of Bubba towering over her, plunging into her, all the time whispering; "this world is ours cousin". She slept soundlessly, a grin creasing her face — the die was cast—.

. . .

Chapter 11

It was becoming harder for Chito and Jesus to keep their double lives separate and secret. Despite their positions within the community they had continued the pretence that they were still working part-time, in security, at one of the casinos. This ruse was necessary for them to have a ready excuse to leave the community and regularly embark on one of their alcohol, drugs and sex binges.

They both lay naked on massage tables in the back room of one of the seedy, gambling institutions they regularly frequented. Two, equally naked brunette, beauties, were easing the two men's tired muscles, but that was merely the prelude for the full-on orgy that would follow. Chito rolled over on his back at the insistence of his masseuse who giggled when she noticed his erect manhood standing tall and proud. Licking her lips she bent down to kiss the tip of his glistening shaft. He reached out and gently massaged her ripe, lush, buttocks before pushing her away.

"Not yet honey; me and my friend are still talking."

He turned his head so he could look directly at Jesus who was busily gobbling his own masseuse's full, factory-generated, breasts.

"Buddy; JC and his family are arriving next week. Are you sure we can pull this off... don't you worry they'll recognise us?"

Jesus stopped his nibbling long enough to regard his friend with a thoughtful look. "Hmmm, I won't lie mate, it's crossed my mind more than once too, but you know what — I'm feeling lucky! Anyway, it's more fun when there's an element of fear involved. Shit Chog, our lives here are way too predictable and way too boring; it'll be fun to be living on edge again. Keeps a fella on his toes!" He grinned at Chito. "Let's live a little bud!"

Chito laughed and grabbed a hold of his masseuse, lifting her one-handed, and plonking her across his waist, one leg straddling either side of him. "OK little lady, time you and I made some serious music."

The masseuse slid down and reached behind her to grab Chito's throbbing erection before she plunged down and thrust it into herself, all the way to the hilt. Chito's breath exploded in a gasp as he felt her warm, wet silkiness envelop him and slowly begin to rise and fall, in an increasingly hypnotic manner. On the other table Jesus had also pinned his masseuse and was busily indulging in his own version of the ancient art of lust.

Both men looked across at each other and an unspoken sense of comradeship passed between them, as they grinned idiotically. They'd always done everything together, since they were kids, and now, nothing had changed.

. . .

It was the family's last day on Pangutaran Island before heading to Manila and then the United States. The island would always be a special place for them — it was where they had truly forged the life-long friendships they enjoyed. For Ronnie and Delia of course it was a real home-coming. They spent much of their time checking on their many business ventures and entertaining their extended family to lavish feasts and parties.

For the others, it was an emotional return, especially for Angelo and Gabriel, who had spent many years working alone there at the Chapel, the Medical Centre and the School.

Like the old days, they'd decided to camp on the beach, just down from the Chapel. When Ronnie and Delia had finally left Pangutaran to join the crusade around Asia it was with some reluctance that they had handed the leadership of the Chapel over to one of the locals, Benjamin Intal, who had been ordained as a minister. Everyone was thrilled to see the wonderful way Benjie had cared for, and maintained their lovely Chapel over the years. They were standing outside admiring the quaint, little building that meant so much to them all. It still looked as beautiful and inspiring as the day they had completed the renovations.

JC was retelling, to his children, the story of their wedding day and the attack by the Abu Sayef, for about the thousandth time; but the children were still fascinated and captivated by the events that had occurred that day.

At one point Angeline tugged on her father's shirt; "Daddy, were you really not scared when you faced those horrible men with guns?"

JC laughed; "Honey-bunch, I was terrified, but I had two things in my favour. I had God looking after me and I had your mother worrying about me. If anything had happened to me I'm pretty sure your mother would have ripped those men apart limb by limb."

Maria placed her arm protectively around JC's shoulder and whispered into his ear. "Well... just remember Mr Hero, you're not Superman anymore, you're just an ordinary man with no special powers."

She kissed him lightly on his cheek; "but, you're *my* ordinary man Mr Hero, and I love you so much." He hugged her tight.

Samantha snorted in disgust; "get a room you two. Sheesh, do you have to do all that lovey-dovey stuff in front of us — it's sort of disgusting."

Maria chuckled and ruffled her daughter's hair. "Ha! It won't be too long before you'll be doing that sort of thing with someone special yourself, young lady, so don't knock it." She kissed Samantha on the cheek before adding; "maybe you'll meet somebody special in America — who knows?"

Sam screwed her face up in annoyance. "No way!" she exclaimed angrily. "I don't want some silly boy fawning all over me... not going to happen!" When her mother laughed even louder at her protestations she just threw her hands up in frustration.

"Enough already;" she shouted. "I'm going for a swim — anything to get away from this conversation."

JC held his hand up; "wait honey, I thought we might go into the Chapel and just worship for a while — you know, ask for guidance and protection for when we leave for America tomorrow."

Her eyes narrowed and she looked sharply at her father. "I don't need or want any protection — got it? I can look after myself!" She turned on her heel and ran full speed toward the shoreline.

JC and Maria stared after her, in shock.

"What brought that on?" Maria asked worriedly.

JC looked at the disappearing figure of his eldest child and scratched his chin. "I don't know babes, but perhaps I'd better go and talk to her."

Maria placed a restraining arm on his; "no honey; let her be — give her some space. I think she's just struggling to come to terms with the break in our crusade. She just needs time to sort it all out; leave her be."

He nodded, before gathering the rest of his children around him. "Right you lot, let's go and pray shall we?"

. . .

Samantha ran straight into the water and splashed out until it was up to her chest. She sank down and let the cool, refreshing water soak all over her. She was so angry and annoyed with her parents. Why couldn't they just let her be?

She was also annoyed at Bubba who hadn't shown again since that time in the coconut tree. She missed him — she missed the strange power he seemed to emanate and the tingling way he had made her feel, when he had held her and kissed her. Coming to the surface spluttering she shouted at the sky; "damn it! Why does everything have to be so damn difficult?"

"What's the problem little one?"

She spun around at the sound of the voice and her face broke into an enormous grin, as she saw Bubba standing there, also waist deep in the water.

"Oh Bubba, thank God you came. I've missed you so much." She flung her arms around his neck and kissed him long and hard.

He finally managed to disentangle himself long enough from her embrace to chortle; "Don't thank God my darling, he's the cause of all the shit I'm in now — thank me!"

She laughed; "Oh Bubba, I do... I do....I do... thank you, thank you, thank you."

Grinning, he took her hand and led her out of the water. "Now come on Sam, I have some important things to tell you about your upcoming trip to the States." He led her compliantly to the nearest sand dune where they sank down out of sight of the main camp. As soon as they were down she grabbed him again and began raining kisses on his old, wrinkled face. He calmly tolerated her youthful enthusiasm for a while before grabbing both her arms and pulling her until they were face to face, just inches apart.

"There'll be plenty of time for that in the future Sam, but for now, just listen to me."

Bubba told her that when the family arrived in the Las Vegas community she was to seek out two members of the leadership group; one Jesus Magtano and one Chito Geurerro. He told her they were part of the leadership team, so she would be bound to be introduced to them.

"You must talk to them, little one, and do whatever they say."

"But, who are they Bubba?" she queried.

He laughed; "who are they Sammy... hmmm, why they are part of *my* leadership team, part of *my* plan to regain *my* true status and power as ruler of the Universe... hehehe."

She looked at him awestruck. "Wow Bubba, and what's my role going to be in this brave, new Universe?"

He grinned widely at her before lifting her up and gently placing her on his lap. "You, my little one; you will rule beside me — you will be my queen. How does that appeal to you Samantha? Queen of the Universe!"

Looking up at his face, she looked past the age, the grey hair, and the wrinkles. All she saw was the exciting, vibrant, youthful, warrior king that he was. Her heart overflowed with a deep and abiding love for this man/God who was to be her salvation and would give her all the power and adulation she needed and wanted.

"Bubba, that appeals to me just fine. All I really want is to be with you."

"And so you shall my Queen... and so you shall."

They spent more time discussing the details of what Bubba required of her and the two men from Las Vegas. As he finished detailing the plan she reached up and grabbed his head between her hands, pulling him down to her level. He allowed himself the luxury of running his hands over her nubile, young frame and he even allowed her to reach and grasp him, before gently disentangling himself.

"This is not the time or place; my darling flower. We cannot and should not despoil that which one day will be married to the Prince of Darkness. We will consummate our wedding — in glory, and you shall be an unspoilt virgin on that day."

Samantha pouted and reached for him again; "but I want you now Bubba... I want to feel your power, inside of me."

He chuckled; "and you will, when we are rulers of the Universe... but not before."

She tossed her hair in annoyance and hugged her knees to her chest, staring out at the gently lapping ocean as it curled into the shore. Sensing her frustration, Bubba leant in close and tickled her ear with his tongue. "You want to know a secret, little one?"

She turned to him with a wicked grin on her face; "Always Bubba, always."

"Well... you know the two men you are going to meet in Las Vegas Chito and Jesus; would you like to know who they really are?"

Excitedly Samantha nodded her head and waved for him to continue;

"You must have heard your father talking about his two "Disciples" that betrayed him, ha? Chog and Dan-dan? Well... Chito and Jesus *are* those two men... Chog and Dan-dan."

The implication of Bubba's words sunk slowly into Samantha's consciousness, but when they did, a positively wicked and evil grin came over her face. She clapped her hands with glee; "Oh Bubba that's so deliciously ironic and fun. Oh... I can't wait to meet the two men that tricked my Daddy... wow, that's awesome... hehehe."

Bubba laughed along with her before leaning over and kissing her chastely on the forehead. "Ok, my little one, you better get back to camp before somebody comes looking for you. Me... well... I better get off and see two men about a plan."

Samantha looked wistfully at him. "Ohhhh... Bubba, I'll miss you."

He grinned; "you'll see me again soon enough;" and with that, he simply disappeared.

She sat there for some time staring at the spot where he had been. Finally, she shook her head sadly, stood and brushed the sand from her clothes before heading, regretfully, back to rejoin her family.

. . .

Chito rolled over gently so as not to cause too much movement inside his skull, which was threatening to explode at any moment. He gave a slight moan as flashes of blue and white light pierced through his cerebellum. God, that was one hell of a bender, he thought. Risking it, he decided to open one eye, immediately regretting it, as a shaft of harsh, florescent light lanced his already throbbing head.

As his eyes slowly focused he could see his partner in crime, lying face down, in a pool of what could only be described as filth. Chito wasn't sure what it was, and frankly he didn't want to know. Jesus was naked and was surrounded by the detritus of a party gone out of control. Broken bottles, syringes, used condoms, and several naked women; none of whom appeared to be the masseuses they'd started the party with, littered the floor around him.

He pushed himself to his knees and glancing down realised his own situation was no better than his mate's. Chito was also naked, and worse; seemed to be covered in a caking of dried blood. Worried, he quickly checked himself and ascertained that wherever the blood had come from, it certainly wasn't him. Breathing a sigh of relief he tottered to his feet and wobbled briefly as he tried to come to terms with the whole standing routine... and then he saw him.

Sitting on one of the massage tables, his feet dangling over the edge; the elderly man was whistling a soft tune. Chito strained to hear the song as it seemed achingly familiar. In a blinding flash, that wobbled his fragile brain, the name of the song came into his head; "The Devil Went Down to Georgia". He grinned; that had been one of his favourite songs ever since he was a kid. He wiped the grime from his eyes and faced the stranger squarely;

"...and just who the fuck might you be, Sunshine?" he enquired belligerently.

The elderly man jumped off the masseuse table with surprising ease and grabbed Chito by the throat, catching him by complete surprise. As he struggled and writhed trying to get a breath, he couldn't believe the strength in the old man's arms. He was holding him like a vice and nothing Chito could do seemed to lessen the stranger's grip. His vision began to cloud over and he began to sink into unconsciousness. The grip suddenly relaxed and he sank to his knees gasping for breath, gingerly holding his bruised neck.

"Who the fuck might I be? I'll tell you just who the fuck I am *Sunshine,* I'm your worst fucking nightmare my friend, I'm the thing you dream about when you have nightmares."

He threw back his head and roared with laughter before reaching down and lifting Chito to his feet. Grinning at him he added; "but you can just call me The Devil".

Dumbfounded Chito stared at him... lost for words.

"Now wake up your mate and come and sit down my friend, I've got a little job for both of you."

Chito briefly considered the option of charging the "Devil", but he remembered the vice-like grip of the old fella and in his hung-over, weakened state, he wasn't too sure he would back himself to win. Instead he knelt beside Jesus and slapped him hard on his face. Jesus warily opened one eye to stare at him with a hurt expression on his face.

"What'd ya do that for buddy? I was having a lovely dream."

Chito's response was to haul Jesus to his feet. "We have company ha!"

Jesus stood there, blinking rapidly, looking at the interloper and sizing him up; "and just who the fuck might you be, Sunshine?" he also ventured.

Bubba held his hand up, wearily. "Let's not go through all that crap again. Chog, you tell Danny boy here what's what and then we'll have a talk." Chito recoiled at the use of their real names.

"How the..." Bubba silenced him with a withering glare.

"All in good time boys... all in good time. First, go and get yourselves cleaned up." He held in nose in disdain. "You buggers don't half stink, so go and have a shower, get dressed, and then come back here and we'll talk eh?"

The pair looked at each other questioningly. Jesus shrugged his shoulders and said; "Ah well... what have we got to lose? Let's go and get showered".

After they'd left, Bubba looked around the room at the absolute tip-site that it was, shaking his head disdainfully. He put both his arms in the air, closed his eyes and his brow furrowed in concentration, before he whipped his arms down and shouted; *"Asmodeus"*. A brilliant flash of light was followed by a sonic boom and when he opened his eyes again, everything in the room was gone; the filth; the tables; the naked, unconscious women; everything had just disappeared. Bubba chuckled softly to himself; "I've still got it!"

When Chito and Jesus finally re-emerged from the bathroom, they recoiled at the room's transformation.

"How did you..." Jesus started to say, but Bubba cut him off.

"Just *my* little, party trick, boys. Now get your arses over here and let's discuss some business."

By the time Bubba had outlined his plan to the two men, they were excited and keen. Chito turned to Jesus and clapped him on his shoulder.

"I knew their coming here was going to be a turning point for us. Finally we have the opportunity to gain some real power and riches. Shit... we're going to rule the Universe."

Bubba laughed; "well technically Samantha and I will rule the Universe guys, but I'm sure there'll be plenty left over for you two."

Jesus' face suddenly turned very serious; "Hey! We're going to go to hell for this aren't we?"

Bubba chuckled; "My friends you were already destined to spend eternity in hell... but no... it's God, JC, that prick Michael and all those other goodie-two-shoe's Angels in Heaven, that are going to hell. You and me we're going to Heaven — we're going to rule the Universe."

Jesus managed to crack a smile at that.

"Ok Chog, we better get moving ha, we have things to prepare before they get here." He turned to say something to Bubba, but he'd already disappeared.

Shaking his head he turned back to his friend; "well buddy it's all happening now eh? Let's go!"

. . .

Damien tossed and turned on the soft sand where they were sleeping that night. He was worried about Samantha. He knew his parents had told him to leave her be, but how could he — she was his twin and more than that they had their supernatural bond. He knew Sammy was greatly troubled. She'd been blocking him entering her mind for quite a long time now. As they had grown older they had managed to master the art of mind-blocking; but neither of them had used it too much — until recently that is. Nowadays it seemed like every time he tried to check on her, she was blocking him.

He looked across at his sister, who was sleeping softly, curled into almost a ball on the sand. He could see her lips fluttering with each breath and the long strands of hair that hung over her face would rise and fall softly with each exhalation. He noticed she had a big grin on her sleeping face. She looked so happy and angelic his heart melted for the little girl he had spent his life with, but who now seemed so distant and so remote.

As an experiment he attempted to probe her mind. As he explored the recesses of her mind, he realised her dream was actually quite horrific and yet she was smiling — she seemed happy. All he could see was tall columns of fire and grotesque creatures; twisted and deformed, kneeling at the base of a double throne; seemingly worshipping something. Looking higher to see what the ugly beasts were worshipping he recoiled as he saw his beloved sister, sitting on one of the twin thrones next to a wizened, bent old man whose hair was ablaze and whose lips were opened in a toothless grin — and they were holding hands!

Samantha was regal in her stature and bearing. She sat, expressionless, her hand just waving airily at the worshippers as if granting them permission to continue their obsequiousness to her. She seemed totally at ease, as the fires of hell roared around her. Damien gasped aloud as he watched the old man transform before his eyes. The wrinkles fell off his face, like scales on a dead fish, to be replaced by fresh, youthful looking skin. The cracked, toothless lips were swept away by a full set of gleaming, razor sharp white teeth, that shone eerily in the firelight — radiating their evil potential. He watched in horror as two, wickedly curved horns slowly began to emerge from the man's forehead. They swept forward from just above his eyebrows and then curved sharply upward ending in glistening, almost needle-like points.

Most horrific of all was the bright red forked tail that rose like some massive phallus from between the creature's legs. It reminded Damien of pictures he had seen of giant king cobras just before they strike the killing bite. It was at least two feet long, tipped by what could only be described as three tines of a fork. It hung there, obscenely waving back and forth, as the creature; for that is truly what he was now, reached for it and gently stroked it. He was horrified and repulsed by what he was witnessing inside his sister's dreams.

What came next though, was so unexpected and so frightening, that Damien couldn't hold back a shocked scream of horror. In a blinding flash of movement the creature grabbed Samantha and impaled her on his disgusting, throbbing tail. As if the act itself wasn't repulsive enough, the sight of Samantha actually appearing to enjoy it was enough to send him into deep, sobbing breaths. Instead of screaming in pain from being impaled by the monster's tail, Samantha was rocking back and forth and mewing softly with pleasure.

He watched in horror; unable to look away, as the "mating" reached a crescendo. With a flash of lightening and a clap of thunder, Samantha screamed in ecstasy as their coupling was fully consummated. She collapsed on his chest sobbing softly as the monster looked out at his vast adoring audience of misshapen, misbegotten, creatures and declared in a surprisingly gentle, and soft voice;

"It is complete — the King and Queen of the Universe are united. Together, we will rule for all eternity." He reached down and lifted Samantha's face, before kissing her gently on the lips.

Damien could take it no longer, quickly withdrawing from her dream and shaking his head to try and clear the horrific images from his mind. He looked across at his beautiful sister and was mortified to see she appeared to be experiencing her dream physically. Her mouth was open and she was panting heavily, beads of perspiration pouring down her perfect, unblemished face. He turned his head in shame and embarrassment when he realised that not only was her dress bunched around her waist, she had thrust her hand deep inside her pants and was rubbing herself vigorously. Quickly he rolled away from her; what does it all mean? What is happening to her? He opened his eyes and looked at the twinkling stars that taunted him from on high. Softly he whispered to the void;

"Michael, where are you when I really, really need you?"

The voice; almost made Damien shout aloud;

"I'm right here Damien, my boy, what's the problem?"

When he sat up, Michael was seated just a few feet away from him.

"Sheesh, Michael, is it really necessary to scare the crap out of me every time you show up?"

Michael just grinned; "Just like to keep you on your toes lad — now what's the problem?"

Damien explained his sister's dream to Michael, asking him what he thought it all meant. Michael sat there scratching his chin for a while before smiling.

"I have no idea Damien, although it does sound pretty awful. Maybe Samantha's just feeling some sexual tension and repression. I mean... she's a beautiful, young woman Damien and all those hormones are rushing around her system. Who knows what drives women, my young friend — I've never been able to figure it out, and I've been around forever. I wouldn't worry, but like I said earlier, keep an eye on your big sister over the next few months ha!"

Damien nodded soberly at him. "Don't worry Michael, I'll be the protective brother, you can be sure of that."

Michael slapped him on the shoulder; "good man, you do that. Time I was elsewhere; I'll catch up with you in America."

He stood and rapidly ascended into the violet vault of stars. Damien stole one last glance at his sister, sleeping peacefully now, before rolling onto his side and finally finding the sweet release of his own dream-time—.

. . .

Chapter 12

As the Castillo family made the long drive from Las Vegas airport to Ezraville, each of them reacted differently to what was the gaudy, neon-lit strip of Las Vegas proper. Angelo, unable to take in all the magnificent sights in one view, was swinging his head from side to side, so rapidly, that it threatened to roll off his shoulders. He and his twin sister were simply awestruck by the shining castles, the towers, the waterfalls and the replicas, that made up this glittering monument to man's ingenuity.

"Oh look Mama, there's the Eiffel Tower," Angeline shrieked. "Oh... Oh... Oh... and look there's Venice, just like in the picture-books."

Maria grinned at her youngest children's enthusiasm. "Yes honey! They say you don't need to travel the world to see the sights anymore — just come to Las Vegas and they're all here waiting for you.

"Mama, mama;" Angelo piped up. "Look over there, it's a pyramid — wow, how do they build those things — it's amazing!"

As they continued down the main strip there was always something to capture the youngsters' attention.

Shannen and Sean was trying their best to be the most mature of the four youngest. They were more restrained in their comments and their exclamations of wonder and glee; but when they passed the "New York, New York" display, even Sean was brought to exclaim;

"Ohhhh... is that the Statue of Liberty? Wow... that is the most amazing thing I've ever seen in my life."

Shannen leant over the seat and hugged her twin brother tight. "Isn't it all just absolutely wonderful Sean... I hope Papa will let us come back and look around properly." She looked at her Father, whose expression seemed stern and set, as he drove steadily down the main street of Vegas.

"Can we papa, please? Can we? Can we come back and look around sometime... please... pretty please?" Shannen wheedled.

JC's face softened at his daughter's entreaties. He looked across at Maria and raised his eyebrows as if to say; "what choice have we got really."

Taking a quick glance backward he saw Shannen eagerly leaning forward, desperate for his positive reply. Despite himself, he grinned; "well... I guess it can't do us much harm just to take a look around one day... but, I want you all to know I don't like or approve of this city."

Damien looked up from his iPad. "What's the problem with Las Vegas Papa — surely it fulfils a need, or it wouldn't be here, right?"

JC smiled at his son's rapid grasp and understanding of the human condition. He took a deep breath before replying; "Yes my boy, it does fill a need, but, it's not a need we should be encouraging."

He shook his head sadly before addressing everyone. "You know guys; Las Vegas is a testament to man's basest needs and desires. It's an exploiter of greed, lust and the need for diversion from life's pains and suffering." He hit his fist in frustration on the steering wheel, which got everyone's attention.

"This... is why we started our communities — to fulfil people's needs, so they wouldn't need to seek the temporary and damning diversions in places like Las Vegas."

Realising he was preaching now, he relaxed his grip on the wheel and smiling widely added; "but, it *is* pretty, and I don't see why we shouldn't enjoy it while we're here."

Samantha, who it seemed was always in some sort of daydream most of the time these days, looked up from where she had been studying her nails for the last thirty minutes and asked; "Papa, is it always wrong to seek pleasure? Isn't that what we were made to do — enjoy ourselves?"

JC's brow wrinkled in consternation at his daughter's odd but challenging question.

"Hmmmm;" he began, "how can I put this? Well... there is pleasure, and then there is *pleasure...* Ummm, what I guess I'm trying to say Sammy is that some pleasure is good and worthwhile, while some is just self-indulgent and destructive. Do you get me?"

Sam leaned forward in her seat; "Yes papa, but..."

Damien jammed her in the side with his elbow in an attempt to shut her up, but she was having none of it. She turned to her brother and scowled at him with a look of pure vitriol and spite, before continuing.

"But papa... who is it that decides, what is good pleasure and what is bad pleasure?"

JC was decidedly unhappy with the turn the conversation had taken. He breathed deeply and told himself to be calm, to be rational, and to remember she was still just a young woman; unaware of much of the evil and filth in the world.

"Well Sammy," he began again; "ultimately it was the Father who set the rules — after all he *is* the creator, it's his planet and we are his creation. He wants us to live in peace, happiness and harmony; and that's what our communities are all about — finding fulfilment and joy while living together and enjoying each other's company." He rubbed his fingers through his hair in frustration; "I hope you realise now why we live the way we do Sam."

Samantha grinned wryly before playing her trump card; "But Papa... if God gave us free will; to choose to live how we desire, why should he now think he can take that free will away from us, and tell us how we should live our lives?"

JC sat there for some time, concentrating on the road ahead. There was complete silence as everyone wondered just how he would answer Samantha's question. The younger kids glared at their *Ate* (elder sister). Everything had been so happy and excited just a short time ago and now Samantha had angered their father.

Damien shrugged his shoulders at the turn of events and mind whispered to his sister; "you cretin Sam... Why do you always have to start arguments, these days?"

His reward was a gleeful grin and a dig in his ribs to rival the one he had given her. "Why should papa get away with telling us how to live — he should justify his words surely?"

Finally JC began to speak; "Yes... we have free will Sam, but within our human consciousness is a deep desire to be loved, to love, and to live in peace. For some people it has been superseded by the need for instant gratification and for experimenting with some of life's more base experiences. What we're seeking to do is to bring people back to what their lives should be. Remember honey, we don't force anyone; we show them the right way and we ask them to follow us. If they choose not to, that's their decision and we won't argue with it. So... they still have their free will Sam, all we're doing is offering them a better opportunity to choose from."

He lifted one hand from the steering wheel and wiped his brow with the back of his hand. "Is that okay honey?"

JC was relieved when she replied; "oh yes papa... that makes total sense. Thank you for explaining it so well."

It was only Damien that heard the additional words whispered by his sister; "but papa... who says it's a better opportunity ha? Perhaps there's another way, did you ever stop and consider that?"

Damien shook his head sadly. Michael's dead right. I need to keep a close eye on this girl. She's starting to worry me big-time.

The remainder of the drive to Ezraville was completed in relative silence as they relaxed inside their own thoughts. JC had told Pastor Nolasco that they didn't want any fuss on their arrival at Ezraville. He wanted them just to be treated like any normal family arriving at the community. In fact, he'd made it clear they wanted to undergo the same initiation and orientation into community life that any new family would be subjected to. They would be staying for several months and JC wanted to get the feel of how it was to enter an unknown, new community, full of fear and trepidation and to be accepted and welcomed. He wanted them all to experience this for themselves; especially Samantha, he thought wryly, so they could get a better understanding of how new recruits felt.

As they approached the grand gates of the community, JC couldn't resist chuckling to himself; "Gosh, they couldn't help themselves, could they?"

Strung across the entire entrance of the community was a tarpaulin that read; *"EZRAVILLE WELCOMES THE CASTILLO*

FAMILY — MABUHAY!" He laughed and turned to Maria; "looks like we're expected then... hehehe".

Maria smiled back warmly; "yes honey... it does look like our anonymous entry has been a trifle sabotaged;" but her mind was on other matters. She had been profoundly disturbed by Samantha's outburst. What's going on in that young lady's mind, she thought? Maria had realised some time ago that Samantha was troubled, but to be actually questioning the entire purpose of their mission and their very existence — that was something new. She resolved to have a very serious mother/daughter chat in the not too distant future.

Turning her mind to their upcoming arrival at Ezraville she plastered a smile on her face as she clambered out of the car to greet and embrace her old friend from Davao; Pastor Jhoemar Nolasco, who neither of them had seen for close to fifteen years. There was much back-slapping and hugging as JC and Maria set about introducing their six children to the Pastor and his lovely wife Vilma.

JC looked around himself at the modern buildings, the clean pathways and the crowds of smiling, happy people, awaiting their arrival inside the complex. He clapped his old friend on the shoulder; "Joe, me old mate, looks like you've done an awesome job here — of course, I always knew you would. How could you fail with someone as wonderful and stern as Vilma to keep you in line?"

Joe's wife blushed at the compliment and spluttered; "Right... right... right... first things first... there's a whole bunch of people that want to meet you, but Joe told me you wanted the full indoctrination and orientation process, so let's head to the office and do that first shall we?"

Jhoemar tried to intervene; "but honey everyone is wait..."

Vilma silenced him with a withering look. "Jhoemar Nolasco! Would you just be quiet and do what you're told, for once in your life. Now take this lovely, new family out of the sun and welcome them properly to Ezraville."

Chastened by his wife's invective, Jhoemar still seemed prepared to argue. "But Vil, everyone's waiting for them..."

She stomped her foot in such a way as to brook no argument. "Joe!" she uttered warningly. He'd clearly heard that tone before now because he immediately set about herding the Castillo's toward the office; although he was heard to mutter loudly enough for everyone to hear;

"Who's the boss here again... did you say?"

JC and Maria laughed and followed the now thoroughly compliant Jhoemar into the cool, air-conditioned, comfort of the offices. The children, lagging behind, were stunned by all the facilities they could see off in the distance.

"Did you see Sean, they have a tennis court — we can play;" Shannen whispered.

Sean grinned; "yeah... and I can see a pool over there... and an enormous playground as well. I think we're going to enjoy it here."

Once the formalities of the orientation were over, Pastor Nolasco escorted them to a large, Spanish style villa where they would be accommodated. "Now, make yourselves at home guys."

He looked at the children; "go and explore and have some fun, there's heaps here for youngsters to do." Looking back to JC and Maria, he added; "and for you old fogies, there's a whole lot of people that are dying to meet you, so when you've had something to eat, come on over to the Glory Hall and we'll introduce you to them all."

As an afterthought he turned to Damien and Samantha.

"Hmmmm... I've been keeping up with you two over the internet. It seems *you* are the real stars of this show now, so please, if you want, come with your Mama and Papa. I know everyone is bursting to meet you both."

Looking at Samantha he added; "and as for you pretty lady, I suspect there is a phalanx of young men just lining up to be introduced to you."

To his surprise Samantha turned away in annoyance and said haughtily; "Hmpth, I certainly didn't come here to meet boys... that's for sure." She turned back to him and added with a cheeky smile; "men on the other hand... now that's a totally different kettle of fish... hehehe."

Maria jumped in to save Jhoemar's blushes, and patting him on the shoulder she assured him they would be there straight after dinner.

When he had departed Maria favoured her daughter with a questioning stare. "While your dad and Damien prepare some dinner, I think it's time you and I had a little talk, young lady." She turned to JC and arched her eyebrows as if to say; "God knows how... but it needs to be done."

JC nodded his head knowingly and allowed Maria to lead Samantha, reluctantly, into one of the many bedrooms of the villa.

JC tuned to Damien; "Right, let's get cooking shall we."

To the younger four he added; "go explore and we'll call you when dinner's ready."

They needed no second invitation and Shannen, Sean, Angeline and Angelo headed out the door, whooping and hollering, to see what they could find.

JC and Damien looked at each other and shrugged. They knew this one was women's talk and well outside of their league or experience.

"Let's just stick to cooking buddy, and let the girls sort out their own things;" JC recommended.

. . .

Jesus and Chito had been in the front line of those waiting for the Castillo family to arrive. They were nervous about being recognised, but equally they were excited to see JC and Maria after all these years. When they emerged from the car, both had a collective inward rush of breath. JC hadn't change too much in the ensuing years. Sure he was a little older now, his long hair a little greyer and the crows-feet around his eyes were more pronounced, but his demeanour, his carriage was still the same, bouncy, youthful JC they remembered so well from their days together on their crusade.

Maria, also, was still the, slightly faded now, beauty they remembered. She still had the big, gorgeous, brown eyes that seemed to have the ability to drill right into your soul. Jesus trembled as he thought about the possibility that they might be recognised. Turning to Chito, he whispered; "I'm guessing if anyone tumbles us it will be Maria, mate. You remember how she always used to seem to know exactly what you were thinking."

Chito looked at him; "yeah, I do! We'll have to be careful around her, that's for sure."

When Samantha stepped from the car, a collective gasp went up from all the young men waiting to meet the Castillo's. In the harsh, Nevada sunlight her hair seemed to sparkle and glisten with a life of its own. As she tossed her head to clear a few stray bangs from her eyes everyone drew a breath. They all edged just a little closer to gain a better view. "Oh wow! She's a goddess!" one voice was heard to exclaim; followed by numerous muttered assents.

Chito turned to Jesus and whispered; "bloody hell! Bubba said that's her, that's our contact. Shit... I'm going to enjoy this. She's mega hot Jesus and I'm betting she's primed and ready for a real man."

He, sure as hell wasn't ready for the fist that thudded into his kidney, from the other side.

Grunting and bending slightly to ease the pain, he turned angrily to see the smiling, old face, of Bubba standing beside him. In a voice, barely audible, yet carrying an intensity that struck deep fear into Chito's entrails, Bubba whispered; "Samantha's mine arseholes. You touch her, or hurt her in any way, and both of you will die an eternal death that will bring you more pain than you've ever imagined in your wildest nightmares. Do I make myself clear? Stick to the plan; nothing more, nothing less. Got it?"

Chito grimaced and nodded his head vigorously. "Sorry Bubba, of course... yeah, stick to the plan."

When it became apparent that the reception committee wasn't going to get the opportunity to meet the Castillo's just yet, one by one people drifted off to partake in their normal daily routines. Still rubbing his kidney gingerly Chito said; "Ah well, they're gonna be here for quite some time — we'll get our chance to test out our disguises soon enough. Shit Jesus, Bubba's one mean dude eh? I don't think we ever want to cross him."

Jesus' rapid nodding of his head was answer enough.

. . .

Maria sat down on the bed with Samantha, and took both her hands in hers. "Honey; what troubles you? Why you are so negative and why, why, are you testing and pushing Daddy — you've never done that before. What's going on inside that head of yours sweetie... please tell me."

Samantha was absolutely livid with her Mother, with everyone in fact. Why could nobody see what a sham this all was. She was sure they all knew, deep down, that what they did was just another way of achieving power and control over people. Her Mother and Father just kept trying to dress it up in platitudes and wish-washy bullshit about it being for the good of everyone and about love and peace. Shit! she thought, I know exactly why I do it — I love the feeling of control and domination it gives me. I love the adulation and worship. Why can't they just be honest with themselves and admit that's what it is for them too? They're all just such fucking hypocrites.

She looked at her mother's expectant face and knew she was going to have to suck it up, lie and be repentant. She could almost hear her beloved Bubba's voice in her ear; "sweetheart, we have to be humble for now in order to gain the greatest reward of all — power over everything in the Universe. Just swallow your pride and anger, my little one, and one day soon you will join me on the throne of heaven."

She swallowed deeply and bowed her head, squeezing some fake tears out from the corners of her eyes. "Oh Mama... I'm so sorry;" she began. "I don't mean to be like this. It's just... just... sometimes, I feel so angry and frustrated about stopping our mission — even if it's only for a short time."

She looked up, directly into her mother's eyes; the tears by now pouring unimpeded down her cheeks. "We were making a difference Mama!"

Maria was so moved by her daughter's contrition she reached for her and pulled her into her arms. "Hush Sammy... I understand. It's okay baby, we'll be back on tour before you know it." She paused for a second before adding; "besides I suspect you'll have some opportunity here in Ezraville to do some preaching. I think Jhoemar has some public rallies planned for our visit."

Samantha pulled out of her Mother's embrace, wiped her eyes with her sleeve and smiled warmly; "really Mama... really?"

Maria nodded her head, thinking even if Jhoemar didn't have something planned, she would damn well make sure he organised something. The two women embraced again and Maria sat there rocking her little baby; just like she had, so many times, on so many nights, so very long ago, in the Mangyan village.

Eventually they disentangled from each other and Maria handed her a handkerchief. "Now blow your nose... wipe away those tears... and go and wash up. Dad and Damien will have dinner prepared by now."

She looked hard at her daughter; "So, we're all settled now Sammy — no more dramas?"

Samantha kissed her Mother on her cheek. "No Mama — no more dramas."

During dinner the conversation was light and playful. The four younger children had found exciting amenity after exciting amenity in the community.

"They have a trampoline near the pool papa — and I had a go." Angeline trumpeted happily.

JC ruffled her hair; "and were you brilliant on it pumpkin?"

Her nose wrinkled up at her father's use of his pet name for her. "Papa... you know I hate you calling me pumpkin — it's such a big, fat, round vegetable and I'm not big, fat, or round — am I? Oh... and yes, of course I was brilliant."

That brought a round of laughter from everyone. It could have been just any normal, middle-class family sitting around the dinner table that evening. There were conflicting and violent undercurrents floating in the air though — that would shortly explode into horrific violence and terror, changing them all forever and splitting their family asunder—.

. . .

Chapter 13

Chito and Jesus sat nervously at the head table in the hall, along with all the other members of the leadership group. Around the sides, the rest of the community, who were able to be present that day, sat on the bleachers of the hall, which doubled as the community's gymnasium.

Every so often their concern would betray them with a quick wringing of their hands, or a hurried wipe at their foreheads at some perceived droplet of perspiration. To cover their unease they chattered endlessly with their fellow leaders. "So, what do you make of JC and his family?" Chito asked Penelope Wright, the community's housing manager, seated on his right.

"Ohhhh, Chito... aren't they just so adorable. I mean we only saw them from a distance, but that young man Damien... isn't he just the cutest thing you've ever seen. I just want to hug him and pinch his cheeks... ohhhh... and don't get me started on Samantha;" she gushed. Taking a deep breath, she continued her outpouring; "wow, that girl just makes you feel so old... isn't she absolutely the most stunning beauty you've ever seen."

Chito grinned at her; "Well Penny, you're not wrong there and even JC and Maria still look pretty good."

Penny turned and regarded him thoughtfully. "Ahhhh... so you've met them before Chito?"

Inwardly he cursed at his stupidity but moved quickly to right his gaffe. "Met them... ohhhh, I wish I'd been so lucky. No...

no... I've just seen photos of them from the early days of the Crusades. They were stunning then and they still are now."

Penny nodded her head and turned to whisper something to the lady on her right. Chito breathed out slowly. Phew, I've got to be on my toes — no more silly mistakes like that.

The hub-bub of conversation in the hall suddenly died away and everyone looked toward the door, as it swung open. Pastor Nolasco entered, leading JC, Maria, Samantha and Damien. You could have heard a pin drop, as everyone's attention focused completely on the newcomers.

Instantaneously the entire room stood as one and began clapping, shouting and cheering, for the arrivals. JC and Maria smiled broadly at the enthusiastic welcome. Samantha was back in her element, the centre of attention again and she responded with grateful smiles and waves to the cheering crowd. Only Damien seemed to be unaffected by the rapturous welcome. His face was stony and concentrated as he studied the people around the hall. This was definitely not his element and he couldn't help but wonder what all these people were actually like — one on one; in person.

He'd never been comfortable in the large crowds. He preferred to sit down with people, to chat, to get to know them and to make friends with them. He valued the personal level, so much more than what he saw as this superficial, hero worship. He looked at Samantha and sighed sadly; she loved it! He knew that.

She was oblivious to his slight disdain. She was so excited that she had left the group, and begun shaking hands and giving hugs to the people crowding around her from the bleachers; like some sort of rock-superstar.

Eventually the procession reached the head table and Pastor Nolasco held up his hands for quiet. Samantha, rather reluctantly, scuttled over to rejoin her family clustered around the Pastor. As the hub-bub eventually died down Jhoemar began to speak:

"My friends, my fellow travellers in God's will, we are truly blessed to have the presence among us..." He looked at JC and smiled; "...I understand, for at least the next six months, of a very special family."

Jhoemar looked out at the crowd, fidgeting expectantly. "Ohhhh... I don't need a big, long, speech do I? You all know who they are. On behalf of the Ezraville Community it gives me enormous pleasure to welcome JC, Maria, Samantha, and Damien to our community hall... Of course, there are four other members of the family..."

He chuckled; "but my understanding is... Shannen, Sean, Angeline and Angelo are swimming in the pool and refuse to get out. They say, it's just too hot to get out of the water... hehehe." He waited for the tittering to die down before continuing.

"Okay my dear friends... I'll just take them down the leadership group and introduce them to everyone and then they're all yours to meet, to chat with and to learn from. We are so, so blessed to have them in our midst; HALLELUJAH!"

As a group they all chorused back; "HALLELUJAH!"

JC was deeply moved by the warmth of the welcome and gathering his brood around him, they quickly made their way down the leadership group. He was keen to get the formalities over with, and take the opportunity to mix and mingle with just the ordinary members of his community. These were the people that had responded to his brave, new world. There was nothing he enjoyed more than listening to his follower's stories of their often sad and sorry past lives before they discovered the Kingdom of God Church. He always took great pleasure and inspiration from the stories of redemption they told him.

Over the years he'd talked to former drug addicts, prostitutes, mafia hit-men, rapists and even murderers; who had all turned their lives around and become respectable, fully committed members, of God's community. He'd never lost his belief in the capability of humanity's redemption... and he never would. This was his life's work and as he briefly nodded to each of Ezraville's leaders and had a quick word with all of them, his mind was already distracted by the multitudes waiting to meet him. He shook hands with Chito and Jesus in turn; smiling and nodding his head, but barely even noticing the two.

Chito grinned to himself. Well... that was easy, he thought, but then he saw Maria bearing down on them and he swallowed hard. She won't be quite so easy!

As Maria approached first Jesus; Chito unconsciously bent his head to try to hide his profile from her probing eyes. She stopped in front of Jesus and graced him with a beatific smile. "Hi! I'm Maria, I'm so happy to be here and to meet you."

Jesus stammered briefly; "Mmmaria, we are so blessed to have you and your lovely family here with us. We hope you enjoy your stay."

She nodded, smiled again and replied; "Thank you so, so much, I'm sure we'll love it here"; before moving on to Chito.

Just as she stood in front of him she glanced back at Jesus and her brow furrowed. Shaking her head she looked up at Chito and did a double-take. Chito wasn't quite sure what to do. Clearly she was having some sort of recognition... but equally clearly, she didn't know what it was she was recognising. She recovered her manners quickly and held out her hand for Chito to shake.

Her hand was warm and soft, and Chito felt overwhelmed with memories of the happy days they'd spent together so long ago.

"Hi," she said; "I'm Maria... have we met before? You look *very* familiar."

Chito's hand was shaking and he released his grip quickly. He looked up at the ceiling in mock concentration; "Ahhhh... no Maria... I'm sure we haven't met. I'd never forget someone as stunningly beautiful and charming as your good self. I'm Chito, by the way; from Mexico."

She blushed at the compliment, but continued to study his face. There *was* something achingly familiar about this man, but she just couldn't put her finger on it. Finally, she shook her head and laughed softly.

"Yes Chito... I guess it must've been someone that looked like you... I meet so many people every year. I think sometimes they all just meld into one long, continuous face... hehehe. Lovely to meet you;" and she moved on to greet Penelope Wright.

Chito held his breath for a few seconds, until Maria was clearly engaged with the chatty Penny. He exhaled loudly and turning to Jesus arched his eyebrows as if to say; "shit... that was a bit too close for comfort."

Once the formalities were over there was a mad rush to surround the visitors, to chat with them, and of course, to take "selfies" with them. Whilst JC and Maria were extremely popular, in their own right, it was Samantha who took centre stage, especially for the younger members of the community. They literally flocked to her and hung on her every word. It appeared that every single, young, man from the community had made the effort to be there that day and they fawned over her.

Damien, who was actually seated at the head table, having a long philosophical discussion about finding your passion in life, with an earnest, young man by the name of Simon Robertson, glanced up at his sister.

There she was; seated on the top row of the bleachers, her skirt spread out around her, her long beautiful legs crossed demurely at the knees, nodding and smiling graciously at her many admirers. Admirers, Damien thought — hmmm, more like subjects! She really did seem like she was the Queen, holding court and granting her loyal subjects the great gift of her attention.

Simon, noticing that Damien was no longer listening to him, followed his gaze. "She's quite something your sister, isn't she?"

Damien chuckled; "she is that Simon... she is something — I'm just not sure quite what yet."

Simon's brow furrowed briefly. "You don't really like her... do you Damien?"

Damien pulled his eyes away from his sister's floor show and focused on Simon's inquiring gaze. "Like her? Hmmmm... I love her like I love my own self. We're twins Simon — we've always been bound by that bond; we've always been inseparable."

He paused and smiled sadly; "but like her Simon? Ahhhh... not always. There have been times lately when I haven't particularly liked her." He suddenly remembered the incident with the trolley when they were children. "Actually Simon... there have been *many* times when I haven't liked Samantha all that much, but recently...;" his voice trailed off as he realised this was possibly the first time he'd admitted to himself that there was something seriously amiss in their relationship.

"Well! That's a bloody nice thing to say, isn't it... you prick?"

The voice inside his head, uninvited, was that of his dear sister. Glancing at her he realised she was watching him and clearly was listening to everything he and Simon had been discussing. Despite her obvious anger, her face betrayed nothing as she continued to smile and drop little graces on her adoring fans.

"You know Damien... you're such an arsehole sometimes. I don't want you talking to me ever again ha! And don't you ever go inside my head again, or so help me, I'll do something terrible to you. As far as I'm concerned... I don't have a brother any more — you got it? You're a spineless little bastard Damien?"

Grief stricken, he looked appealingly at his sister, seeking some relief but her icy stare spoke only of anger... maybe....even hatred. Unable to face the withering look she gave him, he quickly turned away.

Putting his head down, he felt both ashamed and relieved that he'd finally let vent his true feelings. Simon, seeming to understand Damien's pain, put his arm around his shoulders and just stayed there with him until the hurt started to recede. Damien looked at his new friend and realised that here was someone he could identify with and truly be friends with. True friendship was something Damien had missed on tour — he hadn't had a real friend since the days of the Mangyan village.

He smiled at Simon. "Thanks for understanding mate. I hope we can spend a lot of time together over the next few months. You're the first person in a long, long, time that actually seems to get me; and I really want to get to know you better."

Clearly delighted, Simon stuck his hand out. "Shake on it pardner;" he offered. "You and me — we're gonna have some fun together."

Damien grasped his hand, like it was a lifeline thrown to a drowning sailor, and he felt the warmth of real contact with another human being, outside of his family. This is what getting away from the Crusade was meant to achieve, he thought; meeting people — making connections.

Samantha's laugh cascaded around the hall. She was having such a fantastic time, being the centre of all this attention, that she'd completely lost track of her parents. As for her brother... well... she'd told him! She didn't have a brother anymore. Who did that little shit think he was, she thought haughtily to herself. We have so much opportunity for power and he just can't see it. He'd rather sit there and chat with some gay, geek — God, he's so pathetic!

She smiled quickly as yet another group selfie was taken, on yet another cell-phone. No, she thought... this is the only way to be — the centre of attention; the "Queen of the Universe". As she leant forward to give one more male adulator a quick peck on the cheek she inwardly revelled in the thought that very soon she and Bubba really will be "Rulers of the Universe" and then it won't just be the young ones who will hang on her every word. No! Every single person in the world will fear her wrath and will bow down in total obsequiousness to her glory and her beauty. She couldn't restrain herself and she giggled with sheer glee — adding to her admirer's obvious love of her.

She didn't even notice her mother, parting the crowd and sitting down beside her. She jumped when Maria whispered to her; "come on honey, Daddy says we need to go now and let these people get off to bed. They all have to work tomorrow."

Samantha bit back a harsh reply and strangled it in her throat. Turning to her mother she smiled sweetly; "of course Mama, we mustn't keep them from their beds. Ohhhh... Mama, I've had so much fun tonight. I'm going to love it here, I know I am."

Maria leant over and hugged her daughter, relief flowing through her body. Thank God, she thought, perhaps there's hope for this little girl yet.

. . .

The family's first few weeks in the Ezraville community passed quickly into months. They rapidly developed a routine that seemed to suit them admirably.

Once it had become apparent that the younger two sets of twins had not inherited the amazing abilities or knowledge of Damien and Samantha; there had been no question about it — they had to be properly schooled. Being on the move, their schooling had fallen to Maria, which was the natural order of things. Once they arrived in Ezraville, however they discovered a modern, thriving school within the community that Shannen, Sean, Angeline and Angelo happily joined and became an integral part of. This freed Maria up, to spend more time with JC, meeting with the leaders and making plans for the expansion and development of the community.

She never quite got over the feeling that she'd met Chito somewhere before, but she just dismissed it as some sort of "déjà vu" and they got on with the task of working together, to make Ezraville even better than it already was.

JC and Maria were sitting in Pastor Jhoemar's office on a bright, sunny, afternoon. The dappled sunlight was finding its way through the protective window shades and bathing the office in a soft, warm glow. As they sipped their coffee JC regarded his old friend from Davao.

"Joe, I just wanted to say what an amazing job you have done in this community — it represents everything we worked so hard to establish in Davao. I couldn't be happier with what we've found here."

Jhoemar shrunk in his chair from embarrassment at JC's effusive praise.

"Ohhhh... JC... I'm just the co-ordinator. What makes it all work so well is our leadership team and the fact that what people find here is exactly what they've been searching for all their life. We provide a meaning to life that everyone's looking for. I don't deserve the praise... really!" He looked up at the ceiling; "Give the glory to God — this is his doing."

JC smiled; "I couldn't agree more Joe, this truly is God's family here in Ezraville."

He leant forward and placed his elbows on Jhoemar's desk, steepling his fingers. "Joe... Maria and I have been talking and we think it might just be a good idea to run some public revival meetings while we're here — you know, take advantage of having Samantha and Damien here. I'm telling you, when those two kids do their 'party trick' everyone takes notice. They're absolutely awesome!"

Jhoemar threw back his head and laughed. "Oh my goodness JC; I've been thinking exactly the same thing ever since you guys arrived, but I didn't want to raise it because... well... I mean... you're supposed to be on holiday. I didn't want to impinge on that — but... since *you* brought it up; absolutely, I think it's a marvellous idea."

He clapped his hands in excitement; "so, how many can we run JC?"

Maria put her hands up to stop them. They were really getting into the flow now. "Hoy boys; let's not get too carried away ha! The kids need a rest — hell JC and I need a rest. I think we shouldn't have any more than half a dozen rallies at the most."

Jhoemar leaned back in his chair and stared at the ceiling for some time. Finally he straightened up and faced them. "So... how does this sound? We organise a week of praise! How about we hire the Las Vegas Motor Speedway for an entire week? Sheesh, you can get about 130,000 people in there. We hold rallies there every night for a whole week and we see who comes.

JC smiled at his friend. "That's what I like about you Joe, you never think small. I love it." He turned to his wife; "Honey?"

Maria absentmindedly scratched her nose, something she always did when she was thinking. Finally, she grinned; "Perfect... one week of concerted effort and then we can rest again. Sounds like a plan to me." Foremost in Maria's mind was that it would be something to keep Samantha happy.

To be honest, although Sam had showed absolutely no interest in the boys that were constantly courting her — Maria secretly worried that someone might just steal her heart; or worse; convince her that a night of pleasure was worth the risk. She knew the planned rallies would give her something to focus on and keep her mind occupied.

Jhoemar flicked his calendar over to August. "How about we pencil in the week starting August 15th? I'll check on availability and I'll get our leadership team onto the logistics."

He nodded thoughtfully. "You know, it's been a while since we had a major project to work on — this will be great for everyone. I'm so glad we decided to do it."

. . .

Damien's life at Ezraville was about as happy as he could ever remember being, once he got past Samantha's rejection. Initially he'd been devastated by it and in the weeks that followed he tried desperately to mend their relationship. It quickly became clear though, they had reached a turning point in their lives and Samantha no longer needed, or indeed wanted him in her life.

The one time he'd tried to talk to her, telepathically, he had been rudely and violently thrown from her mind by loud music blasting at 120 decibels. He'd clutched his head in agony as the deep, rumbling bass had literally shaken his brain. He had tried to talk to her normally the night after the "meet and greet", but he had been firmly rebuffed. She'd looked at him with disdain, almost like he was something she had scraped off her shoe.

Favouring him with a wry smile she had effectively closed the door to reconciliation... perhaps forever. With a virtually emotionless voices she'd tossed her hair and exclaimed; "Damien... fuck off... I don't want to talk to you *EVER*... unless I absolutely have to... get it?"

He'd bowed his head and even felt a tear squeeze out from under one of his lids. It hurt even more when Sam threw after him, as he turned to leave the room; "God, you're such a bloody cry-baby Damien — get a life; I have."

He'd wondered what she meant by the "I have" bit; but he went out and did exactly what Samantha suggested — he got himself a life.

The farm that was attached to the community was diversified and more than capable of feeding the entire village; with a surplus to sell in the local towns. They had received a water right from the Las Vegas Council and were able to irrigate much of their land, making it productive for more than just livestock. They were able to grow all types of vegetables and a large part of the cropping area was dominated by some massive greenhouses.

It was to these greenhouses that Damien tentatively offered his services. He knew absolutely nothing about agriculture, but he wanted to become, and also to be seen as, an actively contributing member of their new, albeit temporary, home. It wasn't a coincidence that Simon was employed in the greenhouses, as well, that prompted Damien to volunteer there. Their friendship had quickly developed from that first meeting and they would spend many hours together in the warm, sultry evenings, sitting on the community centre's balcony discussing the future and their role in it.

Simon was actually a farmer's son, so he had plenty of experience in agriculture plus he was studying online, part-time, toward a degree in plant science. He was the head curator of a cluster of ten greenhouses that bordered the eastern edge of the community's residential area.

One of their real pleasures was their daily walk to work. The greenhouses were around three kilometres from where Damien and Simon both lived, so they would meet up each morning at around six, before strolling through the village streets, in the crispness that foreshadows another sunny, cloudless day. They both treasured this time together and they would often tell each other of tales and adventures from their younger days.

Damien discovered he absolutely loved and adored working with plants. He thrilled to the feel of the soil, as it ran through his fingers and marvelled at the way the different plants grew. From tiny seedlings they'd planted in small trays, he watched, in wonder, as they grew into large, snaking vines that climbed the trellis in the greenhouse. When they eventually sprouted tiny green balls, that with water, nutrients and heaps of love and care would one day grow into the deep red, plump, ripe and incredibly delicious tomatoes, he was overjoyed. He was as happy as he could ever recall himself being.

One day, as he and Simon sat down to eat their packed lunches of bologna sandwiches; the talk turned to what they wanted from their lives in the future. Damien found himself pouring out his heart to his new friend.

"The truth is Simon, I can't do this travelling circus thing for much longer — it's not what I want out of life; but I just don't know what to do."

He looked at Damien's profile, drooped in sadness and he reached out softly brushing his fingers across his cheek.

"So... walk away Damien... why not? Come and live here — we can work together for as long as you're happy. Come on... just do it!"

Damien reached for Simon's fingers and briefly held them. "If only it were that easy my friend, but there are things you don't know yet; things you may not understand."

Simon looked with compassion at him but gestured with his eyebrows for Damien to continue.

In a rapid gush he quickly told him about Michael's desire; no, requirement; for Damien to carry on his father's work and how they were both just a little scared and worried about what Samantha might be up to. He emphasised that as far as Michael was concerned it was not only Damien's birthright but it was his sacred duty to continue on in this mission.

"So you see, Simon... I really don't have a choice;" he finished.

Simon sat and quietly chewed the last of his sandwiches, before reaching for the water bottle and downing it in a single swallow. "We'll talk about this again my friend. There has to be a way — why should you have to subjugate yourself for the greater good? You're important too... *but* right now we need to hoe some tomato plants, so come on let's get moving."

He added; "I know you really don't want to do it, but I must admit I have a secret desire to see you and Sam in action — I'm really looking forward to the upcoming rallies in Las Vegas."

Damien smiled shyly at him; "I'm not Simon... but I'll tell you something, you will be impressed — it's quite a show".

Simon stood up in one fluid, graceful, motion and reached for Damien's hand to pull him to his feet. There was a brief moment of awkwardness before Damien threw his arms around him and hugged him tight, whispering;

"Thank you Simon — I don't know what I'd do if I didn't have you to talk to."

. . .

Samantha wasn't one to dirty her fingers with manual labour — besides she rationalised, aren't we supposed to be on holiday? She didn't bother looking for any sort of gainful employment while they were at Ezraville. What she did do however was join as many of the community organisations and clubs as she could think of. Oh... it wasn't that she was particularly interested in them or anything as mundane as that — what really motivated her was the opportunity to be the centre of attention, in as many different forums as she could be.

The community's Glee Club was a good example. Now Sam could really sing — her voice had been described by the millions who had witnessed it over the years as; "belonging to an Angel". Her melodic tones and soaring power had brought many an audience to tears, so it was only natural that she joined the Glee Club.

The truth was she had no interest at all in singing, unless it was as a soloist. She loved the worship she received when she sang but couldn't care less about harmonizing with others, or being part of a team. In Samantha's world there was only room for one Diva — Her! No, she joined the Glee Club to show everyone else just how absolutely average and normal they were and just how outstanding and fantastic she was.

While the others loved the camaraderie and joy of singing as part of a large group — Samantha was only ever happy when she was the one out front, and the rest were her backup singers. One positive effect of her involvement in Glee was the recruitment of male voices. Glee Club had always struggled to attract male members, it was seen as a "girl thing" by many of the men, but with Samantha's involvement suddenly male membership numbers soared through the roof.

She did, however, manage to secretly meet with her two allies, Chito and Jesus.

On the pretext of the Glee Club visiting Las Vegas to sing for a local retirement village, she managed to sneak away for a couple of hours to meet with the pair in a local hotel room. As she wandered down the corridor and approached the door number they had surreptitiously slipped her during dinner the previous evening, she wondered just what these two men who had betrayed her father were really like. Knocking tentatively, the door was immediately opened by Jesus, who grabbed her arm and whisked her inside, before looking up and down the corridor to ensure she hadn't been followed.

"What's with all the subterfuge guys? I'm not a wanted criminal you know!"

Jesus roared with laughter; "Maybe not little girl, but we are... hahaha!"

She studied the two men who had betrayed her parents. "So..." she began. "You are the infamous Dan-dan and Chog eh? Hmmm... you don't look like much! How did you manage to trick my Mum and Dad then? They're not stupid."

Chito bridled and unconsciously sucked in his already burgeoning beer gut. "Ahhhh... well... that was a long time ago and we were much younger and trimmer then; besides... your parents are actually dumb-asses; they trust anyone."

Samantha thought about that for a while before she chuckled; "yeah, I guess you're right about that. So... are we all set?"

They sat down around the suite's coffee table and Jesus outlined the details of what they had in mind to fulfil Bubba's desires. As they outlined the plan a smile formed on Samantha's lips..."Shit, that's so clever — it'll be like taking candy from a baby; they won't know what's struck them."

She stood up and patted them both on the shoulder. "Maybe I misjudged you two eh? I think your plan's perfect. Good one! But... I better get back to those idiot singers or they'll put out an APB on me, and we can't have that." She gave them both a winning smile and even pecked them on the cheek, before turning for the door.

It was the peck on the cheek that was the "straw that broke the camel's back" for Chito. Ever since she'd walked in the room he'd been staring lustfully at her shapely body and imagining her writhing in passion beneath him. If you asked him what colour eyes Samantha had, he wouldn't have had a clue. The whole time she'd been talking he had been staring at the point where her breasts challenged her blouse buttons and threatened to escape from their captivity.

He grabbed her arm and hoarsely whispered; "Don't go yet ha, we can have a little fun first... yeah?"

Samantha spun round, her face a mask of contempt and fury. She pulled her hand back to deliver a slap on that pudgy, self-satisfied, little face, with the almost pig-like eyes, but she was a fraction too slow.

Chito collapsed in a screaming heap on the hotel room floor as an unseen boot kicked him right in his most vulnerable spot — his beloved "crown jewels".

Bubba stood there shaking in anger; "I thought I told you; you don't mess with Bubba's girl! When are you going to learn?"

The only reply from the writhing Chito was a strangled moan, followed by the gushing sound of vomit pouring onto the carpet.

Jesus held his hands up in surrender. "Sorry Boss! You know Chito ha — it won't happen again, I promise."

Bubba looked at him and scowled. "It better bloody not! Or once this caper's over, I'll send you both to hell and ram pineapples up your rectums every single hour — Do I make myself clear?"

Jesus' sphincter shrunk instantly at the mention of pineapples and he murmured "Crystal boss... crystal."

Bubba's face changed instantly into a malicious grin as he turned to Samantha; "everything all set to go little one?"

She nodded happily and threw her arms around his neck, raining kisses on his cheeks. He chuckled and gently disentangled himself before favouring her with a kiss on her lips; thrusting his tongue deep inside her mouth. "That should keep you going until you get the real thing;" he giggled releasing her from his embrace.

He turned to Jesus, who was trying to comfort a still moaning Chito. "Okay, you two — make it happen!"

Pecking Samantha on the cheek, he simply disappeared.

She stood there staring at the point where he'd been, for several seconds, before focusing on the pair still sitting on the floor; Jesus cradling his friend in his arms.

"Don't fuck it up guys... I'll see you both real soon." She spun on her heels and slammed the door behind her as she left.

Jesus looked down at Chito and managed a slight smile. "When you gonna learn pardner; Bubba sees everything; Bubba knows everything; and most important of all Bubba can kick your sorry arse from here to Asia... *and* you know it."

Chito nodded weakly before dry-retching the last of the bile from his stomach and uttering a loud moan—.

. . .

Chapter 14

The day of the first revival rally dawned crisp and clear; the dry desert air whispering its promise of the heat the full day would bring. Fortunately, the rally would not start until eight in the evening, when the worst of the day's scorching temperatures had thankfully receded.

Maria was jerked from her blissful slumber, curled up in the arms of her loving husband, by the insistent jangling of the bedside telephone. Groaning softly she rolled over and stared at the digital display on the bedside clock. She blinked several times before the fuzzy, red, numbers finally came into focus. "5.30 am"!

"Oh my goodness;" she exclaimed softly; "who the hell could possibly be ringing at this godforsaken time?"

Glancing over at JC, who hadn't moved since the phone began to ring, she smiled at his ability to sleep through virtually anything. Snatching the phone from its cradle, to stifle the noisy instrument she stuttered; "Hhhhello, who is this?"

"*Mama!*" The voice she knew and loved so well came roaring down the phone at her. "Mama! It's me... Samuel... How are you?"

Maria grinned; she hadn't talked to her first son Samuel for such a long time. He'd been six when she'd first met JC, and he'd been raised mainly by his *Lola,* back in San Jose. It seemed like forever since that day he'd left for New York's Columbia University; to become a man, to discover his purpose in life, and of course to study economics. They were planning to visit him before returning to the Philippines — but why was he ringing them now? What was wrong?

"Sammy darling," she began; "what's the matter? Is something wrong? It's five-thirty in the morning here sweetie. Why are you calling?"

"Oooops... sorry Mama, I totally forgot about the time difference — sorry. No Mama, there's nothing wrong. I just made a decision to quit University and return to San Jose... actually, that's where I'm calling from Mama..." His voice trailed off.

She sat bolt upright in the bed, brushed her hair from her eyes and thought quickly; "Quit University Sammy — but why? You were doing so well; you're an honours student and everything... why... why would you quit now?"

There was a long silence as she sat with the phone pushed up hard against her ear waiting for the reply. "Sammy? Sammy? Are you still there honey?"

"Yes Mama... It's just that... well... it's a bit hard to explain over the phone but I've had... oh I don't know... I guess you'd call it a revelation. I've felt a calling Mama — I know now what I want to do with the rest of my life."

Maria rubbed her forehead. It was just too early in the morning for this sort of drama, she thought. Changing the phone to the other ear she said; "well honey, that's nice. Look, why don't you fly out here to Las Vegas and we can have a proper talk about the future ha!"

There was a loud exhalation over the phone and Maria realised her son had been holding his breath, awaiting her reaction. "I was hoping you'd say that Mama... you see... my revelation has been that I need to join you and JC on your

Crusade. It came to me in a dream Mama... something bad's going to happen and I need to be there to help you guys!"

"Something bad Sam! What?"

Across the miles, she actually felt her son shrug his shoulders. "I really don't know Mama, all I know is, I'm supposed to be beside you and JC"...there was a brief pause before he added..."you and Papa."

That brought a smile to Maria's face. She'd been trying for a long time to get Sammy to call JC his Papa. As far as JC was concerned, Sammy was his child, so to hear her son call him Papa brought a warm feeling to her heart. She looked across at her husband still sleeping soundly. "Okay honey... well you get on the next plane to the States and let us know when you'll arrive; we'll pick you up from the airport. Ohhhh... Sammy, I'm so looking forward to seeing you."

She heard a chuckle from the other end of the line. "Me too Mama... me too."

After she hung up, she sat there hugging her knees and wondering what this premonition of her son's was. She heard JC stir and mumble something before she felt his hand snaking up her leg.

"Good morning honey — how are you feeling this morning?" he murmured.

She playfully slapped his hand away from where it was rapidly heading. "Hmmm... not like that anyway, Mister! We have more important things to do."

His voice was that of a wounded child; "ohhhh... what could be more important than making love to my wife?"

She giggled and hit his hand again, a little harder, this time, as it began its exploratory march up her inner thigh. "Enough my big boy! You get yourself out of that bed and get some breakfast on the stove for that ravenous horde."

Chastened, he grinned at her; "certainly my Liege, but I feel it's only fair to warn you I intend to ravish you later this evening."

Leaning over, she kissed him softly on the lips. "I'd be disappointed if you didn't knave; now go... cook!" Reluctantly, he crawled to the edge of the bed, slipped on his slippers, and padded toward the door.

"Ohhhh... by the way;" Maria called after him; "Sammy called honey; he's coming here."

He turned to look at her with a questioning expression. "Sammy? What did..."

She cut him short with a wave of her hands. "Later hon; I need to clean myself up, and you need to cook. I'll tell you all about it over breakfast."

He nodded and headed for the kitchen. Maria jumped off the bed and began her daily fifteen-minute exercise regime, before heading for the shower.

. . .

Samantha rose through the layers of unconsciousness slowly and reluctantly. She was having the most wonderful dream and she didn't want it to end... ever! In the recesses of her subconscious she pictured Bubba and her sitting on the twin thrones of heaven — with the entire world bowed at their feet worshipping them. The warmth and love that emanated from the masses and flowed over them like a river, was the most blissful, joyful, thing she had ever felt. She looked across at her husband — Beelzebub; the ruler of the Universe and gloried in the knowledge he had chosen her to rule alongside him — as his equal.

Relishing the power she felt running through her veins she lifted just one hand and immediately silenced the simpering masses. "Bring the traitors here so we can humiliate them;" she commanded, in her most imperious tone.

From out of the crowd she watched with a smile playing across her lips, as shackled and bound; hand and foot; her Mother, Father and her siblings were frog-marched across the vast amphitheatre toward them.

When they were finally presented to the Empress and Emperor of the Universe; Samantha chuckled as she saw the pain and hurt in her mother's eyes. "Sorry Mama," she giggled; "I guess I didn't quite turn out the way you and Papa hoped, did I? Ah well... we can't have everything we want in life, now can we... hehehe."

Maria stood silently and turned her head so she didn't have to look at her own flesh and blood that had betrayed them so viciously and hatefully.

"Look at me, you pathetic bitch!" Samantha screamed, but Maria just lowered her head onto JC's shoulder and began to weep gently.

Frustrated, Samantha commanded them; "kneel down and worship your Gods, slaves... kneel down, and give the respect and honour that is due to Beelzebub and his Queen."

JC's response was one of contempt. Unable to place his arm around Maria's shoulders he shuffled them around on their heels until they were facing directly away from Samantha.

She looked across at Beelzebub and smiled sweetly; "Darling," she cooed; "will you please do the honours and remove these misbegotten creatures from my sight forever."

He inclined his head, ever so slightly, before rising to his full height on the podium.

"As the lady wishes;" he intoned, and with a flick of his long, spiked tail; so quick that it was merely a whistling blur, the heads of Samantha's entire family bounced and rolled across the marble floor. She stood and kissed her husband, before throwing her head back and roaring with laughter.

The laughter was still ringing in her ears as she surfaced the final layer of sleep. With the dream still fresh in her mind she lay quietly for a while in her warm, comfortable, bed, allowing the euphoria of that moment to flow all through her body. Finally, she sat up and looking around said aloud, to the walls.

"This is it — today's the day our glorious plan begins. Yes! Today, I start the path to ultimate power." She threw her arms high in the air, as if reaching for the stars, before hugging herself and rocking with glee and excitement; "yes" she whispered; "oh yes, yes, yes!"

. . .

It was a different awakening for Damien, several miles away. Simon and he had been working late the previous evening to ensure all of the seedlings that arrived from the nursery were transplanted into their hydroponic vessels, before they dried out, withered and died.

Damien had quickly discovered that plants did not always keep the same nine to five schedules as people. To be honest, he didn't mind the long hours or the occasional evening when they would end up sleeping in one of the offices attached to the greenhouses. He was loving his life on the farm and he loved working so closely with Simon.

When it was easier to stay the night on the farm, rather than hike the long walk back home, they utilised a large mattress that was kept for that purpose. Throwing it on the floor, they'd usually just collapse on it and sleep the sleep of the dog-tired, but the truly satisfied.

Damien stretched as the first rays of sunlight sneaked through the slats of the vertical blinds. Opening his eyes, he smiled, when he realised Simon had rolled into him during the night. Still asleep, his smooth face was just inches from Damien's eyes. Staring at Simon's youthful face, Damien drank in the feelings of care, love, and concern he had for this friend. He'd known for quite some time he felt differently about Simon than he'd ever felt about anyone before.

He didn't know what to call these feelings he was experiencing; but lying there watching his friend's lips flutter, as he inhaled and exhaled, Damien bathed in his beauty and his closeness. Unconsciously, without willing it, Damien's hand came up and cupped his friend's chin. Gently he stroked his finger across Simon's cheek. He was lost in his own world of wonder and peace. He felt so at ease with everything.

Simon's left eye opened and Damien could see his friend's mind evaluating the situation they found themselves in. He didn't realise that he had been holding his breath, but when Simon's lips widened into a broad smile, he exhaled loudly in relief. Neither of them really seemed to know what to do next — they lay there cheek to cheek staring into each other's eyes. Finally it was Simon who moved; placing his lips on Damien's he kissed him long, hard and passionately.

Damien's head was spinning with emotion, desire and warmth. He kissed his friend back and they remained locked together for what seemed an eternity. Damien was the one to break the embrace eventually and propping himself up on one elbow he raised an eyebrow questioningly at Simon. There were no words; none were needed really. Simon just smiled back at him and cuffed him gently under his chin, before wrapping his arms around him and holding him tight.

When they heard the sounds of movement from the greenhouse they guiltily jumped to their feet, realising that the first of the workers was arriving for the day's shift. They looked at each other and both knew this was a turning point in their relationship. Neither knew where this would eventually head; in fact neither knew what it was they were feeling; but they both knew things would never be the same again. A line had been crossed and it could not be uncrossed. Their relationship was going to the next level and Damien thought to himself — I couldn't be happier about that. What will be; will be!

As they busied themselves tidying up their bedding Simon turned to him and croaked, his voice still full of emotion; "Wwwwell... it's a big day for you today my friend. It's back to the preaching business for you."

Damien shrugged his shoulders wearily; "I don't want to, but I really don't have a choice." Just before they left the office to check out the early arrivals, Simon placed his hand on Damien's forearm;

"I'll be there for you; every step of the way."

Damien spun round and took Simon's face between his hands, kissing him quickly on the lips. "Thank you; that means so very much to me."

. . .

The mood in the room, backstage at the Las Vegas speedway, was one of stark contrast. On one side of the room, in front of a series of mirrors, putting the final touches to her makeup, Samantha sat; whistling softly to herself. With one final brush of her blusher she deemed herself perfect and stood up, twirling in front of the mirror. "Oh my God," she exclaimed; "it's just so good to be back in the limelight again. God, I'm beautiful," she giggled.

Looking up from where they were sat at the far end of the room, Damien and Simon watched Sam prance around and pirouette in front of the mirror.

Simon smiled; "she's right about one thing Damien — she is beautiful."

Damien scowled at his friend; "Hmmpft! You think so Simon?"

He studied his sister more closely. "Well... I guess," he allowed; "in a sort of a cheap, slutty way though".

Simon smacked him playfully on the arm; "That's no way to talk about your twin sister Damien."

He smiled ruefully and looked back down at the table, studying the filmy surface of his already cold cup of coffee. Looking up appealingly at Simon, he said; "Shit mate, I wish I didn't have to do this."

Simon smiled reassuringly at him. "Hey... there's no point in feeling miserable about it. You'll get to do some things on that stage tonight that us mere mortals just dream of. Enjoy it... take pleasure from being unique." He reached out and held Damien's hand, before plunging on. "You are unique Damien. You're the most amazing, wonderful person I've ever met. You *are* special."

He checked to make sure Samantha wasn't looking, then bent and gently kissed each of Damien's fingers one by one. Looking up and smiling he added; "and you wanna know the most incredible thing about it all?"

Damien smiled and nodded.

"You're *my* unique person."

Damien felt a tear forming behind his right eyelid. He wanted desperately to hug and hold Simon, but he knew it was not the time or place. Instead he just wiped his eye and mouthed the words; "Thank You!"

"Damien! You sad sack! Get your arse over here! I want to talk to you."

Reluctantly, Damien disentangled his fingers from Simon's and rose wearily before walking toward his sister. "Yeah Sis! What's up?"

She looked Damien straight in his eyes; "What's Up? What's Up? I'll tell you what's bloody up bro! Here we are about to go back on stage, about to do what we were born to do, and what are you doing? You're moping around the room like some moody teenager. Just what the fuck's your problem Damien?"

Damien jerked away from her; the regular use of profanity was something he'd noticed creeping into her speech over the past few months, but it was still enough to shock him and frankly repel him.

"Samantha..." he remonstrated; "why do you have to use those crude words? What would Mama and Papa say if they heard you now? Do you think they'd be proud of you?"

He saw a brief flash of absolute fury and hatred cross her eyes, before she gained control of it. She just spat out at him; "oh just *fuck* off then — God, you're such a bloody wimp!"

Damien turned away in disgust when he felt Samantha entering his mind. He tried desperately to block her but she was too damn quick for him.

He was mortified when she burst into laughter and spoke to him telepathically; "Oh my God Damien... no... no... surely not... really Damien... really and truly? No... you're joking... hahaha."

She grabbed hold of his arm and spun him round to face her. She was chuckling loudly, but still managed to send her next thought message. "Really Damien... you bat for the other team? Oh my God... this is so absolutely delicious; my brother's gay... wait till I tell Mama and Papa... their precious little Damien likes boys."

He grabbed both her arms so viciously she visibly winced before he sent very slowly and very deliberately, the message. "Sam, if you ever mention this to anyone, I swear I will never, ever, help you perform again, including tonight — It'll be over for good."

She looked thoughtfully at her brother as she considered the implication of what he'd sent her. She nodded her head slowly; "Okay Damien... this will be our little secret". To herself, she added; "for now."

He released her arms and without another word turned and headed back to Simon.

Oblivious to the drama that had just played out a mere few feet away, Simon smiled broadly at him. "All good?"

Damien forced a smile onto his face; "yeah mate, it's all good..."

Their discussion was interrupted by a knock on the door, followed by JC's head poking around it. "Hey guys... you better get upstairs ha — we're on in a few minutes."

Samantha waved to her father; "Coming Papa."

Damien nodded and, with a reassuring pat on the arm from Simon, wandered back over to join his sister. "Alright kiddo;" he muttered; "let's get this charade over with." As an afterthought he added; "and don't forget our agreement eh?"

Sam was already feeling the thrill and anticipation of the coming show. She patted him on the head; "don't worry your secret's safe with me. Now come on it's fun time." She grabbed his hand and dragged him through the door and up the stairs to the wings of the great stage. Simon, caught up in Samantha's enthusiasm, quickly followed them.

. . .

It had been an amazing performance. The crowd, composed of perhaps thirty percent community members and seventy percent non-believers, was in raptures. By the time Samantha and Damien began their "party trick" and rose into the clear, star-lit sky above the arena, most of the unbelievers were rapidly becoming convinced. Samantha was thrilled to be back in her element — the whirling, spinning, beautiful, object of everyone's gaze and attention that she almost forgot what was supposed to happen next.

They were floating, motionless, above the centre of the arena; all necks were craned upward and eyes focused on the two beautiful creatures hovering above them. Damien leant back and prepared to let fly with his deep baritone voice when he felt, rather than heard, the bullet. It made an obscene whistling noise as it flew past his cheek, grazing it slightly, before slamming into Samantha's right shoulder and exiting in a spray of blood and tissue.

Her cry of surprise and pain was not rehearsed. It damn well hurt. She lazily, almost poetically, spun on her axis before twisting and rapidly spiralling to the ground thirty feet beneath them.

The crowd were stunned into utter silence, by the noise her body made when it slammed into the ground of the arena. Nobody moved a muscle. Damien continued to hover; despite the shared pain he felt for Samantha's wound. He was stunned, unsure what had happened, or what to do about it.

JC was the first to react; "Sammy!" he screamed, as he leapt from the stage and began to race through the aisles to the point where he'd seen his daughter land. The audience, re-gathering its senses panicked and a loud rumbling of frightened voices erupted from the arena, as people began to realise they might be in danger also. JC was trying to fight his way through a wall of bodies to get to Samantha, but he was stymied by the fleeing patrons.

Samantha lay in a small, open space between the aisles. Clearly still alive, she was groaning softly. Those closest to her hesitated; scared for their own safety, until one patron finally found the courage to move.

"I'm a paramedic," he shouted. "Let me look at her."

Moving backward, the crowd gave him the space to kneel beside the fallen girl. He leant close, to listen to her heartbeat. His head exploded in a shower of brain tissue, gristle, and pink blood. Everyone instinctively turned to the direction of the shot to see two, hooded men, dressed in boiler suits and carrying large assault rifles, striding down the aisle toward Samantha.

As they walked they constantly cracked the butts of their rifles on the heads of anyone who seemed even remotely in their way. Like magic, the path to Samantha widened and opened. The largest of the two men threw his rifle at his comrade and bent to pick Samantha up in his arms. Cradling her, surprisingly gently, he turned and began to run toward the nearest exit.

His partner fired shots, seemingly randomly into the crowd as they ran, to encourage anyone who was feeling even a tad brave, to crawl down and try to hide beneath their seats. It transpired that five people were killed in this savage act and eighteen people wounded; but for the assailants it had worked perfectly — the path to the exit remained unimpeded.

Racing from the speedway, the two men jumped into a waiting car. The man carrying Samantha gently laid her on the back seat and clambered in beside her. His partner jumped behind the wheel and gunned the engine before racing out of the parking lot and heading south. The man in the back seat breathed a sigh of relief, and dragged off his hooded ski mask. Chito looked worried as he bent down to check if Samantha was still bleeding.

He tentatively asked; "are you all right little one?"

Samantha's eyes flashed open. "No! I'm not fucking-well alright you useless piece of shit. You weren't supposed to hit me... you were supposed to just graze me. Can't you even shoot straight? Ahhhh... fuck me... it bloody well hurts."

Chito smiled apologetically. She was going to be just fine, he thought. If she can get that angry, she'll be fine. "Sorry Sam, but don't blame me ha, Jesus was the shooter, not me. Now just lie there and rest until we get to the motel. You know Bubba will fix that up real quick."

Samantha's anger dissipated at the thought of seeing Bubba again. She closed her eyes and tried to focus on something other than the pain — the look of horror on Damien's face when she got shot. Now that was priceless... hehehe.

That's the first phase of the plan complete, she thought, as she allowed herself to fall into a half sleep for the rest of the journey—.

. . .

Chapter 15

Nobody at the stadium could quite believe what had transpired. For several minutes, after the gunmen had departed, people stood around checking — reassuring themselves they were still alive. Almost on cue, the first person began to scream and within seconds the entire stadium was a cacophony of sound.

One hundred and twenty thousand people collectively decided it was time to get the hell out of this killing ground and as they surged toward the exits the young, the frail and the elderly were knocked to the ground; many of them injured or killed beneath the raging tide of humanity. It was utter chaos and finally several hours later, after order was restored, the police and paramedics were able to make an accurate body count. The horrific aftermath of the night was revealed — forty seven people lost their lives that evening with one hundred and twelve ending up in the local hospitals; injuries ranging from sprains and contusions, through to fractured skulls and broken bones.

Within this scene of complete carnage; JC, Maria, Damien and Simon sat alone on the stage, staring out at the devastation.

"Why JC... why?" Maria looked at her husband and begged him with her eyes to have an answer, but JC was just as lost and bereft as anyone.

He looked up, his eyes raw and swollen with tears. "Hhhoney..." he managed to choke out, but he could go no further. Bowing his head into his hands he began to softly sob and shake.

Maria grasped him around his shoulders, instinctively knowing that this time it was her who needed to be the strong one — it was her who needed to keep this family together, so they could weather this tragedy. She glanced at Simon and Damien who were sitting together, consoling each other. A flash of intuition swept through the mother's mind and despite the dire circumstances facing them she managed a small, wry smile. Ah, so that's how the land lies is it? I wonder when Damien will have the courage to tell us, she thought.

She smiled reassuringly at the two friends and nodded her head in brief acknowledgement of what she now understood.

Deciding it was time for her to "step up to the plate" she stood up and reached down to grasp her husband's arms. She pulled him reluctantly to his feet, where he stood, staring at nothingness, completely wrapped up in his own misery. Grasping his face between her fingers, she dug her nails into his cheeks with some force, to ensure she got through to him.

"*JC!* Now you listen to me;" she slowly and forcefully pronounced. She was rewarded with a flash of understanding in her husband's eyes.

"What has happened here is tragic; horrific — a lot of people have lost their lives and our daughter is who knows where; injured, perhaps even dead." She moved her hands up so they cradled his head and she leant forward so her eyes were just centimetres from his. She could see that he was not totally lost — there was some spark of fire and anger still in his eyes. Good, she thought, I can still reach him.

"Sitting here, feeling sorry for ourselves, and worrying, isn't going to achieve anything my darling. We need to move — we need action; damnit JC we need to start looking for our daughter." The final words Maria spat forcefully and they had the desired effect.

His eyes came into focus as he looked deeply into Maria's angry eyes. "Honey..." He pulled himself out of her grasp and shook his head.

"Honey... I'm sorry babes... you're right — we need to focus on fixing this."

Looking around him and noticing the hundreds of policemen currently scouring the stadium for evidence of bullet cartridges, he drew himself up and visibly shuddered to try and regain control of his emotions.

"Right hon, first things first — the police are going to want to talk to us. I'll go and see if we can put that off; we need to start looking for Sssammy." Despite his new found control he still choked a little when he said her name. With a quick pat on Maria's shoulder and a smile to his son, he headed off in search of the officer in charge.

Maria breathed a sigh of relief; JC was back in control. She was a strong woman, she'd always known that, but there was something incredibly reassuring and powerful about JC. He always gave her additional strength, and he hadn't lost that... when he'd become fully human. She signalled the two boys to join her. When they ambled over she made an immediate, motherly, effort to include Simon into the "inner circle". She put an arm around each of their shoulders and drew them close to her. The effect was instantaneous as both boys grasped onto her loving embrace and they remain locked, motionless, in a group hug; drawing strength from each other, for several seconds.

Releasing them, she smiled at each of them in turn. "Righto boys, we need to find Samantha."

She looked at Damien, who nodded; "yes Mama."

Maria clapped her hands in inspiration; "Damien, you can communicate with Sam; can you feel her now?"

He shook his head sadly; "Mama, when she was shot, I felt the pain also — you know how that happens, right? I was able to follow her as they took her from the stadium, but suddenly she just disappeared..." He shook his head sadly. "I don't know what happened; maybe it was the distance, maybe she was unintentionally blocking me... or perhaps... you know..."

Maria snapped at her son. "No Damien... No! Don't for a second think what you're thinking. Samantha's still very much alive and we will find her, right?" The boy just nodded his head and leaned on Simon's shoulder, seeking comfort.

Maria looked around and spotted JC heading back toward them. "Okay, your father has hopefully put off the police for a short while. What we'll do is we'll tour around Las Vegas and you'll try to get a handle on your sister... try to find her in your mind. Is that how it works Damien?"

He screwed his face up in concentration. "Wait Mama, I have a better idea. Whoever took Sammy, took her for a reason. They didn't kill her, did they? The kidnapped her — they wanted her. Why? There's only one thing I know of that kidnappers want and that's money."

He managed a wry smile; "well, at least we have plenty of that Mama." He continued; "I think one of us needs to be at home, just in case these people call... yes?"

"That's... exactly... what... the... police... just... said;" JC huffed as he arrived beside them just in time to catch Damien's last sentence. "One of us, needs to be at home, with a policeman and their equipment, in case the kidnappers call."

He looked at his wife and shrugged; "honey, it should be you."

He saw Maria bristle and stiffen, but he held up his hand to stop her jumping in. "Babes, let's be honest, you're the most understanding and rational of all of us. The police said a woman is always better at keeping kidnappers talking until the police can get a fix on their position."

Again, Maria looked about to speak. JC gripped both her arms and looked directly into her face. "I'd just lose my temper, you know I would. Honey, the police said it needs to be you — please understand babes, I know you want to go and find her, but this is the best thing for you to be doing."

Her shoulders shrunk in resignation and she nodded. "Okay, but you guys better get going and you *better* damn well find her."

JC turned to Simon and Damien. "Come on boys, let's go." Turning back to Maria he held her briefly and kissed her. "Don't worry honey... Damien will find her, have faith in our boy."

Maria smiled tightly and pushed JC toward the stage stairs. "Go now, you're wasting time."

The three men ran toward the exit, leaving Maria a sad, lonely, figure on the stage.

. . .

As Maria turned the key in the house door, and walked in, she imagined she could smell Samantha's favourite perfume. The other twins were safely asleep in their beds, totally oblivious to the drama that was playing out around them, but the children's *yaya* (nanny) was watching television when Maria walked in.

She quickly jumped to her feet and ran to her adoptive mother. "Ohhhh Maria," she wailed; "I saw it all on television... ohhhh... ohhhh... whatever will become of our Samantha?"

Maria took a deep breath and hugged Marielle tightly. "Calm down sweetie, the police will monitor any phone-calls we get and JC, Damien and Simon are looking for her. They'll find her don't worry."

Drawing strength from Maria's calmness, Marielle quickly set about helping the policemen set up and organising snacks for them while they waited, for what they hoped would be the inevitable phone-call.

. . .

The car skidded to a stop in the gravel car-park of the trucker's stop about fifty miles south of Las Vegas. As was often the case at trucker's stops, there was a service station and restaurant out front, near the expressway and tucked in behind was the ubiquitous, slightly faded, and tatty, motor hotel. The boys had pre-booked a room several days earlier and Jesus spun the car into a spot in front of room seventeen, in a spray of gravel.

"Way to keep a low profile mate;" Chito spat at his partner.

Jesus turned in the seat and grinned; "hehehe... that was fun!"

Chito noticed the door to room seventeen was slightly ajar, as they had arranged. Checking around to ensure there were no prying eyes, he gently leveraged Samantha from the rear seat. Not gently enough apparently as Samantha's eyes ripped open and she snarled; "Careful you big galoot... it still bloody hurts like hell."

Grinning apologetically he dashed them into the room, with Jesus entering just behind them; closing the door and locking the deadlock, as well as placing the security chain in place. Chito carried her as gently as he could to the bed, in the centre of the room, where he laid her down before bending to give her what was meant to be nothing more than a reassuring peck on the cheek. All he got for his troubles however was a string of profanity laced invective, and a stinging slap to his cheek.

"Ahhhh... little one;" he said ruefully rubbing his red cheek; "there's nothing wrong with you. Now is there? Still the fiery, little, monster... hehehe."

Samantha fixed his grinning face with a stony glare. "One day... one day... you will not dare to talk to your Queen like that. Just remember who I am Chito. You forget at your own peril."

The reality of his position did seem to sink through and contritely he stood up from her and waved his arms in apology. Turning to Jesus he muttered; "where the hell's Bubba? He was supposed to meet us here.

Though they were well used to it by now, Bubba's sudden appearances and disappearances, still caught them by surprise. When Chito felt the tap on his shoulder he jumped two feet in the air and gave an involuntary squeal.

Bubba laughed aloud. "Hi boys... and how are we tonight?" Regaining his composure Chito turned to face their boss.

"It went well boss... well... apart from Jesus actually shooting Sam, that part was a trifle unfortunate."

Bubba rubbed his chin thoughtfully. "Hmmm... yes... that *was* a tad unnecessary, but don't worry Jesus, your *reward* for that piece of clumsiness will come in due course... hehehe... you just won't know when. Anyway, we haven't got time for all that crap. You two need to get back and start looking for Samantha. Remember, it has to be you guys that find her... God forbid that idiot brother of hers stumbles across her or even worse... the police. So... get back to Ezraville and offer your services in the search."

Chito nodded effusively. "Yes Bubba!" He grabbed Jesus' arm and headed toward the door. Just as they were leaving he turned back; "what about Sammy, boss? She's hurting."

Bubba looked at him like he was just a piece of crap; "don't you worry about *my* girl Chito, I'll look after her."

As the door slammed behind them Bubba turned to look at Samantha, who was trying to rise off the bed to greet her love. His face softened and all the anger and violence faded from him as he looked at his beautiful bride to be. Her usually pale complexion was even whiter than normal; her skin almost translucent and glowing. His hard-heart melted when he noticed her eyes were screwed up with suppressed agony as she tried to leverage herself from the bed. Despite her clear pain, she was smiling — she was so happy to see her Bubba again.

Rushing to the bed, he placed his arm around her and pushed her gently back down. "Don't move my precious little one. I'll soon have those nasty wounds repaired. You just lie back and relax... you'll feel a warm, tingling sensation, but that will be all and then everything will be fine."

Having total faith in her man, Samantha relaxed and lay back. She refused to close her eyes though, as she didn't want Bubba's face to fade from her sight. He reached down and gently cupped her shoulder in both hands, covering the wound on both sides. She winced slightly as his fingers probed the gaping hole, still leaking blood, but relaxed as she felt this incredible, glowing, warmth, exude from his long, gnarly fingers.

Bubba closed his eyes in deep concentration as his fingers dug deeper and deeper into Samantha's wound. Lifting his head, he shouted just one phrase; *"Tui Gratia Lovis Sit Cura".*

The second the words had left Bubba's lips, Samantha felt an immense power grip her. Like a tidal wave of water it swept her up and up toward a glowing light that grew bigger and bigger within her vision, until that was all she could see. The light pulsed and changed colours from white, through orange, pink and finally blood red before it exploded in a cascade that was purely physical.

She could feel the liquid from the exploded light literally running down her face. She wasn't sure quite what it was but it felt warm, comforting and so, so, relaxing. She just closed her eyes and let the sensations envelop her and flow through her. Time seemed to stand still and she was shocked and surprised when as suddenly as the beautiful sensations had appeared; they were gone — leaving her feeling bereft. As her senses began to return to normal she heard the reassuring voice of Bubba whispering in her ear; "that's it my precious princess — you're all fixed."

She sat up on the bed stunned, and rotated her shoulder — it felt fine. Her hands flew up to feel where the wound had been; but there was nothing there, just the tattered cloth of her ruined dress. A grin came over her face and she clapped her hands with glee. Jumping off the bed she bent over to test her spine, but all the bruises, all the contusions, all the pain, had miraculously disappeared.

She turned to Bubba and grabbing his face in her hands she plastered kisses all over his wrinkles. "Oh, you clever, clever, man;" she gushed as she attempted to take him in her arms.

He gently, but forcefully removed her arms from around him. "No time for that my dear, I have a phone call to make and you... have some acting to do... hehehe."

Samantha giggled, as she watched Bubba reach for the motel phone, by the bed. "This will be fun;" she chortled.

. . .

Maria hadn't moved from the kitchen table, where she'd sat ever since the police had connected their monitoring equipment, to the phone that was placed in front of her. She stared at it with a quiet vehemence. Ring... damn you... ring, she silently commanded the mute instrument.

She jumped from her chair when instead of the jangling of the telephone there came a rapid hammering on the door. One of the policemen quickly rushed to answer it, drawing his sidearm as he went. Maria distractedly looked to see who had arrived and when she saw it was Chito and Jesus, she jumped up and ran toward them.

"Jesus," she shouted. "Have you got any news, have you found my little girl?" Jesus grabbed her, pulling her tight into his embrace and allowing her the luxury of sobbing on his shoulder. She looked up expectantly at the Community's Chief of Police, but Jesus just shook his head sadly.

"Nothing yet Ma'am, I'm so sorry."

He looked at his partner before continuing. "Chito has some ideas though and we're gonna follow through on them. Our jobs at the Casino often bring us into contact with the underworld in this town and we do have our contacts. We're going to use them." His lips tightened and he scowled; "ruthlessly and viciously if we have to, but Maria, we'll find out who did this and we'll find Sammy... trust us!"

Maria's face radiated the hope only a mother can summon in such dire circumstances. She smiled at the two men and patted

Jesus on the shoulder. "Thank you... thank you... thank you... but, you'd better stop wast..."

The sharp, jangle of the phone cut through the room. Everyone turned and stared at the offending instrument — nobody moving a muscle, Maria recovered first and dashed across the room to snatch up the receiver.

As she reached for it, the beefy hand of the Chief of Detectives grabbed her wrist. "Wait Ma'am;" he commanded. "Please don't pick it up till I give the signal." Motioning to the tech experts in the corner of the kitchen they quickly flicked their switches. "Keep him or her talking for as long as you can Ma'am... try anything to keep the caller on the line." Maria nodded her understanding and picked the receiver up.

"Hhhhello"; she stuttered in a cracking voice, "Ttthis is Maria Castillo, who is this pl..."

The voice that interrupted her was harsh, raspy and spoke barely above a whisper. She found herself pushing the receiver hard into her ear, just to catch the words he spoke. She idly wondered if the caller was deliberately trying to disguise his voice.

"Ahhhh... the gorgeous Maria. I have no doubt the police are tracing this call, but I have no intention of speaking long enough for that to happen, so listen carefully."

"Whhhat do you want? Where is my..."

"I told you to listen carefully bitch... not to talk... so shut the fuck up and listen."

Maria gulped, but bit back her words, and although the unseen caller couldn't possibly have seen her, she nodded her head vigorously.

"Okay... Now, I have your lovely Samantha here with me... don't worry she's fine... for *now!* But just to show you how serious I am, I'm going to chop off her two little fingers, and you're going to listen."

Maria screamed as she heard the phone being slammed down harshly at the other end. Seconds later, the ear piercing, heart rending sound of Samantha's agony blasted her eardrums. She dropped the phone and put her hands to her face in horror.

The Police Chief grabbed the phone and held it up to her ear. "I'm sorry," he whispered to her. "You *must* listen and you *must, must* keep him talking."

Tears pouring down her cheeks, she nodded and grabbed the phone, a steely determination replacing the horror on her face.

"Now that was fun;" the voice returned.

Maria could still hear Samantha's pained whimpering in the background. "Wwwhat... is... it... you... wwwant?" she finally managed to squeeze out between deep gasps of air.

"Jesus Christ!" he exploded. "I thought I told you to shut up. Now, I'll call you back in one hour and then I think I'll start on pretty girl's toes... hehehe."

Maria gasped involuntarily; "please, please, just tell me what it is you want from us... we'll do anything, pay anything... just don't hurt my little..."

Realising she was talking to thin air, she stood there, the phone cord drooping from her hand and began to shake.

The Chief of Detectives wrapped his arms around her and allowed her to sob loudly until she'd managed to recover her composure. He glanced across at his head technician who sadly shook his head. "It's ok Ma'am, don't worry we'll find her." Maria nodded slowly and sank back down onto the kitchen chair.

Chito came over and placed a hand on her shoulder. "We'll go Maria, the sooner we find her the better."

She looked up and smiled at him. "Thank you!" was the only thing she could find to say. She took her cell-phone from the table and quickly dialled a number. Summoning up her strength and courage she straightened up and brushed the hair out of her face, wiping her tear stained cheeks as she did so.

When the phone was answered, she spoke very calmly, very quietly, and very controlled, but there was a real undertone of anger and determination in her words. "Honey, he rang. He *has* Samantha and babes; he's hurting her. You and the boys — you have to find her honey. You have to." She listened for a while before pushing the terminate button and gently replacing the phone on the table-top.

She looked up at the circle of concerned policemen and smiled wanly; "Find her please," she pleaded.

The Chief turned away from her entreating look and mumbled; "we'll do our best Ma'am, I promise."

. . .

JC turned off his cell-phone and struggled to contain his emotions. He rubbed his face vigorously, before leaning across to the front seat of the car and tapping Damien on the shoulder.

Damien had been in a trance-like state the whole drive, concentrating deeply on trying to locate even a hint of his sister's thoughts. He jumped, in fright, and turned to face his father.

"Anything Damien?"

Damien shook his head "Look Dad, if she was here in Las Vegas I'd have felt something by now, especially since she's bound to be in pain, after the bullet and the fall and everything. If she's here Dad... then she's definitely..."

JC quickly shook his head; "nope Damien, she's definitely not dead. Your Mum just got a call from the kidnapper... and Damien... he's hurting her. She'll be in real pain, so it should be easy for you to feel her."

Damien studied the pain in his Father's eyes and it broke his heart. Putting out his hand, he stroked his father's cheek. "Okay Papa, if she's alive and in pain — then she's not here. They must have taken her out of town."

He scratched his nose absently; "but which way? North or South?"

JC threw his hands up in the air in frustration. "Your guess is as good as mine boy! I have no idea."

Simon, who was driving, briefly glanced at the pair; "just make a decision then — we've got a fifty-fifty chance of being right. We drive one way for an hour or so and if we get nothing, then we come back and try the other way. But we have to choose something."

Damien smiled at Simon's unerring logic. "You're right of course. Okay then, I'll make a decision."

He thought briefly before looking up at Simon. "Hey, we're at the north end of town already ha, let's just keep going — let's head North on the Interstate."

Simon nodded and pushed his foot hard on the accelerator, heading their posse toward Northern California. As they picked up speed Damien returned to his concentrated trance, and JC relaxed back on his seat, alone with his thoughts and his fears. Without even realising it he'd begun to pray to his Father for guidance.

. . .

Maria watched the minutes tick over slowly on the digital clock on the countertop. It had been exactly one hour and ten minutes since he'd last called. Why hadn't he called back? Horrible, scary scenarios kept running through her head. What was he doing to her precious, beloved, firstborn girl? She was at the point of collapsing on the table, head in hands, uncontrollably sobbing again, when the Chief of Detectives, intuitively recognising her need, placed a hand gently on her shoulder and spoke softly;

"It's okay Ma'am, he probably doesn't have quite the same issue with time that we do. Don't worry! He wants something! — he'll ca..."

Like a summoned demon, that's exactly what happened, as the air was rent by the jangle of the phone again.

Maria snatched it up so quickly the technicians struggled to get their recording equipment running in time and she almost dropped it. Thrusting it into her ear she wasted no time on preliminaries;

"What!" she shouted into the instrument.

That now familiar, evil, voice trickled down the line into her ear;

"Ohhhh Maria... is that any way to greet your Saviour? Never mind, my dear, I'm sure you're just a tad overwrought at the moment. Now, same rules as before — you say nothing; you just listen... right?"

Maria gulped and managed to hold back the flood of questions that were already forming on her lips. She closed her eyes and wordlessly nodded.

"Now, that's a good girl. You're learning quickly;" the smarmy, sarcastic voice oozed back at her.

"You want to know what I want. Well, that's actually very simple really. What I want is one hundred million dollars — just a drop in the bucket for the Kingdom of God Church, I'm sure, but for me, well let's just say; it's a pretty penny for me."

There was a pause and Maria contemplated answering, but before she got a chance the voice continued; "okay, I'll give you instructions next time on where to leave the money, but for now I want you to listen to a little bit more fun. I'm going to chop off Sammy's little toes now... isn't that a hoot?"

Unable to contain herself Maria shouted; "NO!" but it was too late, the phone had already been dropped on the table.

If anything, the screams were louder and more bone-chillingly painful to hear than the first time. Maria sat, stoically, with the phone hard against her ear. She owed it to her daughter to at least try to share her pain with her, she felt. Tears were soundlessly cascading down her face, but she never once took the phone from her ear.

The only time her courage wavered was when she imagined she could hear Samantha whimpering; "mama... mama... please help me." She bowed her head but still kept the phone glued to her ear.

Finally, the man came back on the line. His voice was slightly breathless, but there was a definite undertone of glee in it that sickened Maria to the core. "I'll call you in four hours and tell you where to leave the money. I have some cooking and snacking on 'finger food' to do."

Maria, gasped aloud, and shouted down the phone; "you unspeakable creature — how could you possibly do this; you are... you are... you are... the Devil incarnate."

"Why Maria... How sweet of you to say so... talk to you in a few hours sweetie; bye for now."

The finality of the click was loud in everyone's ears. The Chief looked hopefully to the technicians; "any joy boys?"

The head technician took off his headphones and shrugged. "It wasn't long enough to get an exact location boss, but I think we've narrowed it down to an area of around 100 square miles south of Las Vegas."

The Chief clapped his hands. "Well that's something guys — we're closing in. We'll get him next time." He grabbed his cell-phone from his pocket and turned to organise the searching forces and to concentrate them south of the City.

Maria quickly dialled JC and told him where the police believed the call had come from. He assured her they would quickly head that way.

"Honey, he's still hurting her — please, please find her soon;" she whispered into her phone—.

. . .

Chapter 16

Samantha hugged Bubba tightly; "Oh honey, this is so, so much fun. I wish I could've seen Mama's face as she listened to my screams — it must've been priceless!"

Bubba laughed; "Ah Samantha, you're a girl after my own heart."

He suddenly became very serious. "You know something sweetie... I never thought I would find someone worthy of my love — someone with a heart as purely evil as my own; and then... I found you. You're perfect."

She looked at him with love and adoration; "It's you that makes me perfect Bubba."

They locked in an embrace, uniting the twin forces of evil on earth. Samantha felt the power of evil and hatred flow through her body and revelled in the joy of uniting now and forever with Bubba. She wanted him... and she wanted him now! As they embraced she hungrily began to undo the buttons on his shirt, sliding down to kiss his neck; long, slender and terribly wrinkled. She noticed none of that though — she was interested only in consummating their love. As she slid lower down his body and began to circle his left nipple with her tongue, she heard Bubba give an audible gasp of pleasure; immediately bringing a smile to her lips.

Without warning Bubba grasped both her wrists, pulled her upright and in one furious motion threw her on the motel bed.

She smiled seductively; he wants me too and he wants me now. Briefly it flashed through her head that here she was about to lose her virginity to the most powerful being on Earth. She was about to mate with Beelzebub — The Prince of Darkness; how incredibly delicious. Licking her lips in anticipation, she beckoned him with a crooked finger, to join her on the bed.

Bubba towered over her, his eyes misted with passion or desire or... He gazed down at the perfect creature that lay beneath him, writhing, begging, enticing him to take her; to fill her with his mystical power. With a great force of will, he tore his eyes from her voluptuous curves and focused solely on her face. A smile creased his aged face before he spoke in his "devil" voice — a voice that reverberated round the tiny motel room, bouncing off every wall, and focusing directly on Samantha.

"Oh baby," he began; "if only you knew what lay in store for you little one. Yes, we will be united in marriage and yes we will consummate the perfection of our evil love... but just not yet."

He paused to lean down and kiss her on the lips. She reached out to pull him down beside her, but he squirmed out of her embrace. "You see... my little one, there is just a couple of things I forgot to mention to you."

Looking at him quizzically, she began to push herself upright. Bubba leant over and pushed her back down. He knelt close to her ear and whispered softly.

Her eyes flew open wide and her mouth gaped involuntarily in a mouthed "No!" She twisted her head away from his whispering lips. "No Bubba... you can't ask that of me;" she whimpered.

His face twisted into a vicious scowl as he grabbed her chin and pulled her face back to him. "You *will* do it little one... or, we will never be united." He spat out the next sentence in unrestrained fury; "you *will* do it for Bubba... for me... do you understand?"

Samantha closed her eyes, took a deep breath and slowly nodded her acquiescence to his evil request.

"Good girl, now the second requirement. Yes, you *will* be mine, but sadly for you, you must die first. I can't mate with a living human — you must join me first in the eternity of hell."

From between his legs sprung his enormous forked tail; deep blood red and around two foot in length. He waved it in a circle that Samantha's widening eyes followed in terror. She just had time to form the words; "Bubba No..." on her lips, before he struck with lightening speed. The tail twisted and plunged deep into the centre of her forehead, cleaving her skull in half. The force of the attack was such that the fork of the tail went right through her head to bury itself in the pillow she was lying on.

He looked sadly down at his bride and muttered softly; "Sorry Sammy, but if I'd told you any earlier you might have resisted me. Don't worry... I'll bring you back and then we'll rule the Universe."

He bent down to feast on the gory mess that was flowing unimpeded across the pillow. He was kneeling on the bed, greedily lapping it up, when the door of the motel room swung open and the familiar voices of Chito and Jesus could be heard.

"Hey Bubba; what's up my ma..."

Chito stopped short as he surveyed the horrific scene in the room. "Holy Fuck!" he exclaimed; "what are you doing for Christ's sake?

Bubba sat upright and turned his head to examine his visitors. He wiped the ooze from his chin that was dripping onto the bed. His lips spread in a malicious grin.

"What am I doing Chito? Ahhhh... my good man, I'm just preparing my bride for our wedding ceremony." He giggled uncontrollably. "You could even say I'm making an early start on our wedding breakfast... hehehe."

It was too much for Chito, who turned away from the scene of utter carnage and promptly vomited on Jesus' shoes. Jesus, who hadn't yet seen the full extent of the horror, recoiled, and bent double to vomit his own stream of bile. Bubba climbed slowly off the bed and walked jauntily toward the two; who were now sitting on the floor dry-retching what little was left in their stomachs.

"You boys haven't really got the balls for the tough stuff have you?" Bubba reached down and lifted them both onto their feet, with just one hand. "Pull yourselves together boys; you've got some work to do before you call this one into the police ha!"

The two stood there shaking uncontrollably until Chito finally managed to stutter; "wwwwhat are we supposed to do now?"

He turned to Jesus and muttered; "Oh my God Danny... what have we done? What have we gotten ourselves into?"

Bubba had had enough of this pair of simpering idiots and he smashed their heads together with such force that they slumped to the ground moaning. Kicking them both, a couple of times, for good measure he commanded; "Right... now... first things first. We need to get this mess cleaned up before JC and the police arrive. They must be closing in by now."

Chito and Jesus moaned loudly, but pulled themselves slowly to their feet. They gingerly approached the scene of the carnage; hands held over their noses and looked helplessly at Bubba.

"Hhhhow cccan we clean this up?" Jesus managed to get out.

Bubba laughed; "just give me a few minutes boys and then you can sort it."

He walked over to where Samantha's now lifeless body lay, caked in brain matter, blood and other bodily fluids. Climbing onto the bed, he squatted over her chest and closed his eyes. Grabbing either side of her skull, he began to softly chant.

He swayed back and forth; chanting continuously as Chito and Jesus stood there dumbfounded; looking at each other with expressions of horror and fear. After five minutes of ceaseless chanting Bubba threw his arms to the heavens and boomed;

"Give me the assurance that in Beelzebub I died; and in him I now rise. In my death I live and in his life I flourish. In the Prince of Darkness' victory I triumph and in his resurrection and ascension to Heaven — I WILL BE GLORIFIED!"

Chito and Jesus edged closer to see if they could catch a glimpse of what was happening on the bed. Bubba made it easy for them by lithely jumping off the bed, like a man half his age, and turning to the pair with an enormous grin on his face.

"Well, that's done boys. Sam will awaken in thirty minutes or so and she'll be none the worse for her experience." He laughed loudly at the two men; mouths agape and eyes as wide as saucers.

"When you've picked your jaws up off the floor boys, you might want to get some damp cloths and clean up what little residue there is left — but as for me, I gotta fly. Laterz boys!" With that he was just... gone.

Chito turned to his friend and rubbed his eyes. "Damn! I'll never get used to that."

They looked at the bed and were stunned. Instead of the broken, crumpled body of the beautiful Samantha — her skull split in half and her brains softly oozing onto the pillow, all they saw was a gorgeous young woman. Her long, sandy, hair fanned out across the pillow, with no sign of the horror and violence that had just taken place.

Unconsciously Chito reached for Jesus' hand and grasped it tight; digging his fingernails into the back of it so hard that Jesus gave a small whimper.

He turned to him and almost in tears whispered; "I... I... I... really think we're in over our heads this time Jesus."

Jesus was crying. He wiped his other sleeve across his face and nodded soberly; "yeah... but there 'aint nothing we can do about it now... is there? We're just as tied to Beelzebub as Sam there is." Samantha lay on the bed... to all intents and purposes looking as if she was softly sleeping. Jesus walked over to the bed and bent his head until his ear was directly on Samantha's chest.

"There's no heartbeat Chito, she's definitely dead."

Chito joined his partner and placed his arm around his shoulder. "Well... you heard what Bubba said; she'll be fine in a half hour or so." He wiped his forehead with his sleeve; "and Bubba's never been wrong before has he?"

Samantha did indeed look like she was just sleeping; even her lips were formed into a half smile, as if some deep, satisfying dream was teasing her and playing on her subconscious. On closer inspection Chito realised Bubba had been right. Although there was no obvious sign of the butchery that had taken place, here and there, he did notice some slight staining of the pillow and sheets.

"We'd better get that cleaned up before we call in that we've found her." Jesus urged. They set about carefully sponging off anything that could indicate what might have taken place.

. . .

JC wasn't losing hope, but he was becoming more frantic as the car sped south and still Damien had no inkling of Samantha's presence. He touched him lightly on the shoulder; "anything Son?"

Damien shook his head sadly. "I don't know Papa; perhaps it's true... perhaps..."

JC gave an audible gasp. "No Damien! Don't say it! No! We'll find her."

Damien nodded but exchanged glances with Simon, clearly indicating their doubts over his father's certainty.

When the phone-call came it was so unexpected JC, fumbling in his shirt pocket for his cell-phone, dropped it on the floor of the back seat. He scrambled down, furiously trying to find it but only succeeded in kicking it further under Damien's seat.

Damien reached down and felt the metallic edge of the phone, gently pulling it out. Instead of handing it back to his father he flicked the call button himself. "Yes...

...Where?

...Okay... we're about 15 minutes from there I think. Is she okay?"

Damien listened for a short while before hanging up the phone and handing it back to his father.

"Well... well... who was it? Have they found her?" JC spluttered into his son's face, covering it with spittle.

Damien placed his hands gently on his father's shoulders and began to softly sob. "Ddddad... I'm sorry... but Chito said she doesn't look good. All he would say is we should be prepared for the worst."

JC's face collapsed and he grabbed hold of his son's shoulders and buried his face in his neck, shaking softly and occasionally uttering soft cries of pain.

Damien flicked his eyes across to Simon who was grasping the steering wheel in a vice-like grip and staring straight ahead. He noticed, with compassion, that Simon's face was also streaked with tears.

"Simon; I think we'd better stop for a few minutes buddy. I think we need some time to compose ourselves."

JC's reaction was immediate. He pulled himself up from his son and shouted; "NO! We've got to get to my baby as soon as possible... she needs us!"

Damien nodded and signalled with his eyes for Simon to keep driving. "Buddy... we're heading for the Silver Palms Truck Stop and Diner. It should be on our left, in about thirty miles.

JC took an enormous breath and looked at his son. "It 'aint over till it's over Damien. We need to get there and see what we can do... right?"

Damien looked thoughtful; "Papa," he began, "is there any point in trying to get in touch with Michael? Maybe he can help us."

"Oh my goodness Damien... you're a bloody genius... why didn't I think of that?" JC leant back in the car's rear seat and closed his eyes in concentration. Damien could see him softly muttering the words; but couldn't actually hear them. He decided to join his Father in his entreaties to the Archangel Michael. Two prayers were always better than one, he reasoned.

Simon kept his eyes focused on the blacktop as they streaked toward the motel. They were travelling well over the speed limit but he seemed more than capable of weaving in and out of traffic and keeping them on track. The white lines marking the lanes sped by so fast they merged into one solid line, as they ate up the distance between them and Samantha.

When Michael finally appeared, it was not in the manner of the past. There was no slow, majestic, descent from the heavens; he was just instantaneously present.

"So... what's going on his time; my little rebel buddy?"

JC's eyes flew open at the words of his oldest and dearest friend. "Michael, thank God you're here."

The big, blond warrior chuckled; "Don't thank God JC... you know he'd be pissed if he realised I was interfering... *yet* again, in his beloved earth. So... what's the problem?"

JC quickly summarised the events leading up to where they found themselves now. He was interrupted by an exclamation from the front seat.

"There it is!" Simon yelled excitedly. There it is... just up there on the left."

Damien craned his head to see. "Go around the back of the Diner Simon, that's where the rooms are — they're in room fifteen... go... go... go!"

Simon spun the wheel at the very last minute so as not to waste any time and they skidded onto the petrol station and diner forecourt. Spotting the looped road that would take them to the accommodation area, he gunned the accelerator. They slid to a stop, right outside unit fifteen, in a hail of gravel and dust. Before the car had even stopped JC had the door open and was jumping for the exit. He stumbled once before recovering and crashing straight through the door of unit fifteen, without even opening it. Once inside he skidded to a stop and stared disbelievingly at the scene that confronted him.

Damien had been just one step behind his father and cannoned into his back causing them both to tumble unceremoniously onto the ground. At a much more sedate pace Simon and Michael walked through the door, each bending down to lift one of the Castillo's to his feet. They all turned to look at the tableau spread before them.

"Hello Daddy... thanks for coming to rescue me... but as you can see Chito and Jesus have already done the honours."

They stood there, dumbfounded, staring at Chito, Jesus and Samantha; sitting around the small table in the centre of the room, calmly playing cards... playing cards!

Michael recovered his equilibrium, first. He clapped JC on the shoulder and laughed; "looks like you might have overreacted slightly my friend and that sure as hell wouldn't be a first. I don't think you need me at all."

JC continued to stand there, shaking his head and trying to form a cogent word.

Damien rushed over to his sister and lifted her from her chair where he held her in a giant bear hug for a few seconds.

He whispered in her ear; "just what the hell's happening here Sam. I thought that bastard had hurt you, but you look fine."

She threw back her head and laughed. "Well yes... he did hurt me, very badly." She looked down at herself and grinned; "but as you can see... I'm perfectly fine now."

JC finally recovered from his shock and ran to take his daughter in his arms, cradling her gently and rocking her back and forth.

"Well... I hate to break up this touching family reunion, really I do;" Michael started; "but, it looks like I'm not really needed here so I better get my butt back before the Father misses me and there's all sorts of hell to pay."

JC looked up and smiled at him; "Of course Mickey... you get going... and thanks... I'm just glad we didn't need you."

Michael grinned; "no problem buddy... Ummmm, JC... a quiet word first please;" he added, crooking his finger at him.

Reluctantly letting Samantha go, he headed over to the door, where Michael surprisingly and quickly whisked him outside. "JC, you know I love Samantha as much as the rest of you, but you really need to know something."

JC arched his eyebrows, looking at him quizzically.

"You need to keep an eye on that girl JC; I swear I can sense evil emanating from her."

JC jerked his head back as if Michael had slapped him full in the face. "Evil — no! What on earth do you mean Mickey?"

Michael breathed out long and hard. "Look JC. Samantha's a great kid, but really you need to keep an eye on her."

JC grimaced. It hurt to hear Michael say those words, but there were more important things to worry about than arguing with him so he just nodded his head once. "Trust me Michael... that girl is not going to be out of mine or her Mother's sight for a very long time after this."

He suddenly yelped. "Shit... I haven't even told Maria she's ok. Bloody hell, everything's happened so fast." He dug his cell-phone out of his pocket and slammed his fingers on the numbers.

Michael touched him briefly on the shoulder. "Okay buddy... give my love to Maria — I'd better get back."

JC nodded, smiled at his friend, and continued dialling. This time Michael did perform the glory rise; ascending slowly into the heavens, with one final quick salute to JC before he disappeared from view.

After JC had relayed the news to Maria and assured her that, yes, Samantha was fine and yes, she still did have all her body parts intact, he hung up the phone, promising his wife they would get home as quickly as safety allowed them.

He stood outside the motel door for a few seconds, pondering Michael's words. Evil — his daughter? No... Michael's got to be mistaken. Shaking his head he re-entered, for another longer, more tearful, reunion with Samantha.

. . .

Maria slowly put the phone on the kitchen table. The entire room was focused on her and she didn't disappoint them. Jumping to her feet, she grabbed the nearest person; The Chief of Detectives and began to dance around and around in circles; shouting out with glee; "They've found her... they've found her... She's alive."

Her infectious excitement soon had everyone slapping each other's backs and hugging and dancing. The four younger children, who had no real idea of the gravity of the situation, did however recognise happiness when they saw it. They ran to their mother and holding onto her skirts spun around with her and Chief Rosales.

After the emotion of the last few hours was worked out of their systems, Maria slowed and patted her children on the head. She sat down on her chair and lifted the youngest twins Angeline and Angelo onto her knees.

Just a few minutes prior to the phone call; her face had looked taut, pinched and tired, with the crow's-feet around her eyes that she'd had worked so hard to keep at bay, being her most prominent feature. For the first time ever Maria Castillo had looked every one of her forty-five years. The emotional release was accompanied by a physical release of the tension and pain that had been etched into her face over the hours. She was transformed once again into the carefree, youthful, mother that everyone adored.

Kissing each of the twins in turn, she looked up at the Chief of Detectives with a grin that lasted only a second; to be replaced by a look of utter consternation.

"Okay Chief, obviously it is fantastic news that Samantha's alive and well... but... what in the hell happened to the kidnappers? I mean, that man said he wanted one hundred million dollars and he must have known we not only had it, but would gladly give it to him, in exchange for our daughter's life."

She paused and shook her head. "Why would they run? Why didn't they wait for the money? It's weird... isn't it?"

He sat in the chair opposite Maria and considered her questions carefully. "I've got to admit, I have no idea! Perhaps they got scared... perhaps... maybe... they got tipped off we were closing in on them." He frowned; "Yes, that's probably it. If Mr Magtano and Mr Guerrero had been tapping their underworld connections for information, one of the villains might have tipped them off. Until we catch the bastards... I guess we'll never know."

He studied his hands briefly; "The most important thing for you guys is you have your daughter back safe and sound... just leave the rest of the worry to us."

Maria nodded her head in agreement, but her eyes still betrayed her doubts.

She looked around at the numerous police officers and technicians who were now just standing around chatting among themselves. Maria peered over two of the taller men to spot Marielle on the sofa.

"Ellie honey;" she cooed; "do you think you could find all these fine, young men something to eat. If they're anything like me they must be famished. Whew, what a day!"

Two hours later, the front door to the house opened and JC, with his arm firmly wrapped around the shoulder of his daughter, entered. There was another joyous and tearful reunion. The Chief of Detectives spoke briefly to Chito and Jesus, who assured him they would come into the station tomorrow, to make a statement. He then focused on chatting with Samantha, about her ordeal.

"I'll need you to also come down with Chito and Jesus — we have a lot to discuss."

Samantha nodded briefly. She was already tired of continually recounting her tale to everyone. She just wanted to see Bubba again — she wanted to ask him why? Why had he done that to her?

"Oh hell!"

The shouted exclamation was so out of the general cheerfulness of the gathering that everyone's eyes swivelled to look at Maria.

She waved her hands apologetically; "sorry... I just remembered Samuel's arriving on the 8am flight tomorrow. Oh my goodness, I'd totally forgotten all about it in all the conf..."

Interrupted by the jangle of the telephone, she didn't think twice before unconsciously reaching for it and flicking the switch. "Yes... Hello;" she answered gaily.

"Ahhhh... my lovely Maria;" that familiar voice oozed menacingly down the telephone wires. "Have you got your precious little daughter back now?"

Maria started to reply, but he just issued a guttural laugh. "No need to respond my dear; I know everything."

Maria tried again; "what do you..."

The voice interrupted her again; "What do I want dear lady... what do I want? Well... I just wanted you to know this was never about the money. I don't give a shit about money. Nope! What this was... was just me showing you and your disgusting family that I can get you, whenever and wherever, I want."

There was a brief pause, so Maria tried to interrupt.

"Now you just listen..."

The quick and furious response took her by surprise. "No bitch! *You* just listen here. Nobody in your freak of a family is safe from me. I will strike again, so watch your back bitch." He giggled; "and watch everyone else's back as well... hehehe."

Maria uttered one word..."Why?"

The disembodied voice at the other end of the phone roared with laughter. "Why... you Jesus loving freak? Well... let's just say the Devil made me do it, shall we?"

The line went dead and Maria stood there stony-faced — the receiver dangling from her hand and spinning around and around in mid air—.

. . .

Chapter 17

"Honey, what's happened... was that him?" JC ran to his wife's side.

Maria nodded dumbly at him and buried her face in his shoulders. He cradled her, patting her head, until she was emotionally ready to surface, and talk.

After discussions with the Chief of Detectives, Chito and Jesus; it was agreed there would be no more rallies for Las Vegas at this time. The Chief advised them that sentiment was running high around town about the deaths of the innocent people in the stadium.

"Look;" he said, "I know deep down people don't really blame you for what happened but there are a lot of people hurting in this community and they need someone to vent their anger on. I'm concerned that another rally might just give them a forum to do that." Sources had also suggested that some local underworld characters had used the carnage at the revival meeting to try and stir up trouble for the Ezraville residents.

"The truth is;" he added; "The shadier side of Las Vegas has never been terribly comfortable having such a 'God-fearing' community right next door to them — you're bad for business they reckon; so they'll jump on any opportunity to make you guys look bad, or to cause trouble."

Jesus felt that given the threats made by the kidnapper, it was imperative that nobody from the Castillo family left the compound without an armed bodyguard or minder. He volunteered himself and Chito for the role.

Looking at JC he added; "but truthfully JC, I'd really rather nobody went anywhere — this guy's clearly a psycho and he's sure seems out to get you and your family."

JC nodded sadly; "I don't want to accept that — it's just not the way I want us to live. It's not what we stand for, but you're right, I don't ever want to have to go through again what we just experienced with Sammy. I agree, nobody goes anywhere outside this compound, without talking to us first — is that understood?"

Enthusiastic nods around the table assured JC of their concurrence.

Everyone jumped when Maria slapped her hand on the table.

She smiled a little shamefacedly; "sorry," she murmured. "We have to pick Samuel up from the airport in a few hours. How do we to do that?"

JC, Jesus and Chito looked at each other; JC scratching his overnight bristle and Jesus and Chito raising their eyebrows questioningly.

"Hmmmm..." Chito began, "...can we organise transport for him — a limo service or something?"

Maria bristled; "Listen, this man, whoever he is seems very well informed about us. He threatened all *our* family and Samuel's as much a part of our family as anyone. I'm not risking him to any anonymous limo service."

She slapped her hand firmly on the table. "No! We are going to pick Samuel up from the airport, come hell or high-water."

JC jumped in to support her, arguing that Samuel could well be seen by this man as a soft target and someone they might not have thought to protect. "Jesus... Chito, can we organise a group of armed members to escort us to the airport and back?"

Chito grinned; "that's what we do boss — no problem. Just leave it to me and Jesus."

JC visibly relaxed and when the Chief of Detectives assured him he would organise a police escort from the Airport to Ezraville, he began to feel calmer.

Their worries eased; Maria suggested everyone get some sleep after such a trying twenty-four hours. They would all meet back there at six. "Samuel's plane arrives at 8a.m.," she advised them all.

. . .

Samuel Castillo was a tall, handsome, young man of twenty-four, who'd had the benefit of some great genes. His mother Maria was a true Filipina beauty and his long, lost father had been an extremely handsome, young, lad from San Jose who had stolen his mother's heart; before crushing it and leaving her to cope with a new son. He'd been raised almost exclusively by his *Lola* (Grandmother) Caterina in San Jose.

He'd carried his mother's Manyanan name until he was eight years old. When JC and Maria's first twins had been born, JC had insisted on formally adopting Samuel. They were already great friends and JC had a real soft spot for the boy, having previously saved him from drowning, on their first visit to San Jose.

Reluctantly his parents had agreed with *Lola* Cat's insistence that Samuel would be better to remain with her than to be with them in the Mangyan Village. Maria and JC ensured he'd received the necessary money to attend all the best private schools and ultimately to complete his undergraduate degree at the University of the Philippines, before heading for Columbia University, and a planned doctoral thesis in Economics.

Samuel was trying to stretch his long legs and ease the cramp and tiredness from the interminably long flight from Manila. He glanced out the window and felt rather than saw the plane had begun its long, patient descent down from 35,000 feet to the waiting runway at Las Vegas. Almost there, he thought, as he contemplated what he was going to say to his Mama and JC. How could he explain to them what he was feeling? Why he'd left Columbia and felt this intense desire to be part of the Kingdom of God Church?

More than just a simple dream had shaken him up at Columbia; there was also the mad, passionate, love affair with Petrona. "Oh Petal;" he muttered softly to himself; "I miss you so, so, much already."

Shaking his head to clear his swirling thoughts he tried to focus on seeing his parents again and his half-siblings. He loved them all — they were his family and although he'd grown up separately from them; he absolutely, positively felt he was a Castillo. "I am the son of JC... no matter what the genes say;" he whispered softly to himself. It had been a year since he had seen any of them. Once he'd left for Columbia there was no opportunity to see them again, so he was excited about the prospect of reuniting.

Stepping out of the air-conditioned arrival's lobby of the airport terminal, a wave of intense heat, that even this early in the morning seemed to radiate from the sidewalk like a physical force, struck him. Coming from the Philippines he felt he was well acclimatised to heat, but this was different from back home — this was drier and even breathing made his throat rasp.

Wiping his forehead he scanned the groups of waiting people to see if he could spot his Mom, JC, or any of the rest of the clan.

He was horrified and deeply perplexed when a phalanx of heavily armed men surrounded him. They were dressed half-way between policemen and army assault troops. All wore matching bullet-proof vests with LVPD emblazoned across them but they were also dressed in a variety of mismatched, army, camouflage gear. He was terrified, and immediately threw his arms in the air shouting; "Don't shoot... don't shoot... I'm just a visitor... I'm not armed."

The leader of the group smiled warmly, and walked over to him, gently pulling his arms down. "Sorry Samuel... we didn't mean to scare you — we're here to protect you. My name's Jesus and we're here to escort you to Ezraville."

"Pppprotect me?" Samuel managed to splutter out. "Ppprotect me from who... from what?" Regaining some semblance of control, he snapped at Jesus; "...and where the bloody hell is my family?"

Jesus put one arm around his shoulder and began to steer him toward a large, black SUV, with heavily tinted windows, parked at the apron to the airport entrance; flanked by three LVPD police vehicles. "They're all in there waiting for you Samuel, I'll let them explain." Looking warily around the area, he hustled Samuel into the back seat of the SUV.

"Sammy!" an excited squeal came from the seat behind him. "Sammy, I missed you." He chuckled and turned to look at his little half-sister Angeline bouncing up and down; clapping her hands in glee.

"Missed you too punk'in," he grinned at her before leaning over and plonking a large kiss on the delighted child's cheek.

Turning back he looked at his Mother who was waiting to take him into her arms. His brow furrowed and his eyebrows arched, in that cute, questioning way he had. He couldn't help but notice the tears cascading down Maria's face.

He grabbed her and hugged her for a moment; then pulling back he questioned her again; "Mama?"

She silenced him with a finger to his lips. "All that can come later darling. For now just let me enjoy looking at you, touching you, and kissing you... my little man."

As the SUV started up and headed out of the airport he couldn't help but notice the police car take station in front with the other two swinging directly in behind them. "Looks like we got us a convoy;" he tunelessly sang, softly to himself, but his mind was working overtime. What's been going on here that would warrant this sort of behaviour and police protection? Whatever it was... it was clearly bad, and it was clearly a fulfilment of his premonition of evil. Hmmmm... so... what was it?

Twice on the trip to Ezraville, Samuel broached the issue of what had happened; but was stonewalled each time first by JC and then by his Mother. They both kept insisting that there would be plenty of time to discuss everything; "including young man... what crazy inspiration drove you to walk away from a Doctoral Degree at Columbia University ha!" his mother added with some finality.

Samuel gulped guiltily. Yes... there was still that to try and explain to them. Realizing his entreaties were not going to be met with any success, he settled back to enjoy the ride and the views of Las Vegas; a city he'd heard much about, but had never seen.

Samuel wasn't overly impressed with his first look at the Las Vegas skyline. New York could probably be described as an aging "cougar", still looking to retain her youth and vitality. It was still able to excite and thrill on occasions; yet more often than not was happy to relax in the role of attractive, middle-aged dowager. Las Vegas, though, was the polar opposite. The City stank of excess, of man's need for instant gratification, and seemed to appeal to the lowest common denominator. He found the many fake replica buildings and statues, the garish architecture of many of the hotels, childish and seeking to recreate a teenager's rebellion at authority and conformity. Nope... Las Vegas definitely doesn't do it for me, he thought, as the SUV left the fake city behind and headed for the community of Ezraville.

Many hugs and kisses, especially from his siblings, later; Samuel, JC, Maria, Damien and Samantha sat quietly around the dining room table, sipping coffee and allowing their sumptuous lunch to quietly digest.

Samuel looked up and shrugged his shoulders; "So... who's going to tell me what in the hell's been happening here? Why the armed guards? Why the police escort? Sheesh... I thought I was on some sort of crazy movie set when I first stepped out the airport exit."

JC took the lead in describing the tumultuous events of the previous forty-eight hours. When he got to the part about Samantha's kidnapping, Sam's hands flew to his lips in horror. He turned to his namesake, who he'd always felt a close bond with. Leaning across, his hand rested on hers.

"Oh Sammy baby... that must have been terrible. Are you alright hon? That bastard didn't hurt you did he?"

Samantha gave him her sweetest and most appealing smile. "Nope Samuel... I'm all good. I was scared shitless of course, but he actually wasn't mean to me."

She looked around at the rest. "You know... he didn't really come near me at all. Most of the time it was his two goons who dealt with me." She briefly put her head in her hands before lifting her face up and brushing her hair away from her cheeks.

"Ohhhh... I still have flashbacks to it, but nope... I'm not going to let it define me. I'm fine, and soon we'll all just get back to work again; doing what we've always done — right Daddy? We're not going to let this stop us bringing people to the faith — right Daddy?" she entreated a second time.

JC looked uncomfortable and looked to Maria for assistance.

Always quick, always ready and able to jump in Maria said; "Honey, that's a long way off yet — there's plenty of time to discuss it later."

She looked quickly to Samuel; "and anyway, *Mr* Samuel, you still haven't told us what made you leave University. You had a great career in front of you Sammy... so why?"

He gulped. Damn! It had snuck back round to him much quicker than he'd hoped for. He held both hands up in front of him and exclaimed; "Okay... Okay... I get the picture and I'll tell all... promise; but J... Papa, please finish the story of how you rescued Samantha first."

JC grinned, fully aware that Samuel had dodged his Mother's unerring bullet — for now at least.

After the full recounting of the kidnap and subsequent rescue, Samuel's face was almost white. "My God, that's some tale Papa — I can see now why there was so much security at the airport. So... where does that leave 'the mission'? What is your pl..."

"Not so fast *Mister*" his mother interrupted. "It's your turn now kiddo. What's going on inside that head of yours? I thought

Lola Cat instilled some brains into that thick skull. So... what's with all this running away from school and joining the circus?"

Samuel laughed; "I hadn't actually thought of yours and Dad's mission as being a circus, but yeah... I guess I can see it... and Mama, please... I'm not ten years old anymore — I didn't run away from school."

Everyone laughed as it lightened the atmosphere round the table and released some of the tension. Even Maria tittered slightly, but JC did hear her say, ever so softly, that nobody else could possibly hear; "Sammy darling, you'll always be ten years old to me."

. . .

He explained he'd been sitting in an economic theory class one sweltering afternoon, listening to the professor droning on about why Capitalism was the answer to the world's woes and how globalization was already solving the third-world issues of poverty and wealth distribution, when the student beside him uttered just one word under her breath, but still loud enough for Sam to catch it.

"Bullshit!" was all she'd said, but it was enough to drag Samuel from his dream-like state.

He turned to look at the woman who had dared to question the eminent professor's diatribe and instead of the radical hippie he expected to have uttered the blasphemy he was pleasantly surprised to see a perfectly dressed, elegantly coiffured and extremely pretty, young, lady. Intrigued he gave her a quick smile and leant closer.

"That's an interesting and extremely erudite summation of the professor's work; would you care to expand on it over coffee, after class?"

She tossed her long, wavy, blond hair away from her eyes and regarded him with a quizzical stare. "Well... that's either the strangest pickup line ever, or... you're actually interested in talking about this." Her soft, melodious voice just wafted over Samuel and he was entranced by her sparkling eyes that seemed to be laughing at his obvious discomfort. He managed to stammer;

"Aaaa bbbit of both... if the truth be known."

Trying to regain his composure, he added; "Soooo... would you like to?"

She laughed; right there, in the middle of an Economics lecture; a soft, tinkling laugh that was loud enough for everyone to turn and look; even the professor. Embarrassed, she giggled and put her head down before slyly turning to Sam and whispering;

"Well, that's a new twist — honesty. I'd love to! I'm Petrona, by the way."

Sam smiled and nodded; holding his hand out for her to shake; "Petrona, hmmmm... now there's an interesting name for sure. I'm Sam, and I'm totally stoked to meet you Petrona." The formalities out of the way they refocused on enduring the last few minutes of the boring lecture, before he jumped up and gently holding Petrona's elbow steered her toward the exit.

Sam looked at his family, who were clearly enthralled by his story. Maria's lips were flickering into a smile; aha, so my little boy's growing up, she was thinking.

JC on the other hand was displaying a broad smile; "So... Sam... you met a girl!" He chuckled; "there's always a girl involved isn't there? Whenever a big decision is made, or a change of direction in life, you can usually trace it to there being a girl involved... hehehe."

Samuel waved his hands airily and sighed; "No Dad... it wasn't anything like that... now let me finish!"

Clearly not believing his son's protestations, he grinned and sat back in his chair signalling for Sam to continue his story.

It transpired that the coffee turned into a day-long session of discussion about what was important and necessary to change the corrupt, self-serving nature of the elite few.

Sam looked up and everyone could see his face was shining with excitement at the memories. "Oh Papa... you wouldn't believe Petrona — she's just so... so... oh, I don't know how to describe it... she's so passionate and so committed about what she believes in."

JC grinned and muttered; "passionate and committed ha... I've heard it called many things before... but passionate and committed... hmmmm."

Maria slapped him on the arm; "shut up you cynic... just let the boy speak."

JC chuckled and nodded.

Petrona Fafitis, it seemed, was the daughter of an extremely successful, high-tech entrepreneur billionaire, originally from Athens, Greece; but who now ran his vast technology empire out of Silicon Valley in California. Petrona explained she'd had absolutely every privilege in life and never wanted for anything. "I grew up the perfect, pampered, little rich girl;" she'd told Sam; "but... when I turned 18, I rebelled big time and took my trust fund and headed off to Central America to 'change the world', something I was horribly unsuccessful at doing."

Sam explained that when she'd been duped out of yet more money by unscrupulous government employees and policemen in Nicaragua, she'd realised she was fighting a losing battle and headed home with her tail between her legs; to seek her father's guidance and help. She'd decided the only way to make a real difference in the world was to get inside the system and to change it from the top.

She'd determined that she was going to become President of the United States in thirty year's time and set about doing whatever was necessary to achieve that goal. She'd explained to Sam that studying Economics at Columbia was just one of the steps necessary to achieve her political goals. "I have to look the part;" she'd confided in Samuel; "even if I totally despise the bullshit they teach us in these classes."

Samuel had laughed — it was true he was captivated by her beauty, her wit and her charm; but more than that he was totally captivated by her heart for humanity, her empathy and her compassion for those not as fortunate as her, by accident of birth.

Sam's face was beaming with pride when he pronounced; "Oh Mama... Petrona's such an amazing woman. She's so driven and I'll tell you something for nothing; if anyone can fulfil her dreams and ambitions — that woman can. She's just... just... oh... just awesome."

Maria giggled; "so, my little boy is in love then?"

Samuel blanched; "in love Mama? No... nothing like that.......oh, for goodness sake Mother, can't a man and a woman have a relationship on just an intellectual level? Why does everyone just assume there has to be a romantic thing going on... it's not like that — Petrona has a beautiful mind and a beautiful heart!"

Maria leant across the table and patted her agitated son's hand. "Whatever you say Sam... whatever you say... hehehe."

When Samuel told Petrona about his own background she was absolutely aghast. She couldn't understand what Sam was doing in Columbia and why he wasn't out there with his mother and father helping to change the world, at the ground level.

"Do you not understand Sam;" she'd almost shouted at him. "Politics and economics is such bullshit — the only way to make a real difference in this world is to actually change the hearts and the mindsets of ordinary people. If just enough of them alter their lifelong routines and have the opportunity to live different, loving, caring lives — Oh my God, the entire world will change for the better."

Petrona had reached up and grasped Samuel's cheeks in either hand, her eyes blazing, she was so excited. "Sam;" she'd begun. "You don't seem to realise what an incredible gift you've been given. By sheer chance you were born into one of the most influential families on this planet; a bit like me... hehehe. You are the adopted son of Jesus Christ. Your parents and your family are making a massive difference in this world. They're changing lives!"

She'd paused to gather herself for the final assault. "So tell me Samuel Castillo, just what the hell are you doing here in New York, pretending to study economics — for what purpose ha? Will economics change the world ha?" she'd squeezed her fingers into his cheekbones until he'd begun to wince. "Damn right it won't... damn right! So why aren't you with them... making a difference?" she had finished, finally releasing his cheeks.

Unconsciously Samuel reached up and rubbed his cheeks at the memory of the moment.

Damien spoke up; "So that was what convinced you to come here Sam? A girl's speech?"

Sam laughed uncertainly; "Ahhhhm; no... what Petrona said certainly got me to thinking; I won't deny that, but it wasn't just her that made me realise I should be here with you guys. No — it was the dream that was the final clincher.

JC leant forward expectantly; "The dream? Did you have a vision Samuel?"

He waved his hands. "I don't know if it qualifies as a vision Dad; but yeah, I certainly had the most realistic dream I've ever had."

JC nodded; his face unable to contain his growing excitement and waved for Sam to continue the story.

Sam and Petrona had spent every spare hour together, after that first thrilling day at the coffee shop, where they'd happily forgone their daily lecture schedule to "right the world". Several days later they were relaxing at Petrona's up-market apartment — "all paid for by Daddy"; she assured him. They were listening to music and lying on large bean bags that had been strewn across her floor. Both had had an intensive day of lectures and were tired and a little groggy, from the wine Petrona had served, before they settled down to listen to the hypnotic beats of the Caribbean Reggae music she so favoured.

Sam shut his eyes and let his mind drift in and out of consciousness; in that half asleep, never-never land that precedes deep, relaxing sleep. He wasn't sure if he was asleep or awake but his mind had transported him to an enormous stone cavern. He stood at the entrance of the cavern, unsure whether to enter or not. Looking up at the vault of the ceiling, it seemed an impossible distance away.

The subdued lighting was provided by individual flaming torches spaced along the walls at intervals of around a hundred metres or so. He strained his eyes to see further, to the very end; where he could just make out a raised platform of stone and the back of someone; someone that had long, blond, flowing hair cascading down his back. He was dressed in what Samuel could only describe as battle gear. He wore a burnished breastplate that seemed to glow with a life of its own.

Samuel had met the Archangel Michael on only two occasions, but instinctively he knew it was Michael standing astride the raised stone dais. Taking a tentative step into the cavern he stuttered; "Mmmichael? Is that you? Mmmichael?" His soft voice reverberated off the cavern walls and seemed to rise in intensity as each echo fired back at him. Frightened, he took a step back toward the entrance when the answer came.

"Samuel; you came. Yes it's Michael." The figure turned and faced him directly. Samuel let out a loud exhalation of relief and began to trot toward him.

Michael held up his enormous broadsword and gestured for Samuel to come no further. "Samuel... I have a message for you;" Michael began; "an important message... one that could save your parents and your entire family from disaster."

Frightened by the intensity of the words Samuel began to move forward again toward his father's friend.

Michael again held his sword up to stop the advance. "Listen carefully Samuel; evil has been released into the world — Beelzebub is free and is wreaking his havoc on earth and on humanity. Your father and mother — in fact, all of your family are in peril. You must go and join them and help them in the fight against the evil one."

Samuel stood dumbstruck by the words. What did Michael think *he* could possibly do against the Devil? He was just a mere mortal.

"But Michael;" he managed; "wwwwhat can I..." Michael thrust his massive sword down in a wide arc that sent a current of air whistling past Samuel's face.

"United... a family can do anything Samuel. You need to join them. Do you understand?"

Samuel just nodded dumbly and stood there in utter shock. Michael turned his back on the boy and raised his hands above his head before just... disappearing.

. . .

"Sammy... Sammy... wake up you idiot... you're dreaming... and shouting in your sleep."

He opened his eyes to see Petrona leaning over him shaking him furiously. "Whew... are you ok Sam? I think you had a bad dream."

He smiled wanly at her and nodded.

Sam looked around the table. There was not a single one of them that wasn't enraptured by what he had just told them. He smiled brightly; "So, there you go guys, that's why I'm here."

Everyone started talking at once, trying to talk over the other person. Finally JC clapped his hands for silence. "You're sure it was Michael; Sammy?"

Sam looked at his Dad..."It's not a mistake I'm likely to make, now is it Dad? Yes, it was Michael."

JC looked thoughtful, before addressing everyone.

"Okay... so we already knew evil was afoot in the world. Hell! As if what just happened with the kidnapping wasn't enough — Samuel's pretty much confirmed it for us now and straight from Michael's mouth. We just didn't realise how evil up till now. So, the question is what do we do about it?" He looked around the table expectantly.

Maria, ever the practical one, suggested; "Well... for a start... we should finish up here and head back home, I think. I mean we're not really equipped to fight the Devil are we? You're just a man now JC... and don't you forget it please!"

She looked at Damien and Samantha, before adding; "okay... our two kids are special, but bloody hell; I'm damned if I'm going to risk their lives by fighting this Beelzebub. We need to return home, regroup, and figure out what to do next. Well... that's what I think anyway."

Everyone chipped in with their opinions, except Samantha, who hadn't said a word since Samuel had begun talking. She was looking ashen-faced and appeared to be shaking slightly.

Noticing her, Samuel got up from the table and put his arm around her shoulder before leaning down and whispering to her; "I'm sorry Samantha... I guess all this talk, so soon after your horrible experience, has frightened you. It's going to be alright... trust me. If we all stick together, as a family, we'll be fine."

Samantha gulped at having been found out — I must keep this facade up at all times, I can't let it slip she thought. She nodded slowly; "yyyes, that's it Samuel, I'm frightened." She straightened up and grinned at him. "We'll be fine... you're right."

Damien was distraught about the thought of leaving Ezraville and he voiced his opinions loudly and forcefully.

"We shouldn't run away guys — if there's a war to be fought then we should stand and fight. Samantha and I have more power than any of you realise. We're ready to stand and fight and so should you be."

Maria knew there was much more behind Damien's reluctance to leave than just a desire to fight... and she knew they would have to address *that* particular issue, sooner rather than later. Oh dear, she thought... life's getting *very* complicated.

Damien wondered how Simon would react to him leaving — he really didn't want to think about it and resolved there and then, in his own mind, that it wasn't going to happen. We're not going to be parted he decided. Besides which, he thought, I really need to get Samuel alone and have a chat with him about Michael. I want him to know that Michael's been talking to me also.

After much discussion, JC held up one hand to signal it was at an end. He looked around at his family and smiled.

"Okay... So here's what I've decided we'll do. We'll head back to The Philippines — to Pangutaran initially, but that's flex..."

Damien began to interrupt, but JC gave him a withering glance.

"No Damien... this is not up for discussion. As head of this family, and this mission, I *have* decided." He continued; "as I was saying going to Pangutaran is our first option, but I'm flexible on that. We need to go somewhere where we can plan our strategy. We *will* fight the evil force that's loose on this earth... *BUT* we will fight it on our terms, not his."

He looked at Damien; "we're not running away son, we're just getting ready. We'll leave in five days time, so everyone has time to say their goodbyes." Again he looked pointedly at Damien, who dropped his head away from his father's penetrative stare.

Samuel walked over to his adopted father and placed his hands on his shoulders. "Oh... by the way... one thing I forgot to mention. Petrona will arrive here in two days."

Maria clapped her hands in glee laughing..."Not in love Samuel?....really Samuel?" she giggled—.

. . .

Chapter 18

Damien wandered over to Samuel and clapped his elder brother on the shoulder. "Well... now all that's out of the way Sam; what say you and me go for a walk and catch up eh? I'll show you the greenhouses where I work."

Samuel had always loved his little brother and nodded enthusiastically. "Yeah sure bro!"

Strolling along in the sunshine, Samuel enquired as to how he was enjoying the break from the travelling, the teaching and the sermons. Damien looked at his older brother, and Samuel could see there was something he desperately wanted to say to him. He grabbed his arm and steered him toward a nearby park bench.

"Ok Bro... I can see something's bothering you big time... tell me... perhaps I can help."

Damien shrugged his shoulders sheepishly. "There's not much to tell Sammy... the truth is; I'm loving the break way too much. I don't want to go back. It's just not me."

Sam looked hard into his eyes and could see that Damien was deeply troubled by the revelation. "So... have you talked to Mom and Dad about the way you feel? I mean, there's always Samantha to carry on the mission... she has everything you have; right?"

Damien hung his head and tears began to well in his eyes. Samuel reached around him and pulled him tight. "Hey... hey... it can't possibly be that bad surely? Come on... give me the full story eh!"

He looked up at his older brother; a lone tear tumbling down his cheek. "Ohhhh Sam, it's jjjust not that simple... if only it was."

The dam burst and Damien began to sob uncontrollably; Samuel cradled his little brother in his arms and allowed him to get the emotions out of his system.

When he'd finally calmed down and regained some semblance of control; he managed to explain to Samuel about Michael's visit and his insistence that it had to be him that carried on their father's work... and not Samantha.

"Why not Samantha? She's just as qualified as you are and from what I hear she absolutely loves it. Mama said she was distraught when the tour was stopped for a year," Samuel queried.

After Damien had communicated Michael's fears and worries about Samantha; Samuel sat quietly for a while digesting the surprising news. "Samantha... evil? Nope... I don't think I can buy that one. She's so sweet and loving — how can she be evil?"

Frustrated, Damien pulled himself out of Samuel's grasp. "Well. try telling that to Michael ha! He's convinced there's something wrong with her and now it's all down to me."

"Okay," Samuel finally said; "I get why you're a bit frustrated and annoyed. I don't know... all I know is what Michael told me... that I needed to be here to stand beside my family against Beelzebub... that's why I came."

He sat back on the park bench and contemplated for a while before adding; "Anyway Damien, we need to get through whatever's coming and then worry about the future."

He clapped Damien on the shoulder. "Who knows... things might change... don't be too hard on yourself and don't allow it to get you down." He looked around at the park-like surroundings, the beautiful homes, the flowers, the trees; and he stretched his arms out wide reaching for the sunshine. "This is way too beautiful a place to let ourselves get miserable... now 'aint it?"

Damien slowly nodded his head; and smiled hesitatingly at Samuel; "There is sort of something else too bro... I think I'm in love."

Samuel gave a whoop of pure joy and jumped to his feet; "join the club bro! It's freakin' awesome, isn't it?"

Damien, caught up in his brother's infectious enthusiasm, grinned widely; "yeah" he chuckled..."it's the best thing I've ever felt." Immediately his face fell and he sobered up. "Actually Samuel *he* works here in the greenhouses with me... we're off to meet him."

Samuel didn't fail to recognise the significance of his brother's use of the masculine, personal pronoun, but he made sure nothing reflected on his face as he hugged his brother and danced him around in a circle. "That's just brilliant. What are we standing here for then... let's go meet this wonderful man of yours."

Damien was so gratified that Sam's answer had not only indicated he understood Simon was a boy — but that it didn't matter to him. Grabbing his brother's arm he shouted; "Okay... okay... come on... this way then."

The three of them spent the afternoon together and Samuel was genuinely impressed by Simon's sincerity, his demeanour and his attitude to life in general. He couldn't help but like the young man his brother was so besotted with. As the work day wound down Simon went off to the nearby greenhouse to sort out some seeds for the next day. Alone, for the first time in a few hours Damien turned to the brother, whose opinion he respected more than anyone else in the world; except perhaps his father.

The excitement and anticipation was written all over his face, like a little kid seeking approval from his big brother, for something he'd done. "So... so... Sam... what do you think of him?"

Samuel placed an arm around his shoulder and gently rubbed his balled fist into Damien's forehead. "What do I think? I think he's bloody amazing Damien... I think you should be very happy to have met him. I'm thrilled for you both."

The look of utter and complete gratitude on his brother's face was reward enough for Samuel. "and... and... what do you think of me? I mean... now you know I'm gggay." Damien had some trouble expressing the word; but once he got it out he quickly repeated himself. "So... I'm gay Samuel... how does that make you feel?"

Samuel was overcome with emotion and empathy for his poor, young, brother; clearly struggling with his identity, and so desperate for his approval. He turned to Damien so they were looking eye to eye, just inches apart.

"Damien," he began; "I love you for who you are... regardless of who that is. I'm not going to lie and pretend I understand... honestly, I don't. I don't have those feelings." He paused for a deep breath; "but what I do understand is falling in love, because that's exactly what I've done. I am so, so happy for you both because love is the most wonderful, treasured thing in the world."

The relief on Damien's face at his big brother's reassuring words was palpable. He hugged Samuel tight and whispered in his ear; "thank you, thank you, thank you."

Finally releasing him; Samuel looked at him questioningly; "So... have you told Mum and Dad yet?"

Damien's face fell and he shook his head sadly from side to side.

"You know, you should Damien... they'll understand, I just know they will. Damien, they love you unconditionally; you should know that by n..."

He was interrupted by Simon's return to the room. Samuel nodded warmly to him and seemed about to say something before Damien tapped him rapidly on his arm and shook his head furiously. Aha, Samuel thought, he hasn't actually professed anything yet to Simon. Ah well... plenty of time.

Placing his arm firmly around Damien's shoulders he announced; "well guys, I don't know about you two, but I'm hot, I'm thirsty and I could sure use a cold one. How about we head over to the Community Centre, sit on the balcony and watch the sun go down, with a cold beer in our hands."

Simon chuckled and punched Samuel lightly on his arm. "Hey Samuel, I knew your brother could read minds... but I never realised you could too. I was thinking just the same thing."

Samuel grinned, but Damien just turned bright red and stammered; "Ccccome on then, the beer's getting warm." The three of them strolled companionably through the fields until they came to the first of the community's paved streets. Turning a corner they ran headlong into Jesus and Chito, heading the other way.

Jesus backed up and held up his arms in apology. "Ahhhh, Damien... Simon and..."

Samuel smiled; "Samuel actually... you picked me up from the airport I think. You were the guy in charge of security".

Jesus grinned broadly; "yep, that be me alright, Jesus Magtano, Chief of Police of this here borough and this is my best buddy Chito Guerrero — he looks after all the money in our happy little community. Sorry we didn't have a chance to have a proper introduction at the airport... but as you know things have been a little bit tense around here of late and we needed to ensure your safe arrival."

Samuel thrust out his hand for Jesus and Chito to shake; "no probs guys — I know you had a job to do... and might I add, you did it fantastically. I couldn't have felt safer if I'd been surrounded by armed marines."

Jesus beamed in the reflection of the compliment. "Why thank you my boy... I does appreciate someone who understands the requirements of the job. So... where are you three off to, this delightful evening?"

Samuel explained they were going to have a quiet drink at the Community Centre and watch the sun sink below the horizon. Jesus rubbed his chin and turned to Chito seeking confirmation with his eyes. Turning back to Samuel he drawled; "weeell, boys, I'll tell ya summat for nothing, shall I... the best darn view of the Las Vegas sunset is to be had from mine and Chito's balcony."

Looking at Chito, who was nodding amiably he added; "why... me and Chito here... we sit out there just about every night and admire God's awesome handiwork. Now why don't you boys join us tonight? We'd be mighty proud and happy to have you with us."

Jesus turned to Damien and said conspiratorially; "actually young Damien, me and Chito here was hoping to catch up with you sometime soon anyway, as we wanted to have a wee chat with you. This would be perfect timing. So boys... you fancy a beer with a couple of old codgers?

The three friends looked at each other and shrugged their shoulders in unison; Simon answered for all of them. "Sounds like a plan Jesus... let's go."

Jesus placed an arm around Simon's shoulder and led them all off in the direction of their unit.

The five of them were relaxing around a large table on Jesus and Chito's balcony. Chito turned to Samuel; then looked across the valley at the distant mountains that were burnished a deep gold by the setting sun. He smiled happily; "any second now guys... it's about to happen."

They all turned and followed his gaze; marvelling at the subtle hues the desert sands had taken on. It was like a graduated palette of deep gold's and red's as their gaze settled on the fiery ball hanging, half visible, between two mountain peaks. They were dumbstruck by the sheer magnificence of nature's beauty.

Suddenly there was an explosion of colour as the sun finally dipped behind the mountain. The gold's spun into deep purple's and the velvet skyline began to twinkle with the vista of a billion stars. They all drew in their breaths simultaneously as the light show entered it's finale. As quickly as they had come — the colours and the light disappeared and the sky took on a deep impenetrable blackness, pierced only by the still glittering starlight.

"See... I told ya now... didn't I?" Jesus broke the silence. "When God made this; he got it right... there's no denying it." Everyone nodded their heads in agreement and slowly exhaled, revelling in the beauty of the display they had witnessed.

Chito rocked back on his chair, and broke the magical spell when he flicked on the balcony's lights. Flooded with light, the group now lost the magic of the sunset they had just witnessed and returned to their conversations.

Damien looked at Jesus; "so, what was it you wanted to discuss with me, Jesus?"

He nodded rapidly and rubbed his forehead a little nervously before explaining. He told Damien that he and Chito had become very close to the Castillo family over the past few months and given all that had happened, especially with Samantha, they were very keen to officially join the group and return to The Philippines with them.

Chito barged in during Jesus' explanation. "You see guys... when we rescued Samantha, we realised that now we're tied to her forever."

He laughed softly; "you save someone's life... you're responsible for them from then on."

Jesus carried on; "Chito's right, we do feel something like that with Samantha... but it's more than that, we just both feel we're wasted here." He grasped Chito's arm before continuing.

"Me and Chito... well... we're security experts and if anyone needs security right now; it's you guys."

Having got it all out he looked at the three men — "so... what do you think? Would JC want us?"

Damien sipped his beer thoughtfully and glanced at Simon and Samuel, who he noted were both smiling broadly. It made total sense he thought — we do need security and these two have already proved their loyalty, and their capability. Of course it's the way to go. He grinned at the pair; "Guys... I think that's an awesome idea. Would you like me to talk to Papa about it?"

Chito and Jesus visibly relaxed in their chairs. They had, without even realising it, been leaning forward expectantly, waiting for Damien's answer. Chito agreed it would be the perfect solution for everyone, if Damien were to raise it with JC.

"Now boys! How's about another beer ha?" Chito suggested.

Damien had already risen from his chair and pulled Simon up with him. "Ah, not for us thanks Chito; we'll head back now... and besides I want to talk to..." He looked at Simon adoringly; "actually, *we* want to talk to Papa and Mama about something before they go to bed."

Samuel smiled inwardly. Good for him, he thought.

Wanting to give the boys some breathing space Samuel smiled at Chito; "I'll stay for another beer mate... this is really hitting the spot."

. . .

Damien gently pushed open the door to their unit and pulling Simon behind him by the hand they headed for the living room, where they could hear the muted voices of his father, mother... and he suspected, Samantha. All three looked up in pleasure at their arrival.

"Ah, there you are Damien, we've been getting worried about you — what with all the drama of late... and... I see Simon's with you;" his mother added. Aha, she thought, I guess I know what this is all about. I've been waiting for this moment.

"Oh Mama... don't be such a worry-wart; nothing bad can happen to us here in Ezraville; we're totally safe here."

Maria nodded, although she had her misgivings that any of them were actually safe, anywhere.

"We just stopped for a beer on our way home after work, but we're here now."

Dragging Simon along reluctantly behind him he led them to the unoccupied of the two sofas in the room. Damien immediately began fussing with his trousers, not looking at anyone.

"Well boys," Maria began. "We've just been talking about going home and planning for the future, so it's good that you're here."

She looked at Damien long and hard and emphasised her next phrase very slowly and deliberately. "After all Damien, *you* are an enormous part of that future; right?" Damien looked up and tried to smile as best he could, but in the end, he just nodded his head sadly.

Maria went on to discuss the family's travel plans back to Manila. They were to leave at the end of the week. They would spend a couple of days in Davao, at the Church's headquarters, before heading to Pangutaran Island to retreat, regroup, and plan their next move.

Damien physically puffed himself up, as if to give himself some extra courage, and then interrupted his mother's spiel.

"Mama... Papa... there's really something much more important that I need to tell you, before we go on any further."

Maria sat up and smiled at her son; "yes Damien... I suspect there is." She reached for JC's hand and gave it a quick squeeze and flicked him a reassuring look.

She'd already discussed her suspicions about Damien's preferences, with her husband, some time ago so both were ready and primed to deal with the revelation and both were determined to be supportive and loving of their son; who was clearly in some turmoil. JC squeezed her hand back to assure her he understood his role perfectly, in this little family drama.

Maria looked at Damien and indicated, with an arch of her eyebrows, that he should carry on. Despite his carefully rehearsed and planned big speech, it all came out as a non-stop splurge of words, crashing one over the other.

He told them he thought he was gay and that he was in love with Simon and if Simon wasn't coming to Manila with them, then damnit, he wasn't going either. By the end of his speech he was spluttering and repeating himself.

JC, feeling deep compassion for his son and admiring the courage it had taken him to make this admission leant forward and rescued him from the enormous hole he seemed to be digging.

"Son," he began; "your Mom and I guessed it a long time ago — don't fret yourself. It's okay! We love you and we support you one hundred percent in whatever you do. Now... if you want Simon to come with us to Manila; then Simon comes with us... it's not a problem."

JC looked up at Simon, who sat there with a look of utter shock on his face. He sat back in the sofa and JC noticed tears slowly dripping down the young man's cheeks.

"Simon, welcome to the family... I think;" JC chuckled, to try to lighten the mood. "I'm not sure if you know quite what you're letting yourself in for, but you are very welcome."

Simon grinned and reached for Damien's hand. "Well!" he breathed out loudly. "I wish Damien had discussed this with me first..."

Damien looked up at him and cringed in a gesture of apology.

"...But... it doesn't really matter — I was searching for a way for us to be together still, and this seems like the perfect solution."

He grasped Damien around his shoulders and hugged him tight. "I'm so excited actually;" he beamed at JC and Maria.

Samantha hadn't uttered a word the entire time. She'd sat there with her arms folded across her chest and just stared piteously at her twin brother. For the first time in a long time she transmitted a thought to him. "So, this is what you really want little brother? God, you're so weak! We could have dominion over the entire Universe, if we wanted it, and you want to settle for a comfy, soft, domestic situation with your little friend. God, you're pathetic! Well, I'll tell you this *little* brother — not for me ha! I'm not going to be a slave to domesticity — I *am* going to rule the Universe one day; with or without you."

Damien realised just how much he and his darling big sister had diverged over the past year or so. We just don't have anything in common any more, he thought.

His thoughts strayed back to Michael's seemingly prophetic words;*"There's something evil lurking in that young woman, something I can't quite put my finger on."* He grimaced; "I think I know what you mean Michael", he whispered to himself. "I think there's something evil in her too. I couldn't possibly leave now; someone's got to keep that girl in check."

His only answer to Samantha was a curt; "nope Sis... I'm going to stay right here beside you, keeping an eye on you."

Her response was a one word screamed curse; *"Fuckwit!"* Damien grinned at her before returning his attention back to Simon.

Maria suddenly remembered that her daughter was there and she turned and questioned; "So, what do you make of all these exciting developments Sam? Are you happy for your brother?"

Samantha smiled her absolutely sweetest smile and cocking her head slightly to one side she gushed; "Oh Mama... I'm just so thrilled Damien has found someone to love. I'm so glad Simon's joining us; isn't it just wonderful?"

Damien almost laughed aloud at her answer. Only he knew her real feelings and he glanced across at her. She was all, little miss sweetness and light, and secretly he had to admire her skills as an actress. Damn she's good; he thought.

"Oh... I almost forgot Papa; we were talking to Chito and Jesus earlier — actually that's who we had the beer with. They were saying they wanted to come to Manila with us, if we'll have them."

JC looked quizzically at his son; "what's prompted this, do you think?"

Damien ploughed on; "well Papa... they think we need better security and they feel like they owe a debt to the family... something about saving Samantha's life and now always being responsible for her."

He glanced across at Samantha who had leant forward, following the conversation intently.

JC looked at Maria and raised an eyebrow questioningly; "well hon? What do you think?"

Maria's lips tightened a bit and her eyelids hooded. "Mmmm," she began; "I'm not sure we actually kno..."

Samantha immediately jumped in. "Mama... how can you even consider, thinking about it? Those two men saved my life; they're my heroes... I would feel so much safer if I knew Chito and Jesus had my back. Oh Mama... they have to come. They're right, we need as much security as we can manage — and I trust them Mama."

JC took control and made the decision; "well, that settles it then; Chito and Jesus are now head of the group's security team."

He turned to Maria. "Yes hon... you agree?"

Maria's bottom lip came out in a pout, but then she smiled tightly, nodded softly and murmured; "Well... I guess... if that's what Sammy wants... if it makes her happy; then I guess they'd better come."

. . .

After Damien and Simon had left; Chito, Jesus and Samuel sat quietly, sipping their beers, in enjoyable, companionable company; relishing the gentle warmth of the evening breeze. Finally Chito looked at Samuel. Secretly he was thinking what a fine, young man little Sammy had become. He could well remember the fun they'd all had together on the beach at San Jose, all those years ago, and the terror and then relief at Sammy's near drowning. He found himself admiring the man that sat before him. Perhaps it was the memories that slipped through and allowed him to lower his guard.

"Another beer Sam;" he asked as Samuel placed the empty glass on the table.

He wasn't too used to drinking all that much of recent times, although during his College days he'd garnered a reputation for being the "life of the party"; with his enormous capacity for downing the brown stuff and yet still remaining sober enough to stand up.

He sighed contentedly and thought that Damien and Simon were going to need a bit more private time with Papa and Mama. He grinned at Chito; "why not? One for the road eh!"

Chito headed back inside the unit to grab some more cold ones from the fridge.

Jesus and Samuel chatted briefly about New York, and Columbia, while they waited his return. Chito strode through the sliding doors and placed a brand, new frosted can on the table in front of Sam.

"There you go my little Sammy boy; get that down ya!"

There was something in the intonation, or the words, or the phrasing that struck deeply into Samuel's memory banks. He sat there and tipped his head quizzically to one side; alternately looking closely at Chito and Jesus' faces.

Finally... after an eternity... his brow furrowed, and almost apologetically, he whispered; "*Tito* Chog... *Tito* Dan-dan... it is you..isn't it?"

Chito was the first to react. He reached behind him and pulled a pistol from the back of his waistband, pointing it directly at Samuel's forehead.

"Damn you Sammy! Why, of all the people that could have found us out... why did it have to be you? We love you Sammy — we always have. Ohhhh Sammy... I'm so sorry son."

He shot Samuel, point blank, directly in the middle of his forehead, just above the eyebrows, a few inches above where his nose flared out. The bullet unerringly sliced through the skull, split Samuel's brain almost asymmetrically and finally lodged itself in the hard skull shell at the rear.

A dribble of blood oozed from the gaping wound and Samuel was dead, even before his face hit the table. As he slumped forward, crashing into the tabletop, his body slid off the chair and onto the balcony deck—.

. . .

Chapter 19

"Oh shit! What the fuck have you done?" Jesus muttered, as he stared at Samuel's lifeless body, lying prostrate on the deck.

Chito just stood there looking at the body. His bottom lip started to quiver. "Ohhhh Sammy... my little man... I'm so, so sorry! Why, oh why, did you have to recognise us?" he managed to strangle out.

Jesus moved forward and placed one hand on his partner's shoulder. "Never mind Sammy, buddy, although yeah, I liked the kid too — it's a real shame you had to waste him; but what the fuck Chog, he recognised us. Really, what other option did you have?"

Chito stared at his partner with, hazy, unfocused eyes, until suddenly a thought struck him and clarity reappeared behind his eyelids. His mouth dropped open and he uttered; "Oh my God... what's Bubba gonna say about this shit going down? Jesus, he might even waste *us*... oh shit... oh shit... oh...;" his voice trailed off in despair.

"What's Bubba gonna say?" The voice came from behind them and gave them such a fright they momentarily jumped in the air and gave an involuntary squeal.

"I'll tell you what Bubba's gonna say... shall I?" the voice continued. "Bubba's gonna be mightily pissed... that's what Bubba's gonna be... and as to what Bubba's gonna say; well let's start with this shall we? *YOU FUCKING CRETINS!* What the bloody hell did you think you were doing? I keep making all these clever plans and you two just keep screwing them up."

They slowly turned to face their leader, dreading to see the look on his face.

To their absolute shock Bubba didn't even look terribly upset. He had a wry grin on his face and was softly shaking his head. "Just funning with ya boys ha! So what! A member of the Castillo family is dead... can't be nothing too bad about that; now can there?"

Chito and Jesus let their collective breaths out and Chito nervously chuckled. "I got him right in the head Bubba; there's no coming back for that boy."

Bubba clapped him a little unnecessarily hard on his shoulder. "Yeah... well... like I said, one less Castillo's all good in my book... even if he was a bastard Castillo; but that does put a bit of a damper on the idea of you two returning to Manila with them."

He looked thoughtfully at the pair; "how the hell are we going to explain you putting a bullet in the forehead of number one son eh?"

Chito rubbed his shoulder ruefully; "well Bubb..."

"Shut the fuck up Chito; it was a bloody rhetorical question. Now both of you shut up and let me think."

He moved over to the table and sat down; Samuel's body slumped at his feet. He bent down and touched the now clammy, cold skin and couldn't restrain a soft giggle. Looking out over the darkness of the desert he gazed at the vault of twinkling stars and lost himself in his thoughts.

Chito and Jesus exchanged glances, but neither was willing to risk the danger of saying anything, or God forbid, interrupting Bubba's train of thought. After five minutes, they noticed an evil grin come over Bubba's face. Jesus looked at his partner; smiled and nodded his head. It was gonna be alright — Bubba had an answer.

He looked at the two of them, eagerly leaning forward awaiting instructions. Sighing; he once again reminded himself that this was all he had to work with. Sad as it might be; these two bullocking buffoons were an integral part of his plan to dominate the Universe. He needed them and that annoyed the crap out of him.

Forcing a warm smile onto his face he addressed them; "Right... well... I think I have a solution. We'll take the body somewhere and leave it, for whoever happens to wander along, to find."

Jesus wrinkled his forehead and screwed up his nose. "But Bubba, how are we going to explain the bullet hole and the fact that we were the last people to see him alive. It's going to get pretty hot around here and we're supposed to leave with JC and the others in a couple of days."

Losing patience with the two idiots Bubba snapped; "leave the damn thinking to me will you... I've got everything covered. Now let's get this body somewhere else first eh?"

Chastened; Chito and Jesus grabbed Samuel's body under each arm and began to drag him toward the door of the unit.

"At least lift him upright you damn fools so if anyone spots you, you can at least pretend he's drunk and you're carrying him home." They hoisted the body upright and placed supporting arms around its shoulders.

The trio rapidly made their way through the maze of streets until they reached the point where the residential area of Ezraville melded into the agricultural area. In order to move quicker Chito had hoisted the body over his shoulder, and the three men were trotting toward the centre of the first paddock; a milk cow, holding paddock.

"Right;" Bubba commanded; "this is as good a place as any... just drop the body there in the middle of that big hunk of cow shit."

Chito unceremoniously dropped Samuel's body into the designated pat. He looked down at the sprawled body and felt a twinge of remorse. Bending down to at least close poor Samuel's eyes he felt a strong, vice-like grip, on his arm.

"Don't go getting all sentimental on us now Chito. He's just fine the way he is;" Bubba instructed.

Jesus looked at the desolate scene and asked; "Bubba, what about the bullet hole and what about us? How are we going to explain it all to the authorities?"

Bubba looked at the bereft pair; standing there in blackness, illuminated only by the pale reflection of a quarter-moon and his face split in an enormous grin. "Ah boys... I think we can handle the bullet hole — no problem."

Kneeling down beside the body he grasped his bony fingers tightly on either side of the ugly, blood encrusted, wound. Looking up at the stars he began to softly chant, so softly the other two couldn't even catch the words, let alone their meaning. They stood entranced, as the macabre scene played out in front of them.

After two minutes of whispered chanting Bubba rose and waved both his hands downward, pointing at the body. Chito and Jesus craned forward to see what was happening and to their utter astonishment they watched as the crushed remnants of a bullet slowly began to ooze out of the wound. Bubba reached down and plucked the metal fragment, like he was plucking a flower from its stem. He held it in the air to display it to them before grinning and slipping it into his pocket. He now knelt beside the corpse and pulled his fingers together from either side of the wound. When he removed his hand so the other two could see; there simply wasn't a wound there anymore. The skin was totally unblemished.

They gasped in complete amazement. Bubba turned and looked up at them, cackling; "and that my boy's is pure evil magic at work. That repair will even pass an autopsy report... hehehe."

Noticing there was still some residue of blood left on the body's forehead, Chito and Jesus stared in disgust, as Bubba bent closer and flicked his long, forked tongue out; licking and cleaning the area fastidiously. Finally... apparently satisfied with his work, Bubba stood and stretched in the chill, night air.

"Problem solved!" he pronounced.

Jesus shook his head. Damn, he thought, this is all just way too fucking much — but he knew there was no way out now. They were in it... for the long haul.

Chito turned away from the body as if to cleanse the vision he had just witnessed, from his mind's eye. "But Bubba;" he began; "we still haven't got a story to tell the auth..."

"I didn't say I was finished yet, did I?" Bubba interrupted him.

Both had previously witnessed the speed and viciousness of Bubba's tail; but it was still a terrifying sight when suddenly it appeared from between his legs again. Involuntarily they both took a step back from the evil instrument. One second it wasn't there and the next second it was.

"Bloody hell!" Chito exclaimed.

Bubba just smiled and lent down close to the body. With his bottom lip curled up between his teeth and his eyes narrowed in intense concentration; he set to work on mutilating the corpse.

First he struck with two wide swathes across the body's torso, exposing its chest cavity. The razor sharp prongs of the tail met no resistance from the skin and ribs of the body. With the chest cavity wide open and exposed to the night air; he moved up the body, to the point where the bullet hole had been. Gently, almost reverently, the sharp tip of the tail began to carve delicately into the flesh; cutting it, but not slicing right through to the skull. He worked in total silence for five minutes before reaching up with his sleeve to wipe his forehead, which despite the chill of the evening was dripping perspiration. Seemingly satisfied with his handiwork he stood up and spread his arms in pride; imploring them to look at what he had achieved.

When Chito and Jesus looked down at the head they were amazed to see the most delicately carved and intricately decorated inverted cross, right next to a pentacle, in the middle of what had once been Samuel's forehead. "Holy mother of Christ!" Chito muttered.

"Not bad work for an old fella... even if I do say so myself;" Bubba murmured. He looked down and pronounced; "There 'aint no doubt about the cause of death now is there? And my little artwork should give everyone some food for thought... hehehe."

Chito gave Bubba what he hoped was an approving smile and tried again;

"But Bubba what about our alib..."

His plea was cut off in mid stream as Bubba's tail whipped around and caught him high on his left arm. He screamed in agony as the razor tip entered the flesh and sliced through, almost to the bone. Grasping his wounded arm with his good hand and trying to staunch the blood flow; he squealed in a high-pitched voice; "Bubba!" But Bubba had no time for formalities.

His tail swept down and sliced through both of Chito's calf muscles, causing him to collapse in a heap on the ground. For good measure he then ran the tip of his tail up Chito's body from the top of his groin right up to his bobbing adam's apple. The cut was deep enough to slice his clothing and to leave a perfectly straight-line of oozing blood, but not deep enough to penetrate, or damage, any of his vital organs. Chito lay writhing on the ground, mewling softly and clutching various parts of his anatomy with his one good arm, unsure of how, or what to do, to stop the infernal pain. Finally; mercifully, his brain gave up to the intense agony and allowed him to slip into unconsciousness.

Jesus had staggered and fallen backwards at the ferocity of Bubba's assault on Chito and was sitting, terrified, in a large pile of cow shit. He started to scrabble away from Bubba, as he approached him, still grinning and gently swinging his tail.

In a blinding flash the tail shot out from his hands and sliced off all the toes on Jesus' right foot; clean as a whistle, right through Jesus' shoes. Bubba began to whistle softly as he got into his work. The tail swivelled and sliced upward in a similar fashion to the manner he had carved up Chito. Mercifully; Jesus slipped into unconsciousness almost instantly and Bubba frowned as he realised he wasn't going to get any more pleasure from seeing Jesus' reaction.

Shrugging his shoulders resignedly he knelt beside the unconscious forms of first Jesus and then Chito; copying the same intricate design on their foreheads, as well. Finally, complete and satisfied with his efforts, he stood up and surveyed the carnage.

"Not a bad effort for a night's work;" he chuckled.

He looked at Chito and Jesus, almost feeling a modicum of compassion for them. They so wanted to help... but they were such useless losers, he thought. Grinning at his artwork on all three men he muttered softly; "now... all three of you belong to Beelzebub... for eternity."

He looked up at the twinkling stars, laughed maniacally, and waved his arms like a magician with his cape. Instantaneously, he was gone, and all that was left; sprawled helplessly around the cow paddock was one corpse and two very badly wounded soldiers.

. . .

Samantha awoke the second Bubba's warm breath kissed her exposed neck. She moaned softly and rolled over with an ease and subtly sexual movement that was intended to arouse her visitor. Automatically she reached her arms up to grasp his face and pull him closer to her. She'd been dreaming a turbulent nightmare, filled with visions of death and destruction, and Bubba's arrival gave her the opportunity to rise from those depths of depravity and embrace the true, perfect love, that she had for this aged devil.

Her ruse worked and Bubba found himself beginning to breathe heavily and become deeply excited at the insistent probing of Samantha's tongue inside his mouth and the unceasing caressing mission that her fingers were engaged on. She kneaded his flesh, wherever she could find it, and as the passion rose between them he found himself struggling to keep focused on the purpose of his visit. He needed to bring Samantha up to speed on the happenings of the evening.

Pulling all his self-restraint to the fore he pulled back, panting, and stood above the semi-naked Samantha, as she lay on the bed writhing and complaining bitterly about him stopping the growing passion. In her excitement, her flimsy pyjama top had become undone and one breast; nipple brown, large and strikingly erect was staring at Bubba begging to be teased and pleasured by his tongue. He tore his eyes away from the entreating, offending party, and focused completely on Samantha's already lust-filled eyes.

"Sammy baby;" he purred softly, his voice breathless from want; "we haven't got time for that right now. A lot has happened tonight that might change our plans, we need to talk." He took one last, long, desirous look at the peek-a-boo nipple, before dismissing it from his mind; "now cover that up, before I go crazy; and listen closely."

He relayed the events of Samuel's death and what it meant for their plans. She was horrified to learn of her half-brother's death. She wasn't as close to Samuel as Damien was; but growing up, she'd always admired the tall, strong boy from San Jose. She'd looked up to him the way a sister; who desperately wants an elder brother to idolise, only could.

From an early age her mother had fed her on a diet of tales about little Sammy growing up, and the adventures they'd all had together in those early days — and now little Samuel was dead... just a pile of decomposing, rotting meat, lying unloved and uncared for, in a field just out of town. The thought of him lying cold and lifeless on the chilly, pre-dawn earth, quickly brought a tear to her eye. She brushed it away impatiently as she waited for Bubba to explain what this meant to them all and especially their plans for the future. When finally he appeared to have finished she looked up at him and in a voice croaking with emotion asked;

"Dddid hhhhe die quickly Bubba — was he in pain?"

For just a brief nanosecond, she thought she saw the unfamiliar image of empathy, or sympathy, or even just plain sadness in Bubba's eyes; but it was a brief interlude. Instantly his eyes hardened and shockingly; he slapped Samantha viciously on the side of her face, slamming her backward flat on her back on the bed.

She didn't cry out and she didn't fight back. She continued lying there, ruefully rubbing her already reddening face and just looking at him, with that sorrowful, little-girl hurt look, of one who has just been chastised by her Daddy. Bubba's hard countenance softened marginally as her looked at her.

"I'm sorry little one, but we just can't afford to be emotional about these things. Remember... by the time we're crowned King and Queen of this Universe, many of your family will be dead; or at the very least consigned to the furnaces of hell, to live eternity in deep pain and suffering." He paused, as his face screwed up in bile and hatred; "just like those motherfuckers in Heaven have done to me for the past millennia."

She took a deep breath, wiped away the tears from the corner of her eyes and sat upright; nodding her head and leaned forward to give Bubba a chaste, but loving kiss on the cheek. He smiled gratifyingly at his beautiful, little protégé; "now that's my girl — so... we're all good honey? We know what comes next... right?"

She nodded her head rapidly in agreement, but Bubba could see there was still more going on, inside that head, than just some residual grief over Samuel's death. He fixed her with a withering stare but forced himself to keep a smile on his face, despite his impatience with her attitude.

"What still bothers you little one?"

Samantha forced herself to grin at him. "No... no... no... there's nothing Bubba... really there's nothing. Let's just do this thing!"

He laughed softly — the last thing he wanted to do was to wake anyone else in the house. "That's the girl I know and love. Okay my dear, you get back to sleep and I'll see you soon."

Like a vampire from all those old Dracula movies, Bubba dramatically flung his cape around himself and simply vanished into thin air. Samantha sat there for some time, contemplating the spot where he'd stood. She knew the die was cast and there was no turning back now, but, could she really do what Bubba had asked of her, to prove her ultimate loyalty to him? She'd gone over it, in her head, so many times — it would be the ultimate act of betrayal and yet it would be the action that would open up all power and glory for her. She was to be the Queen of the Universe and all she had to do was to follow Bubba's instructions to the letter... so why did it seem so hard?.

Eventually, she lay back on the bed and fell into a troubled sleep; vivid again with dreams of violence, slaughter and blood — always the blood; ceaselessly dripping from the mutilated bodies, covering her in its vile, metallic-smelling, viscosity. She tossed and turned; never quite able to reach that depth, where soothing, calming, dreamless sleep exists — forever trapped on the plateau of her nightmares—.

. . .

Chapter 20

The knock on the door, when it came, was very early; just after 5.30am. Maria was busily rushing around the kitchen assisting Marielle with breakfast preparations for the family. Marielle was a god-send to them; "Mama," she had told Maria over coffee one day; "God sent me all these lovely children to me to care for. Why do I need any of my own; I have six wonderful children to help to grow into adults — that's my mission here on earth."

As she watched Marielle's efficient and cheerful organisation, Maria remembered how those simple words spoken so long ago had brought her to tears. Marielle's happy, open outlook on life was a constant that her children had been able to hang onto all those years of touring Asia, never having a permanent home for much longer than a month. JC and Maria may have been the parents; but it was Marielle who kept the family together, happy, and ultimately sane.

Maria always loved cooking the family breakfast together with her because it was *their* special bonding time. It was their chance when they could enjoy the mother / daughter relationship that had been robbed from Marielle when she was just eight — her mother having died from breast cancer, within months of the diagnosis. Besides, Maria thought, I'm the only one who can brew the coffee just the way JC likes it — Marielle tries, but she can never get it perfect.

She giggled to herself; that's because my special ingredient is a touch of love and a pinch of lust... hehehe. Feeling an enormous burst of love and affection for the young woman who had dedicated her life to them she jumped to her feet and spontaneously grabbed Marielle in a bear hug; spinning her around and kissing her on the cheek. "I love you so much *anak* (my child); you truly were sent to us from God."

"Ohhhh... Maria, I love you so much and all..." and then came the insistent rapping on the front door.

They looked at each other in surprise. Who could be calling at this time of the morning? Maria knew it was too early for the car to take them to the airport to pick up Petrona. Oh it's so exciting, she thought, to realise that my little man is finally in love. She must be quite a woman to have stolen Samuel's heart. I'm so looking forward to meeting her. Shrugging her shoulders at Marielle's quizzical look, Maria unconsciously brushed her hands against the sides of her pyjama pants and reached up to tuck a recalcitrant lock of hair, back behind her ears. Sneaking a quick glance at the mirror to ensure she was totally presentable she headed for the front door to see who could possibly be calling at this early hour.

The instant she opened the door and saw Pastor Jhoemar Nolasco's downcast features she knew something terrible had happened. Her hands flew to her mouth, regarding the Pastor with wide eyes, filled with fear and terror, at the news she knew he was bringing them. Joe reached out a hand and placed it gently on her shoulder trying to impart some strength into the woman whose emotions were already in turmoil.

"Mmmmaria;" he only just managed to choke out. "I... I... I... have some awful news for you and JC... cccan we talk inside?"

She tried desperately to pull herself together... awful news? Oh my God, she thought, what now? So many terrible things had happened, and now something more.

"Tell me Joe... ppplease... what's happened?"

Joe's lips tightened as he squeezed her gently on the shoulder. "No Maria, I need to talk to both of you together."

Realising the futility of pressing him any more, on the doorstep and remembering her manners she tried to smile a feeble smile. "Of cccourse Joe, please come in. I'll get JC."

She led him into the living room where he sat uncomfortably and fidgeting on the very edge of one of the large, comfortable sofas. Maria looked around frantically before she spotted Marielle peering around the kitchen door frame; her face a mask of worry and concern.

"Marielle, I'll get JC — can you please wake up Samantha, Damien and Samuel. I think they probably need to hear what Pastor Nolasco has to say."

She didn't see the momentary look of pain pass across the Pastor's face at the mention of Samuel's name. By the time she looked back at him for confirmation of the older children being there, he had recovered his poise and just softly nodded his head.

JC and Maria walked from the bedroom; JC holding tightly around his wife's waist to try and control her trembling; but also for his own support. He was as frightened as Maria and was struggling mightily to contain his rising concern at this early morning visit.

"Maria!" she heard Marielle scream. "Maria... come quick!"

She ran to the hallway that connected the living room to the bedrooms. Marielle was standing outside Samuel's room, one hand to her face.

"Marielle;" Maria called, "what's the matter, what's happening?"

Marielle turned slowly, her face shrouded in fear. "Samuel's not in his bed Mama... it hasn't even been slept in."

Maria screwed her face up in consternation.

"Well, perhaps he just spent the night with Chito and Jesus ha! Remember, Damien said they were drinking a lot. Maybe he just passed out... hehehe."

She looked back at the open doorway where she could see Pastor Nolasco's sorrowful face. She watched, as he took his handkerchief from his pocket, and despite the frigidness of the desert morning, he wiped perspiration from his forehead. It was then that the truth hit her. Jhoemar's here because of Samuel, she thought. Oh my God, something's happened to Samuel — something really bad.

Uttering a loud sob, she spun on her heels and ran back to the lounge, falling to her knees at Jhoemar's feet.

"It's Samuel, isn't it? Something's happened to Samuel... tell me... tell me."

Maria began to beat her fists on Jhoemar's knees as she keened; "Pleeeease, pleeeeease, tell me my little boy's alright....pleeeease."

JC rose to his feet and gently placed his hands on either side of Maria's shoulders. "Come on honey;" he begged; "come and sit down and listen to what Joe has to tell us. Losing our cool isn't going to help anyone. Now, come on sweetie... let's sit down and see what's what."

Reluctantly, Maria allowed herself to be lifted to her feet and steered toward the couch; where she sat, hands twisting together, face a mask of uncertainty and pain, looking at Jhoemar with absolute pleading — mentally begging him to please put her out of her misery.

As matter-of-factly as he could the Pastor relayed the events of that morning. He told them a passing worker, Terry Gunderson, from the dairy farm, had been heading for that morning's milking when he had seen what he thought was an injured animal laying in the middle of the paddock. Rushing over to check he was shocked and horrified by the scene of carnage and mutilation that awaited him. The three bodies had been arranged at right angles, with just their feet touching each other.

Once Terry realised that at least two of the bodies were in fact alive he quickly called 999 and then Pastor Nolasco, to tell him of his discovery. Using the basic first aid that he had learnt in the Boy Scouts, many years previously, Terry did what he could to assist the two men who were still alive; until the Paramedics arrived. Their wounds, although serious, were clearly not life-threatening once Terry had managed to staunch the blood flow from Chito's arm and Jesus' foot.

Jhoemar looked up at the five of them who were following his every word with a mixture of horror, fear, and trepidation. He took a deep breath and addressed JC directly.

"JC; I'm sorry, but the three men were Chito, Jesus and your son Samuel."

Maria gasped aloud.

"Joe; what about Samuel — please; is he one of the ones still alive?"

She knew the answer before he even responded; the expression on his face betrayed him.

"I'm sorry Maria... it seems Samuel was already dead when Terry arrived at the scene. He'd bled out from his injuries... I'm so... so... sorry... but there was nothing either Terry or anyone cccould...." His voice tailed off as it cracked with emotion.

The scream that rent the air inside the living room was as mournful as it was piercing. Maria's mouth kept opening and closing, as she tried to scream more and more, for her lost Samuel, but nothing more came out. The room was just silent as they all looked at, and took their cues, from the grieving mother. Maria slumped down in the chair and buried her face in JC's lap, her body racked by endless, inaudible sobbing. JC placed an arm across the back of her head and slowly, almost rhythmically, continued to gently stroke and pat her. His face was frozen in a mask of sheer horror. He had no idea how to comfort his wife, but he knew instinctively that he must just wait for her to resurface from her despair, in her own time. All he knew was that he had to retain the warmth and care of his loving touch on the back of her head.

Samuel may well have been JC's adopted son, but JC had never thought of him that way. He had joked on several occasions with Maria that when he fell in love with her; he'd bought the entire package — and that included Samuel. He loved that boy with every fibre of his being and although he could never truly experience the agony of a mother losing her son, especially to such a senseless and violent act, he nonetheless was feeling the intense pain of the loss himself. I must be strong, he thought, I must be the strong one for this family — that's my role. I have to be the one to get us through this.

Competing with his desire to be the rock, on which they could all anchor themselves, was this nagging suspicion that somehow he was to blame for all the pain and all the suffering his family was going through. Did I bring all this on them; he agonised. Was it my determination to become human and to spread the word to all the world that has done this? His face reflected the inner turmoil he was struggling with; alternating between anger, concern for his wife, and an immense sadness at the loss of someone with so much potential as Samuel. My Samuel, he thought, as the tears began to stream down his face unchecked,

Damien and Marielle had sought comfort and solace, from the news, in each other's arms. They sat together, locked in a tight embrace, rocking backward and forward, just gently sobbing into each other's chests. Samantha, of all of them, appeared the least affected. Her face was statue-like, as she sat bolt upright on her lounge chair, just staring fixedly at a large wall clock that hung about a foot above Pastor Nolasco's head.

She watched, as the second-hand relentlessly ticked around the dial — each second that passed, another second closer to the ultimate conflagration that she knew was coming. It would not only tear this family to pieces but climactically would tear the earth, and the entire universe, to shreds. She would be right at the centre of it, orchestrating and leading the revolt. The thought of what she had allowed herself to become involved in resonated loudly inside her head.

Her heart actually ached for the loss of Samuel. Illogically, and paradoxically, she felt sad and depressed about the loss of Samuel's undoubted potential; of his youthful exuberance and of the skills and wisdom that he would now never have the opportunity to present to the world. Yet she knew that she was actually the principal architect of his demise. The emotion of elation at another step down the road to her crown of glory was tempered by the sorrow she felt for the pain she had to cause to the people she loved; along the way. All this swirled inside her as the second hand swept remorselessly onward, to her final date with destiny.

Jhoemar had been through this experience of delivering bad news to families on many occasions in the past; but perhaps not quite such horrific news, under such terrible circumstances, as this. Over the years as Pastor of Ezraville, people had died, people had had accidents, and it usually fell to Joe to be the bearer of the bad tidings, to the families of the victims. This was different though; this wasn't a man caught in a threshing machine, or someone having a heart attack in the fields; this was violence and evil incarnate, that he, as a man of God, had never had to witness in his life.

He knew families needed that quiet time to grieve for their lost member before they could face the practicalities of what came next; so he just sat motionless for a while waiting for the right moment to begin. He was feeling pretty helpless as to how to deal with a death as horrific as this one, so in the end he went back inside himself and drew on the two certainties he always imparted in these situations.

"Samuel's with God now, and he's totally at peace;" he said softly and in measured tones to the assembled room.

At his words, Maria raised her head from JC's lap and looked straight into her husband's eyes. "Can you swear, with all certainty, that Samuel's in heaven and that he will be happy and content there?"

JC smiled very thinly and almost inaudibly whispered back; "Honey, that is the *only* thing I'm one hundred percent certain of, at the moment."

Maria reached up and kissed away one of the tears that clung tenaciously to JC's jaw. "Well, for now JC, I guess that will have to be enough for me."

She looked at Jhoemar whose tensed shoulders had relaxed, as he had watched Maria pull back from the black abyss of grief that threatened to swallow her; just as he had seen so many widows, mothers and children do over the years.

Maria suddenly opened her mouth in surprise. "Oh Joe, how incredibly selfish and thoughtless of me. What about Jesus and Chito; how are they? Will they survive? Those poor, poor, men!"

JC grabbed his wife's hand and squeezed it in relief. If she was worrying about others then JC knew she was going to cope with this. There would be months of sadness, sorrow, and even recriminations ahead, but he knew that he and Maria had what it took as human beings and as husband and wife to get through this agony. He breathed a gentle sigh of relief.

Jhoemar also breathed out audibly at Maria's questions — she would be okay, was his relieved thought. He went on to explain that the police were still trying to piece together the events of the morning, but that it appeared to them that Samuel, Jesus and Chito were clearly set upon by someone. He added rather ominously... or something, on their way home from their drinking session.

JC just uttered one word that hung in the air like an invitation, for someone to grab. *"Beelzebub!"*

Jhoemar grimaced at the mention of the feared and reviled name, but he nodded his head sagely; "yes JC... quite possibly... yes."

He looked at them and continued; "as for Chito and Jesus, well they were seriously wounded. It looked like some sort of frenzied knife attack, but hopefully the forensics will give us a better idea of the weapon. Anyway, both of them are hurt, but I suspect it is their pride that's more hurt than anything. I got a chance to grab a word with Chito as they were loading him into the ambulance."

He paused briefly and ran his fingers through his already thinning scalp, the tiredness and stress of the events clearly beginning to catch up with him. He explained that Chito said they tried to fight off the attacker, but he was way too strong for them.

"He kept repeating a phrase which may be enlightening. Remember, he was pretty pumped up by painkillers by that time, but he just kept saying... that damn tail....that damn tail... it's just too fast."

Again JC's lips tightened noticeably and this time he absolutely spat the word out, in disgust; *"Beelzebub!"*

Jhoemar nodded again sadly. "I think..." he was interrupted by another insistent rapping on the door.

Marielle let go of Damien's hand and jumped to her feet, wiping her tear-stained face with the back of her sleeve. She said; "I'll get it Maria."

When she returned she looked a little lost.

"Mama... it's... it's... the car to go to the airport to pick up Petrona."

Maria's jaw dropped and her eyes began to tear up again. "Oh my God... Petrona! Oh hell! What are we going to tell her? She's come all this way to see her beloved Samuel and now... well, now..." her voice tailed off as she began to cry again.

JC quickly took control of the situation, before it had the chance to spiral into another session of inconsolable grieving. He told Damien and Samantha to go and get dressed and he grabbed Maria by her arms pulling her to her feet.

"Honey;" he implored her; "We have to do this, we have to be there for Petrona. She loved Samuel and now we are all she has of him. We need to get ready and go to the airport."

Maria shook her head firmly, as if to clear the last remaining vestiges of pain and sadness before regaining her clarity. "Of course we do... of course."

She looked at Jhoemar, who was by now standing in the middle of the room, looking sheepish and unsure of what to do.

Maria walked over to him and hugged him, kissing him softly on his cheek.

"Now... you... you wonderful man... thank you for your understanding and most of all thank you for your gentleness in telling us. I do appreciate it."

She smiled softly. "Now you hotfoot down to the hospital and make sure those two are going to be alright. Please tell them we'll come and see them tonight; after we settle everything with Petrona."

As Jhoemar hugged her back briefly, and headed for the door, she turned to her husband; again totally in control of her emotions and her usual businesslike and efficient self; "as for you — you look like crap. Go and clean yourself up, have a shave and get dressed, then we'll go."

JC crossed the distance to his wife in just two strides, swept her up in his arms and kissed her long and deeply. "Honey... speak for yourself ha! You don't exactly look like a million dollars either. Let's both go and get cleaned up." Despite everything Maria still managed a wan smile at the man she adored before linking her arm through his and half frogmarching him toward the bedroom.

As Damien rapidly dressed, his mind was racing at a hundred miles an hour. He was devastated by Samuel's death — his *kuya,* his mentor, his friend, his older brother had been taken ruthlessly and violently by the Devil. If a few hours ago he had any doubts about his continuing on in this crusade; they had been swept away by the brutal slaying of his brother.

"I will avenge you Sammy" he whispered at the ceiling. "I will make that bastard pay for ever thinking he could take on the Castillo clan, and win."

As soon as he was dressed he tore outside; shouting to Marielle, who was keeping busy by "making work" for herself in the kitchen; "tell Mum and Dad I'll be back in a few minutes. I'm just going to grab Simon to come with us."

Damien needed to be comforted and loved by Simon, but that could wait. What he needed more than anything right now was to share and talk through his feelings with someone who truly understood him; that person was, and Damien suspected, always would be Simon. Besides, he thought, as he banged on his door, I can't face meeting Petrona, and all that will entail, without having someone to hold my hand through it all.

As the door opened and Simon's smiling face was framed in it, Damien forgot everything — just threw himself into the welcoming comfort of Simon's arms. Everything would be alright now—.

. . .

Chapter 21

They stood in a cluster just outside the final exit point for passengers arriving on internal flights. A quick explanation to the airport manager, and a generous donation to the airport staff social club, had garnered them a private room where they could take Petrona and explain the situation to her.

Angeline had made a special sign with "PETRONA" written on it in large capital letters, so there would be no chance of her missing it. Still unaware of the tragedy that had befallen them all Angeline was excited about meeting her brother's girlfriend and was hopping from one foot to the other, waving the sign above her head. Maria looked ruefully at her younger children; Shannen, Sean, Angeline and Angelo; still blissfully unaware of what had happened. She and JC had agreed that after introductions she would take the four younger children to another room and explain, as gently as possible, what had befallen Samuel — they'd only told them he was feeling unwell at this point. JC, the two eldest children and Simon would be doing the same with Petrona. It was an awful task, but one that had to be done, and Maria was mentally steeling herself for what lay ahead.

In the end, they need not have bothered with the sign. When Petrona finally strode through the concourse they recognised her instantly. She was exactly as Samuel had described her; a tall, willowy, blond, beauty that walked with an air of authority and power, that only the truly wealthy seem to exude, so effortlessly. When they rushed to greet her though there was no sign of any pretentiousness; she was friendly, sweet and totally down to earth. The four children warmed instantly to her and were clutching her hand and seeking the favour of a glance, a pat, or a quiet word.

Obviously elated at meeting Samuel's family; Petrona was clearly worried and upset at his absence. They quickly whisked her away to the private room to explain. Prying the little children away from her was not such an easy task, but this was something Maria knew had to be done, and done quickly.

An hour and a half later, when both groups emerged from their respective rooms, there was a pall of sadness hanging over them all. Everyone was wiping away the tears and both physically and emotionally supporting each other as they left the airport and climbed into the car that would take them back to Ezraville. Once they were organised and seated in the car Maria looked around at everyone and her heart broke at the pain and suffering she saw etched in each of their faces. She longed to bury her own face in her hands and beg God for a release from this agony, but she knew that this was her and JC's life now and they needed to face the reality of what had happened and deal with it. She took a deep breath and reminded herself; "I need to be the strong one here, for everyone's sake; even I just want to curl up into a little ball and cry myself into oblivion."

Petrona was sitting beside her in the middle row of the SUV. She reached for the young woman's hand and squeezed it gently just to let her know that she was still there and that they were in this horror story together. The reciprocal squeeze back that she got was enough to give her the strength to carry on, for that moment anyway. Petrona turned to Maria and gave her a wan smile that spoke volumes of the pain she felt; but still held the warmth that just naturally flowed from her. Maria smiled back tentatively and instinctively leaned forward and kissed her on the cheek.

"Petrona, we're so glad to meet you, even in such a horrible way..." Maria stopped and looked directly into her eyes. "Samuel loved you so much; his face would light up with sheer joy whenever he talked about you."

The corner of Petrona's eye leaked a single tear that rolled unimpeded down her cheek. She made no move to sweep it away but whispered back to Maria; "oh Maria, I've felt like I've known you ever since the first day I met Samuel..." she paused briefly and just leant in, so the two women's foreheads were lightly touching. "Do you have any idea how proud your little boy was of his Mama?" she gave a sad giggle; "he never stopped talking about you... but now... he's... he's... gone..." her voice tailed off as it cracked with the emotion.

Maria's response was to place her hand around Petrona's head and hold it there for the remainder of the journey home, just gently stroking her hair the whole time. They sat in complete silence for the rest of the trip, each of them thinking about, and remembering, their lost brother, son and friend.

Back at the house Damien declared he and Simon were going to the hospital to check on Chito and Jesus. JC nodded that it was a good idea and to tell them that he and Maria would pop in that evening to see them. Samantha asked if she could accompany the boys to see them, which came as no surprise — they were her heroes after all. He shrugged his shoulders; it will keep us all busy anyway and maybe help us forget everything that has happened, at least for a short time anyway. He nodded his assent to her request.

Marielle took the four younger children to their rooms to try and cheer them up a little, as they were clearly devastated by the news. As for Petrona; she asked if they would mind if she lay down for a while — begging a headache and tiredness from the travel. Eventually just Maria and JC remained on the couch.

They sat there, close together, holding hands; each waiting for the other to begin to speak. When JC finally turned to his wife, he kissed her softly on her lips and began to quietly sob; tears rolling, like giant rain drops down his cheeks. It was too much for Maria and she finally gave into the pain and loss that had been hammering at the door to her mind; seeking release. They clung together, for what seemed like hours, wordlessly pouring out their heart's emotions to each other, until both were empty and spiritually cleansed.

As they separated and looked into each other's eyes, JC realised the fire, the love and the passion that had always been there was still undiminished. For not the first time in their relationship he marvelled at the sheer strength and indomitable spirit of the woman he had fallen in love with. People often remarked just how much JC had given up, to marry Maria — but he'd always scoffed at the suggestions;

"I'd do it all over again... in a heartbeat;" was his standard response, but it was more than just a pat answer. Looking into his wife's eyes he knew with an absolute certainty that he'd made the right decision. He loved her with all his being... everything he ever was or ever would be.

With his voice cracking, and just above a whisper he mouthed to her; "I... I... love you Maria... thhhank you!"

Just as she had done so many times in the past, she answered her husband's heart-felt message with her "stock" phrase for the occasion; "Ditto, big boy... ditto."

Even though it had become a standard answer over the life of their marriage, it never sounded glib or contrived. When she said it, she said it with every ounce of love and adoration she could muster.

JC smiled softly at her; "it's been a damn awful few week's honey, but sadly this is what we signed up for when I gave up immortality, for the human experience. There's great joy and passion in humanity; but equally there's intense sorrow and hurt — it is just part of being truly human.

Maria sat back on the sofa and looked out into space, seemingly thinking.

"Now honey... I don't want you to think I'm crazy, or desperate, or a mad, neurotic, woman;" she began; "but I've been thinking."

He sat forward eagerly to listen to his wife's ideas.

"Is there truly nothing you can do to help Samuel? I mean... you are still the son of God; even you've given up your birthright. Is there really nothing you can do? We have to explore every option right? We owe it to ourselves, and to our son."

This hadn't been quite what JC had expected, but he sat back and pondered her words. Finally, with a sad smile, he grabbed her hand and held it tight.

"Sweetheart; don't think I haven't thought about this myself? If I could, I would bring Samuel back right this very second... but no, you're right, I did give up my birthright and with it all the power and authority that that contained. I really don't think there's anything I can do."

Maria digested this, her brow furrowing in concentration before she leant forward to JC again. "What about Sam and Damien hon; they have powers right? We just don't know yet how powerful they are. Maybe they could do something?"

A light began to dawn in JC's eyes..."Oh my God;" he whispered softly. "What if Damien, and Sam, plus Michael, and me, tried? You know, it's possible... who knows if we don't try."

She jumped to her feet in excitement; "you think babes? Really? You think?" She paused, as something occurred to her; "but will Michael do it hon, you know he's supposedly not allowed here."

JC grinned at her. "Honey, Michael would walk across broken glass for me; calm volcanoes for me; even risk his life for me... we go back to eternity sweetheart. He's my brother... nope... you just leave Michael to me."

Their enthusiasm was rising as they considered the possibility that maybe, just maybe, there was a chance to save their beloved son. He looked at Maria and grinned conspiratorially; "you know what we have to do, don't you?"

Maria thought briefly and then her lips formed a smile also; "I think I do yeah — we have to go back to Pangutaran Island; to that magical, little chapel where it all started for you and me — where my faith and my love raised you from the dead... am I right babes?"

JC actually laughed aloud; "Got it in one hon! You read my mind almost as well and Damien and Sam... hehehe."

Infused with hope now; the layers of grief and despair fell away, like autumn leaves off the trees. Maria took control. "Okay; we need to get going tomorrow — I don't know why, but I just have this feeling that the longer we wait, the harder it will be. I'll start getting everyone sorted and you ring the airline and organise our tickets... right?"

JC nodded enthusiastically, excited and relieved that they had thought of a way out of this dilemma. Before they rushed off to their respective tasks they both automatically walked into the other's arms and just held each other tight for several minutes; gently rocking back and forth, and saying nothing verbally, but saying buckets emotionally.

Maria broke the spell in the end, and whispered; "Right; get your arse moving sunshine, we have work to do... and honey... I love you so much."

JC giggled; "right back at ya sweetie."

. . .

Chito lay on his back, staring endlessly at the hospital room's ceiling tiles; white they were — with little dimples all over them. To pass the time, he mentally tried to calculate how many dimples were on each tile and then how many dimples were in his field of his vision. His mental arithmetic just wasn't up to the task and Jesus constantly interrupting his calculations, with his non-stop whinging, didn't make it any easier.

Chito hurt; plain and simple — he hurt. Sure the hospital had given them both ample pain medication, but that only served to take the sharpness off it, leaving a constant background chatter of frazzled nerves and misfiring pain neurons. Damn, he thought, what I wouldn't give right now for a sweet, brown, mellow bottle of Jack Daniels or hell; even one of those cheaper gut-rot whiskeys... now there was a good pain-killer.

"Hey Chog... what the fuck Bubba do that for ha?" this was Jesus' regular complaint. "Why he had to hurt us so bad... couldn't he just of roughed us up a bit? Damn... it hurts Chog... it bloody well hurts."

Chito turned his head to survey his friend in the next bed; his expression one of frustration, and annoyance, rapidly turning to outright anger and hostility.

"Shit Jesus, just shut the fuck up and stop calling me Chog... how many times do we have to go through this... my name is Chito and yours is Jesus... end of bloody story. Sheesh, you're becoming such a pain, my fr..."

The hospital room swing door creaked slightly as it opened. Quickly glancing at Jesus he whispered; "we have company fool, think before you speak ha!"

Chito raised himself painfully to see who the visitors were. When he saw Damien and Simon come through the door he wearily tried to manage a brief wave at them.

"Boys, boys, so good of you to come and see us. We're getting sick to death of each other's company already... hehehe... it'll be good to have someone else to chat to."

He couldn't help but notice that Samantha was also with them; albeit hanging back behind the two boys and positioning herself just inside the door, leaning on the jamb. A slight smile played across her lips, as she surveyed Jesus and Chito — swathed as they were in bandages, and pretty much helpless.

Bitch! Chito thought, she's enjoying this. The pain he felt quickly disappeared, to be replaced by a cold, bitter anger. I'll wipe that goddamn smile off that bitch's face one of these days... see if I don't. Despite the intense fury that was roiling inside of his soul, outwardly; Chito maintained a look of sheer pleasure at his visitors' arrival.

The two boys split up, with Simon sitting beside Jesus' bed and Damien coming across to Chito. Samantha, perhaps realising the incongruousness of standing alone beside the door tentatively wandered over to Simon. She pulled up another chair, and moved it around to sit on the opposite side of Jesus' bed.

Chito looked over at Damien and forced himself to shed a tear from his right eye.

"Samuel didn't make it... did he?"

Damien just shook his head sadly and Chito's single tear became a constant stream.

"Oh Ddddamien," he wailed; "we tried so hard, but that guy... no! He's not a guy... he's bloody supernatural... he was just too much for Jesus and me. I'm so, so sorry Damien... we should have saved him."

Overcome, Damien leant in and hugged Chito, who winced at the pain the embrace caused, definitely helping with the crocodile tears.

"It's ok Chito... it's ok... nobody blames you. We're so proud of what you tried to do for our brother. You're right though, that was no ordinary man you two tangled with — that was the devil himself; Beelzebub. Thank you both for trying... from all of us."

At Damien's words, Chito pulled back and wiped the tears from his eyes.

"Thank you Damien... you don't know how much that means to me."

Damien patted him gently on his undamaged arm. "Why don't you tell me what actually happened after we left you last night."

Samantha had half an ear cocked to the conversation, at her bed, and half cocked to Chito's bed. She shook her head softly; give that man an "Oscar", she thought... damn he's good!

Chito relayed the events of the evening that led up to the confrontation with Beelzebub. He omitted anything that might cast aspersions on his and Jesus' role and embellished the part they had played in the fight, insisting he did manage to land a couple of telling blows on Beelzebub; before succumbing to the wicked evilness of the devil's tail.

"I might be a mess Damien... but I've got a feeling that bastard's nursing a sore jaw and a black eye today."

Despite the circumstances Damien couldn't help but chuckle softly at his friend's bravado, in the face of such devastating injuries.

"Oh... by the way..." Damien began, but was cut off by the chirp of his cell-phone. He pulled it from his pocket and glanced at the screen.

"Oh... it's Mama, I'd better answer this ha!"

Chito smiled bravely and nodded his head. Damien stood up from the bed and moved away a short distance before clicking the accept icon.

"Mama... what's up?"

Chito watched him carefully trying to discern from Damien's words the gist of the phone call. His responses, were unfortunately, fairly monosyllabic and consisted of a series of "aha's, okays, and sure Mama's." He hit the disconnect button and turned thoughtfully to Simon and Samantha.

"That was Mama;" he announced.

Samantha, who had automatically tuned into Damien's mind as soon as he answered the call, already knew what it was about, but that didn't stop her sarcastically replying; "really... we would never have guessed... hehehe."

Damien looked at his sister in annoyance and consternation. Sheesh... she becomes more of a bitch every day, he thought.

"I heard that, arsehole," Samantha rapidly countered in his mind.

Damien immediately put up his mental block to keep her out. "Bitch!" he repeated in his head.

"So, what's up Dame;" Simon spoke up.

Damien looked over to his boyfriend with adoration; "ahhhh... uhhhm... Mama said we're leaving for Manila first thing in the morning. She said Papa and her have an idea and it's to do with Samuel."

Samantha showed her annoyance at the news. "Tomorrow! Tomorrow! God... what's with all the rush?"

Damien smiled a little too sweetly at his beloved sister. "Who knows... but one thing I do know is that what Mama and Papa says... goes... right! You're not the boss yet Sammy!"

Samantha scowled at him, but instead of replying just leaned over Jesus' bed and grinned at Simon. Speaking in a voice clearly designed for everyone in the room to hear she whispered; "Simon dear, how on earth do you ever put up with that pompous, little prig?"

Simon threw his head back and roared with laughter. "Well sweetie," he simpered in the most effeminate voice he could muster; "it helps when you're in love with the pompous, little prig."

That brought a smile to even Samantha's scowling face and lightened the heavy atmosphere of the room. Their interchange was interrupted by the sounds of movement from the other bed.

"Chito! What *are* you doing? You're in no condition to get out of bed." Damien shouted.

Chito looked at him determinedly. "We're going back with you... it was all agreed wasn't it?"

Damien sighed; "Of course we want you both to join us... but come on... look at the mess the pair of you are. There's no way you can travel in that state."

Chito swung his legs off the bed and struggled to stand; balancing on his one good foot. He reached for the IV-line holder to try and gain some support, but before he grasped it, Damien had crossed the distance between them and grabbed him around the waist, holding him up.

"Now get back into bed pleeease Chito;" Damien implored him.

Ignoring him, Chito sat on the edge of the bed and fixed Damien with a hard stare.

"Listen my friend; we are part of this mission now — part of the family. We've all been through hell together and neither of us is prepared to be left behind, languishing in a Las Vegas hospital bed."

He took a deep breath and grimaced as a spasm of pain swept through him. "We're not going to be separated now Damien — you, JC, Maria, all of you, are our life now, so please don't suggest that we can't come with you. We can and we will!" he added with absolute finality.

Damien looked in awe at Chito and recognised his determination and indomitable spirit. "Well... what can I say? I can't argue with you, can I?" Chito just shook his head, smiling.

"Okay guys, well if you and Jesus are coming, I'd better talk to the hospital about organising some transport to the airport and some stretchers... or at the very least some wheelchairs." He rubbed his hand across his forehead and looked at Chito. "Are you absolutely sure? You don't want to wait a week or so and follows us later?"

Chito dropped his head. "Damien, something big is about to happen. Evil is loose in the world. If the worst comes to the worst... well, we want to be with you guys."

Damien was so touched by his speech that he struggled for words.

"Alright... alright, ahhhm... okay....ahhhh, yeah, right, yes, ah, okay, I'll go and talk to the hospital administrators." He looked across at Samantha.

"Sam, you get on the phone to Papa — tell him what's happening and get him to organise two extra seats for Chito and Jesus." Damien looked at Chito's grateful face and chuckled...."better make that room for a couple of stretchers eh Sammy."

Samantha breathed a sigh of relief. She knew Bubba wanted them all there with the family, but she guessed he hadn't banked on their sudden return to Pangutaran Island; so at least this way Chito and Jesus would be with them.

She pulled her cell phone out of her bag and began to call her father. Damien, meantime, had turned a full circle twice and still seemed flustered about what to do next. It was Simon who saved the situation by grabbing him by the shoulders, turning him toward the hospital room door, and pushing him toward it.

Damien responded with a quick wave over his shoulder; "right, right... hospital administrator, right!"

Simon meantime busied himself helping Chito to struggle into some clothes suitable for travelling in; rather than the old, floppy hospital gowns in which it was almost impossible to maintain one's dignity.

. . .

They were standing, clustered, in a tight group outside the house that had been their home for several months; just waiting for their driver to load all the suitcases into the limousine they had hired to take them to the airport. Chito and Jesus would be delivered directly to the plane by ambulance and would be loaded on, to await the arrival of the others.

Damien and Simon stood off to one side, heads close together whispering to each other. Samantha glanced over at them and shuddered slightly. Damn, I hate those two, she thought, but then images of what Bubba required of her came flooding back into her mind and she gulped. It's a long way from over she thought. I need to keep my focus.

Nobody had even asked Simon if he was coming with them and he had never even asked if it was alright. It was just a given! He was very much part of their family now and Damien was filled with gratitude that they had not only accepted Simon and shown their love for him right from the beginning, but that they had so readily and happily accepted Damien for who he really was. He reached up one finger and gently brushed it across Simon's face, marvelling in how lucky he was to have found this wonderful companion who could share his life with him. To think, I wasn't all that keen on coming here in the first place, he grinned to himself. It just shows you how circumstance and fate really work.

Perhaps surprisingly, Petrona stood with the group also — still slightly apart, but she was going with them too. She had spent several hours the previous evening with Maria, relating the joys and highlights of her and Sammy's whirlwind romance in New York. For Maria it was so wonderful to just revel in her son's life and exploits through the eyes of this beautiful, smart, young woman. For a brief time she forgot the pain, and laughed along with Petrona, at her tales of Samuel's incredible shyness around women, his funny mannerisms, and his ridiculously annoying habits.

At one point both woman had collapsed on the bed in hysterics before Petrona sat up and asked Maria if she could join their mission. Maria was moved and stunned by the request.

"I want to do something special for the world. I told Sammy that what you were doing was making a difference and that he should join you."

She wiped away a tear that had started to form; "so... in a way it's my fault."

Maria reached out to comfort her, but she pulled back and smiled. "It's okay Maria, it was still the right decision and I want to honour his memory by joining with you guys... if you'll have me."

Maria was delighted with her offer and immediately told her so. It did occur to her that having Samuel's true love there when they tried to bring him back might be just the impetus needed to make it work. After all, it was her own undying love of JC that brought *him* back... wasn't it? She hadn't told anyone of their plan, so it was slightly cryptic, for Petronas, when she said;

"That's a wonderful idea... you might make all the difference."

Everything settled the two women hugged and resumed their hilarious recounting of their mutual love's life until the very early hours of the morning.

. . .

Pastor Nolasco came bustling up to the group and embraced them one by one, wishing them God-speed and safe travels. His face seemed to have aged considerably since that carefree day just a few months earlier when they had embraced at the gate. So much had happened in the intervening weeks that would change them all forever. He seemed to have taken much of the pain and responsibility, for the horrors, on his own shoulders and it reflected in his lined and weary visage. When he reached JC and Maria, he hugged them both long and hard.

"I'm so... so... sorry it all had to end like this JC... I had such dreams and visions of your both being here, and such high hopes of bringing so many more souls to redemption... but....it all went so horribly wrong..." His voice faded as he broke down in tears.

JC reached for the man, his heart full of compassion, and placing one hand on either shoulder he commanded Joe to look at him.

"Joe, my dear, old friend... none of this is your doing. Evil is loose in the world and sooner or later we will have to confront it head on. The job you and your team has done here has been extraordinary — don't you ever forget that."

Still sobbing lightly, Jhoemar smiled and nodded his head. JC gave him one last hug and then waved for everyone to board the limousine. As he climbed into his seat, he turned to Pastor Nolasco and ominously added;

"The battle for Earth has just begun my friend... and *we* intend to win it—.

. . .

Chapter 22

As the tarmac whizzed by underneath the plane's wings and the giant metal bird rose ponderously, into the skies, Maria lay back in her seat and breathed a long, deep sigh. It had been an enormously gut-wrenching few days for her and the family, but especially for her, and she knew she hadn't had much time to grieve for the loss of her little man. She closed her eyes and allowed herself the luxury of remembering long lost, happy, halcyon days, when their only concern seemed to be what flavour ice-cream to buy.

Samuel's body was safely stored inside a large refrigerated container in the aircraft's hull. Maria had no idea whether her crazy idea of trying to bring Samuel back had any validity, or possibility of success, but she knew she had to try.

I brought JC back from the dead, didn't I? So why not Samuel? Her mind wandered endlessly through the corridors of her memory. When she had married JC she knew this was not going to be a life so ordinary — but nothing had prepared her for the shock and horror of losing her first-born. Unconsciously she reached for JC's hand beside her and felt the comforting, reassuring squeeze back, just to let her know that he was there, as always, and willing to talk.

She wasn't ready to talk yet; not about this anyway. In her mind, she truly felt that talking about Samuel's death would be presumptuous, whilst they still had dreams of reviving him. To discuss her dead son would be tantamount to having given up on him and there was no damn way she was ready to do that yet.

She found herself wondering about JC's father — the Lord God Almighty! Just what sort of being was he? Was he truly as seemingly heartless as he was sometimes painted by authors and theologians? She'd always felt just a little cheated, that unlike other women, she'd never had the opportunity to meet her husband's family. JC talked very little about his days before "them". Oh sure... he joked, and played around, with Michael and gave the impression that everything in heaven had been sweetness and light, but Maria always knew that his first experience on earth, those 2,000 odd years ago had changed him indelibly.

He had begun to glimpse just exactly what the human experience was and despite the horror and pain of his death on the cross at Calvary he had gained a deep insight into the depth of the human spirit — the great joys and sorrows that humanity endured on their journey of life. She had little doubt that the past two millennia had been very hard on him. He had seen and experienced something that few in heaven, least of all his father, could possibly understand.

She understood why he had been drawn to her and why they had ended up together. Yes... it was love that brought them into this life together, but it was more than that — it was, as if she was destined to be the one to bring JC back to where he truly belonged; back to earth and back to his humanity. His previous time on earth had changed him forever and it was love that would be the catalyst for him to discover his true mission — that of saving humanity.

She smiled softly to herself; yes, no matter what happens, I'm truly blessed to have found him and to have loved him. She opened her eyes to look on the profile of her husband and was totally unsurprised to see that he was actually staring at her. She blushed slightly and smiled shyly at him.

"Thinking about me were you? he asked, with a grin.

"Oh...." she exclaimed; "don't be so damn presumptuous ha! It's not all about you, you know;" smacking him on his shoulder as she said it.

Rubbing his shoulder furiously in mock pain he just kept on grinning in that slightly infuriating way of his. "Aha!" was his only comment, before he turned back to the movie he had been watching on his entertainment console.

Maria just poked her tongue out at him and closed her eyes, turning her head back to the window. Grrrrr, she thought, why the hell does he always have to be so right about everything; it can be so bloody annoying sometimes. She allowed herself to drift off into a comfortable, deep sleep letting the rhythmic thrum of the plane's giant engines gently rock her into dreamland. Her last conscious thought was; well that proves he's truly human — he can be a pompous prig... hehehe.

. . .

They were back where so much of their previous adventure had begun — the tiny island of Pangutaran, in the South Sulu Sea, but this time they were returning with heavy hearts and a large refrigerated box that contained the frozen mortal remains of one Samuel Castillo.

Angelo, Gabriel, Ronnie and Delia were all there to meet them off the boat but their delight at seeing their friends again was quickly tempered by the horrific news that Samuel had been slain by Beelzebub. They stood just outside the tiny chapel that had marked the true beginnings of their journeys.

For Ronnie and Delia; JC and Maria, it had been the place where their lives together had started. For Angelo and Gabriel, it had for many years been their sanctuary, their home and their place of worship. Lovingly restored, all those years ago, by the original team and maintained in the years since by an eager procession of loyal islanders, the chapel was more than a place of worship to them — it was their spiritual home.

The four younger children had been sent to Ronnie and Delia's house, to play with their children, for the duration of the planned ceremony; JC believing they were just too young to witness what might happen there that day. He moved slowly into the middle of the group of his family and friends that were gathered there that sunlit morning and gently explained to them what Maria and he had in mind to try and bring Samuel back.

Strangely enough, nobody expressed too much shock or surprise at what was in store. It was as if they had known all along the reason for returning to this beautiful island and this magical, little chapel. Part of the group, but also feeling slightly apart, Chito and Jesus, still swathed in bandages and seated in wheelchairs, exchanged glances.

Both men were wearing baseball caps, pulled low over their forehead, ostensibly to protect them from the harsh tropical sun, but there was also an element of hiding the shame that screamed out from their foreheads. The twin carvings of an inverted cross and a pentacle were still raw, livid and sharp, and marked them as something different; something to be feared even.

Ironically, they were as proud of their marks, as they were embarrassed by them. Part of them longed to proudly display to the world that they were indeed an integral part of the Evil Alliance and yet deep down they knew the marks were to be feared. Chito leant slightly toward his friend and whispered;

"shit Danny, I'm not so sure this is such a good idea... I mean, it's sure as hell gonna piss Bubba off."

Jesus raised his eyebrows in assent and slowly shook his head. "JC's playing with fire, this time;" he murmured back.

Elsewhere in the group reactions were varied; the "originals" Gabes, Ange, Delia and Ronnie had seen it all before. They were there when the power of Maria's love and faith had raised JC from the dead. Nothing would shock or surprise them when it came to their leader and his amazing wife. They were thrilled and excited about the possibility that their little Samuel could be brought back to them.

For Petrona, the news was like a last minute reprieve, to a death-row inmate. The entire flight back to Manila she had been trying to reconcile herself to not having the opportunity to experience the wonderful, loving, relationship that she was sure Samuel had beckoned her with, albeit so tantalisingly briefly. It hurt so bad to know they would never have the chance to experience all those things that lifetime partners get to experience together; both the joys and the sorrows. She felt cheated, and she felt such sorrow for the loss of Samuel's potential for the world. She knew he had greatness inside him — a greatness the world would now never get to see.

By the time they had landed in Manila, however, she had convinced herself that what she needed to do was to throw herself wholeheartedly into JC and Maria's mission — to honour the memory of her beautiful man; her Samuel. The idea that there might be a chance at resurrection was like an offer of a glass of cool, clear, crystal water to a man dying of thirst. She just hoped the glass would not cruelly be snatched away again at the last minute. She was filled with excitement, anticipation and an equal amount of fear and trepidation.

Simon and Damien had automatically grabbed each other and hugged, when Damien's father had imparted the plan to try to bring Samuel back. Both men had secretly and independently blamed themselves for what had happened to him. If only we hadn't left early and if only we'd waited for him and walked home with him, things might have turned out very differently; Damien had chastised himself on more than one occasion. Equally, Simon had agonised over the fact that it was their selfish behaviour in wanting to share their relationship with JC and Maria that had led to Samuel, Chito and Jesus being alone on their walk home.

Maybe he and Damien couldn't have made that much of a difference, especially given the carnage Beelzebub had wreaked, but that didn't stop him feeling guilty for not being there. The idea that their guilt could be salved by Samuel's resurrection appealed greatly to both of them.

Only Samantha seemed upset by JC's news.

She stomped her foot hard on the ground and bit her lip furiously to stop herself from screaming out; No... no... no... you can't undo what Beelzebub has done. Samuel is gone... leave him be!

She knew two things for sure. Bubba would be furious about this crazy scheme and she couldn't do anything to stop it. Bubba had made it quite clear what her role was to be and it wasn't to declare her loyalties just yet. The time would come for that, he had purred to her, last time they had been together. With enormous willpower she plastered a smile on her face and tried to look as happy and excited as everyone else.

She could feel Damien probing the outer perimeter of her mind. He wanted to know what she thought about their father's plans. She immediately focused on blocking him, and keeping him from discovering exactly what it was she *was* thinking. My time will come, she reminded herself. She cast a glance over at her twin; currently embracing his little boyfriend; and she spat out in a harsh whisper; "and so will yours little man... so will yours!"

. . .

JC had announced that the ritual, the ceremony, the resurrection, call it what you will, would be held just on sundown that evening, commencing exactly at 6.27p.m. the advertised sunset time for the South Sulu Sea. He had suggested that everyone get some rest, as he suspected it would be a long and arduous night.

Jesus and Chito had been given a tent to shelter in during the day as some recognition of their injuries and their still fragile condition. Jesus was reclining on the stretcher that had been provided, shifting himself occasionally to try and find a more comfortable position that didn't chafe his wounds. Chito sat at a small table in the centre of the tent, his head bowed and his fingers steepled, resembling an attitude of prayer.

"Whose ya praying to Chog?" Jesus teased him.

Chito looked up and fixed his compadre with a stare that would have terrified a lesser man. Jesus though, wasn't frightened of his friend — he would back himself to kick Chito's butt, if he had to.

"I was just thinking arsehole," Chito hissed at him. "It's just a shame you don't do more of that sometimes."

The constant pain was getting on Jesus' nerves and he wasn't about to take any shit from Chito. He seemed about to leap off the cot and go for him, when the tent-flap flew open and

Samantha strode in. Chito looked at Jesus and waved him back down; "save your strength buddy, you might need it later."

He fixed his gaze on Samantha, and even though he was swathed in bandages and wracked with pain, he couldn't help smiling at and lusting after her. "Well... if it isn't the Queen herself;" he sneered, "and to what do we owe the honour of your personal appearance."

Samantha was in no mood for Chito's innuendoes, or his childish goading. She walked across to him and slapped him hard across the face.

"Just don't you forget who I'll be very, very soon! Fine... if you want to spend eternity in torment and pain; then go on... go right ahead and fuck with me... but, I wouldn't advise it ha!"

As Chito sat ruefully rubbing his stinging cheek and contemplating whether to actually let it ride, Samantha's face softened and she almost tenderly reached out and patted the back of his hand.

"Ay, Ay, Ay," she remonstrated, "why must we always argue ha? We're on the same team remember."

She brushed her hair out of her face and grabbing a camp stool sat down next to Chito. "So," she addressed the pair of them, "what do you make of Daddy's plans?" Her face tightened before she added; "what's Bubba going to have to say about it... I mean... shit... what do you think he'll do?"

"Bubba will do... what Bubba does best!" As usual his sudden appearance caused everyone to jump.

I don't think I'll ever get used to him just turning up unannounced, Samantha thought, as she turned toward the voice and rushed to hug her future lover.

Jesus painfully pushed himself off the bed;

"Bubba," he exclaimed, "why the hell you had to hurt us so bad....sheesh, a flesh wound or two would have done, but this... bloody..."

Bubba cut off his protests with a wave of his hand.

"Had to make it look realistic now didn't I boys? Had to make them think you battled me hard... right?"

Jesus pouted sourly and looked about to launch into another tirade when a sharp look from Chito pulled him up. He slowly nodded his head and mumbled; "yeah... yeah... guess so;" the surly pout remaining though.

Bubba just breezed past it and announced cheerily; "Oh yeah... Bubba boy has a plan."

He fixed his eyes on Jesus and Chito; "you two... all you have to do is go along with that idiot JC... just agree to everything, right? Don't give away your hand yet, just be a part of their silly, little team. You got it?"

Chito and Jesus looked at each other and shrugged their shoulders before nodding.

"Good... good;" Bubba looked at Samantha; "and you my Queen, you have to keep playing your role of the dutiful daughter... yes?" Samantha smiled and kissed his cheek.

"Of course Bubba, whatever you want."

Bubba's lips cracked wide and his eyes twinkled. "This is going to be fun guys. We gonna give 'em something they never bargained for... hehehe."

Pulling Samantha over to the corner of the tent he whispered to her; "you know what your duty is Sammy; but now's not the time... it will be soon though; very soon... so you be ready."

Samantha gulped hard. In all the excitement of the past few days she had forgotten her most important and difficult assignment still lay ahead. She sought strength from his fiery red eyes, before smiling and nodding. "Of course Bubba, I'm ready."

He patted her gently on the head and then he was gone. No puff of smoke, no dramatic gestures — just gone. Samantha breathed deeply — damn she hated that!

. . .

At just before 6pm everyone slowly filed into the little chapel. Samuel's body had been carefully removed from the refrigerated container, earlier in the day, and was now at the head of the church on a raised dais, just in front of the altar. There was a palpable sense of anticipation in the air, but it was tempered by a degree of fear and reverence at what they expected to witness there that night.

The chapel had been lit by a succession of around a hundred candles that lined the walls every few feet and surrounded the lifeless form of Samuel. Their flickering wicks, in the gentle breeze that wafted in off the sea, plus the dying light of the setting sun gave the entire scene an ethereal, perhaps even macabre perspective.

Nobody spoke as they all filed slowly past Samuel's body; each leaning down and whispering something, or softly kissing his face. JC had done his best to cover the hateful inverted cross and pentacle scar on Samuel's forehead, with a linen cloth that he had wrapped around his head.

When Maria came level with the body of her beloved son, she stumbled briefly and JC thrust out an arm to stop her from falling. Smiling tightly her thanks to him, she turned to face the body. In a quavering, yet strong voice she addressed him. "Sssammy, mmmy darling. I don't know what will happen here this evening, but if this truly is to be the last time we spend together, just know two things; Mama and Papa love you very much, and one day we will all be together again."

As the tears rolled down her cheeks she turned, smiled to everyone and added; "but... that's not going to happen is it? We're going to see Samuel rise from this altar tonight... I just know it."

JC placed an arm around her shoulder and with a final glance at the body, led her to her seat in the front row of pews. Returning to stand behind the body he waited until everyone had filed past and had an opportunity to say their possible goodbyes to a friend, a lover, a brother, and a son. When Damien, who had been last in line, had filed past, JC signalled for Samantha and him to join him on the raised platform.

He held his arms up and addressed his small family. "I'm not even sure if we have the moral right to be trying to do what we are doing here tonight, but I know we must, for my sake and for Samuel's mother's sake. I believe that with the special powers Damien and Samantha both possess, the magical power of this very special place we are sitting in, the power of our united prayer and our love for Samuel, we may have an opportunity to bring our baby back."

He paused, placing one arm around Damien's shoulder and one arm around Samantha's. "But... even our power I suspect is not enough so... first we need to ask the Archangel Michael to come and assist us."

JC knelt behind Samuel's body, pulling Damien and Samantha down with him. He stretched both arms toward the beautiful, exposed roof beams of the Chapel and very softly intoned; "Michael, my dearest, my oldest friend, if ever there was an occasion when I needed your help, your comfort and your solace, this is such a time. Michael, I implore you, please come —

help your brother." JC lowered his arms and continued kneeling, his head bowed and his eyes closed.

An eerie silence descended over the chapel, the wind died away and the candles ceased to flutter. The candle light, direct now, brought sharpness, where previously there had been shadows. It was Simon; seated two rows back who heard it first — a soft buzzing, like a swarm of angry bees, getting closer and closer.

"It's coming from just outside," he exclaimed excitedly.

Heads turned and craned to try and catch a glimpse of what might be making the noise. Like a beacon of hope, the last dying ray of the tropical sun, as it gently sank beneath the surface of the South Sulu Sea, illuminated the entrance to the Chapel in a burst of orange light. Into the light slowly descended the warrior figure that was, the Archangel Michael.

He was dressed in his full battle regalia — burnished gold breastplate and helmet, with his robes of deepest purple. His helmet shone and sparkled in that last ray of light, with the twinkling of a thousand precious gems. The multicoloured feathers of his headdress, with his long, flowing blond hair, just added the final touch to his impressive arrival. At well over six feet he cut an imposing figure and appeared to fill the entire doorway with his frame. With no preamble he strode into the chapel, heading directly for JC — his face drawn, in anger, or perhaps annoyance.

As he passed Chito and Jesus he visibly winced when he noticed the twin marks of Beelzebub on their foreheads, and his right hand tightened on the jewel encrusted handle of his mighty broadsword. Giving them as wide a berth as possible he continued to the front and planted himself, feet wide apart, in front of the still kneeling JC.

"Get up boy!" that stentorian voice of his boomed out. "Get up and talk to me."

JC rose tentatively and when he saw the expression on his friend's face he visibly blanched.

"Ahhhhm, Michael;" he managed; "I see you still have the flair for the dramatic entrance," he added, trying to lighten the tension everyone was feeling.

"Ahhhh... well... the reason we asked you here..."

Michael cut him off with a sweep of his hand that grazed JC's cheek.

"Of course I know why you called me here;" he boomed; "do you think I haven't been watching you... I know exactly what you're up to".

JC tried a smile; "and... so... will you help us?"

Michael's countenance relaxed and he let out a long, frustrated, sigh.

"Ohhhh... JC my boy. What you want to do here... it's... it's just too much ha! Samuel's gone my friend and much as it pains me to say so, I don't think we really have the right to bring him back."

Maria jumped up from her seat and ran to Michael, falling to her knees in front of him, tears streaming down her face. She tugged on the hem of his tunic, like a peasant seeking favour from a Lord.

"Mmmmichael," she blubbered; "ppplease don't deny me this... pppplease. I can't lose my little boy. Oh Michael... ppplease, you must help us."

Seeing her so desperate and tearful just broke his heart. He knelt down beside her and grasping her underneath her arms easily lifted her to her feet, where he placed an arm around her waist and held her tight.

"Mich..." she began.

He put a finger to her lips and merely said; "hush now".

Turning back to JC and shaking his head sadly, he scolded him; "Have you forgotten your big speech to your father already ha!"

JC hung his head shamefully... of course he had not forgotten.

"Well let me remind you, shall I? If I remember rightly it went something along the lines of; earth is better, and more exciting than heaven, because there is a permanent sense of urgency — the knowledge that today might be your last day. Humanity lives in the moment; something like that JC?"

JC nodded but couldn't bear to look at Michael's mocking face.

"Two things JC! If, and I do mean if, I decide to do this for you..." he gently cuffed JC under his right ear; "well... for Maria really... then there are a couple of conditions that must apply."

JC looked hopefully at his old friend and signalled with a slight nod of his head for Michael to continue. "Like I said, a couple of conditions. Number one: When the battle comes... and trust me JC it is coming; and we have to rid this Universe of that evil, twisted, creature Beelzebub, you must promise that you will return to heaven and fight alongside me."

JC's face looked forlorn as he contemplated the possible consequences of such a decision. He would have to leave Maria again and take on his Godly persona. He wasn't sure if he was ready for that. Michael saw the conflict in his face and continued on;

"JC, this is going to be a battle for eternity, for all humanity and everything we hold dear... I need you by my side."

He put his left hand on JC's right shoulder; "so... will you agree to the rules?"

JC smiled wryly; "But Michael I'm not sure what my father will say to such a request;" his voice tailed off as he sadly added; "not after what I said to him anyway...".

Michael grinned broadly; "Ha! When it comes to war JC, our father will listen to me. He knows nothing of the art of battle... you just leave him to me."

JC squinted up at Michael, wavering on his decision.

"JC, my dearest friend, Beelzebub will array the most powerful army of evil souls against us. He can call on the most evil of humanity's failures to fight for him, while we only have, the good and the righteous... I truly fear that even with you beside me... this is a war we could lose. Without you, we are surely lost."

Kneeling in front of Michael he bowed his head and briefly sought his own counsel. To everyone in the chapel's relief, who had been hanging on every word of the exchange, he finally looked up, grinned and said;

"I'm in Mickey... but... you said there were two conditions."

Michael giggled; "the second condition is perhaps harder than the first. I'm craving a kiss from your beautiful wife. Unless Maria kisses me, I will not help... hehehe."

The tension was broken and all around the small chapel everyone giggled and laughed aloud.

JC smiled wryly; bloody typical of Mickey, he thought... always the amateur theatrics. He looked to Maria who was kneeling beside him, but he was too slow. She had already jumped to her feet, flung her arms around Michael's neck and was raining kisses all over his face.

"Ohhhh, Michael... thank you, thank you, thank you... just consider this an advance payment ha! There's more to come."

Grinning broadly Michael gently unwound Maria from around his neck and patted her sweetly on the head.

"Thank you my dear, I shall look forward to the next instalment... hehehe."

All business-like now Michael bent down and raised JC to his feet. "So, I guess I'm cornered now and have no choice."

JC looked into his friend's eyes and realised he was now just playing with him.

"So, you'll do it Mickey?"

Michael nodded; "yeah, of course I will... how I could possibly refuse now?"

He paused and looked around the congregation. "Okay... so, you're right about one thing JC, I can't do this on my own. I'm going to need Samantha and Damien to help me with their power and I'm going to need all of you to focus and pray like you've never focused and prayed before... you got it?"

He quickly signalled everyone to gather around Samuel's body, which still lay unmoving in his coffin on the dais. He instructed the congregation to kneel in a circle around the dais, link hands and begin to pray.

"Think of nothing else but Samuel — when he was alive. Remember his smile, his walk, his way of talking. I want your minds to be totally filled with a living, joyous Samuel."

Nodding assent, they quickly knelt and linked hands and followed his instructions.

He reached for Damien and Samantha's hands and took them away from the others. Speaking so softly they had to lean in to make sure they caught his words exactly, he told them they would climb up on the coffin, and link hands across it, over Samuel's body.

"You and Samantha, unlike the others are not to pray, not to close your eyes — you are to focus your eyes and your minds at one exact point on Sammy's body — his heart and you are to just will in your minds for his heart to start again. You don't say anything, you don't look anywhere else, you don't think anything else... just will that heart to start beating again. Okay?"

Both of them quickly looked at each other before shrugging their shoulders and nodding their understanding.

Once they were all in position, Michael turned his face to the heavens and slowly, quietly began to chant. The words were not any language anyone there, except JC had ever heard. It was the language of heaven; mysterious, mystical, powerful and steeped in eons of tradition. As Michael chanted there began a small vibration deep within the earth, which rose in volume and intensity the longer he spoke. Pretty soon the entire chapel was shaking and the three of them struggled to maintain their upright position above the body.

When the voice came, it came with such an explosive force, that Michael, Damien and Samantha were all tossed to the ground in a tangled heap.

"STOP!"

That single, vehement word stopped everything dead in its tracks. The shaking and the rumbling ceased. All eyes on the dais turned toward the door.

Framed in the doorway, the flickering candles casting shadows across his face, was the massive, naked form of the true

Beelzebub. Gone was the pretence of a simple, elderly man, and in its place, the pure personification of evil, in humanoid form.

He stood over seven feet tall and filled the entire doorway of the tiny chapel. His head was crowned with seven horns of fire that burst from it, in waves of heat. The door frame of the chapel was already blackening slightly under the ferocious onslaught.

Beelzebub held his hands out almost in a gesture, of entreaty, of friendship, but when he spoke there was no tone of reconciliation or grace in his words, or his manner.

Holding one hand out; the long gnarly finger, with its twelve inch nails that tapered to a needle point; gesturing directly to Michael, his voice boomed again. The chapel seemed to physically shudder under the violence of his words and many of the hundreds of candles within the chapel, flickered and died.

"How dare you! That soul is mine; it bears my mark — the mark of the beast. How dare you try to steal that soul from me?"

He began to stride down the chapel aisle, the vicious, evil, tail swinging menacingly behind him. "Leave him be, you hear. He's mine!"

Recovering his poise Michael drew his flaming broadsword and ran to face Beelzebub in the chapel aisle. Samantha's immediate thought was one of immense excitement and utter pleasure. She had never seen the true Bubba revealed and he enthralled her. She wanted to rush to his side, throw her arms around his neck, and proclaim her love for him. She so desperately wanted to join him in this battle against her family. She half moved to stand, before she remembered her role in this play.

"Not yet little one" she could hear Bubba's soft, loving tones in her mind. "Not yet my Queen — you know when; your time will come."

She checked herself and realising that Damien and JC had both rushed to Michael's side, she ran to join them.

Michael turned and smiled at them, but gestured them back with his sword.

"No my friends, this little argument is between Bubba and me." He turned back to face the monstrous apparition who had stopped a few feet short of Michael's sword-sweep arc.

He grinned at Michael, revealing a perfect set of gleaming white teeth, honed to a razor-sharpness.

"Ahhhh, Mickey, finally we see each other again... it's been too long my old friend."

Michael threw his head back and laughed. "No Bubba, we were never friends. You were always an arsehole and I always despised you... nice to see some things never change."

He shifted his broadsword into both hands and held it in front of him, so that its gleaming tip was just mere feet from Bubba's face.

Bubba involuntarily took a small step backward and grinned back at him.

"You're right... nothing changes Mickey; you're still the arrogant, little, self-righteous prick you always were — never mind that tiresome, bloody mate of yours, JC there. Now give me back my hard-earned soul. He's mine and you can't argue about that. He bears my mark... he's mine."

Michael took a step forward and raised the sword over his head; "so... if, he's yours, you better come and take him then."

"So be it!" Bubba exclaimed, and in one single motion, with lightening speed, that fearsome tail whipped between Bubba's legs and sliced for Michael's face.

Michael rolled his head slightly and the tail whistled past, just catching the edge of his left cheek, tearing the skin, but not reaching bone.

He smiled ruefully and spat at the blood that was already pooling in the corner of his mouth.

"You're going to have to do better than that," he taunted, before crouching and thrusting upward with the sword. It entered Bubba's body just above his right knee, slicing through muscle, tendon and bone like a hot knife through butter.

His right leg almost severed, Bubba sank to the ground on his good knee and looked up at Michael imploringly.

"No Mickey... no... don't kill me... please... please... not again," he begged.

Michael hesitated before leaning in even closer and reverse swinging his broadsword, as he sought to slice off the head of the beast.

Bubba bent his head, it seemed almost in resignation at what was coming, exposing his neck for the inevitable final cut. The broadsword; trailing flame, whistled mournfully as it sliced through the air, before clattering harmlessly and nosily onto the marble tiles.

Michael looked down, shock and disbelief mirrored in his face. The triple prong of Bubba's wickedly barbed tail had entered his chest just below his left nipple, splitting his ribs into splinters, piercing his heart and exiting through his back; where it stayed, quivering and covered in blood.

As Bubba flicked his tail sharply and withdrew it with a flourish, there was an enormous sucking noise that caused everyone in the Chapel to shudder. He pushed himself to his feet and balancing on his one leg he began to chuckle.

"That *was* fun! The impetuous little prick thought he had me. Ah well... we live and learn."

He spat down onto Michael's body. "Well... in his case, we die and learn... hehehe. Still, that's the bastard about being immortal — he'll come back again to haunt me someday." He looked at the crowd on the dais who were still cowering in fear, shock and disbelief at what they had just witnessed.

Almost friendly-like, Bubba spread his arms and added; "still, that'll be fun too; killing him over and over again."

He reached over to a pew beside him and with immense strength just ripped out the backing rail behind it. Snapping the four inch by four inch solid Narra rail in half, as if it was a mere toothpick, he placed one end under his right armpit and using it as a crutch advanced toward the cowering group, and Samuel's body.

They backed away from him as he got closer and chuckling he reached down into the coffin and effortlessly picked up Samuel's dead body, throwing it over his shoulder, like a fireman with a rescued victim.

"Right, my lad, time we got you home ha! It's been quite a day! I haven't had to work this hard to win back one of my souls for centuries... hehehe."

"NO!"

Maria's scream of anguish pierced the chapel as she jumped to her feet and ran at Beelzebub, fully intending to knock him from there to kingdom come.

"You can't have him! He's my little boy! You..."

Bubba's tail whipped up and smashed into her chest, knocking her sideways across the dais, but fortunately not piercing her skin. She flew into the altar and slid to the ground unconscious. JC looked at Bubba, glanced at Michael's prostrate body, and then at his wife's unconscious form.

Love won out and he ran to her motionless body, kneeling and trying to revive her.

Bubba looked over toward the fallen Maria and murmured;

"Not only can I have your precious son my dear Maria, one day, soon, I'll have you as well... hehehe."

Turning to the rest of the cowering group and with a smile; a conspiratorial wink, to Samantha; and a nod of his head, to Chito and Jesus... he and Samuel were just gone; just disappeared—.

. . .

Chapter 23

The only sound that could be heard in the gloom of the old chapel came from Petrona; curled up in the foetal position at the back of the altar, sobbing and wailing mournfully. Damien and Simon were the first to react, rushing over to her and lifting her to her feet; hugging her, rocking her, comforting her and whispering words of encouragement to her. Samantha ran to her parents and knelt beside JC who by this stage had managed to revive Maria, who was sitting upright, coughing and wincing in pain at her obviously damaged side. Angelo and Gabriel had rushed over to the still motionless form of Michael.

Angelo looked at his friend;

"Michael's immortal right? So... he's got to come back to life sometime... doesn't he?" Gabriel shrugged his shoulders and began to examine Michael's wounds.

"God knows Ange, I'm no expert on this stuff. I guess you're right, but bloody hell! Looking at that hole in his chest... I'm damned if I know. It's an absolute mess!"

With Maria managing to stagger to her feet, wincing terribly from the pain and clutching onto JC for dear life, they hobbled over to join Angelo and Gabriel. Ignoring her pain, Maria pulled away and walked across to the small cluster of Petrona, Simon and Damien.

Smiling reassuringly at the two boys, she waved for them to join JC and the others. "This takes a woman's touch;" she said softly to her son.

Petrona was still shaking and whimpering incoherently. A woman's touch was exactly what was needed Maria thought to herself. She slapped Petrona on the side of her face with as much force as she was able to muster in her weakened condition.

The tough love seemed to do the trick, and as Petrona's eyes opened wide in shock, Maria saw anger and determination flash briefly in them. She'll be fine Maria thought and was ill-prepared for the return slap that hit her full in the face.

Shaking her head and managing to laugh softly she grabbed Petrona's hands and held them tightly in hers to prevent any repeat.

"Wow, that's quite a swing you've got there Petrona. Now we're not going to get anywhere by being all girly-girly about this right? We have to be strong warriors and fight back with everything we have — not simpering, cowering, little girls. Am I right?"

Petrona took a deep breath and clarity returned to her eyes. She nodded her head to Maria, who released her hands gently and then steered the girl over to join everyone else, who by this stage were all clustered around Michael's body.

"So what happens, JC?" Ronnie was just asking. "Does his body rejuvenate... or what? Do we have to do anything?"

JC looked around at his team and despite the circumstances, he tried to keep them positive.

"Oh, don't worry about Michael; he'll be fine in a few hours — or perhaps I should say his body will."

The looks of confusion and consternation from the others prompted him to continue; "you see, Michael's actually not here anymore. As soon as his body died, Michael... ahhhm, how do I put this? The true essence of Michael left the body and went back to heaven."

"But;" Angelo began, "what happens to his body... do we bury it? What do we do?"

JC managed a chuckle. "No Ange, we sure as hell don't bury it. Michael will want it back soon enough. The body will repair itself in a few hours and he'll come back to claim it again. Shit, if we'd stuck it under six feet of dirt, there'd be hell to pay. Michael would be screaming blue, bloody, murder... hahaha."

His attempt at levity lightened the mood considerably.

"So, what do we do now then?" Gabs ventured.

"Ahhhh... well, for now we just sit and wait for Michael to return and then we plan our strategy."

Maria's punch on JC's shoulder was so hard and so unexpected that he jumped and squealed; "Owwww!"

She immediately launched into him; "sit and wait... sit and wait... I'm not bloody well sitting and waiting for anyone JC. That horrible, evil thing has stolen my son. You're the great Jesus Christ for goodness sake — wwwwe have to do something... there must be something we can do, surely... hhhhe's my son JC..." As her voice started to break, JC turned to her and placing one hand on either shoulder he softly spoke.

"Honey, Michael's right; war *is* coming — a war between good and evil."

He paused. "Do you really think Beelzebub is going to be happy with dominion over some of the Earth? No my darling, he wants it all, the whole damn shooting box. He wants to be the ruler of the Universe and he wants you, me and all of us to spend eternity right where he has been for the past eons — in hell.

There's no way that we *can't* fight him honey — This is going to be a *Holy War*. We just wait for Michael okay babes?"

Maria breathed in deeply and nodded, although JC could see the tears pooling in her eyes; "you're right, I know you are... but it is just so hard..."

He clasped her tight and together they silently rocked.

Samantha secretly grinned; yes Bubba did want it all, and *we* will have it all! I *will* be the Queen of this Universe and I *will* take great pleasure in sending you all to hell... hehehe.

. . .

It was a reflective and quiet group that gathered around the outside dining table that evening to discuss their plans for the future. Nothing had changed; JC was still their leader and they all looked to him for guidance and counsel.

JC, for his part, wasn't so sure he had any good guidance or counsel. He meant what he'd said to Maria earlier, they really did have to just wait and see what Michael had to say. Knowing he needed to show leadership and strength during these trying times he placed both hands on the table, and looking around at his band of "disciples", he addressed them.

"Alright guys... so, we've had a bit of a setback..."

There were a few collective groans around the table, so JC hurried on; "...but that doesn't mean we're going to give up. You heard what Michael said, there's going to be a war; we have to put Beelzebub back where he belongs — in the pits of Hades. We'll be at the forefront of this war and trust me on this; it's going to be brutal."

Ronnie was rubbing his forehead with his hand, looking perplexed.

JC glanced over at him smiling; "ever the practical Ronnie ha; so what's on your mind my friend? What troubles you?"

Ronnie looked a bit sheepish but ventured an opinion;

"I... I... don't know JC... I mean I guess you know about these things better than me, but it seems to me that if the hosts of heaven go up against one man... well, I mean to say... where's the war in that? Surely you all have the collective power to just crush this Beelzebub like a pesky little ant?"

He smiled awkwardly at them and shrugged his shoulders, but noted that more than one of them nodded, indicating either they agreed with him, or it was something that had crossed their minds also.

JC acknowledged the logic of what Ronnie had said but reminded them that it wasn't just Beelzebub they would be up against.

"The Prince of Darkness has his own army, my friends, it's not just him."

He sighed at the thought; "he can call on every evil man that ever walked this earth, to fight for him, and believe me there's no shortage of them."

Angelo was the first to grasp exactly what JC was saying; "Oh my God;" he exclaimed. "You mean to say we will be facing the likes of; Atilla the Hun, Napoleon, Idi Amin, Hitler, Pol Pot... all those evil bastards?"

JC chuckled; "well yeah... them... and a few more besides..."

He actually grinned at them before adding; "...although some of you might be genuinely surprised who actually ended up where, in the end. History's written by the victors and sometimes they do have a tendency to over-embellish the evil character of the vanquished... but yeah... there's definitely going to be some pretty evil people that we're going up against."

This deepened the darkness of the mood at the table even more, so JC acted quickly and thumping the table with the flat of his hand, he shouted; "come on peoples, not so glum ha! At the end of the day we still have God and the power of right on our side. We *will* win!"

He slammed his fist hard onto the table at the end of his words, causing everyone to jump in fright, but there were tentative nods from everyone, and one particularly loud ***"YEAH!"*** from Maria.

JC gave her a special thank you glance for her support.

She nodded back and then quietly asked; "So, JC... where do we go from here?"

He quickly explained that he had already been on the radio to the founding church in Davao and instructed them to contact Adonis and Jonny so they could rush back and join them. "We're going to need everyone on deck for this one;" he explained.

He was less forthcoming about their overall plans though, knowing full well they needed to discuss things with Michael first, but... he was still not back with them.

"First, we go to Davao and regroup," he said; "then we..."

"Then we get ready for war;" the voice behind him added.

Spinning round, JC leapt to his feet to embrace his dear friend. Michael was strutting toward them in all his glory, fully restored, and still resplendent in his armour and his finery.

JC noted gladly that all remnants of blood and tissue seemed to have been wiped clean in the restoration of his body. Michael cut an imposing figure at the best of times and this was no different. Despite them having just witnessed him being bested in a fight, just his mere presence back with them was enough to fill them with hope and promise for the future.

JC and Michael separated and JC led him to his seat at the head of the table. Michael smiled shyly at everyone as he sat down; "sorry you all had to witness that humiliation — I always was a sucker for someone begging for their life and I hesitated a millisecond too long." He clamped his mouth tight and ground his teeth before completing the thought; "it sure as hell won't happen again."

JC took charge and questioned Michael about the response from Heaven to what was happening down here at the moment. This time Michael did actually laugh out loud. "Oh JC... you know your Father. I think it was fair to say he was mighty pissed. First at you asking me to come and help, but more at me, for actually doing it."

Michael carried on to explain that when God realised the import of what had just gone down here in Pangutaran and that Satan was on the loose again and wreaking havoc, he was all for destroying earth again, and everyone in it — including the Devil. A collective gasp from everyone was met by Michael's smile; "but don't worry guys I gently reminded him that, firstly his beloved son was still here and also that humanity had come a long way forward since JC first came back — Earth was just too beautiful to destroy now, and all we really needed to do was to crush the little weasel Bubba, once and for all."

JC clapped his friend on the shoulder to thank him. "So what's the plan Michael?"

Michael looked a little worried; "well, ahhhhm, to be perfectly honest... I haven't quite fine-tuned it yet; but ummmm... but I will." he hastily added.

JC nodded slowly; "ahhhh, okay, no problem, but what do you want us to do in the meantime?"

"That's easy JC! This isn't really a war about territory; about dominion over Earth. This is a war about souls. Bubba doesn't just want earth he wants everyone in it to worship him and proclaim him God. We need to keep winning souls for our side JC. What I want you and the others to do is to go back on tour; as if nothing had happened. Carry on doing what Samantha and Damien there, do best - winning people for the Kingdom of God Church."

JC nodded and admitted that it made sense.

Down one end of the table Samantha, Chito and Jesus had been hanging into every single word of the interchange between JC and Michael. All three of them had visions of being Bubba's number one super-spy. All of them desperately wanted to be the ones who would provide the best information for their Lord and master.

When Michael had said that they should go back on tour, it was like music to Samantha's ears. That was exactly what she wanted to do; not so much for the adulation and love she received, although that would be nice to feel again. No, going back on tour would give her the perfect opportunity to carry out Bubba's instructions to her — to the letter. She grinned inwardly at finally getting the chance to prove her undying loyalty to him.

Gabriel voiced a concern that many of them were feeling;

"Michael, it just bothers me a bit; how are we supposed to fight the demons of hell? I mean, we're just men and women; we don't have any special abilities and we sure as hell aren't immortal... so... how?"

Michael chortled; "Don't worry Gabs! I'm not going to throw my broadsword at you and ask you to battle with Attila, no..."

Gabriel bristled at the put-down and sneered at him; "Hey, I might be getting on a bit, but I'm still the strongest one of this bunch. I keep fit... sort of... I reckon I could swing that sword of yours just as hard and just as accurately as you can."

Michael roared with laughter; "Oh you do... do you?"

He stood up and beckoned Gabriel toward him. Drawing his massive, double-edged sword he dextrously flicked it this way and that, making the air whistle, until the blade become just a blur to the eyes. Finally, he smiled, and turning the handle toward Gabriel he raised his eyebrows in invitation. Gabriel was beginning to get annoyed by now and angrily snatched the sword from him, immediately falling to his knees; the swords tip ploughing into the sand in front of him. He staggered to his feet, the sword's point still buried deep in the ground.

An ex-professional boxer, Gabriel was no small-fry. As he had intimated he had kept up a rigorous training regime all his life and summoning all the strength he could muster, he slowly raised the mighty sword above his head. The veins on his forehead were boldly standing out as he struggled with the immense weight of the object. His arms and his muscles were quivering under the strain as he sought to keep the sword steady. No amount of strength, however, was enough to defy the laws of gravity for too long, and almost in slow motion he began to topple over backwards. His fall gained momentum, as he tumbled to the ground, the sword burying itself in the sand, behind his head.

It was such a comical sight — the mighty Gabs — flat on his back; the sword lying useless above his head, that it set everyone at the table into fits of giggles.

Michael motioned them, with a finger to his lips, to show a little more respect and reached down to offer his hand to the gasping Gabriel. As he lifted him to his feet, Gabriel huffed and puffed shamefully;

"Ah... ha... Ah... ha... okay... okay, I guess I was wrong... that sword is way too heavy for anyone but you to lift Michael."

Michael put a comforting arm around the big man's shoulders and patted him in appreciation.

"Gabs, my friend, don't feel so bad. No human being has ever been able to even lift this sword... yet you managed to get it all the way over your head. Trust me that was a super-human feat of strength. I'm totally in awe of you right now."

The warm words quickly bucked up Gabs' wounded pride and he shrugged his shoulders self-deprecatingly before heading back to his seat; as spontaneous applause broke out among the team. Gabs just smiled shyly and said nothing.

Walking over to pick up and sheath his sword Michael continued; "as I was saying... we're not going to ask you guys to fight, not physically anyway."

He explained that once the *Holy War* actually began there was going to be a great, philosophical battle for the hearts and souls of humanity. The war wasn't going to be fought solely on the battlefield, but also in convincing individuals that they should choose their side — the good side.

"That's why you and your teams, all over the world, have to be out there, still fighting for the cause of right and good. We need people to see that what we offer is better than what Beelzebub can offer... and trust me, he'll have some pretty cool gifts to offer people."

JC nodded; "we get it Michael." He looked at his group; "okay, we need to get back to Davao and get our revival mission up and running again. There's no time to lose, so we'll leave first thing in the morning. Is everyone okay with that?"

The vigorous nods around the table told him everything he needed to know. His people were onboard and they were loyal.

Michael embraced JC;

"I'd better get back guys. I have a lot of preparation to do. It's been a long time since our people went to war — they're a bit rusty."

As he turned away; he threw back over his shoulder; "Oh, by the way, it's not just the Devil we have to fight. Very soon there will be a new, powerful, more acceptable, face of Satan appearing on earth. This person will do Bubba's bidding and will be much more enticing to potential followers than that ugly, old, evil, creature. He or she will be Bubba's ruler on Earth."

JC walked toward Michael; "Who's this person Michael? he asked slowly and deliberately.

Facing him square on, Michael just shook his head softly; "I have no idea my friend; all I know is he will be called *The AntiChrist.* We are about to witness *The Rise of the AntiChrist."*

Michael's words sent a shiver of fear down JC's spine. He knew of *The AntiChrist,* it was something they had discussed in heaven for eons, but he had never realised that it was any more than just a myth, a story to keep young children quiet and obedient.

He mouthed the words softly to himself; *"The Rise of the AntiChrist".*

The moment she had heard Michael say that word, Samantha had shuddered. *The AntiChrist;* it was such a dramatic name, one that evoked horror and fear. She smiled to herself and rolled the name over her lips, deciding that yes, she liked the term very, very much. She hugged herself to stop from shouting with glee. Oh yes, she thought; this really is going to be fun.

Michael smiled and added; "but don't worry JC it's not something you can't handle." He lifted his arms and dramatically ascended into the skies, slowly sliding upward and out of view.

JC spun on his heels and commanded; "okay people, let's get this show on the road. We have a lot to do—.

. . .

Chapter 24

Maria lay in the crook of her husband's arm as they rested on the bed of the guest accommodation of the Davao Church. The tears were softly running down her cheeks as she thought of her lost son, Samuel. She sniffed loudly and wiped her face, not wanting her tears to fall on JC and wake him. It had been a very rushed trip back to Davao, from the island, and everyone was feeling the strain. They all needed the rest, especially JC, who carried the weight of their mission on his own broad shoulders.

As she lay there she reflected on the past turbulent year. So much had happened, and yet, if JC and Michael were to be believed, there was so much more still to come. She breathed deeply, unsure in her own mind just how much more pain she could endure. The loss of Samuel had cut her to her soul. She knew JC still didn't believe he was truly gone and that they would somehow be able to rescue him from Bubba's clutches. She wanted to believe that so badly, but her intuition was telling her that he really was, truly gone. A strangled sob escaped from her lips as she began to weep again.

JC stirred beside her and opening one eye he watched her try to keep her tears from dropping onto his naked chest. That simple action of love reached deep inside him and stirred all the emotions that symbolised his marriage to Maria. There was nothing he wouldn't do for this woman and yet he knew, for now anyway, there was nothing he could do to ease her pain and loss.

He would do the only thing he could — just be there for her, hold her and comfort her through this horrible time.

He propped himself up on one elbow and took her hands in his;

She started; "Ohhhh, I'm sorry honey, did I wake you?"

His answer was to reach up and trace the outline of her cheeks with his fingers. She opened her mouth and kissed each of his fingers in turn.

"It's ok babes;" he began, "I was only napping, but you — you need to get some serious sleep. We have so much to do over the next few days. I know how hard it is for you right now, but we have to be strong... if only for the sake of the rest of our children."

He paused and smiled softly, before adding; "our literal children as well as the rest of our figurative children... hehehe." That brought a small smile to her lips, but she shook her head sadly.

"The truth is honey, I'm just not sleepy... tell me a story."

JC groaned inwardly. He knew "tell me a story" was code for "I can't sleep honey and I need you to bore me to sleep". He'd been through this many times before. He'd start to tell her something really interesting and then a minute or so after he'd started he would hear her rhythmic breathing indicating that she was already asleep and he was just talking to a brick wall. He chuckled to himself; nothing ever changes, does it?

Propping himself up again and getting comfortable he smiled into his wife's clear, sparkling eyes; "No story tonight, straight to bed and no supper for you!"

She played along with his little game and pouted, before whiningly replying; "Ohhhh, honey, just one story, pleeeeease!" He smiled at her, and kissed her on the lips.

"So, what story would my beloved like tonight?"

Maria's face turned deadly serious; "Tell me about the *AntiChrist* honey. What is it, where does it come from and what's it going to do to us?"

JC gulped and frowned; "That's hardly a bed-time story sweetie. Are you sure you want to get into it now?"

Maria sat upright in the bed and reached up to touch JC's cheek gently. "Honey, this is going to be a very important part of our lives from now on. I can feel it — woman's intuition eh! I just want to know what we're up against."

JC nodded and began to explain the legend, story, myth of the famed *AntiChrist*.

. . .

He explained that the *AntiChrist* was a story they would tell the young ones, in heaven, when they wanted them to behave — but that it was more than just a myth or a fable. Behind the story lay a real element of truth. When Beelzebub began his reign of terror in Heaven, he tried desperately to get some of the other Angels to side with him, in his argument with God.

He smiled at her; "Beelzebub wasn't always an evil, vicious old man honey — once he was the most favoured of all Angels. He was undoubtedly my father's favourite."

This time there would be no falling asleep for Maria. She really wanted to hear this story and she was listening intently.

"Beelzebub was simply the number one Angel in heaven; regarded with greater favour and love than even Michael, Gabriel or Peter. I often used to think of him as my brother; that's how much my father doted on him — almost like a second son." Maria's eyes widened at the implication of JC's words.

"You were that close babes? Oh my! How hard it must be for you now; to oppose him." JC nodded sadly and continued with the tale.

The day to day operations of heaven, and the duties of all the Angels, were never handled directly by God — that task always fell to the Archangels and foremost among them, was Beelzebub. He was beloved as a kind, wise and fair Angel, who would never ask too much of his fellow citizens. He was always prepared to pitch in and help when necessary and was widely respected and loved throughout the kingdom of heaven.

Nobody actually knows what happened, but the change that came over him was so monstrous and so rapid, that it was nothing less than a giant shock to everyone. He went from being this sweet, endearing, helpful old man; almost overnight, into an overbearing, demanding and positively hateful person. Those close to him were so shocked at the change in his personality that they tried desperately to discover what had come over him. Beelzebub's response to their interference was swift, brutal and vicious. He made it crystal clear that he was the boss and what he said, was what would happen. People began to fear him and deliberately attempt to avoid contact with him.

It wasn't long before he was heard to be boasting to anyone that would listen that very soon all of heaven would be his. "It's time for a change"; he would pronounce. "Time that old man retired and let some new blood run this place." To Gabriel, he once had the absolute temerity to announce in no uncertain terms that; "I will be the ruler over all of the Universe very soon; you mark my words".

Gabriel was no fool and quickly reported what was happening to the Father. It appeared that Gabriel was just one of a long line of petitioners to God, who were sick to death, of the arrogant, strutting, little peacock, that Beelzebub had clearly become.

When summoned to appear before him; Beelzebub just brushed off the "invitation". "You tell him"; he sneered; "that Beelzebub is too busy to waste time in silly conferences." He had giggled. "You tell the Lord God Almighty that I will pop in and chat when I have some time."

He'd patronisingly patted the messenger, St Peter, on the head before adding; "now run along little man and deliver the message... there's a good boy".

Needless to say God was livid and stormed down to confront Beelzebub. Again he had the utter gall to keep God waiting and by the time the two eventually confronted each other there was little doubt what the outcome was going to be. He strolled up to the Father and grinned sarcastically at him:

"What's up old man? Have you come to give me control? Finally decided to retire have you?" He'd laughed aloud. 'Well, I can only say that it's about time? You've been well past it for years now. I mean, look at the bloody mess you've allowed earth to get into. You've done nothing really since you sent the flood... now, when was that again?"

He'd looked up, tapping his finger on his chin. "Ah well... it was a long, long time ago anyway."

God spluttered and tried to interject, but Beelzebub wasn't finished yet. "Hmmmm... so... what else have you achieved? Ahhhh, that's right, you sent the *boy* to do a man's job didn't you — and that turned out real well, didn't it? They killed him... hehehe."

He'd taken a deep breath and carried on berating God; totally oblivious to the fury and anger that was suffusing God's face. "Well, let me tell you something Daddy, things will change under my leadership. Humanity needs direction, humanity needs discipline, humanity needs a leader and by *GOD*, I'm going to give it to them."

Apparently finished his tirade, he just stepped back one small step and smiled sweetly at the Father.

There was utter silence; nobody moved and nobody even whispered a word; they all stood waiting for the explosion that surely must come — and come it did, but perhaps not quite in the way they had expected. God sat down and held his head in his hands for a minute or more. His eyes were crinkled in pain, his long grey hair and beard seemed to have even deepened in their greyness. His face was pinched, and in his eyes they could see such complete and utter sadness. In a voice just above a whisper he softly spoke;

"Oh... what pain you've given me Beelzebub, my favoured. I can't express the complete sorrow and sadness I feel at this moment. You have shown yourself to be truly the epitome of evil. I cannot allow you to pollute our beautiful world anymore. You must be banished and much as it pains me, you must be sent away from my sight for eternity — never again to look into the face of God."

Taking a deep breath, he signalled with a nod of his head, to Michael and Gabriel who quickly moved into position beside Beelzebub, each of them grabbing one of his arms to stop him potentially escaping. Beelzebub pulled against his captors, but was no match for their vice-like grips. His voice breaking with emotion God continued;

"I sentence you; to... to... be cast down, below even humanity, to the very fiery pits of the earth's crust. There you will spend eternity, with all of the evil spawn that humanity has ever produced."

He looked sadly, almost pityingly, at Beelzebub; "You wanted a kingdom to rule over my son? I'll give you one — you are now the ruler of Hell!" Nodding his head to Gabriel and Michael, they began to drag Beelzebub away.

Beelzebub wasn't quite finished yet though, and with a surprising show of strength he managed to turn around and rip his arms free from his captors. He made no moves toward the Father. He just placed his legs wide apart and assumed a stance of arrogance. Hands on hips; with a sneer on his lips, he spat back at him;

"You mark my words *Lord!"* He looked around at the gathered hosts of heaven before he began again;

"All of you... mark my words and mark them damn closely. This is not the last you will see of me. I *will* escape from my prison one day and when I do there will be a war like none you have ever seen. I will raise a mythical creature from humanity..."

Raising his voice, almost shouting, he added; *"I WILL RAISE THE ANTICHRIST!* Yes, you heard me, out of humanity will come a person who will help to win the souls of the world for Beelzebub, that person will be the *AntiChrist*. He..."

He smiled thoughtfully before continuing; "he... or she, will rise above the rest of the human race and lead them to their true Saviour, their true salvation — yours truly; The Prince of Darkness, the Devil, Satan, *BEELZEBUB*! *I WILL* have total dominion over all the Universe. I swear it!'

By this time he was frothing at the mouth, and drooling down his chin. He was totally consumed and crazed with anger and power. God just shook his head and wearily turned to walk away.

. . .

JC looked at his wife, whose eyes were as wide as saucers, and whose bottom lip was quivering with emotion.

"So, honey... that's the story of the *AntiChrist*. You know... I don't think any of us truly believed this day would ever come, but there you go. Here we are, facing a *Holy War*, just as Bubba predicted."

Maria said nothing for quite some time and suddenly a thought occurred to her;

"So, who will be the *AntiChrist* JC, have you any inkling?" He shrugged his shoulders and raised his eyebrows.

"Hon, it could be anyone at all — anyone! Mind you..." he added; "I suspect it will need to be somebody who is already famous, or well-known; someone who already has a following in the world — a politician perhaps; an actor or singer; or maybe even someone from the established religions. Hell! We just have no way of knowing until he... or she... shows themselves."

She looked thoughtful; "So it could be... say, President Santiago... or Pope Pedro... or even that new President of the European Union, that horrible, old, man Putin...;" her voice trailed off; "...anyone..."

JC chuckled; "I don't think it would be Pope Pedro. You know, I knew Antonio when he was still just a Cardinal in Manila — he doesn't have a malicious bone in his body, that man. He *truly* is a man of God. As for Miriam, well... she can be a bit dodgy at times; but I'm sure her heart's in the right place. Now Putin... there's a thought — he's got some real form for evil."

His face turned a little hard. "Actually hon, you know who I'd have my money on; that new, little, trumped up dictator in North Korea. His daddy and grand-daddy were pretty much evil personified and the rumours are that he's no better. Hell, he's only twenty-two, but I've been hearing some pretty horrific stories of persecution and excesses coming out of our two missions in North Korea. I think he'd be a prime candidate for Bubba's recruitment drive."

JC gazed around the room; "but you're right about one thing, it really could be anybody. We have to be ready, no matter who it is."

He kissed his wife softly on her lips; "now... let's get some sleep ha, or we'll be no use to anyone in the morning."

. . .

The next morning, the entire team was seated around a giant conference table in what Angelo had jokingly called; "The Situation Room". He had even gone as far as to get a notice printed for the door.

Jonny and Adonis had flown in from the States overnight, so there was a long round of back-slapping and hugging, before the conference could begin.

Adonis addressed the group first and informed them that apart from the problems that had occurred in Ezraville, which of course, they were well aware of — every other Kingdom of God community across the US were doing wonderfully well, growing daily and prospering. "We're in great shape all across America, Europe and Asia. We're still a bit thin on the ground in South America, Africa and the Pacific, but it's all in the plan."

He finished by adding that if the Devil wanted a *Holy War*, then his communities were ready and able to withstand it. "He won't win the souls of our people very damn easy; they love their God."

JC was effusive in his praise of Adonis and Jonny's work, adding; "I'm thrilled you're both back — apart from having the old team together, which feels great, I want you Adonis to take up some of the slack in the teaching. I just can't do it all myself."

Adonis looked thoughtful for a second; "does that mean what I think it means JC — are we sending out more than one team?"

JC grinned at his comrade's perception. "Got it in one my friend. We need to move fast. I'll take one team and you will lead the second. I've sort of got the teams worked out in my head, but we'll sort out who goes with what team later. I am going to be selfish though and keep my family together — I hope nobody objects to that."

There was a general ripple of laughter around the room and everyone nodded their heads vigorously.

JC's cell-phone began to chirp. He looked down at it with a look of complete embarrassment. He'd already asked everyone to turn off their phones, for the meeting, and here he was with his still on. Glancing at the screen he noticed it was Jhoemar Nolasco calling from Las Vegas. He looked up at everyone and couldn't help but note the self-satisfied grins on everyone's faces. He giggled and held his phone up to cover his embarrassment.

"Hey! Sorry guys! I really should take this. I know... I know... I know!" he half chuckled as he got up from the table and began to walk around the room, talking to the good Pastor.

Simon took the opportunity of the break to surreptitiously reach for Damien's hand under the table. He leant in very close and whispered;

"I'm worried Dame. What if we get split up? What if JC sends me in Adonis' team?" Damien looked up in horror. The thought clearly hadn't occurred to him. He scratched his chin slightly before breaking out in a wide smile.

"Simon;" he whispered back; "that's just not going to happen is it? You heard Dad, he said he's keeping the family together... well... you *are* part of the family now. You're part of my family."

Simon's ears turned red and his face shone with love and adoration. With their faces just inches apart he mouthed a silent kiss at Damien who just grinned back and reached his hand up to catch it and place it next to his heart.

They could all hear snatches of JC's conversation with Jhoemar, but none of them were able to get the full gist of what was happening. JC's answers were often just; "aha, no, really, and the odd hmmmm," thrown in for good measure. After a few minutes they heard him say; "Thanks Joe, I'll be in touch."

He held the phone up for everyone to see, before turning it off with a flourish. As he sat back down he looked down the table at Jesus and Chito, still well bandaged and looking slightly the worse for wear. His eyebrows knitted, just ever so briefly, before he looked back at the full table and smiled; "now... where were we?"

He then went on to explain his plan of action to everyone. There would be a lot of work to do in a very short time and he had allocated them assignments to take care of, before the planned departure date, just over a week away. As they started to gather up their papers to head off and begin work, it was Ronnie who asked the inevitable question;

"Ahhhh... JC... where are we actually going? It sort of might help us... you know... to book airfares and vans etc... hehehe."

JC laughed; "ooops, did I forget to mention that little point... sorry. Okay... Adonis' team will head to Baghdad. I've been totally overwhelmed by the support and response we've had over the past fourteen odd years from our Muslim brothers, but, understandably there are still some very large pockets of resistance out there — especially in the Middle East. You've all read the papers. You know what some of them are saying; that our teachings are blasphemous."

He grinned at Adonis; "so you've got the easy job Adonis — of convincing them to follow the true path; good luck with that!"

Adonis just saluted JC and snapped to attention.

"We will make it so; JC!"

"So;" Samantha finally piped up; "where are *we* going Daddy?"

JC grinned and looked at Maria; "why honey, were going not too far actually. We're off to Pyongyang."

Maria smiled secretly; I should have guessed, she thought—.

. . .

Chapter 25

As the plane rolled down the runway and cruised to a halt at the newly christened Kim Jong-Un International Airport, JC glanced out the window at the place they would call home, for at least the next month. The grey sky, with its dark snow-laden clouds that threatened to swamp them all in a blanket of white, for now appeared to be holding off. He hoped the darkness of the skies and the drabness of the airport facilities were not portents of their mission's success.

There were two Kingdom of God missions in North Korea. The first, just 10klm from the International Airport, was where they would be staying for the first part of their crusade. Their second stronghold was in the very far north of the country near a small town called Onsong, right on the border with China. If the truth be told JC was keen to get to Onsong as quickly as possible. He knew, the further away they got from the bullies in Pyongyang, the easier life would be. It seemed the simple, country-folk on the North Korean border were less prone to interference to their way of life from the bureaucrats in the Capital than were the leaders of Adamston, the settlement right next door to the capital.

The harassment began the second they exited the plane. Instead of following the other passengers to the terminal and customs, the Castillo party was met at the bottom of the plane's steps by a phalanx of goose-stepping, heavily armed soldiers.

Each soldier carried an automatic sub-machine gun; apparently quite willing to use it at the slightest provocation. JC made it clear to everyone that they should just smile at the guards and go along happily with everything they had to say.

"We have nothing to hide guys — we come in peace, remember;" he reminded them.

It took over six hours of constant questioning and grilling by a series of military personnel, each one higher in rank than the one that preceded him; before finally a certain General Tiu indicated that their visas would be approved for their visit to the Democratic People's Republic of Korea. Their principal concern appeared to be that JC and his group were intent on undermining and criticizing the leadership of the Country. JC continually repeated the same phrase to a number of North Korean officers; "we have come to support our brothers and sisters in Adamston and in Maryville, up north. While we are here we plan to hold some rallies, but they are for the garnering of hearts not to undermine this beautiful country of yours."

Hard as it was, everyone managed to keep a smile on their lips and a welcome in their eyes, as they endured the hard-line questioning. By the time they eventually straggled out of the airport terminal they felt like they had been put through a meat processing plant and squeezed out the other end as minced pork. They literally fell into the vans that had been sent from the settlement to pick them up, for the short thirty minute drive to the camp. Most, immediately fell off to sleep but for some it was an opportunity to view the capital that they had heard and read so much about, but few had ever seen.

The one thing that struck JC most of all was the sheer lack of traffic on the roads. Coming from Manila, it was incredible to be travelling on smooth, broad highways that were congestion free.

He wasn't entirely sure if the lack of vehicles was a reflection of the many oil embargoes the country had endured over the years, or just the sheer poverty of the common folk to be able to afford cars. Nonetheless, it made for a quick and smooth drive to the front gate of the Adamston compound.

Visions of prisons or even concentration camps filled JC's mind as he first laid eyes on Adamston. The walls of the village were at least seven foot high and disconcertingly, topped with coils of razor wire. He tapped Maria on the shoulder and jokingly asked; "Is the razor wire to keep the inmates in... or to keep the bad guys out?"

Maria just raised her eyebrows and gave a nervous giggle. This was so, so different from any of the settlements they had visited in the past. JC remonstrated with himself for not having allowed himself the luxury of visiting more of the "frontier" outposts of the Church over the years. Nudging Maria again he commented; "we tend to forget, it's not all sweetness and light for some of our followers, ha?"

She smiled indulgently and nodded.

The outer rim of the compound was surrounded by military vehicles. JC counted seven armoured personnel carriers and no less than three full size tanks. Sheesh, he thought, are they planning on starting a war with us sometime soon? Once through the entrance gates to Adamston however, the outlook changed dramatically. Adamston was built to the same layout and basic design as all of the other communities. Within each community, however, their architects had been given a free hand to design the properties to reflect the culture and history of the country in which they were founded.

Adamston was a beautiful sight to behold. It stuck JC with such force that this is what the rest of North Korea should look like — a peaceful, pastoral, scene with modern, functional and culturally accurate and pleasant residences. He had noted with distaste the drab, grey, monolithic apartment blocks as they had driven through Pongyang and out into the countryside. Nobody should be forced to live like rabbits in a warren, he thought, when they have a heritage like this to fall back on.

Each house within the village was simple and functional, made just of hardened mud brick and topped with the traditional sloping tiled roof. Whereas the city had been drab and uniform, no two houses in Adamston looked exactly the same. Each house was festooned in colour; whether it be traditional decorations hanging from the eaves or colourful, flowering vines that wound themselves around the balustrades. It was a welcoming sight for the weary travellers.

As they exited their vehicles they were met by the resident pastor; Robertini Aguirre, yet another Davaoan native who had given up the comforts of the headquarters' Church to go out into the masses and minister to the newly believed and newly faithful.

Tini Aguirre greeted JC and his exhausted band, with effusive hugs and welcomes. JC and Tini were old friends, from the early days of the mission work, and both were thrilled to be reunited for this time.

"I'm sorry! I'm the only one to greet you my friend," Tini began, "we did have a welcoming committee all planned, but what, with your delay at the airport and everyone's need to get on with their work, well... it's just me left..."

JC laughed; "and you — you old reprobate, you're the only one we need to feel welcome. We're just thrilled to be here, but we really would like to get some sleep before anything else. I'm sure you understand."

Pastor Aguirre rushed around assuring everyone that their rooms were ready and that yes, the first order of business was definitely for them all to get some rest. He showed them to their quarters; a series of identical houses set in a rectangle around a beautiful, delightfully green, and lush garden of pink, yellow and flaming red flowers. In the centre of the rectangle was small pond, with a tiny bridge over it. JC noted with a smile the miniscule, yet delicately made, and intricate, porcelain figurines of ancient Koreans that were perched on the bridge, fishing poles in hand, clearly catching the evening's supper for their families. It was an idyllic, little spot and one that JC was sure they would all spend some time relaxing around, in the days to come.

Once they were all safely settled, everyone in the group headed straight for their bedrooms; everyone that is except the three elder children; the twins; Damien and Samantha and of course Simon. Damien expressed that his body clock was telling him it wasn't time to rest just yet. The other two nodded their agreement and they all settled down in the lounge to discover what delights the local Korean television fare might hold.

It was the first time Damien had found himself alone with Samantha for a long time. The enmity between them had been palpable for some time and Damien was tired of it frankly and he just wanted it to end. After all, he thought, I love my sister so much, but I hate what she seems to have become. I really want to talk to her and see if we can't somehow sort this whole thing out, for our own sakes, as much as for Mum and Dad's.

As Simon flicked through the very few channels that were available on the local service, Damien tried a probing thought into his sister's mind; "Sis, can we talk?" The response when it came was polite enough, but in Damien's confused mind he was unable to avoid placing a sarcastic tag on it;

"Of course, little bro... we can talk anytime, can't we? So what's up?"

He launched into a long explanation that he was concerned that Samantha wasn't happy; that perhaps she was looking for something, but she didn't know what. He ended by saying that he couldn't understand why she was still so angry at him and why they couldn't just let things go and move on, as twins should — close and loving. Unconsciously, while he was communicating with her he had reached for Simon's hand and was softly squeezing it for reassurance and comfort.

Well! That was enough, for Samantha;

"Bloody hell Damien!" she exclaimed; "can't you do anything by yourself — you're just so damn weak. You always have to have little Simon with you to hold your hand and kiss you better. God, you make me sick sometimes!"

Damien, devastated by the ferocity of her attack on him, and the obvious pointlessness of trying to mend their relationship, grimaced and sat back on the couch, slowly shaking his head.

"anyway;" Samantha continued; "I'm sick to death of all this bullshit and you and this bloody family. I'm going to bed." She jumped to her feet and stalked off toward the hallway. Just as the door closed behind her Damien heard her final thought before she put up her mind shutters and blocked him out.

"Thank the fuck this is going to be over soon and I can end all this bullshit pretence. God, I hate these people."

Beside Damien; Simon, blissfully unaware of the drama that had just played out next to him looked up from the screen; "talk about a load of rubbish and propaganda on the television Dam, I think it's time I hit the sack too."

He looked where Samantha had sat and added; "Oh, has Sammy gone to bed already?" Damien nodded briefly before saying;

"I'll sit a bit yet Simon — you go off ha."

Simon stood, but before he left he leant down to kiss Damien's cheek. "I love you Dam." he added as he left.

Damien smiled and nodded; "right back at ya. See you later."

He sat there for another hour just running Samantha's last thought through his mind. What on earth did she mean by "it's going to be over soon"...what is she planning? Is she going to leave us? Unable to come up with a satisfactory answer, eventually he rose wearily and headed in the same direction as the rest of the family — the blessed relief of sleep.

. . .

When the Castillo family and their entourage finally got to meet the residents of Adamston the next day, they were astounded by the sheer joy and happiness that reflected on the faces of their brothers and sisters.

Pastor Tini tried to explain to them that for many of these people this was the *very* first time in their lives that they had felt safe, contented, and most of all not hungry. They love their community, with an absolute passion, he revealed.

"Actually, I think that's one of the reasons the Government is so anti-us. We offer the North Korean's something they haven't experienced in a long, long time — hope, peace and belonging. I think the Government's terrified of us and if it was up to that little upstart Kim Jong-Teng I'm pretty sure he would have nuked us off the planet a long time ago... us... and Maryville."

Horrified JC asked the inevitable question; "he won't though... will he?"

Tini grinned and related that he couldn't afford to do anything because the rest of the world was watching. The last thing this country needs right now is an international conflict. Tini explained that roughly seventy percent of the population lived below the poverty line and were officially ranked as "poor". A war — or even, tougher sanctions could well be enough to push the people to desperation measures.

"Teng's a canny bugger — at the moment he has the military on his side, but if the country slides too far into the abyss, they could easily turn on him. So — for now anyway; they leave us alone, sort of, although they do continually harass our people. I mean... you saw their military presence outside, right? Nobody can leave the village without at least one military vehicle following them, wherever they go. It's a bit nerve-wracking sometimes, but hey... you get used to it."

JC just shook his head in amazement, at the matter of fact way the people put up with living under constant threat.

"So Tini, what have you got planned for us while we're here."

Pastor Aguirre shook his head softly and went on to tell JC that in actual fact there was only one rally planned for their time in Pyongyang. When JC raised his eyebrows in surprise at the news, he hurried on to explain that even getting permission for one rally had been an almost insurmountable hurdle.

He coughed slightly in embarrassment; "I have to admit JC I even resorted to a little bit of bribery to get the final permits signed. I hated it, but what can you do?"

JC grinned and slapped him on the shoulder.

"Let it go my friend... you know the old saying..."When in Pyongyang do as the Pyongyangians do... hehehe....or perhaps you'd prefer; Render under Kim Jong-Teng that which is due to Kim Jong-Teng and render unto God, that which is due to God. Hahaha! So, when's the big day Tini?"

Robertini breathed a sigh of relief; "the day after tomorrow actually. I've hired the Rungrado 1st of May stadium for the event — it's enormous, a capacity of something like 150,000."

He smiled almost apologetically; "but I'm not sure if we'll be able to fill it. A lot of people are terrified of being seen identifying with our group and you can bet that however many we do get — half of them will be armed forces personnel or the dreaded State Security Department, which is Teng's very own secret police force."

JC just chuckled; "well... that will be some coup then; if we can convert a big number of Teng's minions then who knows just what will happen to the Government. Hehehe... it could be fairly interesting."

Tini added that he was still trying to get permission for more rallies, later in the month, but he didn't hold out much hope of success.

"So much will depend, on how this first one goes, JC."

After his chat with the Pastor, JC wandered around the hall catching up with family members and meeting some wonderful, down to earth and happy North Koreans. He had no idea what the rally would be like and how it would be received, but with the confidence of a man on a mission from God; he put any concerns out of his mind and determined to enjoy his time in North Korea—.

. . .

Chapter 26

The next day was spent planning the performance — the show, and by the time the morning of the rally dawned, everyone was ready; clear on the roles they would play that day.

JC had decided very early on in the piece, that the show-stopper; Damien and Samantha's flying routine, was just way too risky for them to perform. "Given the tension that's gonna be in that stadium guys, I'm just not sure that something as magical, as flying, will go down too well. There will be thousands of people with guns at the ready and if you two start flying over them... well, who knows how they might react. You both could get yourselves killed... and I'm not having that!"

Samantha had been furious and had remonstrated loudly with her father;

"So, what you're saying Dad is that you don't have enough faith ha! Well, that's pretty rich in my opinion, especially coming from the Son of God himself. Of course we must do the routine — it's what the punters want, it's what they expect, and let's be honest, it's what tips them over the edge to committing to our cause. We have to do it Dad, really we do."

JC was still doubtful and Maria had been pushing him also to take that part out of the show. He looked at his wife and shrugged his shoulders. A little hurt by Samantha's withering attack on his faith he mumbled to Maria; "Hon... she has a point."

Maria grimaced; "maybe she does... but does she always have to be so damn rude at putting it across. I swear sometimes I don't even know this little girl anymore."

She looked directly at Samantha and creased her brows, before looking back to her husband. "Ah well hon, I guess we will just have to risk it... if only to keep Samantha happy."

That settled, the rest of the preparations for the big rally were expedited.

. . .

Samantha woke early that morning and lay for some time in her bed just contemplating the day that lay in store for her. Bubba had visited her briefly last night and explained that this was it — this was the moment they would make their move; their declaration. After tomorrow, he'd told her, nothing would ever be the same again. Their march to their rightful Kingdom would begin — and it was all to start with her. She assured Bubba she knew what she had to do and despite all her misgivings and a nagging doubt, in the back of her mind, about betrayal; Bubba's warm embrace and his loving words were enough to sweep them away.

"YES!" she exclaimed to herself.

"Today marks the start of the rise of Samantha and the decline of Damien. I'll show that little, trumped-up brother of mine what real power is... hehehe."

She jumped out of bed, excited and nervous, throwing open her curtains to gaze at this momentous day. The sky was slate grey, menacing almost; with dark clouds that rapidly scudded across the horizon, driven by a mean, vicious wind straight from the Arctic, full of chill and the promise of snow. She decided, as a portent, the weather was perfect. Very soon the world will feel the darkness and chill of Bubba and her reign, so this bleak day was entirely appropriate.

Whistling softly to herself, she dressed, and made herself up very carefully, so as to accentuate both the natural beauty of her flawless face and skin, plus the seductive curves of her long, willowy body. Satisfied with her efforts she examined herself carefully in the room's full-length mirror. She grinned back at the image that was presented to her.

"Damn I'm hot!" she whispered softly to her reflection. She continued to gaze at herself for several minutes, turning this way and that; admiring the curve of her long, sinewy neck, the gentle hillock that was her buttocks and the face that spoke so much of her mixed heritage and gave her that dusky, exotic look that men seemed to find irresistible.

Declaring herself satisfied, she spun on her heels and grabbing her bag headed out to join her family for breakfast and to make an official beginning to this day — this most momentous of days.

. . .

The rally had progressed exceptionally well up to that point. The stadium wasn't full to capacity by any means, but JC had estimated there must have been at least a hundred thousand people out there.

He jokingly remarked to Maria; "well... if half are Government stooges that still means over fifty thousand people braved these elements to come and hear us in such miserable conditions. I think the North Korean people are just grasping for hope; any sort of hope for a better life — and in us they see that possibility. I can't blame them".

Maria patted him gently on the shoulder in agreement.

She looked out also at the sea of people, wrapped up in whatever they could lay their hands on, to try and keep warm and dry. It had been a futile gesture however as the icy wind cut through everyone, chilling them to the bone and now she noted a gentle snow was falling on the assembled. Her heart went out to them, but like her husband she rationalised they were here for a reason, seeking a better life and they were used to suffering, so they could cope with a bit of bad weather.

She had been especially proud of the message her husband had brought to them today. JC hadn't addressed a crowd this size since Las Vegas and even he had expressed concerns he might be a bit rusty. He needn't have worried, Maria thought; he was superb. The crowd was moved to tears in many places, during his lesson. She smiled inwardly... as had she and many of their team.

His message had been one of love and reconciliation — of communities living together and supporting one another. It was clearly something that struck a chord deep within the hearts of the poor, North Korean populace. They were searching for and longing for something different and JC gave them that in bucketfuls. Worryingly, she knew it wouldn't have gone down well with the country's leadership, but that was something they would have to worry about later. For now, it was just a marvellous opportunity to bask in God's Glory. She was loving it!

She looked over to Damien and Samantha. It would be their big moment soon. After everyone had finished singing the final Hymn, it would be time for her two eldest children to do their thing. Who would have thought the two of them would have grown up to become such different people, she thought. They were so similar as youngsters and then something happened and their paths diverged.

A twinge of regret passed through her mind that she hadn't had more time to spend with her beloved twins, but it truly was, just a fleeting moment. When I married JC I knew what the future held — and this is it; as she sang along to the last lines of the beautiful hymn; "How Great Thou Art".

Glancing back at her kids she shuddered as she saw the brevity of their clothing. They would literally freeze up there when they began to circle the stadium. She knew Samantha was very proud of her body, as she should be — she was beautiful, but did she really have to expose quite so much of it to the audience?

Maria giggled softly; well... after this little display, I have no doubt both of them will investigate "winter" outfits before the next show. The last bar of the song signalled the moment of truth for Damien and Samantha, as they stepped forward to take centre-stage.

. . .

Samantha breathed deeply; finally... my moment has come. Raising her hands high above her head she led Damien to the centre of the large stage. The gloom of the dark day and the brilliance of the whiteness of the sweeping snow combined with the powerful spotlight focused on the pair, to give them an other-worldly, almost ethereal look. Both appeared to be wreathed in glistening, sparkling halos. There was an audible gasp from the audience at their appearance, as all eyes focused directly on them.

This truly was the part that Samantha adored; and had missed so terribly over the past year. *She* was the centre of attention and she positively glowed in the adulation of the crowd. Dramatically she lowered her arms and her sweet, sing-song voice began to effortlessly echo around the giant stadium.

"Good people of Pyongyang, I come to you today with greetings and love from the child of the child of God! *I* am a direct descendent of the Almighty and today *I* will show you the true path of salvation."

Damien looked askance at his sister.

What the bloody hell was she up to? This isn't in the script! He tried to message her mind, but was blocked by an impenetrable wall. Samantha was way too caught up in herself to allow him in.

She raised her arms above her head again and gently rose up into the air, oblivious to the harsh winds that buffeted her. The Arctic storm had no clear effect on her and she rose higher and higher until she was thirty feet above the audience, now craning their necks desperately to see her.

The man operating the spotlight was caught unawares, as Damien stayed where he was on stage. He was unsure whether to follow her with the light or to remain focused on Damien. He ended up wavering between the two, constantly flicking back and forth.

Damien turned to look at his father at the back of the stage. He spread his arms in confusion and mouthed the question; "what do I do now?"

A flustered JC just indicated with an upward movement of both hands, that he should follow his sister. His ascent was much more rapid than hers had been and when he reached her, he had to shout above the roaring wind just to be heard; "what the fuck are you doing Sam?" he exploded at her.

Samantha turned to face him; her eyes glazed over and she smiled angelically.

"Why Damien, my darling, little, twin brother... I'm just taking my birthright back... nothing too amazing."

He realised she had mind messaged him that, so he responded angrily;

"What the hell are you on about Sam?"

This time, when she stared at him, he didn't recognise her anymore. The smile was gone, replaced instead by a twisted scowl. In her eyes he saw the years of jealousy, malevolence and hatred boil up, until her eyes actually changed colour, to black, bottomless pools of nothingness.

Horrified by what he saw; he moved backward away from her — but there was no escaping Samantha's wrath this time.

She leant forward and whispered softly; "Kiss me Bro."

Reaching for him, she wrapped her left arm around his neck and pulled his face close to her. Planting a kiss on his forehead she sighed;

"Goodbye brother"

From nowhere, in her right hand, appeared a needle-sharp, ten-inch stiletto, which, with one final exclamation of *"Beelzebub!"* she thrust deep into Damien's chest.

His eyes opened wide, as the stiletto bounced off a rib, before burying itself deep inside his heart. He breathed just one word; "Sammy?" before his lifeless body cart-wheeled and tumbled to the ground, slamming into the edge of the stage, before dropping crumpled onto the snowy grass.

Samantha screamed and clutched her chest frantically, succumbing to the exact, same pain that Damien had just felt; before she also began to fall. As consciousness began to depart from her she felt strong arms wrap around her and hold her tight. A voice whispered in her ear; "block him out Sammy... block him out."

With Bubba's reassurance she found the strength to fight back against the pain and to block Damien from her head — for the very last time.

As Bubba soared back into the swirling snow, she wrapped her arms tight around his chest and just breathed in that familiar scent, that was her beloved.

When he felt she was ready, he pried her fingers from around his neck and holding her by the hand they faced the panicking crowd.

"BEHOLD!"

Bubba's voice boomed out around the stadium. People automatically stopped and looked up again.

Bubba grinned maniacally;

"BEHOLD!

This is the new order — *this* is the beginning of the dawn of Beelzebub."

In the crowd, many had drawn pistols, or were pointing rifles directly at the pair. Beelzebub looked down and sneered;

"Your pop-guns cannot harm us. *I* am the ruler of the Universe — *I* am Beelzebub! Remember my name well."

He took Samantha's still shaking arm and raised it high above her head.

"BEHOLD!

I hold the hand of Earth's new leader — I hold the hand, of the daughter, of the son of God."

He paused for effect, before screaming so loudly the stadium actually began to vibrate and sway;

"I HOLD THE VERY HAND OF THE ANTICHRIST! HAJULELLAH!"

With that pronouncement Samantha and Beelzebub just simply disappeared.

. . .

Below, in total shock and disbelief; JC, tears streaming down his face turned to his wife and said; "It has begun — *Holy War*, has begun!"

THE END